Marcia Willett was born in Somerset, the youngest of five girls. After training to become a ballet dancer, she joined her sister's Dance Academy as a ballet mistress. She then became a naval wife and her son was born in 1970. She now lives in Devon with her husband, Rodney, who first encouraged Marcia to write, and their Newfoundlands, Bessie and Trubshawe. *Holding On* is the second novel in the Chadwick Family Chronicles, which began with *Looking Forward* and depict the moving and entertaining story of the generations of Chadwicks who live at The Keep. As Willa Marsh, Marcia Willett writes novels published by Sceptre.

Praise for Marcia Willett's previous novels:

'A genuine voice of our times'   *The Times*

'A fascinating study of character . . . A cleverly woven story with lots of human interest'   *Publishing News*

'A very readable book'   *Prima*

'Rich characterisation here, and not a little humour, too. Enjoyable'   *Manchester Evening News*

'A delightful journey'   *Lancashire Evening Telegraph*

'Filled with closely drawn observations on human nature . . . A real winner'   *Kingsbridge Gazette*

'Poignantly told, with fine characterisation and a lavish sprinkling of humour'   *Evening Herald*

'An excellent storyteller, whose characters are delineated with compassion, humour and generosity'   *Totnes Times*

Also by Marcia Willett

Holding On

The Chadwick Family Chronicles
The Middle Years

Marcia Willett

HEADLINE

First published in 1999
by HEADLINE BOOK PUBLISHING

First published in paperback in 2000
by HEADLINE BOOK PUBLISHING

10 9 8 7 6 5 4 3 2 1

ISBN 0 7472 5997 6

Typeset by
Letterpart Limited, Reigate, Surrey

Printed and bound in Great Britain by
Clays Ltd, St Ives plc

HEADLINE BOOK PUBLISHING
A division of the Hodder Headline Group
338 Euston Road
London NW1 3BH
www.headline.co.uk
www.hodderheadline.com

To James and Nicola

ACKNOWLEDGEMENT

I should like to thank Father Iain Matthew OCD for his
permission to use his translation of St John of
The Cross's Prayer of a soul in love

THE CHADWICK FAMILY

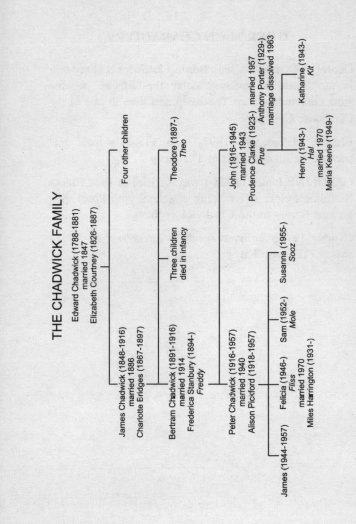

Edward Chadwick (1788–1881)
married 1847
Elizabeth Courtney (1826–1887)

James Chadwick (1848–1916)
married 1886
Charlotte Bridges (1867–1897)

Four other children

Bertram Chadwick (1891–1916)
married 1914
Frederica Stanbury (1894–)
Freddy

Three children
died in infancy

Theodore (1897–)
Theo

Peter Chadwick (1916–1957)
married 1940
Alison Pickford (1918–1957)

John (1916–1945)
married 1943
Prudence Clarke (1923–) married 1957
Anthony Porter (1929–)
marriage dissolved 1963
Prue

James (1944–1957)

Felicia (1946–)
Fliss
married 1970
Miles Harrington (1931–)

Sam (1952–)
Mole

Susanna (1955–)
Sooz

Henry (1943–)
Hal
married 1970
Maria Keene (1949–)

Katharine (1943–)
Kit

OTHER MAIN CHARACTERS

George FOX (1892-) was Bertie Chadwick's Gun-layer at the Battle of Jutland. After the war he became gardener/handyman at The Keep and lives in one of the Gatehouse Cottages.

ELLEN Makepeace (1897-) was Freddy's maid and became the housekeeper at The Keep.

CAROLINE James (1928-) was a friend of Prue Clarke (Caroline's elder sister being at school with Prue). She became Nanny to the Chadwick orphans.

Cynthia Janice Tulliver – otherwise known as SIN – shares a flat with Kit.

Book One
Summer 1972

Chapter One

The lark was somewhere high above her, filling the blue air
with his song. Fliss stared upwards, shielding her eyes with
her hands, dazzled by the brilliant, golden light. The land
was drenched in sunlight; it soaked into the rich red earth,
plunged into the clear cold waters of the river and bathed
the trees with vivid colour. Close to, each long blade of
grass showed separately, bright, clear cut, with its own thin,
sharp, black shadow; far off, the hills rose up, indigo and
violet, their heads touched with gilt. Across the river, sheep
with lambs still at heel nibbled lazily as they strayed across
the meadow, ignored by the cows that lay in the shade of the
pollarded willows at the water's edge.

Fliss stepped back into the darkness of the spinney. Here
and there the sunshine penetrated the thick green roof,
splashing golden coins upon the earthy floor and dripping
molten fingers down rough-barked trunks and smooth grey
boles. Now that the bluebells were over, very little blossomed in this dim interior. Amongst the roots of a mighty
beech, the pale pink flowerets of the campion stretched
hopefully on leggy stalks toward the distant light, whilst
brambles encroached stealthily across a fallen branch.

As her eyes grew accustomed to the shadow, Fliss battled with a now-familiar surge of fear. She found it quite impossible to believe that in three months' time she would be in Hong Kong, about to become a mother, preparing for a two-year naval posting. She simply could not imagine either of these two events. Becoming a mother must be a sufficiently world-shattering experience without it taking place so many thousands of miles away from all that she knew and loved. She looked about her, lightly touching an overhanging spray of leaves, feeling the sappy resilience as she rolled a beech leaf between her fingers. In the past – her past – the spinney had been a symbol, a landmark, a challenge. It was her younger siblings, Mole and Susanna, who had begun it. Running round the spinney had started simply as a race to be timed by Fox, their grandmother's gardener and handyman. Watch in hand he would stand on the hill, beneath the walls of The Keep, whilst they ran round the stand of trees. Then it had been just a game. Later, for Mole it had become more significant, a symbol of achievement; to run round the spinney alone, to pass the point where he could no longer see the walls of The Keep, had demanded all his courage.

Even now, Fliss did not know why Mole had been so completely devastated by the news of their parents' and elder brother's ambush and murder by the Mau-Mau in Kenya fifteen years before. Her own grief had been agonising enough but Mole, at four years old, had been struck dumb for months and even now was sometimes unable to control the stammer which had accompanied the return of his powers of speech. He'd suffered terrible nightmares and had dreaded being left alone. Back at The Keep, however, in

4

the care of his grandmother, Frederica Chadwick, he had gradually learned to control his terror. Now he had passed the Admiralty Interview Board and entered the Royal Navy, as generations of Chadwicks had done before him.

Fliss leaned against the beech tree and closed her eyes. How far they had come since that day of desolation in Kenya. Mole – a naval cadet; Susanna – about to leave school to train as a graphic artist; and she, Fliss – married to a naval officer, pregnant with her first child and soon to leave the safety of familiar surroundings for Hong Kong. Her husband, Miles, had no idea of the depth of her fear. It seemed perfectly natural to him that she should pack and follow wherever the Navy should send him, and she was unable to share her anxieties with him. Fifteen years older than she, he was so adult, so much more experienced, so determined . . .

Fliss thought: He has no family, no roots and he is so confident, so *sure* . . .

She sighed a little, pressing back her fear, remembering how she had come through the anguish of the death of her parents and her beloved big brother, Jamie. From the shadow of the spinney she looked out across the fields to the hills, breathing deeply until a measure of courage returned. If Mole could batten down his weakness and his terror then so could she. She stared up at the trees, whose long shadows stretched out towards The Keep, remembering how much she had worried about him, how frightened she had been for him. No need to worry about either of them now. Mole was settled at Dartmouth and Susanna still had the happy confidence which had been her birthright; there was no reason why she, Fliss, could not go out to

Hong Kong quite free from anxiety.

Fliss thought: But there're still Grandmother and Uncle Theo. And Fox and Ellen. They're getting old . . .

These two first years of marriage had been fun, with Miles based at Devonport in a shore job, and their little house in Dartmouth barely half an hour's drive from The Keep, but Hong Kong was such a long way away and her baby would be nearly two years old when she returned home. Two years old: the same age as Susanna when they'd first arrived from Kenya. She could remember how alone and frightened she'd felt until Grandmother had arrived at the station, bundled them into the car and driven them home to The Keep: home to Ellen, the housekeeper, and Fox, and the dogs . . . She simply mustn't let them see that she was nervous, they would worry so. No, she must show them that she saw it as great fun, a huge adventure.

Squaring her shoulders Fliss moved out into the sunlight and, without glancing back at the spinney, she began to climb the path that led to the green door in the high stone wall.

Her grandmother was waiting for her in the big, cool hall. By tradition tea was always eaten here. In the winter a log fire burned in the huge granite fireplace but today the front door was open wide to the courtyard, to the drifting scent of the Albertine and to the birdsong. On either side of the fireplace two high-backed sofas faced each other across a long, low table. A third chair had been placed at the end of the table making a little room within the vaster spaces of the hall. The rubbed and faded chintz, the fat cushions and worn tartan rugs gave it a homely, comfortable air, and the tea, brought in by Caroline, the children's nanny, a few moments earlier and set out upon the table, completed the picture.

Frederica Chadwick was thinking about Fliss. It had been such fun to have her living so close during these last two years. She was a regular visitor to The Keep and it was clear to see that she was enjoying her new life with Miles, relishing her married status. How proud she was to welcome them all to the house in Dartmouth, doing the honours and showing off her new home. Occasionally she'd drop Miles off at the dockyard and spend the whole day with them at The Keep and, during the holidays, Susanna and Mole had spent days at a time with her in Dartmouth, although not both together, the little house wasn't big enough to boast two spare bedrooms and Miles was unhappy about bodies in sleeping bags on the drawing-room floor. He was a stickler for tidiness and good manners, of which Freddy thoroughly approved, but she often felt that he was much more of her own generation than that of her grandchildren. The truth of it was, of course, that he belonged to the generation in between and it had to be said that he was often rather more like a father to Fliss and her siblings than husband and brother-in-law.

Freddy stirred restlessly. If only it were possible to send Caroline out to Hong Kong with Fliss, just until she'd had the baby; to settle her in and make certain that all was well. Miles had pooh-poohed the idea when she'd tentatively suggested it. It was quite normal now, he said, for wives to manage without the entourage of nanny and staff which had moved around with naval families of the officer class in Freddy's day. He'd assured her that Fliss would be well cared for in the British Military Hospital, that she would have an amah to help her look after the baby, that a fellow officer, already out in Hong Kong, was organising accommodation. There had been nothing else for her to do but to trust him. Freddy knew that she was fussing, being mother hen-ish, but Fliss was so very special. They were all going to miss her terribly . . .

Theo Chadwick, watching his sister-in-law across the table, was aware that she was unconscious of any of the afternoon's delights. Although her head was turned towards the open door, he was convinced that she neither heard the birds nor was aware of the scent of roses. Even the plate of Ellen's new-baked scones and the pot of home-made bramble jelly could not hold her attention. He'd searched about for something with which to distract her, knowing that her thoughts were with Fliss, but his mind remained unhelpfully blank. The silence lengthened and presently he spoke the words which he hoped might offer some kind of comfort.

'She will be well cared for, you know,' he said gently. 'It will all be very much a home from home. A little England. Hong Kong is a crown colony, after all.'

She made no attempt to dissemble or to deny her anxieties. 'But it is so far away,' she said despairingly.

Theo was silent. Although the Chadwicks made their money from china clay there had been a naval tradition in the family for well over a hundred years. Theo's father had been an admiral, his elder brother, Bertie – Freddy's husband – had been killed at Jutland during the First World War and he himself had become a naval chaplain. Nobody knew better than he that Freddy was no stranger to separation and loss. Left a widow with twin baby boys,

Peter and John, she had managed with the help of Ellen and Fox: Ellen, who as Freddy's maid, had arrived with her at The Keep more than fifty years before, and Fox, who had served under Bertie as a gun-layer in 1916. After the war Fox had made his way to The Keep, so as to tell Lieutenant Chadwick's family the truth of his courageous last battle, and had stayed on to look after The Keep and to protect the young widow and her babies. The twins had grown up in time to serve in the Second World War. History repeated itself with uncanny relentlessness. John died when his ship was torpedoed on convoy duty, leaving his young widow, Prue, to bring up their twins, and although Peter had survived the war, he had died later in Kenya along with his wife and eldest son . . .

Theo sighed, a silent internal sigh. No, Freddy was no stranger to grief – and already the next generation was taking up the challenge. Hal, John's son, was a naval lieutenant and Mole, Peter's younger boy, was determined to become a submariner . . . and now Fliss was preparing to pack and follow.

'You were quite happy when Hal's ship went out to the Far East for two years,' he ventured at last. 'It's much the same, isn't it?'

'It's not the same at all,' said Freddy sharply. 'Hal is a man. And he wasn't pregnant.'

Once more Theo was silenced. He heard her words but he felt that there was something much deeper here; something beyond her natural concern for her granddaughter. She glanced at him almost defiantly, chin lifted in the old way, and his great love for her shook his heart and increased his feeling of inadequacy.

'Say something,' she cried. 'Don't just sit there.'

'But what can I say?' he asked helplessly. 'Hong Kong *is* a long way off. Hal *is* a man and he certainly wasn't pregnant when he went out to Singapore.'

To his horror he saw tears glinting in her eyes. 'I might die before she comes back,' she muttered. 'I might never see Fliss's child.'

'My dear Freddy,' he answered, trying for a lighter tone, 'this could be true for any of us, even for Susanna or Mole – accidents might happen to any one of us at any time. But why should we be morbid? You are fit and healthy and come from a long-lived family—'

'I am seventy-seven years old,' interrupted Freddy crossly, rather as if she resented Theo's positive view. 'Anything could happen.'

'Another undeniable truth,' agreed Theo, reaching for the teapot. 'Earthquake, flood, famine. A plague or two . . .'

She glared at him but, as usual, he had cheered her a little by refusing to panic with her. If only she could be certain that Fliss was truly happy, that she had been right to marry Miles.

She took her tea from Theo, managing to return his smile, just as the door which led to the back of the house opened and Fliss came in. She smiled at the two elderly people who waited for her.

'Sorry I'm late,' she said. 'It's so beautiful out there I could hardly bear to leave it. I've just been round the spinney.'

The familiarity of the scene before her was both soothing and poignant. Since she'd known that she was expecting a child her emotions had been unreliable, teetering unsteadily between tears and laughter, confidence and terror. The picture of her grandmother and great-uncle sitting opposite each other at the tea table was a comforting one, representing continuity and serenity; yet her contentment at the sight was undermined by the fear that they might not be here when she returned from Hong Kong. She tried hard to control these emotions, mocking herself for childishness, telling herself that she was being pathetic, but still she wished that she need not have had to cope with both the posting and the baby at once.

Uncle Theo was pouring tea for her whilst Grandmother talked gently on the subject of greenfly on the roses. Fliss took a scone and reached for the bramble jelly.

'I've been spoiled, living so close to home,' she said cheerfully. 'I'm going to have to write down some of Ellen's recipes to take out with me. I hope I'll be able to buy the ingredients. Isn't it odd to think that in three months' time I shall be shopping in Hong Kong?'

Chapter Two

It was later, in the solitude of her room, that Fliss wished that she had not used the words 'I've just been round the spinney'. She suspected that the significance of them had not been lost on her grandmother and great-uncle. Although she had chattered all through tea about the excitement of going to Hong Kong there had been an air of – of what? Fliss turned her back on the view from the window and, sitting on the window seat, took stock of the little room which had been hers for the last fifteen years. Apart from a few precious things which had gone to the house in Dartmouth, it remained much the same as when she had taken possession of it.

'You'll want to come and stay sometimes,' Caroline had said, 'when Miles is away at sea. Home from home. Leave a few things . . .'

Fliss had taken her advice. Anyway, her bits and pieces didn't quite fit into the narrow house in Above Town which Miles had bought when he was first married as a very young officer. His delicate wife had died after only a few years of marriage but he had kept the house, and his personality was stamped firmly upon it. Fliss's Victorian flower prints would have looked incongruous beside his original watercolours and antique prints of naval ports; the small painted chest would have been out of place amongst the expensive reproduction furniture. He had selected his furnishings with care and there was a certain austerity combined with practicality which was faintly daunting. Fliss was used to a more organic style of living. The pieces in the rooms at The Keep had accumulated gradually, each generation adding, replacing, repairing, so that modern and Edwardian jostled with Regency and Victorian, yet all blended together in an entirely natural way.

She stood up and wandered over to the washstand. She had removed the small china pot which had belonged to her mother, and the alabaster box which had once held her father's cufflinks, and taken them with her to Dartmouth but she had left the looking-glass, age-spotted, in its battered mahogany frame. In this frame were stuck some photographs. To begin with she had simply forgotten them, although she had taken the silver-framed studio photograph which showed her father with Jamie standing next to him, her mother with Susanna on her knee, Mole leaning against her and Fliss sitting beside her. It was a charming portrait of a happy, normal little family and now it stood on the mahogany chest of drawers in her bedroom in Dartmouth. There, it did not seem out of place. Yet, for some reason, she had left these other photographs, familiar, comforting, important, stuck in the frame. Jamie was there, hands in pocket, smiling out at her; Susanna astride Fliss's old bicycle, beaming proudly; Kit their cousin, kneeling beside the now long-dead dog, Mrs Pooter, an arm about her furry neck, Mole squinting out at her, a blurred Fox behind him.

Fliss bent to look at the snapshot of her parents at Nairobi's Ngong Racecourse; her father tall, confident, handsome, and her mother with a look which was almost censorious. Fliss bent closer. Did she resemble her mother? That look on her mother's face had kept her and Jamie on their toes. Alison had expected great things of her children, and living up to her expectations had been something of a strain. Fliss was certain that her mother would not sympathise with her present fears. Had she not gone to Kenya with Fliss only seven and Mole barely a year old? Susanna had been born in Africa. Alison had been efficient, calm, competent; had she ever been frightened?

Another photograph caught her attention. It was of her own wedding but not taken by the official photographer; those she kept in the smart album bought for her by Miles. This one had simply been stuck in the frame with the others. Fliss took it from the mahogany frame and studied it closely. It had been taken in the courtyard on the central rectangle of grass. She was holding Mole's arm and they were laughing together. Susanna crouched beside them fiddling with her shoe, her bouquet of sweet peas flung down beside her on the grass. Miles was in the background, smart in his uniform, one arm raised, a finger pointing at some unseen companion. It was what her cousin Kit called his '. . . and furthermore . . .' stance.

For a brief moment Fliss was transported back to the June day, two years before; she could almost feel the sun on her back, smell the scent of the roses. The whole family had risen to the occasion, giving of their utmost, determined to make it her happiest day, showing their pride and love in different, special ways. Since Miles was a widower she had

15

decided to keep the whole thing simple and quiet, just family and close friends, and it had worked very well. Susanna had looked so pretty in that strange dark, dusky pink; she'd been thrilled with the bracelet of delicately wrought silver and coral which Miles had given her. Fliss's own dress was made of thick, cream, cotton lace, ankle-length, slender and faintly Victorian in style. She loved it and often wore it to Ladies' Nights and formal parties. Mole, in his best Sunday suit, had given her away and later, the champagne having gone to his head, he'd given a most amusing and rather touching speech without a trace of his stammer. She'd been so proud of him . . .

Fliss turned away from the washstand and sat on the edge of the narrow iron bed, her fingers unconsciously brushing the patchwork quilt, another of her talismans which had not quite fitted into the house at Dartmouth. The quilt was a history of the family, her family. Oh, how could she bear to leave them and go so far away? How could she endure it that she and her baby would miss such vital contact? No Grandmother to give her that private smile of approval, no Uncle Theo with his immense inner strength, no Ellen to cluck with joy and pride, no Fox to tell her that the baby was a proper Chadwick, no Caroline with her good sense nor Kit to think up fantastic names for the newest member of the family. No Aunt Prue with her motherly warmth, no Susanna or Mole, the baby's aunt and uncle. No Hal . . .

She stood up quickly as the knock at the door was followed by the appearance of Caroline. It was years now since Caroline had ceased to be her nanny and become her friend but Fliss smiled at her automatically, assuming the mantle of bright cheerfulness which she had adopted from the moment she'd arrived at The Keep the evening before.

'Come down to the kitchen for a chat while I do the vegetables for dinner,' suggested Caroline. 'We're all longing to hear about Hong Kong. It's wonderful about the baby, isn't it? Are you as happy as you look or are you being brave? I should be terrified at the thought of going out to Hong Kong to have my first baby.'

Fliss looked at her quickly. What a fool she'd been to think she could hide anything from Caroline.

'Have the others guessed?' she asked anxiously. 'I don't want anyone worrying about me.'

Caroline reached out and gave Fliss's arm an affectionate little squeeze.

'You're probably overdoing it,' she admitted gently. 'Just a touch. We can't *quite* believe that you're so delighted at the idea of being so far away from us. We have our pride, you know. We want to think that you'll miss us. Just a bit.'

'Of course I shall miss you,' said Fliss wretchedly. 'Of course I'm frightened – but what can I do? I don't want Grandmother worrying. It's not so much the idea of going to Hong Kong – that's quite exciting – it's just the thought of having my baby so far from home. And what if something should happen to any of you while I'm there . . .'

She turned away, staring out of the window, unwilling to let Caroline see the tears in her eyes.

Caroline watched her compassionately. She had come to The Keep soon after the arrival of the children when it had been decided that help was needed. Mrs Chadwick had been sixty-two, Ellen sixty, Fox sixty-five; an old household for such young children. So Caroline had come to look after them and never, in all her jobs as a nanny, had she been so

17

happy as at The Keep. It had been a mutual decision that, when the children no longer needed her care, she should stay on, gradually shouldering the tasks which for fifty years had belonged to Ellen and Fox. Ellen was still fairly active but crippling arthritis prevented Fox from carrying out most of his former duties. There was no question, however, that he should be pensioned off. He remained in his quarters in the gatehouse, pottering about at smaller tasks, content to let the responsibility pass to Caroline and young Josh, who came up from the village to do the heavy work about the grounds.

These three, Fox, Ellen and Caroline, had formed the framework for the children's lives and Caroline knew how deeply Fliss's roots had sunk into the ground from which her family had sprung, sending out tender feelers which climbed and twined themselves about that framework. Of all the children she was most deeply knitted into the fabric of The Keep and the family. She had gone off bravely to school and to college, and later to her job in Gloucestershire, but it was here that she belonged, where she most loved to be.

Caroline thought: It would be easier for her to go to Hong Kong if she wasn't pregnant. Fliss will hate to have her baby so far away from us all.

Aloud, she said, 'Come on down and talk about it. You can't stop people worrying. It's best to be open about it. Stiff upper lips are all very well but sometimes a good weep is just as beneficial. Don't bottle things up, Flissy dear.'

Fliss smiled at her gratefully. 'I'm a bit wound up about it all,' she admitted. 'Silly, isn't it? There's nothing to it, really. Miles says that it's what naval wives have to expect. They have a saying, you know: "If you can't take a joke you shouldn't have joined." You shouldn't marry a sailor and expect him to stay at home.'

'That's quite true,' agreed Caroline, following Fliss out on to the landing. 'But then Miles has no family to leave. And it isn't him having the baby.'

Fliss descended the stairs from the nursery quarters on the second floor thoughtfully. She couldn't argue with Caroline's observations but in the end it made no difference. The situation had to be faced and there was no use whining about it.

'I've been very lucky,' she said as they reached the landing. 'Starting as a naval wife with Miles in a shore job was a tremendous bonus. He's hardly been away at all. I can't tell you how thrilled he is to be given the command of HMS *Yarnton*. He's terribly excited about the whole thing.'

'Yes,' said Caroline, remembering a time when she had imagined herself to be in love with Miles. 'Yes, he would be. And about the baby, too, I expect.'

Fliss's answer was rather a long time in coming and slightly confused. 'Well, he is but it's rather . . . You know. Perhaps the timing is a bit unfortunate . . . Of course, I'd rather have my baby here but I couldn't possibly leave Miles for that long. He'd be very hurt . . .'

Watching Fliss, noting the downcast face, the thick fair hair pulled back into a loose plait, the slender figure with a long Indian skirt wrapped about the still-narrow waist and a cheesecloth shirt knotted above it, Caroline was seized by a variety of sensations. She felt the old tenderness for the child she had known, a new respect for the woman Fliss was becoming, and an overwhelming relief that she herself had stood aside from the complex bonds which tied the wife and mother. As she watched Fliss struggling with her confused emotions, she was profoundly thankful that she would never know that particular division of loyalty. Who should come first: husband or child? She slipped an arm about the slim, square shoulders as they passed through the hall.

'A glass of sherry,' she suggested. 'Yes? You shall sit and have a drink while I peel the potatoes. Ellen is over with Fox, changing his sheets and sorting him out. We'll have a quiet half an hour.'

In the kitchen Mrs Pooter's descendent, Polly Perkins, lay in the enormous dog basket. Mrs Pooter and her son, Mugwump, were both dead, but Perks was just such another large, woolly Border collie, crossed with spaniel or retriever, with a rusty coloured coat, flopping ears and dark brown eyes. She was of a more passive disposition than the greedy, cunning and ungrateful Mrs Pooter but she had Mugwump's sense of fun, and she enjoyed her walks on the hill behind The Keep or in the deep, quiet lane where Caroline had exercised her earlier, after tea. She lay curled in a ball, nose on tail, sleeping peacefully, and the mere sight of her brought some measure of tranquillity to Fliss's anxious mind.

As usual she looked around the kitchen with pleasure. For as long as she could remember it seemed unchanged, her favourite place. Here, when they had returned from Kenya, she had felt safest, sharing the responsibility of her siblings with Ellen and Fox, playing dominoes at the kitchen table or kneeling on the window seat, staring out over the neat, multicoloured fields to the distant hills. The hill sloped away so steeply behind the house that the kitchen was poised high up in the air and the small Fliss had been enchanted to be able to look down upon the birds that circled below her.

Fliss sat down in the rocking chair by the Aga and watched Caroline's sturdy reassuring figure moving to and fro, fetching glasses, pouring sherry. The warmth from the Aga, the slow ticking of the clock, the geraniums on the deep windowsill and the soft gleam of the china on the dresser, all these things soothed the senses and Fliss felt, suddenly, pleasantly drowsy.

It had been almost a relief when Miles had gone off to Portsmouth on a course and she had been left alone to brood over the news of his posting to Hong Kong. It had come swiftly on the heels of the discovery that she was pregnant and she had barely had time to digest either piece of information.

'Did we want a baby this soon?' Miles had asked. It had been a cheerful enough question but Fliss's stomach had lurched oddly. She had expected him to be as thrilled as she was and she did not know how to answer him. A childish disappointment had gripped her and she'd remained silent. He'd glanced round at her, puzzled, and then smiled at her expression. 'Silly child,' he'd said, going to her and taking her into his arms. 'I'm delighted, of course. That goes without saying, surely? It's just a bit of a shock. I thought we were going to wait for a while. Enjoy ourselves and so on. It's going to be rather a tie, you know.'

'It must have been when we were on leave,' she'd said, almost apologetically, trying to hide her own feelings. 'We were a bit careless . . .'

'I *told* you to go on the Pill,' he'd said reprovingly. 'Too late now . . . This'll bump the mess bill up a few quid, I can tell you . . .'

Now, as she sat sipping her sherry, listening to Caroline recounting Perks's latest exploits, Fliss realised that what she'd felt was a kind of resentment. Miles's attitude was that of an adult reproving a child for some thoughtless misdemeanour rather than husband and wife discussing their first child. When he'd returned from his visit to the Appointer, jubilant with the news of his posting to Hong Kong, it had been her turn to be shocked.

'But how can we?' she'd asked anxiously. 'With the baby and things. Of course, it's wonderful news, darling. Terribly exciting. But how will I manage with . . . you know, having the baby and so on?'

'Good heavens, there's a British military hospital in Hong Kong,' he'd cried impatiently. 'That's not a problem. Don't worry about that. God, it'll be fantastic to have my own command. Tell you what, I'll book a table at the Cherub. This calls for a bit of a celebration.'

It had hurt that he'd been so much more excited at the news of his posting than the discovery that she was expecting their child. She'd told herself to grow up and had made a determined effort to enjoy their evening out. Still, it was a relief to be on her own, to have the small, narrow house to herself for a while and to come over to see her family at The Keep. As she finished her sherry she decided that she was simply feeling tired – probably quite normal under the circumstances – and that she'd been suffering from a sense of humour failure.

'Come on,' she said, getting up and joining Caroline at the sink, 'I'll help you with the vegetables. Have you heard from Kit lately? She was thrilled about the baby. She wants to be a godmother . . .'

Chapter Three

Later that day in London, in the roomy second-floor flat in Pembridge Square, Kit was thinking about her cousin Fliss, and musing happily over the news of the expected child.

'Hannah,' said Kit thoughtfully. 'Hannah's a nice name, isn't it? Or Humphrey, if it's a boy? We want something different. A name that will make him or her stick in the memory. What do you think?'

Her flatmate Cynthia Jane – nicknamed Sin by Kit in student days – poured some more wine into her glass and propped her chin in her hands.

'Hannibal,' she suggested idly. 'Got a bit of a ring to it, wouldn't you say? Imagine his first day at school and Fliss saying, "This is Hannibal Harrington." That would stick in the memory all right.'

'Oh, shut up,' said Kit good-humouredly. 'But you could be right. Perhaps not an alliteration. Pity. I really like Hannah. OK then . . .' She riffled the pages of the little book which she was studying. 'Georgina. Or George, of course.'

Sin rolled her eyes. 'You really think that they're going to allow you to choose the name of their first-born?'

'I always think up the names for the family,' protested Kit. 'I'm known for it.'

'For the dogs, yes,' admitted Sin. 'And for cars. Nicknames, even. But for new babies? Do you honestly think that Miles is going to stand by while you christen his child?'

'Fliss said, "You must come up with a really good name,",' said Kit. 'I *am* the child's cousin and godmother.'

'Can you be a cousin and a godmother to the same child?' mused Sin.

'Why not?' demanded Kit. 'I've always longed to be somebody's godmother. It sounds such fun. You take them out from school and buy them tea and leave them all your money when you die.'

'Well, that'll be a treat for the poor thing,' murmured Sin. 'I can't imagine why, but I always thought that there was some religious connection . . .'

'Well, of course there is,' answered Kit impatiently, seizing the bottle and eyeing the inch or two left in the bottom meaningly. 'I shall get Uncle Theo to help me out with that bit.'

Sin sat up straight. 'Gosh,' she said softly. 'I never thought of that. Hours closeted with darling Theo discussing the state of my soul.'

'What d'you mean?' asked Kit suspiciously. 'What has *your* soul got to do with this?'

'Listen,' said Sin earnestly, pushing her plate aside and leaning forward. 'How about if *I* become the kid's godmother and you just stick with being good old Cousin Kit? You can still have terrific fun—'

'Forget it,' said Kit firmly. 'I know your game. This has

nothing to do with the baby; it's simply a ruse to spend time with Uncle Theo. Everyone knows of your passion for him. It's shocking. And him a man of the cloth and in his seventies to boot!'

'He has ruined my life,' sighed Sin. 'Are you sure I couldn't be godmother? It might be the making of me.'

'I can just see Miles agreeing to it,' scoffed Kit. 'Especially when you flirt outrageously with him at every opportunity, even at his own wedding. What with him and Uncle Theo . . .'

'I have a thing about older men.' Sin sipped sadly at her wine.

'True. And every other sort of man.' Kit closed the book. 'Maria is going to do for you one of these days if you're not careful. She's terribly jealous.'

'Maria's so *easy*,' admitted Sin. 'I hardly have to work at it at all. Just one glance at dear Hal, a meaningful little smile, and her hackles are up and she's practically snarling. Dear old Flissy doesn't mind a bit when I do the same with Miles, but then . . .' She paused.

'But then what?' asked Kit curiously, when the silence lengthened.

Sin shrugged, frowning a little, and shook her head.

'Come on,' persisted Kit, surprised. 'What were you going to say?'

'Look,' said Sin at last, 'I haven't really thought this through. It just came into my mind. I'm not sure . . .'

'Oh, for goodness' sake,' cried Kit impatiently. 'Spit it out. Who do you think you are? Wittgenstein, or what? It's not going to be cast in tablets of stone. Just say it.'

'I was going to say that Fliss isn't in love with Miles. Not

25

like Maria is with Hal. That's all. Except that I hadn't really thought about it before but now I *have* thought about it, it still seems that it's true.'

London sounds drifted through the open windows: the rumble of distant traffic, children playing cricket in the little square, snatches of music from someone's radio . . .

Kit thought: She's right. There isn't that passion between Fliss and Miles. Of course, he's so much older, and Fliss is much more serious than Maria, but it *was* there, that kind of battened-down excitement, between Hal and Fliss before the family found out and put the mockers on it. Oh hell . . .

'Of course it means nothing,' Sin was saying rapidly, 'they're such completely different types. Fliss and Maria, I mean. Well, come to that, so are Miles and Hal but—'

'It's OK,' said Kit. 'I can cope with this. Don't go on about it.'

'And they're having a baby,' added Sin, unable to prevent herself attempting to cover the fact that she'd put her foot in it. 'So you see I'm probably quite wrong.'

'Oh, shut up,' said Kit crossly. 'It's too late now. You've made me think about it. And you're right. There's something missing. But what is it? It could be that they're simply a staid, happily married couple, not given to flights of fancy and so on, but it's not quite like that, is it?'

Sin sighed again. 'It's like he's her father. He's kind and considerate and just the tiniest bit condescending. You know? The pat on the head, run along, darling, kind of thing. He loves her, no question about that, but now that he's won her he's settled back into his previous middle-aged routines, except that now he's got a wife in tow.'

'Perhaps going to Hong Kong will help,' suggested Kit hopefully.

Sin raised her eyebrows and said nothing.

'She sounded a bit strange when she talked about it yesterday,' pursued Kit, 'but I just assumed that she was more excited about the baby than going to Hong Kong. Miles is delighted, of course.'

'Of course,' said Sin neutrally.

Kit looked at her sharply. 'Why are you saying it like that?' she demanded. 'Of course he's delighted. A baby on the way and his own command. What could be better?'

'What indeed?' murmured Sin. 'Let's forget it, shall we? Let's go and walk in the park. I feel an urge coming on to drown myself in the Serpentine. It happens each time we talk about love and marriage and babies and so on.'

'We might as well,' said Kit. 'Perhaps I'll join you. We can die together. Relationships are so damned complicated.'

'Talking of which,' said Sin innocently, 'Jake telephoned earlier. Didn't leave a message except to send his love. Want to call him back before we go?'

'No,' said Kit grumpily. 'I'm not in the mood now. That's another problem. I do love dear old Jake the Rake but is it the real thing? I'm even more confused after this little bombshell. We have such fun but if I let him get serious will it rock the boat? Does that mean I don't really love him? How is one to know?'

'Never mind,' said Sin. 'Of course, as you pointed out, I'm not Wittgenstein but you know what he said? "Love which can't be classified is best." Got a point, hasn't he?'

'Your death wish may be gratified before we reach the park,' said Kit grimly. 'You've ruined my evening. Let that be enough for you. Oh, and bring your purse. I might want an ice cream.'

During the journey from Portsmouth to Devon, Maria sat wrapped in preoccupation while Hal talked about his post-ing to the frigate HMS *Falmouth*, the fun of returning to Devon, the possibilities of the married quarter available in Compton Road near HMS *Manadon* in Plymouth. She murmured appropriately, trying to inject enthusiasm into her voice, but her thoughts were busy elsewhere. The prospect of their few days of leave was ruined by the knowledge that Fliss was at The Keep. Maria had been delighted when Hal suggested that they should go down to see the married quarter, staying for a few nights with his grandmother. She loved to be fussed over by Ellen and Fox, to be approved by Mrs Chadwick and Uncle Theo, spoiled by Caroline. She felt like a beloved child returning home from school – and Hal was such a favourite with his family. Although she stared straight ahead she visualised his face; determined, confident, handsome, open. People took to him, warming to his friendly smile and good-natured laugh. He had a handclasp and a redeeming word for all; everyone loved him.

This, of course, was where the root of the matter lay. Maria did not want everyone to love Hal, or rather she wished he were not so indiscriminate in his returning of this love. In her more rational moments she knew that Hal's easy affection was given to male and female alike – but when was jealousy ever rational? It came at her from nowhere, swooping in to undermine her fragile confidence, to shake her belief in his love for her. It drove her to be bitchy and cruel, it kept her awake at nights when he was away, it made her dread the other wives' gossip, hating to hear that he was enjoying himself in any way which might involve other women. She knew that, wherever the ship docked, the officers were invited to parties and dinners, entertained royally during their 'showing the flag visits', fêted when they were in foreign ports. She waited eagerly for his letters, for the occasional telephone call, for every reaffirmation of his love.

This sunny June morning, as the road fled away behind them, she wondered if it would have been the same if Hal had never told her about Fliss. Was it Hal's 'confession' – that he and his cousin had been romantically involved – which was to blame for her insecurity? It was so unfair. Manlike, he had been determined to get it off his chest, unaware of the effect on her. He'd explained that the romance had been adolescent and quite innocent but there was something so horribly Romeo-and-Juliet-ish about the whole business and, or so it seemed to Maria, if his family hadn't forbidden it then presumably he and Fliss would have continued to love one another. She had never quite been able to pin him down. Hal's stance was 'well, it didn't happen so what's all the fuss about? I'm married to you now and that's that.'

Maria thought: There's something still there, though, I just know it. I can feel it when they're together. I'm second best, that's the problem. How can I compete with her? God, I hate her!

The truly irritating thing was that Fliss was so nice to her. In fact, during one of Hal's longer patrols at sea, she had accepted an invitation to stay with Fliss in the little house in

Dartmouth. For a brief, sane moment, Maria had seen that she might neutralise the whole thing by making friends with Fliss; they would form an alliance so that she had nothing to fear from her.

To begin with it actually seemed as if it might work. Without Hal around, the two girls had settled into a delightfully friendly relationship and had a wonderful week together. Fliss introduced Maria to the beaches and moors, took her into the small market towns; they even went to choral evensong at Exeter cathedral after a glorious afternoon of shopping in the city. They had barely mentioned Hal, except as he related to Maria's being utterly miserable when he was away. His absence had allowed her to talk about him as if he were a different Hal, one whom Fliss knew only slightly but whom *she* knew intimately. She had been worldly-wise, tolerant about his shortcomings, joking and light-hearted about his lack of domesticity. Fliss had made no attempt to be proprietorial, made no mention of her own particular knowledge of Hal. She'd been so understanding, so sympathetic, and they'd laughed together over the problems facing the naval wife. By the end of the week Maria was convinced that she'd laid the ghost.

Her certainty had lasted until the next time that she saw Hal and Fliss together at the Birthday weekend at The Keep. The Chadwicks had an old tradition of celebrating several birthdays in one big festivity. Mrs Chadwick, Hal and Kit, and Mole all had birthdays at the end of October and, by some miracle, these always managed to fit in with half term, which was why this celebration had become so important over the years. Everyone made an effort to get to The Keep for it.

This particular Birthday, just after their first wedding anniversary, Hal was home from sea and he and Maria went down to Devon for the festivities. She had felt quite confident, actually looking forward to it – until she'd seen the look in Hal's eyes when he first saw Fliss . . .

They'd been in the hall with Uncle Theo and Mole, having arrived much earlier than they'd expected to, when Fliss had come in with Caroline, helping her to carry the tea things. They'd been laughing together and had paused just inside the door to finish their conversation, heads bent together and looking suddenly serious, before they turned to look at the group around the fire. Maria had heard the phrase about faces 'lighting up' and, at that moment, she knew exactly what it meant. Fliss's small face had smoothed out, her eyes had widened and her lips had curved upward. Glancing involuntarily at Hal, Maria saw that his face, too, was bright with love; it were as though something invisible but almost tangible stretched between them. Her heart had beat fast with terror and she knew a longing to smash something, to scream, anything to snap the thread which seemed to draw her husband and his cousin together.

She'd been silly then, she'd turned to Mole, asking why they still used his nickname now that he was grown up, when he was much too big to burrow under rugs or hide beneath furniture. Sam was a nice name, she'd told him, and from now on she would call him Sam. He had watched her, puzzled, and she knew that her voice was too high, her gestures too exaggerated, but knew, also, that she must do something to break the tension between Hal and Fliss. Then Prue, Hal's mother, had appeared and the charge of electricity had faltered, dwindling into the affection of two members of the same family greeting each other with perfectly natural friendliness. Maria had melted into her mother-in-law's hug with relief and gratitude. Prue was so motherly, so sweet, so delighted to see them . . .

'Honiton,' Hal's cheerful voice broke into her thoughts, startling her. 'We're making very good time. How about stopping for coffee?'

Chapter Four

The Keep had been built on the site of an old hill fort between the moors and the sea, and the three-storeyed castellated tower stood with its back to the north, its grounds sheltering beneath high stone walls. Its courtyard faced south whilst the garden, bounded by orchards, stretched away to the west. To the north and east, however, the hill fell sharply away, the rough, grassy slopes descending to the valley through which the river passed. Later generations had added two wings, set back a little on each side of the original tower whose austere grey stone remained unadorned, although old-fashioned roses and wisteria climbed the wings and the courtyard walls. Exposed to the capriciousness of the West Country weather, The Keep looked older than its one hundred and thirty years. It appeared to have grown quite naturally out of the earth, at one with its surroundings.

This misty, rainy morning Ellen, arriving in the kitchen to begin the morning's tasks, was glad of the Aga's warmth. Never was she foolhardy enough to believe that summer had really arrived or the Aga no longer needed. Despite the new electric stove in the scullery, Ellen clung to tried and trusted ways. Where else could you dry the laundry but on the wooden airer that swung on its pulleys from the ceiling high above? What else would keep the kitchen cosy and warm on such a chill day? It was Caroline now who took out the ashes and carried in the coke, but to Ellen's relief – and Fox's – she did not complain of this back-breaking grind nor did she suggest that the new electric stove might be more convenient. A silent object of reproach, it remained in all its virginal whiteness, unused and a constant reminder of the waste of Mrs Chadwick's money.

Fox was already installed in the rocker, a cup of tea in his hand, whilst Ellen bustled about preparing breakfast. On days such as these, Caroline had taken over the dog walking, too. Fox's arthritis prevented him from venturing far afield, although he enjoyed pottering out on to the hill when the weather permitted. It had taken him a while to adjust to the loss of independence, to give in gracefully. It was his beloved mistress, whom he had served for fifty years, who had removed the sting which threatened to poison the contentment of his old age. He had attempted to express his gratitude at being her pensioner, apologising for his inadequacy, and she had listened to him thoughtfully.

Her words still touched and warmed his heart, allowing him finally to take an honourable ease '. . . you are part of my family. You must be gracious now and accept our care for you as we have accepted your protection and service in the past. It is no more than you deserve . . . You have been with me from the beginning, Fox, and we shall see things out together, you and I.'

She had given him back his dignity so that he did not have to go away, to leave The Keep, to struggle alone without family or friends around him.

'I can't like it,' said Ellen suddenly, putting the marma-lade down upon the table with a thump. 'It's no good. I must have my say or burst. I'm worried sick and that's the truth. Going to the other side of the world to have her baby. Whatever next, I wonder. She'll be no good in that sort of climate. She's not strong, Fliss isn't. Whatever can the Commander be thinking about to allow it?'

Fox painfully flexed his knotted fingers and patted the only bit of Ellen he could reach. She twitched resentfully, like a horse resisting a fly, and then abruptly nodded recognition of his attempted comfort.

'It happens all the time,' he told her. ''Tis British, Hong Kong is. There'll be hospitals and everything. No call to get upset. The Commander can't leave her behind for two years, leastways, he won't want to. He'll be there with her.'

'And a fat lot of good that'll be,' cried Ellen. 'It's your family you need at times like this.'

'He *is* her family,' pointed out Fox mildly. 'He's her husband.'

'You know quite well what I mean,' snapped Ellen. 'Hus-bands might be all very well in their place but their place isn't with a pregnant girl thousands of miles from home. Like as not he'll be off at sea, anyway, and she'll be all alone. Oh, I'm that worried I can't think straight.'

'Fliss is a sailor's wife now,' said Fox gently. 'Her duty is with the Commander. There's nowt nor summat any of us can do about that, maid. Just be thankful there's so much more medical know-how these days.'

'She's frightened,' said Ellen miserably, sitting down suddenly. 'I can see it, for all her bright chatter. She doesn't deceive me.'

Fox stared at her, shocked by this revelation. He had been quite taken in by Fliss's cheerfulness but now, as he looked at the uncharacteristic slump of Ellen's shoulders, he began to feel infected by her anxiety.

'It reminds of me when they first arrived from Kenya,' said Ellen. 'Remember? She was always pushing down her own grief because of Mole being struck dumb by the shock. I can see her now at this very table, panic-stricken because she thought he'd never talk again and him swallowing and swallowing, trying to get the words out. She'd never let him see it, though. Always bright and cheerful, trying to distract him, hiding her fear. She's doing it again now but she doesn't fool *me*.'

Fox could think of nothing to say. He felt inadequate and helpless, guessing that anything he suggested would be rejected by Ellen in her present frame of mind. He gave a sigh of relief as Caroline and Perks came in to the kitchen together.

'It never ceases to amaze me how quickly the weather can change,' said Caroline, shutting the door behind her as Perks headed for her basket. 'Summer one day, autumn the next . . .'

She paused, sensing the atmosphere, her glance passing between the two of them. Fox shook his head slightly, jerking it towards Ellen, pulling down the corners of his mouth warningly. Caroline raised her eyebrows questioningly and put her hand lightly on Ellen's shoulder as she passed.

'I need a cup of tea,' she said. 'It's not that it's *cold* exactly, but there's a kind of dankness. Thank goodness for a nice warm kitchen. Cuppa, Ellen? I see Fox has got one already.'

'I think I will,' said Ellen, not moving. 'I've got the hump today and that's all there is to it.'

'Poor old Ellen.' Caroline lifted the big brown teapot from the Aga and put it on the table. 'Any particular reason or is it Mole's old "black dog" kind of depression?'

'It's that Fliss,' wailed Ellen, plaiting her fingers together and wringing her hands. 'She's not happy, Caroline. No two ways about it.'

'No,' said Caroline after a moment. 'No, I realise that. Here.' She poured Ellen's tea and pushed the cup towards her. 'I've been thinking about it, too. She's trying to be brave about it but there's a lot on her mind. The baby, going to Hong Kong, being away from us all for two years. The trouble is there's nothing to be done about it. If she stays behind to have the baby at home and then waits for it to be old enough to travel, half of Miles's time will be over before she gets out there.'

'In my young days,' said Ellen grimly, unimpressed by this argument, 'young navy wives didn't go gadding round the world with their husbands. They stayed at home sensibly, bringing up their children. I recall fathers not seeing children till they were two years old and upwards.'

'No aeroplanes in those days,' put in Fox. 'The sea voyage out to the China station and suchlike was enough to put off most young wives.'

'But it's not new,' said Caroline gently. 'Think of the British out in India. And surely you wouldn't want Miles not to see his child until it was two years old, Ellen?'

'It's not the Commander I'm thinking of,' said Ellen stubbornly. 'It's Fliss. A young mother should be contented and happy, not scared and lonely for her people.'

'There's the British Military Hospital in Kowloon. There will be other young wives just like Fliss having babies. She'll make lots of friends. The Navy looks after its own, Ellen. The naval base is called HMS *Tamar* after the river. That's a nice familiar Devonshire name, isn't it?'

'Even so what the name of the base has to do with whether Fliss is happy or not I *can't* see.'

Caroline and Fox exchanged glances while Ellen sipped angrily at her tea and set down the cup with a clatter in its saucer.

'The point is,' said Caroline, who came from an army background and could sympathise with both points of view, 'there is nothing we can do. If Fliss senses our fears for her she'll be even more distressed. The way I see it, the less she has to think about, the better. Of course she's worried about leaving us all and going so far away, let alone the anxiety about having her first baby among strangers, but there are no options. She thinks it would be wrong – and I agree with her – to stay behind. The least we can do is to go along with her brave attitude that it's all a great adventure otherwise we shall undermine her courage—'

The door opened and Fliss came into the kitchen. The instant silence was so charged with emotion that she stood for a moment looking at them each in turn. They stared back at her, shocked and unmoving, as if they were all playing the game known as statues.

'Sorry,' she said, smiling but looking faintly anxious. 'Did I interrupt something?'

'Only,' said Ellen, rising heavily to her feet, '*only* the old argument about that dratted cooker. Terrible waste of money to my mind, though Mrs Chadwick meant well. It may be cleaner and more convenient but *what* we'd do without the Aga on a morning like this I *don't* know. But I *do* know that sitting talking about it is getting us nowhere. And me behind with the breakfasts.'

Caroline smiled at Fliss as she slid into a chair. 'Tea?'

'Please.' Fliss sighed contentedly. 'I must say I agree with Ellen. I love this kitchen. I was always so cold when we came back from Kenya and it was such a lovely cosy place to be. It was my favourite room in those days.'

'Remember our games of dominoes?' Fox beamed at her from his rocking chair. 'And Ellen's tin of Sharps toffees?'

'Oh, yes, I do,' said Fliss. 'See-through paper with different coloured squiggles on them. I always liked the red best although I suspect the toffees all tasted the same.'

'And that Susanna,' said Ellen, bustling back again, 'always wanting one in each hand. Terror, she was.'

'Rather typical of Susanna, wouldn't you say?' suggested Caroline. 'Seizing life with both hands and refusing to let go. She hasn't changed.'

'I'm glad she's decided to do her art course at Bristol,' said Fliss, leaning both elbows on the table and cradling her cup in her hands. 'It's a comfort to know that she'll be staying with Aunt Prue to start with. She doesn't know anyone in Bristol and she'd be terribly lonely.'

There was a tiny silence.

'Make friends in no time, she will,' said Fox bracingly. 'Right taking little maid, she be.'

'I quite agree,' smiled Caroline. 'Poor old Mole used to have such difficulty with her on the train going to and from school. She'd talk to anyone.'

'That's why I'm glad she'll be with Aunt Prue,' said Fliss.

'Dear old Sooz has no discrimination. Everyone's a friend. Goodness knows who she'd find herself sharing a room with. This way she'll have a bit of a breathing space. Time to settle in a bit and get to know people.'

'Of course,' said Caroline thoughtfully, 'that's the good thing about the Navy, isn't it? Wherever you go there's that framework. People you know, old friends you meet up with.'

'That's quite true,' said Fliss at once. 'It's surprising how many of Miles's oppos are out in Hong Kong. It'll be quite a reunion by the sound of it. The wives will be able to show me the ropes. It's a comforting thought, I must say.'

'You'll be a real old hand by the time you get home again,' said Fox cheerfully. 'What a lot there'll be to tell us. Mind you take lots of photos, maid. We'll want to see it all.'

'Of course I will,' Fliss assured him. She swallowed, pressing her lips together, and tried to smile. 'I only wish I could take you all with me.'

'And that's a fine thought I must say,' said Ellen, passing behind her and pausing for a second to grip Fliss's shoulder. 'Carting a lot of old folk out to Hong Kong. Whatever next, I wonder. But we shall be here waiting for you to come back, just you be certain of that. Now finish that tea and you shall have some porridge.'

Chapter Five

Freddy moved slowly along the path under the courtyard wall, dead-heading the roses which climbed and flourished amongst the branches of the wisteria and clematis. Her thick hair had faded now to silver but she still wore it in a heavy bun on the nape of her neck, an old linen hat tilted above it to shield her eyes from the sun. Her arms were bare, tanned a deep brown from hours in the garden, her old tweed skirt snagged and pulled out of shape from years of bending and kneeling amongst her beloved flowers and plants. Yet there was still an elegance and grace about her, emphasised by her tall slenderness. A robin was keeping her company, trilling his tune from the branches above her, cocking his head to see if she were enjoying his song. Occasionally he darted down to forage amongst the woody roots or flew up to the top of the wall to preen his feathers. Freddy talked to him quietly, glad that he was there.

The children had returned to their respective homes and The Keep seemed quieter than usual without them. There was, she decided as she snipped, a particular feeling when any of the children were about, yet each child created a different atmosphere. She paused for a moment, wondering if this were a flight of fancy, deciding that it was true. Take Hal, for instance. Hal made you feel alert and ready for action. Your privacy might be disrupted at any moment: a carful of young people was likely to roll in beneath the arch of the gatehouse or there might be a complete stranger at the breakfast table, invited back after a jolly evening at the pub. Whenever she felt inclined to resent this somewhat cavalier attitude, Freddy strove to remember that Hal, at some distant time – perhaps not too distant now – might be master here. He was the executor for her will and a trustee, for she had been persuaded at last to take proper legal advice and put the whole estate into a trust, and she had given him power of attorney. She had been grieved to go back on her word for he was no longer her heir – she had no heir as such – but it was understood and accepted by the family that he was the most likely of her grandchildren to use The Keep as his home and to have the salary to help to maintain it. It was good that he felt so at home here, good that The Keep would be thrown open by his generous hospitality. For so many years now it had been more of a refuge: a refuge for herself and her fatherless twins; a refuge for the three orphaned children returning from Kenya; a refuge, too, for Theo when he decided to give up his flat in Southsea and come home at last. Now all the children were gone – or nearly so. Susanna, the last to leave, would be off to Bristol in the autumn, although she would be back for the holidays, but once Mole had passed out from Dartmouth and Susanna had finished her course, The Keep would be left simply as a shelter for the elderly people within its walls.

Freddy dropped her secateurs into her basket and looked about her. It was a faintly depressing thought – and a foolish one. After all, Caroline was not elderly and the children were always returning for weekends and short holidays or simply passing through. This would not cease because none of them actually lived at The Keep. Nevertheless, it did seem that the family was reaching the end of an era.

The robin hopped on to a nearby twig and sang a stave or two, his bright eye encouraging her. She smiled and nodded as if in answer – she simply must not allow herself to become depressed – and, in an attempt to distract herself, continued to pursue her earlier interesting idea regarding the question of atmospheres. Having dwelled on Hal, she moved on to his twin, Kit. Well, darling Kit was simply an eccentric in the making, no question about that. She reminded Freddy of an elderly aunt whom, as a child, she had adored; quite potty but so delightfully unexpected. Just such a one was Kit. She was young yet but all the signs were there: her tendency to curl up in the huge dog basket with the dogs, her penchant for unusual people – Sin and the delightful Jacques, whom she called Jake the Rake – and her loyalty to her old Morris, called Eppyjay because of its number plate, EPJ 43. She was unpunctual, lazy and vague, but there was, thought Freddy, a warmth in your heart when Kit slid an arm around your neck and whispered, 'Hello, honey' in your ear. None of the other children had ever called her 'honey' . . .

Fliss, of course, was terribly special, not least because she reminded Freddy of herself when young. She masked her insecurity with the same lift of the chin and the squaring of the shoulders; she cared deeply about the family, and beneath her fragile appearance was a sinewy, springy strength. Having Fliss around seemed utterly natural to Freddy, as though she had a younger, stronger version of herself about the place. If only it had been possible to allow Fliss and Hal to marry. They would have made the perfect pair, the ideal owners of The Keep. His liveliness would have leavened her seriousness and her good sense would have kept a restraining hand upon his recklessness.

The robin flipped up and over the wall and Freddy sat down on the wooden seat, gazing out across the courtyard with a sigh. Well, it was over and done with and no use brooding about it. Hal had Maria; such a pretty child but taking a while to mature. There was a lack of confidence which Freddy was at a loss to understand, in fact there had been moments during this last visit when she had felt almost irritated by Maria. At times she had looked quite sulky and when Fliss had told them that she was expecting a child Maria had behaved in the oddest manner.

Freddy thought: I think she was jealous. But what nonsense! Surely she and Hal are quite capable of having babies. It must have been something else.

She lifted her face to the sunshine and closed her eyes. Where had she got to? Ah, yes, Mole. Now Mole was different again. A true Chadwick, so like Theo, dark-haired, brown-eyed, he was quiet, undemanding, companionable, astute, yet – unlike Theo – there was just the suggestion of strain in having him about. It was all those years of worry, of course. First he had been unable to speak and then, once he regained his voice, there were the nightmares and sleepwalking, the terror of being left, his anxiety that the members of his family might disappear in the same way as his parents and his brother. Poor Mole. For the thousandth time she wondered exactly what dreadful details Mole had heard on the terrible day when he'd been playing under the kitchen table and the policeman had come rushing in, recounting the tragic news of the murders to Cookie. For years this had been her own private anguish. The official story was that the car had been ambushed and its occupants shot by Mau-Mau, but since then many other stories of atrocities had filtered back and she guessed that their end had not been so straightforward.

Freddy forced her mind away from such horror and thought about Susanna. Happy, friendly, well balanced: Susanna was the easiest of all the children. Since she had been too young to remember her parents and brother, she had settled contentedly into The Keep and now had no other memories. This was her home and these were her people. She belonged here – as they all did in one way or another, which was why Freddy had insisted that The Keep must be kept as a refuge for them all. Hal might be the natural candidate to take over the reins, to preserve the trust for his own children and their cousins, but this was the condition attached to his 'inheritance'. After all, there were not only the children to consider.

Freddy thought: I suppose we're an odd collection. Dear old Ellen and Fox who have been with me for ever. Caroline. What in the world would we have done without Caroline? And Theo . . .

Sitting there in the sun, her basket beside her on the seat, Freddy smiled sadly. All those years in which she had loved him and yet he had never guessed. How terrible it had been to marry the man you thought you loved only to fall in love with his youngest brother. It had been hard to live without any return of that particular kind of love . . . At least he had never married. No doubt being a priest had had something to do with that, although as a naval chaplain he might have done so. Even now, all passion supposedly spent, Freddy experienced a faint thrill of jealousy at the thought of Theo romantically involved with another woman. How happy she had been when he had decided to come home at last, how precious his companionship had been for these last seven years. She had railed at him, spurned his faith, leaned on him and loved him for more than fifty years. Life without Theo was unimaginable.

The robin flew down, pecking at the cracks between the paving stone beside her shoe, peering at her with his bright, knowing eye.

'Quite right,' she told him. 'I'm slacking,' and, climbing to her feet, Freddy picked up her basket and went back to the roses.

Mole, climbing the hill to the narrow house in Above Town, was thinking what luck it had been to have Fliss living in Dartmouth during his first two years at the college. He loved the town with its narrow streets and quaint old houses, its life centred round the river, busy now with pleasure steamers plying between Dartmouth and Totnes, or taking the visitors out to sea for trips along the coast. The castle guarded the mouth of the river and beneath the wooded shoulder of the hill called Gallants Bower huddled the small stone church of St Petrox.

Mole thought: I feel as if I belong here. Perhaps one day I shall buy a house on the river and come to live here.

During the last year he had begun, at last, to free himself from the nightmare of his family's death; not just to push the horror down where it might spring back at him at any moment but actually to grow away from it. He had begun to think that this would never be possible but his new life – Dartmouth, the Navy, a sense of real belonging – this combination seemed to put his burden into some kind of proportion. For years it had filled his mind, corroding anything else it touched, the words and images blinding and suffocating him. None but he had heard the police-man's account, blurted out to Cookie on that hot afternoon '. . . Oh my Christ! The blood was everywhere. They had machetes, axes, sticks . . . The boy's shirt was soaked with blood . . . They'd smashed his head to pulp and nearly severed it from his body . . .' Sudden death striking out of a bright sunny day. His beloved big brother dead – and in such a way. Only, he, Mole, of all the family carried this burden of the real truth, learning gradually to live with it, coming to terms with it, and, now, it seemed, with the chance to overcome it. He had believed that if he could only hold on, not to be overborne and dragged down into the black pit with those terrible visions, he would eventu-ally control the fear but he had never hoped for absolute freedom from it. Yet he was wise enough not to test himself too far, to hope for too much too soon. It had been his companion for fifteen years and he suspected that it would not relinquish its hold too readily.

He whistled beneath his breath as he climbed Crowders Hill and turned into Above Town. The door was open and he beat a tattoo as he passed into the narrow hall with a shouted greeting. Fliss came out of the kitchen to meet him and they hugged. She was wearing one of her wrap-around Indian skirts and a short-sleeved cheesecloth shirt, its tails tied around her waist. Mole was very conscious of women's clothes and he preferred, on the whole, a more tailored look, but he thought that she looked rather charming in the long flowing skirt with her thick, fair hair twisted casually into a knot. It was difficult to see her dispassionately. She was his sister, friend, confidante, but he looked at her critically, seeing the shadows beneath her eyes and lines of strain about her mouth.

'Are you OK?' he asked, following her into the living room across the hall from the kitchen. 'Everything all right at home? How were Hal and Maria?'

'Everyone's fine,' she assured him. 'Mixed feelings about Hong Kong and the baby, of course.'

'That's understandable, I suppose.' He glanced about the room as he sat down in a Habitat chair, green corduroy slung hammock-like on stainless-steel tubing. He liked this room best. 'Was Maria jealous about the baby?'

She glanced at him sharply. It still surprised her that Mole should be so observant, so quick to assess the thoughts and feelings of others.

'It's funny that you should say that,' she said slowly, curling up in the matching chair. 'She was rather odd about it all. She went very still, expressionless . . .'

'As if her features are icing over,' assisted Mole when Fliss seemed lost for words. 'I know. But her eyes are alive, as if all her feelings have gone into her eyes.'

'What an extraordinary thing to say.' Fliss began to laugh – and then frowned. 'It's true, though. There's something painful about it, somehow.'

'She's not a very confident person,' said Mole. 'I feel rather sorry for her. It's silly really because she's so pretty and all that. But she's too busy thinking about Hal to relax. And dear old Hal is such a friendly person that her life must be hell. She's jealous of you because he's so fond of you. And now there's the baby as well.'

'Why should she mind about the baby?' asked Fliss quickly, sheering away from the subject of Hal's affection for her. 'There's nothing to stop her and Hal having a baby.'

Mole watched her thoughtfully, seeing her expression cloud, noting the brusque note in her voice.

'True,' he said, 'but she won't be first, will she? I expect she would have preferred to produce the first child of the next generation.'

'She's had two years,' Fliss pointed out. 'No one was stopping her. They said that they were going to start a family straight away.'

'Hal's been at sea a lot,' said Mole. 'Perhaps she's been unlucky, which is why she's so upset.'

'We didn't discuss it.' Fliss stretched and shook her head. 'Never mind. Everyone sent their love. Ellen baked me a wonderful chocolate cake which we'll have in a minute. Caroline was muttering about an Aran jersey you wanted her to wash. Grandmother and Uncle Theo were still railing against joining the Common Market. Grandmother does not, she informs me, feel like a European. "We are an island race . . ." and so on. Poor Fox is still suffering agonies but being very brave. Nothing changes at The Keep, thank goodness.'

'Thank goodness,' he echoed. 'I forgot to leave the jersey for Caroline. I brought it back in my grip. Never mind. By the way, I had a letter from Sooz yesterday. She's on the brink of her exams and all of a twitter.'

'She's longing for Bristol,' said Fliss. 'All those stories Kit told her about student parties and going to the Old Vic.'

'Thank God she's going to be staying with Aunt Prue,' said Mole, a flicker of the old terror touching his heart. 'The thought of Sooz loose amongst the student life of Bristol hardly bears thinking about.'

Fliss grinned at him, guessing at the terror, knowing how Mole felt about the safety of his loved ones.

'It's the students I feel sorry for,' she said. 'They have no idea, poor things, what is about to be unleashed amongst them. Come and help me make the tea and we'll pig out on Ellen's cake.'

Chapter Six

'I *know* the quarter in Compton Road isn't as nice as this,' said Hal, 'but we were terrifically lucky that old Mike and Sarah were going off to Singapore and let us rent their cottage. It's been great being out in the country but we can't expect this sort of luck every time. Once we're down in Devon we'll explore and see if we can find a hiring or a cottage to rent. You could have looked into it before, darling, when I was at sea, couldn't you? No good moaning about it now.'

The atmosphere in the tiny kitchen tingled with unspoken irritation, contrasting sharply with the peace of early evening. The door stood open on to the small patch of grass, edged about with cottage-garden flowers; heart's-ease and cornflowers, lavender and feverfew. Beside the door a bush of jasmine blossomed, an old stone trough bright with pot marigolds tucked beneath its delicate sprays. A tall ragged fuchsia hedge sheltered this sunny corner from the narrow village street, and camomile grew between the paving slabs which led to the wooden gate. House martins were busy feeding their babies who crowded at the nest's edge, jostling for position, clamouring for food, and a blackbird was singing in the ash tree by the old shed which doubled as a garage.

Maria stood with her back to Hal, waiting for the potatoes to finish cooking. She heard the tinge of exasperation in his voice but was unable to pull herself out of her mood. She hated it when he criticised her, even obliquely. Surely he must see how impossible it was for her to go down to Devon on her own and sort out hirings? She fiddled with the saucepan, knowing that the usual crossroad was before her. She could turn to him, smiling, agreeing that they had been lucky with the little cottage in Boarhunt, that the quarter would be fine, that they could look for something else later. She could let herself fall in with his attitude that life was good fun, that problems were there to be solved and so on, but it meant relinquishing her grievances, allowing him to get away scot-free. It was important that he saw the sacrifices she was obliged to make, that the life of a naval wife wasn't all coffee mornings and Ladies' Nights.

'How could I go down?' she asked. 'How could I manage to get about? Can you imagine trying to view hirings by public transport?'

Behind her, Hal closed his eyes for a moment. Ducking his head beneath the oak beam, he picked up his glass and swallowed back some beer, waiting for his patience to return.

'You could learn to drive,' he said reasonably. 'The car is there, standing in the garage for weeks on end while I'm away. I know you're nervous because it's a sports car but it's only a Sprite, for God's sake, not a Lamborghini. I've offered to teach you myself but you've always refused.'

Maria picked up a small sharp knife and, lifting the

saucepan lid, prodded at the new potatoes boiling with the freshly picked mint, which grew with other herbs at the edge of the minute vegetable patch, where sweet peas, and runner beans with bright scarlet flowers climbed together on the tall bamboo sticks.

'Daddy always says that there's no quicker road to divorce than a husband teaching his wife to drive,' she said.

Hal bit back the retort that, at this rate, they wouldn't be needing driving lessons to achieve that end, knowing that Maria would take even such a lightly uttered observance to heart and probably burst into tears.

'He might be right,' he said, 'but you have to admit it's silly going on like this. Anyway, Caroline would have run you about. She'd have fetched you from the train and taken you anywhere you'd wanted to go. She'd have enjoyed it, too. It would have been a bit of a variety for her. She loves a challenge.'

'Perhaps she should have been a naval wife then,' said Maria sulkily, lifting the saucepan and carrying it to the sink. 'Plenty of challenges there.'

Hal was silent, wondering how other men coped with this kind of problem. It was clear that Maria resented it every time he went to sea – but what had she expected? The other worrying thing was that she'd made hardly any friends during the last two years, apart from one or two of his fellow officers' wives. Then there was all the fuss about Fliss being pregnant . . . Hal strove to be fair. It was hard that Maria had been unable to conceive, that his brief spells at home had been the wrong time of the month or she had been too tense.

'Look,' he said gently, 'let's not make this a big deal. We

can use the married quarter as a base to find somewhere else to live and we'll organise driving lessons for you. I'll probably have more shore time when I join *Falmouth*. I'm sorry that we haven't managed to get you pregnant but don't begrudge Fliss her baby. Poor old Fliss. If you think you've had a hard time think how she must be feeling about going out to Hong Kong. Of course, she puts a brave face on it but it must be a bit unnerving, being pregnant as well.'

Nothing could have been more calculated to make her angry. As she put the potatoes into the dish with some butter, Maria was seized with a furious envy of Fliss.

'She hasn't done too badly,' she said bitterly. 'She's had Miles with her for the last two years in that lovely house in Dartmouth and she's been within half an hour of her old home. Hardly a great hardship, would you say? You've no idea how difficult it is to move into a completely strange area, not knowing anyone, miles from your family, and have your husband go off to sea for months on end. It's OK for you, surrounded by all your friends, in a world of your own.'

'So you've said many times before,' said Hal quietly. 'I did suggest that you might feel happier if you lived on a married patch with other wives of your own age, just until you got used to things. It was you who insisted that you wanted to bury yourself in a little village, miles from the base and with no transport.'

'They were beastly houses,' she cried. 'And I didn't want to go to boring Tupperware parties or have the other wives in and out all day long, thank you very much. I'm not interested in listening to gossip for hours on end.'

'I should have thought that it's better to listen to a bit of gossip than sit weeping on your own for weeks at a time,' said Hal impatiently. 'Just what *is* it that you want, Maria?'

She was silent, head bent, near to tears. Why couldn't he understand and sympathise? After looking at the available married quarters in the Portsmouth area, this little cottage had been heaven-sent. It hadn't mattered then that she'd be isolated. The low-beamed ceilings and private garden, the charm of Sarah's choice of decoration and furniture was bliss after the unimaginative uniformity of the quarters. Hal had simply no idea of the horror she had felt at being transported from her parents' comfortable home to the vulnerability of the married patch. She'd felt safe in this tiny, fairytale cottage. The thought of moving from it, of going to a new place, of living in the semi in Compton Road, filled her with alarm. How could she say this to Hal, especially when Fliss seemed to be facing the thought of Hong Kong with such equanimity? She finished the preparations without answering, stepping past him as if he didn't exist, confused and miserable.

Hal watched her, his anger evaporating. Her long dark hair swung loose, hiding her down-slanted face, and her bare arms and legs were tanned from hours of sunbathing. She disliked the long Indian clothes which Fliss had adopted and continued to wear miniskirts or jeans. This evening she wore one of his own cotton shirts, left loose over her bikini, but for once he was unaroused. He was too tired. She told him that she longed for them to be together, said that she felt every moment apart was wasted time, yet these bickerings broke out so often. He knew that one way to solve the problem would be to catch her in his arms and make love to her. She would pretend to put up a fight but she would be relieved to allow their mutual passion to sweep away the anger and the tears.

Hal thought: But I don't want to. I'm fed up with this coaxing and pleading. Anyway, I'm damned hungry.

Aloud he said, 'Come on. Have a drink and let's forget it. Thank goodness I shall be home for the move. At least that's a bonus. Gosh, that looks good. What a clever wife I've got.'

He slipped an arm about her, nuzzling her hair, but keeping everything light and easy. Torn between self-righteousness and loneliness, Maria allowed herself to relax against him, accepting the glass of wine. She longed for his approval, to be admired and desired.

'It's only a salmon,' she said, 'and new potatoes and salad. Nothing really.'

She smiled reluctantly at him and he bent to kiss her, putting as much passion into it as he could commensurate with it not distracting her from supper. Once or twice he'd been obliged to take her to bed early and the food had been ruined. Tonight things were not quite that bad. There would be time later to reassure her in the only way which really seemed to matter to her, time to show her that she was the only one he loved, the only one he'd ever want. Perhaps this time she'd become pregnant . . .

In this hour before dinner all was quiet at The Keep. Theo crossed the cool, shadowy hall and, selecting a walking stick from the tall brass container by the door, stepped out into the courtyard. Earlier, Josh had been mowing the central rectangle of grass and the scent lingered, evoking other summers of years long past. He passed beneath the gatehouse roof, between the tall wooden gates which were rarely shut now that there were no small children to keep inside, and out on to the drive which led to the lane.

Fields stretched away on either side and he paused from time to time to examine the beauty of the minutiae which grew on the old stone boundary walls. It never ceased to amaze him that such a dry, even hostile, environment could produce such magic. He bent to look more closely at the English stonecrop, its white flowers faintly flushed with pink, its stems and leaves tinged with red, preferring this delicate sedum to the mustard yellow of the biting stonecrop, its close relative. A tall foxglove leaned perilously from its narrow crevice between two stones, a slender column of purple bells, and Theo wondered anew that any root should gain purchase in nothing but a grain or two of soil. Along the wall, clumps of red valerian clung tenaciously at intervals and patches of powdery lichen stained the pitted surface of the stone with golden rust. A spider darted from its web, scurried between the stems of the herb Robert sprawling over the top of the wall, and disappeared into a dark recess.

Theo walked on, noting the trees' long shadows reaching across the green turf and the brilliance of the western sky. He turned from the drive into the deep, narrow lane, plunging abruptly from light into darkness. The banks were high, narrowing the sky, creating a density of shade. Long gone were the bright, fresh colours of spring but thick, creamy meadowsweet and yellow ragwort lent cheerful colour to the brittle tawniness of the feathery grasses and luminously pale honeysuckle trailed over the mixed hedgerow – nut, thorn, oak, beech – which grew along the top of the bank.

As he walked, Theo brooded on his family. His inner peace was regularly disturbed by the knowledge of his inadequacies. As a priest, he felt that he had done little to promote the spiritual wellbeing of those he loved. His natural reluctance to proselytise had prevented him from doing much more than advise when pressed, or encourage and comfort whoever required support from him. As he grew older his belief became simpler, more concentrated. A constant, secret inflowing of God enabled one to be used as a channel, a conduit; this love was passed on to those nearest to one at any given moment. This was the most, he had decided, that anyone could hope to achieve in this life.

Leaning heavily on his stick, he paused to consider the deep, burning blue of the tufted vetch which scrambled up the bank, reaching out with its tendrils to climb the cow parsley and alexanders. How new and miraculous each shift of season was. It was over seventy years since first he'd walked in this lane and yet there was always something different, something exciting, something at which to marvel. At the same time, there was the calm reassurance of continuity and a comforting sense of belonging.

Theo thought: It is this needing to belong that is making it hard for Fliss to leave. She is more deeply rooted here than any of the other children.

He remembered how often he had walked here, meeting the children coming home from the village school. Susanna had run to him, shouting out her news, recounting the details of her achievements, seizing his knees, laughing up at him. Mole had usually been silent with relief, another day successfully negotiated, his loved ones about to be safely gathered in beneath the same roof; he had carried Theo's arm around his small shoulders, holding his wrist tightly as he stumbled along beside him, listening to Susanna's chatter, frowning in an effort to keep up. Fliss had greeted him with a deep gladness, beaming at him as she took his hand, attempting to match her stride to his. She rarely spoke about her day at school but was more interested in all that had happened at The Keep in her absence. No detail was too small, no convention too banal to be repeated. *Home is where the heart is.* Theo feared that Fliss's heart would be always here, in this small corner of Devon.

Theo knew that the depth of his anxiety for Fliss was the measure of his guilt. He, alone, had attempted to prevent her marriage to Miles. He'd suspected that it was a reaction to Hal's engagement and believed that she should not surrender her strength and independence in a desperate gesture of pride. He had attempted to show it to Freddy in this light, had even raised it – tentatively – with Fliss herself, but he had allowed himself to be convinced, or at least distracted, and he had been unwilling to make any more trouble. How nearly he and Freddy had come to grief over the discovery of the love between Hal and Fliss.

His own love for Freddy was another of his humiliations. To fall in love with your brother's wife was shameful and he thanked God that he had never by a look or word betrayed it to her, that he had been given the strength to keep away. It might have been so tempting to abuse her affection for him, to have made himself necessary to her. Despite her confidence, there had been occasions when she had been ready to submit her will to his. It had been she who had suggested that he should live at The Keep but he returned only when he was certain that her own strength was too well developed to be open to his influence. It had been neither too early nor too late and they had had seven years of quiet happiness. It had been this happiness which he had been reluctant to disturb by pursuing his suspicions about Fliss's sudden decision to marry Miles.

Well, it was too late now. Fliss would go to Hong Kong and have her baby in the British Military Hospital in Kowloon, thousands of miles from her home in Devon.

Theo thought: But had she married Hal the same thing might have happened. He, too, might be posted abroad.

Yet he knew that, somehow, this would have been different, that Fliss would not have minded if she had been with Hal . . .

Chapter Seven

'They haven't got faces any more,' mourned Susanna, kneeling on the window seat. 'They're just trees. I didn't notice them change.'

Mole went to stand beside her, gazing across the garden and the orchard to the three tall fir trees. For as long as they could remember these trees had seemed like guardians, facing north, south and east, watching over the gardens and The Keep. Overlapping branches had allowed glimpses of the sky which looked like eyes and teeth, and Susanna had invested them with personalities and had looked upon them as friends.

'I can see what you mean,' said Mole. 'They've grown out, like hair. Never mind. I expect they'll look more like people again when the wind blows. Then you can see the sky through the branches and they'll have new, different faces.'

'Probably,' said Susanna, slipping off the window seat. 'Gosh, it's good to be home.'

She wandered over to the bed upon whose pillow sat a row of much-loved, if battered, toys. They'd entered into many games and adventures and had suffered a great deal in the consequence. Mole envied Susanna's confidence, which allowed her to leave her toys on public view. When he had reluctantly decided that having toys on his bed was a bit childish for a putative naval cadet, his old teddy and the dashing golliwog knitted by Ellen had been put on the top of his wardrobe. For some reason – which he knew to be utterly ridiculous – he couldn't bear to think of these two stalwart companions shut into a box. 'They won't be able to b-breathe' he'd said to Caroline, a hot wave of embarrassment suffusing his face. Caroline had remained unmoved by his foolishness, her eyes roving about his bedroom. 'Tell you what,' she'd said, 'they can sit up here.' She'd placed them together on the wardrobe. 'How about that?' He liked to see them there, leaning together, when he entered his room. Golly's bright red jacket seemed undimmed with the years, and Teddy still wore a pale strip on the bottom of his foot, which was the name tape bearing the legend 'S CHADWICK', a reminder to Mole of prep school days.

Susanna pushed a pile of clothes to the end of the bed and flung herself down, her head amongst the toys. 'No more school,' she said gleefully. 'I simply can't believe it.' Looking at her, Mole could hardly believe it either. It was impossible to realise that his small sister was growing up at last. It had been difficult enough keeping her under control as a child but what might not happen to her as she moved beyond his control, as friendly as ever but now pretty and desirable, too? At least during these last two years he'd had a chance to become slowly accustomed to it. Apart from anything else, the Navy kept him too busy to think about it much but his own growing confidence had also enabled him to be a little more balanced about his ingrained fear for his loved ones.

'I suppose it didn't seem much of a change to you,' she was saying, 'going straight from one educational establishment to another. Still in dormitories and people bossing you about. You're happy, though, aren't you?'

'It's not really like school,' said Mole. 'It's great, and there's much more freedom than we had at school, but I shall be glad to specialise; to be joining a boat and going to sea.'

She grinned at him. 'Still submarines, of course?'

'Oh yes. Still submarines.'

Susanna looked about her happily. As usual her room was in a state of chaos, clothes spilling out of the chest of drawers, books on the floor, a clutter of belongings on the small table.

'Two months,' she said. 'Two months' holiday to enjoy. What shall we do?'

She still sounded like the little sister who had asked that very question so many times before. Well, they were too old now to play their games of make-believe in the little stone shed in the orchard or to ride their bicycles into Dartington to buy sweets.

'To begin with,' he replied, 'I thought we might take Perks for a walk. Poor old Fox can hardly manage it these days and Caroline's busy this afternoon. We can catch up on all our news. Fliss and the baby and things.'

'Imagine.' Susanna looked at him awestruck. 'Imagine us being an uncle and aunt.'

Mole shook his head. 'I can't really,' he admitted. 'It's weird.'

'I had a letter from Kit,' said Susanna, sitting up and reaching for her shoes, 'and she said that she wants to be a godmother. She sent me a list of names as a joke. It was really funny. I kept it to show you. Now where did I put it?'

She finished lacing her shoe and glanced about her.

'Never mind,' said Mole hastily, knowing they might spend at least an hour searching for it in all the muddle. 'Later will do, when you've properly unpacked. It's probably in your writing case. Come on.' He pushed himself up from the window seat and made for the door. 'This place wouldn't pass an inspection, that's all I can say. Make mincemeat of you, our CPO Manners would.'

'I dare say,' said Susanna, kicking a stray shirt under the bed and seizing her jersey. 'That's why I'm glad to be going to Aunt Prue. She's as bad as I am.'

'What a frightening thought,' murmured Mole. 'Who will keep an eye on you both?'

'Kit,' answered Susanna promptly, slamming her bedroom door behind them. 'She's going to come down regularly and check on us. She doesn't trust us, she says. Aunt Prue has all sorts of things planned.'

'I believe you,' said Mole, grimly. 'And I can just see Kit taking charge of you. She's worse than you and Aunt Prue put together.'

Susanna beamed back at him as she raced down the stairs. 'I know,' she said cheerfully. 'Oh, Mole, it's going to be such *fun.*'

'End of an era,' said Ellen gloomily. 'That's what it is. Fliss off to Hong Kong. Mole off to sea and Susanna finished at school. Things'll be changing now and no mistake.'

'It won't be much of a change,' said Caroline soothingly, slicing the first picking of runner beans as she sat at the table. 'Going to college in Bristol isn't too different from being at school, you know. The term times and holidays will be much the same. There will be cases to pack and all the problems of getting her to and fro. And Mole won't be going to sea for another two years. He'll have fourth-year courses after Dartmouth. It's only Fliss, really.'

Ellen put a tray of scones in the oven and sat down in the rocking chair. 'I'm getting old and foolish,' she admitted. 'That's what. I don't know what's come over me and that's a fact.'

Caroline was silent. Slicing the beans neatly into a colander she reflected that some sort of change had certainly affected Ellen. Hitherto it had been she who was the strong one: acerbic, sharp, keeping them on their toes. Negativity had never been one of Ellen's faults.

Caroline thought: It is as if she has a kind of premonition which is depressing her spirits.

'It gets me here,' cried Ellen miserably, striking her breast, unconsciously corroborating Caroline's thoughts. 'Like a heavy weight it is. Painful. And don't tell me it's indigestion.'

Caroline was unable to control a little smile. 'I wouldn't dream of it,' she said gently. 'Who said it might be?'

'That Fox,' said Ellen grimly. 'Should've known better than to tell him. Never get no sympathy from a man, that's my experience. Like babies they are, when *they* have a twinge of something but as to anyone else having something wrong . . .' she sniffed expressively.

'He's worried about you,' explained Caroline. 'He was hoping to cheer you up, I expect.'

Ellen rocked glumly. She wasn't accustomed to analysing

her thoughts. In her view thinking or talking about yourself too much was simply self-indulgence and should not be encouraged, but just lately she seemed quite incapable of rising above this terrible depression. It occurred to her that she might simply be feeling the lowness of knowing that she was beginning to be useless. Caroline had taken over so much of the burden of her work that she was hardly needed, and now, with the children leaving home, there would be even fewer calls on her energy. Fox, she knew, had already come to terms with this. She remembered how restless and unhappy he had been at first, yet he had been able to accept it with a kind of grace which she was beginning truly to appreciate. He pottered about, finding small jobs and making himself as useful as his knotted hands and painful joints would allow, and for the rest of it he took his ease calmly, refusing to make a martyr of himself, which would have irritated those around him.

'At least I have my health,' she said – and realised that she had spoken aloud.

'And a great many other things, too,' agreed Caroline. 'No one makes scones and sponges like you do, Ellen, or bramble jelly. And you've a much lighter hand with the pastry than I have. Just because the children won't be around quite so much doesn't mean that the rest of us have to go hungry. You'll still have five people to feed.'

'Talking of which,' said Ellen more cheerfully, 'that sponge will be ready to ice. Now where did I put the sieve . . .'

'Baker's here.' Fox put his head round the door. 'Wants to know if you need extra.'

'Money,' said Ellen, distracted from the sponge. 'Where's

the tin? How much is it? And that's another thing. All these silly bits of money. Decimalisation indeed. Whatever next, I wonder. Here, let me have a word with him . . .'

'She do be looking a bit brighter,' said Fox hopefully, when Ellen was out of earshot. 'Found out what's wrong?'

'Not really.' Caroline gathered the waste from the beans neatly into a sheet of newspaper. 'It could simply be that there's another change ahead. Susanna off to Bristol and Fliss off to Hong Kong. She's not a one for change, Ellen.'

'Says she's got a pain in her chest.' Fox sounded studiedly casual. 'Indigestion, I told her, hoping to calm her down. Proper bit my head off, she did. Couldn't be anything more serious, perhaps?'

'I don't think it's physical,' Caroline assured him. 'She's just low in spirits and worrying about Fliss. It's odd, really. Before the children came there were just the three of you here. She didn't mind about that, I imagine?'

'It was different somehow.' Fox tried to cast his mind back to those days. 'We'd had the boys growing up, Peter and John, that is. Lots of coming and going then, especially when they went to Dartmouth and began bringing friends home. Then there was the war. Well, that was different again. Everyone in the same boat and trying to keep going. After the war Prue and the twins came down often and so did Peter and Alison, with Jamie and Fliss as little ones. Quite a houseful we had then. There was a bit of a gap when Peter went off to Kenya but Prue still came often with Hal and Kit so there wasn't an absolute break, if you take my meaning. Once the twins started school the visits got a bit less and we began to settle into a routine down here. What a shock it was when we heard the news and hardly had time to take it in when we had three small children to look after. Shook us all up, it did.' He laughed a little. 'Funny, really, I remember we felt a right set of old fogeys when they small ones arrived. Didn't know how we'd manage. Looking back, we were still young 'uns. Though I have to say, maid, it was a great relief when you turned up.'

Caroline smiled at him. 'It was a good day for me, too. I still think that Ellen's problem is that she doesn't like change. And the children are growing up, of course. It's a great pity that Fliss will be abroad when she has the baby. A new baby would have been just what was needed to cheer Ellen up and take her mind off things.'

'Keeps saying she won't live to see it,' mumbled Fox. He shot a glance at Caroline and looked away. 'Told her it's morbid. No reason to think such a thing.'

Caroline felt a tiny stab of fear pierce her heart and pushed it resolutely away.

'Susanna will cheer her up,' she said hopefully. 'Suppose we get everyone together for a weekend? Fliss can come over and we'll get Kit down from London. Hal and Maria will be here in a week or so anyway. A big family party, that's what we need. It'll take Ellen's mind off things. What d'you think?'

'That young man's asking for a thick ear,' said Ellen, reappearing before Fox could answer. 'Making games of me, cheeky monkey. Never shall I get this new money sorted out. "Can't teach an old dog new tricks," I told him and he said it was a good thing my bark was worse than my bite. Now, where's that sieve?'

'I'll put the kettle on and give Josh a call,' said Caroline. 'He's in the orchard scything the grass. He'll be glad of a break.'

'I'll go,' said Fox with alacrity. 'Hot work that is. The boy'll be ready for a cuppa.'

Ellen opened her mouth – and closed it again, biting her lip as Fox hobbled out. She'd been about to observe that Josh's tea would be cold long before Fox reached the orchard and that Caroline should go instead but she was becoming more and more sensitive to Fox's need still to feel a part of the working household. Even more was she aware of the courage he was showing in accepting his disabilities. To begin with he had been morose, railing against the passage of time, reluctant to allow Josh free rein in the garden, but now he was cheerful, not bearing his pain and lack of usefulness mechanically, as a suffered tragedy, but using it to help himself to grow, turning it into a kind of grace which benefited them all. She had always been anxious for his physical wellbeing; now she saw that there was the inner man, another important part of Fox which was still painfully developing.

'No need to hurry with that tea,' she said sharply to Caroline. 'I'll get this icing done before those men come cluttering up the kitchen. Plenty of time.'

Chapter Eight

'I'm bored,' declared Kit. 'Fed up. I need a change. Do you realise I've been in the same job for seven years. A bit longer if you count working there while I was at university. I need pastures new.'

'Marry me,' suggested Jake, stretched full length on his deep, cushiony sofa amidst the Sunday papers. 'Give in. Accept that we were made for each other. We've been going for seven years, too. I hope you're not bored with me.'

Kit stopped prowling about Jake's large sitting room and looked at him thoughtfully. 'It's habit,' she suggested cautiously. 'We're used to one another, like an old married couple already.'

'We're nothing of the sort,' said Jake indignantly. 'Did our passionate night of love mean nothing to you, ungrateful wench? I love you. God knows I've told you often enough.'

'That's what I mean,' insisted Kit. 'It's become a habit.'

Jake sighed deeply. 'How can I convince you?' he asked. 'Surely my regular proposals are indicative of my serious intention. I don't go about asking every nubile young woman to marry me, you know. I've even resisted Sin. No easy matter, I assure you.'

'No man is safe with Sin,' grumbled Kit. 'I can't imagine why I like her so much. She's got a new chap. Twice her age and terribly rich. It's a bit suspicious if you ask me . . .'

'Don't change the subject,' said Jake calmly. 'Sin was merely brought in to back up my argument. We're talking about you and me. Your mother likes me. Your grandmother and great-uncle like me. Even Hal likes me—'

'Why *even* Hal?' interrupted Kit, interested.

'I'm a Frenchman,' said Jake simply. 'Jacques Villon – my very name is against me. Hal's so English, isn't he? Doesn't like frogs as a rule. England's natural enemy and so on. But he does quite like *me* in a cautious, reluctant sort of way.'

'But you *are* English,' argued Kit. 'Your mother is English. You were educated at Ampleforth . . .'

'Aah,' said Jake, shaking his head sadly, 'and that's another thing. I'm a Roman Catholic. Scarlet woman and all that.'

'You've lapsed,' said Kit severely. 'So don't try to get sympathy on that score.'

'I wasn't angling for sympathy,' said Jake. 'I just want an answer to my proposal. Will you marry me? I have a good position in a merchant bank. I own this nice flat. I am kind to children and animals. I stay awake at the opera . . . You're going to say "no" again, I can see it. I need a drink. Did we have lunch? Never mind. I still need a drink.'

Kit watched him affectionately as he rolled off the sofa, felt about amongst the mass of newspaper for his horn-rimmed spectacles and wandered away towards the kitchen.

She thought: I *do* love him, but is it the grand passion? Supposing I married him and then met someone else who really swept me off my feet. The trouble is I know him so well. He's almost like a brother – except for sex . . .

She felt a familiar languorous sinking of her stomach, a deep warm glow, when she remembered the preceding night of love. Jake was the best lover she'd ever had – and the best friend – but was that enough? Sin thought so. Sin thought she was a fool to keep rejecting Jake. 'You'll lose him one day,' she'd warned her, 'and you'll never forgive yourself. Who wants a grand passion anyway? Seven years he's been faithful to you.'

Kit had laughed. 'I very much doubt it,' she'd said. 'Jake loves women far too much to be faithful to just one. Why do you think I nicknamed him Jake the Rake?'

'That's just sex,' Sin had replied. 'I'm not talking about that. He's never married, has he?'

Kit looked about the room. Jake had plenty of family money behind him, and this large flat in a big Georgian house in Bayswater Road opposite the park was delightful. The rooms looked out across the tops of tall trees and caught all the evening sun. He collected paintings of lesser-known artists – August Macke, Eugène Delacroix, Paul Klee – especially loving those works influenced by the brilliant colours and Moorish architecture of Morocco and Tunisia. His taste, generally, was an odd mixture of modern comfort and a by-gone elegance which worked surprisingly well. On reflection, it was rather like Jake himself . . .

'Come down to Devon with me,' she said impulsively, as he returned carrying two glasses of chilled white wine, so cold that a mist had formed on the outside of the bowls. 'We're having a family weekend. Everyone will be there. Why not? It'll be fun.'

He looked at her thoughtfully, wondering if this were a kind of answer, that this invitation might be a form of acceptance.

'Won't I be in the way?' he asked. 'If it's a family weekend . . .?' He hesitated, his heart knocking erratically with a new hope. If only he were brave enough to drop the mask of humour, to be as truly serious as he sometimes longed to be with her – but then supposing he frightened her right away? She was so elusive, so . . . so *unexpected*. 'I do love you, Kit,' he said, 'so very much.'

'Oh, Jake,' she said, setting down her glass. 'So do I. Love you, I mean. It's just . . . You know . . . Oh hell, I get so muddled . . .'

He put his own glass beside hers on the pretty, inlaid side table and put his arms round her, rocking her, comforting her. 'I know,' he murmured, sighing. 'I know exactly how it is. Never mind . . .'

Fliss lay awake, watching the cool early light spilling into the room. Once she was in bed, here on the top floor of the house in Above Town, all she could see was sky. This morning it was mother-of-pearl, sheeny soft, with the faintest tinge of oyster. From time to time the shadow of a gull's wing drifted past the window, the harsh, haunting cry, so evocative of the coast and seaside holidays, heralding the new day. Fliss drew her arm cautiously from beneath the sheet and peered at her wristwatch: only just after five. She sighed. It seemed as if she had been awake for hours. Lying still for another moment or two to check on the regularity of Miles's steady breathing, she slid carefully to the edge of the bed. She simply couldn't lie there another moment. Lifting her dressing gown from the chair by the window, she slipped noiselessly from the room and padded down the two flights of stairs to the kitchen.

From the kitchen window and from the room across the passage she could see the river, at its busiest at this time of the summer. Small boats rocked lightly at their moorings, their reflections shimmering, breaking and re-forming as the rising tide rippled under their bows and swung them round to point downstream. A cormorant flew with slow steady wingbeats, heading out to sea in the wake of a smack chugging out to the fishing grounds. Soon, across the river, the sun would roll up from behind the hill to fill the house with its warmth and brightness.

Taking her mug of coffee, Fliss crossed the passage and curled up in the hammock chair. She was still feeling heavy-hearted after the row she'd had with Miles the evening before. As she sipped reflectively at her coffee, Fliss decided that 'row' wasn't the right word. One didn't row with Miles. He simply took a stand and stuck with it, formulating his answers carefully and merely repeating them with a kind of tolerant patience – the recollection of which, even some hours later, caused Fliss's fingers to clench on the handle of her mug. The infuriating thing was that though his reasoning was often perfectly rational, terribly sensible, there was, nevertheless, something in the patient reiteration of his views which infuriated her.

Fliss thought: Simply because I am fifteen years younger doesn't mean that I can never be right.

To begin with, this almost paternal approach had been rather nice. After the years of anxiety for her siblings, of being the eldest, there had been something comforting in being able to relax, in being the one who needed to be looked after and protected. It reminded her of being a little girl again, when her father was alive to order her existence and her big brother had been the one taking decisions for the children. The first two years of their marriage had been very happy. As Staff Operations Officer, Miles had been to sea for a few days once or twice, and away on courses, but generally he had driven each day to the dockyard at Devonport and, except when he was on duty, had returned each evening.

It had been such a novelty for Fliss to wake up with no classes to teach, no lessons to prepare, no timetables to consult. Though she might have found a position in one of the local schools, Miles had protested against such an idea. He didn't want her to work; he wanted her to be always available. He wouldn't always have shore jobs, he pointed out, and they must take full advantage of this opportunity. Once he had left for the dockyard the day was her own but, since he took the car, Fliss was obliged to find her way about by foot and other means of transport. Taking a picnic she'd go by ferry out to the castle, climbing behind Sugary Cove up to the cliffs, or she'd take one of the riverboats up to Totnes and meet Caroline in the town for a quick cup of coffee. Her time – between the hours of nine and four – was her own and she used it to explore the Devon countryside. It surprised her that Miles rarely went out of Dartmouth except on a fine Sunday when he might suggest a walk at Start Point or on Torcross beach. This was very pleasant, usually ending with a pub lunch somewhere, or a cream tea if they'd set out after lunch, but it had come as a shock to discover that he knew very little about the country. It was then that she realised how much she had taken in through the pores during her childhood at The Keep. Walks with Fox and the dogs on the hill, playing on the moors and beaches with Caroline, pottering about in the garden with grandmother – all these things had taught Fliss about the natural world.

'Can you hear the wren?' she'd say, as they walked amongst the heather and the gorse, high on the cliffs above the sea. 'Look, there she is. She's scolding us. She's probably got a nest somewhere close.' Miles would put an arm about her affectionately. 'What a clever little girl it is,' he'd reply. 'Haven't a clue, myself . . .' It hadn't really mattered but, after a while, Fliss began to realise that she preferred the walks which she took alone, listening, watching, immersing herself in the colour and sound of the countryside about her. Anyway, Miles was more of a townsman, more at home in the Vic with a pint on the bar than wandering on a cliff or strolling in a lane, and she had plenty of time for her own pursuits.

Fliss set down her empty mug on the glass coffee table and folded her arms beneath her breast, looking about her. This room was the cosiest in the house. It had been used as nothing much more than a hall when she'd moved in two years ago. Miles kept it as a place to pay tradesmen or to give a passing acquaintance a quick cup of coffee. His friends were taken upstairs to the drawing room, which had such a spectacular view of the river and out to sea. Fliss had suggested that the sunny ground-floor room could be a comfortable place to have breakfast and read the morning paper. It was so convenient to the kitchen, she'd pointed out, and a small table could be placed beneath the window . . .

Miles had shrugged tolerantly. He didn't eat breakfast but merely sat on a stool at the bar in the kitchen to drink coffee and glance at the headlines before he hurried off. If she preferred to eat there then that was entirely up to her.

Fliss had looked at the room with new eyes. Like the kitchen, this room had a French window which looked into the narrow strip of garden at the back, whilst the front window faced into the morning sunshine and the reflections from sky and river filled the room with a pearly, luminous light. She'd begun to feel rather excited about her project and had decided that, as well as the table, there should be one or two comfortable chairs, a bookcase, perhaps, and some paintings on the walls.

She'd discussed her idea with Miles, telling him that she planned to potter about in the second-hand shops, hoping to pick up a bargain or two. How quickly Miles had vetoed this idea – they didn't need people's cast-offs and tatty old stuff – no, if it were worth doing it must be done properly. He'd arranged to have the Habitat catalogue sent and had become interested in the plan. It would have seemed churlish to fight him over it but Fliss had stood firm about one or two things – such as the corduroy hammock chairs – which he'd agreed with eventually. She'd accepted his final decisions – after all, he was paying for it and it was his house . . .

It was at this point, Fliss had realised, this was exactly how she felt about it. She loved the house, felt happy and safe in it, but it was not *her* house. Trying to be fair, she'd remembered that Miles had suggested, right at the beginning, that they could sell the house, buy something together. She'd refused, guessing that he was worried whether she minded because he'd lived in it with his first wife. It had not occurred to Fliss to mind. After all, there was nothing to remind her of poor Belinda.

Now, as she looked about the room, she remembered the argument they'd had earlier. The row had been about the house.

'Shall we try to sell it before we go to Hong Kong?' she'd asked. 'Or shall we rent it and put it on the market when we come back?'

'Sell it?' he'd asked, puzzled. 'Why ever should we sell the house?'

She'd stared at him in surprise. 'It would be a terribly difficult house to have a baby in,' she'd pointed out. 'Two flights of stairs. I'd be up and down all day long.'

'No worse than The Keep.' He'd smiled at her. 'No one seems to mind it there.'

'But that's different,' she'd frowned. 'There are lots of rooms on each floor at The Keep. When Daddy and Uncle Peter were small they lived almost permanently on the nursery floor. I couldn't do that here.'

It had been Miles's turn to frown. 'Honestly, darling, it's a bit of a bore, isn't it? I like it here. Surely we can cope. At least there's a garden.'

Fliss had glanced through the window at the narrow strip and Miles had burst out laughing. 'Your face, my sweet, says it all. Not quite up to The Keep, I agree, but lots of kids are brought up in flats.'

'But ours don't have to be,' Fliss had protested. 'It's a dear little house, I love it, but is there a real problem about selling it and buying something a bit bigger? Out in the country, perhaps.'

'I don't particularly want to live in the country,' he'd said flatly. 'I think you're exaggerating the difficulties.'

'I don't think so,' she'd answered, anxious now but trying to keep calm. 'You suggested selling it when we were engaged, remember? If you would have done it then, why not now?'

He'd shrugged. 'I've been here for twenty years,' he'd said. 'I was glad you didn't want to go somewhere else, I must admit, but I wanted everything to be perfect for you.'

'Only then?' she'd asked lightly. 'Not now?'

'Of course now,' he'd answered irritably. 'But since you've been so happy here for the last two years I don't think the question arises.'

'It arises because of the baby,' Fliss had managed to hold on to her temper. 'You must be able to see that. Most couples move on when they start a family.'

'But I didn't want a family,' Miles had said. 'I only wanted you. And it's been wonderful. Heaven knows, the baby will change all that. I don't see why I should have to move house as well.'

Fliss had stared at him, shocked. 'You really don't want the baby?'

He'd stared back coolly, on the defensive. 'To be truthful, no. We never discussed having a family, although I did say you ought to be on the Pill, if you remember.'

'But why not?' She hadn't quite been able to take it in. 'I knew you weren't really excited about it but I didn't realise that you didn't want it at all.'

'Look,' he'd said impatiently, 'I'm not a kid. I'm forty-one. I'll be in my sixties before it's even finished school. I wanted you, that was all, and I thought you felt the same. We were happy, having fun, free. What's it going to be like now with nappies airing all over the house and a screaming baby keeping us awake at night?'

There was silence.

'Nobody could accuse you of having a romantic view of fatherhood,' she'd observed drily, after a few moments.

He'd laughed shortly. 'I've seen it all before,' he'd said. 'All my oppos have been caught sooner or later. Look, no good whingeing about it, I accept that it's happened. But I don't want to sell the house if we don't have to. Let's wait and see what happens when we get back from Hong Kong, shall we? As for letting, I'm thinking about it. I don't want people scratching the furniture and burning holes in the carpet.' He'd glanced at his watch. 'I'm going up to watch the news. I want to see what's happening about this dock strike business. Make some coffee, would you, darling?'

So that had been that. He'd seemed unaware of her silence or her misery and she'd gone early to bed, though not to sleep . . .

Now Fliss uncurled her legs, stood up and wandered over to the window. The heaviness in her heart, which had kept her awake, would not go away. Now she had to go out to Hong Kong for two years, knowing that he did not want their child, managing alone. She swallowed back her tears, raising her chin and biting her lips as she watched the sun rise over the hill, filling the world with brilliance.

Chapter Nine

Sitting by the window on the train from Bristol, Prue Chadwick was brooding. An earlier telephone conversation with her son, Hal, had made her slightly anxious and she was trying to decide if there was anything serious to worry about or whether it was simply that Hal was being super-sensitive. Not that her son was given to being overly sensitive but, since his marriage, he had matured and was now more aware of other people's feelings, especially those of his wife.

He'd talked at some length about her worries and her fears. Prue had agreed that it was terribly disappointing that darling Maria had not yet conceived a child, but surely there was plenty of time? They'd been married for barely two years and Hal had been at sea for so much of it. Clearly, Maria had been very lonely and it was natural that she should want to go home to her own parents when Hal was away – which she did very frequently – but Prue had been delighted on the several occasions when Maria had asked if she might come and stay with her in Bristol. They'd had a great deal of fun. In a very charming way, Maria bossed Prue about, pretending that she wasn't very good at looking after herself and spoiling her. Prue loved it. Kit and Hal did much the same thing and Prue was content to sit back and let them. After all, she'd managed more or less alone for over twenty-five years, ever since darling Johnny was killed, but if it made the children feel grown up and responsible she was quite happy to go along with the pretence.

Prue smiled sympathetically at the harassed young mother in the seat opposite, remembering how many journeys she had made with the twins in the past. Each summer they had come down to The Keep for the long holiday, the children wild with excitement. She remembered, too, how in awe she'd been of her mother-in-law, well aware that she was not quite the competent wife Freddy would have chosen for her brilliant, clever son.

Prue breathed a tiny sigh of contentment. How glad she was that she and Maria got along so happily together. She'd been rather anxious when she'd heard that Freddy had decided to reconsider her will, wondering how much the thought of inheriting The Keep had influenced Maria's decision to accept Hal's proposal of marriage. Hal had taken it very well when his grandmother explained that she'd been advised that The Keep should be left in trust for her great-grandchildren. It was all very complicated and difficult to explain but it was understood that Hal was her executor, she had given him power of attorney and he was still expected to be the one to live there after his grandmother's death. Freddy had been anxious that he should not feel hurt or dispossessed, insisted that he must have a session with her lawyer so that he quite understood the position, but Hal was perfectly sensible about the situation, quite happy to accept the new arrangements. He'd been too busy with his new marriage and his career to worry about it and, after all, there was no great change as far as he could see; it was not as if he would have ever considered selling The Keep. Prue, however, wondered how much he had told Maria and if she had quite grasped the finer details. She suspected that he had not been absolutely open with his wife, knowing her tendency to insecurity and her readiness to worry.

'Please come down, Ma,' Hal had pleaded on the telephone. 'There's a plan for a family gathering at The Keep next weekend and I don't think Maria can face it without you . . . I know, I know. But she's a bit wound up about Fliss being pregnant. You know how she's longing to have a baby, and Kit's inclined to tease her. All in good fun, of course, but Maria's a touch sensitive just at present . . . Yes, Grandmother's great. They get along terrifically well in the main but she's a bit – well, she's a bit *austere*, if you know what I mean . . .?'

Prue knew exactly what he meant. How often she herself had been the object of Freddy's critical gaze, conscious of being judged . . . but surely Maria was a great favourite with Freddy? Of course, she was getting old – she must be nearly eighty – and she could be disconcertingly direct. With Peter and Alison in Kenya and Johnny no longer there for moral support, Prue had felt all the weight of Freddy's expectations. It had been a relief when The Keep was full of children again and dear old Caroline *in situ*. Finding Caroline had been Prue's brainwave and it was this – and the love that Peter's children had for their Aunt Prue – that had softened Freddy's attitude towards her. Luckily, Theo had always been on her side.

What, Prue wondered, would she have done without

darling Theo? However would she have managed without his love and support, especially his financial support? How often he had saved her from embarrassment. The estate had paid her the dividends that would have been Johnny's and, added to this, Freddy had been extremely generous, buying Prue the little mews house in Bristol and paying for the twins' education. Nevertheless, there had been some difficult moments, especially during her short and disastrous marriage with Tony.

Prue thought: How odd. I can barely remember him and yet I thought I loved him so much. How treacherous love is. How it deceives us and makes fools of us.

She felt a surge of relief that Maria so clearly adored Hal. Of course, Hal was such an easy person to love – although Prue realised this might be a mother's prejudice – but she knew that a naval wife's lot was not always a happy one and Maria seemed to be having difficulty in coming to terms with the regular separations. Babies were the answer here. Babies would keep her busy and happy, leaving her no time for moping or feeling sorry for herself. In the terrible months after Johnny's death, it was the twins who had kept her sane. What a comfort they had been to her and, as they grew up, had become more like her friends than her children. It was so important that Hal and Maria should be happy together, to know the kind of bliss she and Johnny had experienced. If only Kit would find someone, too; someone like that nice Jake . . .

Out of habit, as the train pulled into Totnes, Prue reached for her bag and then sank back into her seat smiling. For the first time, in all the years of travelling west, she would be going on to Plymouth. Hal and Maria were now living in their quarter and had promised to meet her at the station.

'To be honest,' Hal had said during that telephone call, 'it's a bit of an anticlimax after the cottage, but that's life, I'm afraid. Maria's fed up. *Do* come, Ma. I know you'll cheer her up.'

For some reason, Prue found herself thinking about Fliss. She wondered how she was feeling about going off to Hong Kong, about having her baby so far from home. It would be lovely to see her – and everybody else, all together once more – and especially lovely to see Kit, who was coming down from London at the weekend . . .

She settled back in her seat, concentrating on this part of the journey which was new to her; speeding through South Brent, rattling across the viaduct high above the Glazebrook, curving round the edge of the moor towards Ivybridge. Prue felt a twinge of excitement mixed with sadness. It seemed so odd that she should be coming to stay with her grown-up son and his wife. Her memories were still full of two excited children, watching eagerly from the window, pointing out the landmarks, asking if it were too early to eat the picnic lunch. How quickly the years had passed since she and Johnny had been like Hal and Maria, setting out together and so much in love. Now Johnny and Peter were gone, their children grown up and she was forty-nine, older than Freddy had been when she'd first met her thirty years ago. Thirty years . . .

Prue was filled with an odd kind of terror. How profligate she'd been with her time, how careless of its preciousness – except for those too few years with Johnny. Then, each minute had been so special, treasured up, relived. If only her two children could know this kind of happiness.

'Nearly there.' The young mother was smiling at her,

signalling relief that the long journey was over. 'It's hell with small kids, isn't it?'

'Hell,' agreed Prue, 'but don't wish their lives away. They'll go quite quickly enough. Mine are your age, now, but I'd be very happy to put the clock back. Now, tell me, how long it is till we actually arrive? I've never done this trip before so it's all very exciting. My son will be meeting me. He's a naval officer . . .'

The Saturday evening party had spilled out of the drawing room into the hall and beyond to the courtyard. At the last moment, plans for it had spiralled out of control, invitations being extended to others apart from the members of the family. Kit had brought Jake and Sin, driving them down in Eppyjay. 'Safety in numbers,' she'd said to Sin. 'You *must* come. You can chat up Uncle Theo and tease Maria but *please* come,' and Sin, torn between feeling sorry for poor Jake and tempted by Kit's lure, had given in. Susanna had Janie, a school chum, staying, and Freddy had invited her own friend, Julia Blakiston, so that they could make up a bridge four with Theo and Prue if things became too noisy.

The party had begun at teatime with Kit's arrival, moved on to a buffet supper elegantly orchestrated by Caroline, Ellen and Fliss, and was now in full swing.

'Hello, partner,' Julia said to Prue as the bridge party assembled. 'How proud you must be of your beautiful children. What a sweet child Maria is . . .' and Prue, weak with relief that she was not to be partnered with the formidable Freddy, chattered happily whilst her mother-in-law fetched the cards and Theo set up the table.

'Am I to have the pleasure of your company at last?' Freddy asked amiably, if pointedly, of Theo – and he smiled that particular smile which crinkled his eyes and barely touched his lips.

'Sin sees me as a challenge,' he replied serenely. 'She can't imagine why I don't wish to make her repent of her wicked ways.'

'Far beyond your abilities, I should have thought,' Freddy said, with a touch of her old asperity. 'You never even managed to convert *me* . . .'

'I know my place, I hope,' he murmured. 'You've always been out of my league,' and beamed upon her as she glared at him, trying to decide if he were complimenting or insulting her.

'Let's fetch Fliss's old gramophone down,' Susanna was saying to Mole. 'Janie's brought some really good records. Beach Boys and things. We could play them out in the courtyard and dance. She's gone upstairs to get them. She's nice, isn't she? Don't you think she's pretty?'

'She's lovely,' said Mole, who was suffering all sorts of pleasing – and uncomfortable – sensations at the proximity of the delightful Janie. 'The thing is, I'm not very good at d-dancing.'

He shook his head, angry with himself that his hated stammer had suddenly reappeared, and Susanna squeezed his arm sympathetically.

'Don't worry about that,' she said comfortingly. 'She thinks you're fab. Really sexy.'

Mole blushed hotly and fought to prevent a foolish – he could feel that it was foolish – smile lingering on his lips. 'Nonsense,' he said severely.

''Tisn't nonsense!' replied Susanna indignantly. 'Anyway, be sure to dance with her. I bet Hal will, once we get going. And that Jake. You have to be assertive. Women like assertive men.'

She dashed off and Mole took a turn about the courtyard, practising being assertive to himself.

'Hello there,' said Sin, appearing beside him and slipping an arm through his. 'How's tricks?'

Mole found himself seriously nervous now. There might be the faint possibility that the seventeen-year-old Janie could look upon him favourably but Sin was way out of his class.

'G-great,' he said – and cursed himself. 'Pretty good, actually.' He attempted a kind of nonchalance, conscious of her warm arm pressing through his shirt. 'How are things with you?'

'Pretty good, actually.'

She was smiling, and he looked at her suspiciously. Was she sending him up?

'I've just noticed,' she was saying, 'how very much like Theo you are. Lots younger, of course, but otherwise terribly like him.' She sighed dreamily. 'I think he's the sexiest man in the world.'

Mole stumbled, righted himself and looked down at her anxiously. 'He's a priest,' he mumbled.

'Dear old Mole,' said Sin, pressing herself a little closer. 'So he is. But *you're* not.'

Mole's tongue suddenly felt several sizes too large for his mouth and his collar appeared to be strangling him. He cleared his throat and gargled inarticulately. Sin's blonde head was very near his shoulder and her scent was quite dizzying. She was wearing a short black dress which looked, to Mole's uneducated eye, terribly simple, and he tried hard not to look at the front of this little masterpiece, which was cut dangerously low.

'No,' he said, suddenly remembering Susanna's advice and affecting an offhandedness which he did not feel. 'I'm not, am I? But where does that lead us?'

Sin gave a gurgle of laughter. 'It leads us rather conveniently into this nice dark corner. Comfort me, Mole, for I am weary of rejection . . .'

She put her arms about him and turned up her face. Mole didn't hesitate. He managed to get the hang of things surprisingly quickly and began to enjoy himself. The music had been playing for several minutes before either of them noticed. They drew apart, looking at each other with a kind of amused delight, and Sin burst out laughing.

'Well,' she said, smoothing back her unruly mane, 'I think I might just have to demote Theo to second place. Come on. We'll stroll back nice and casual, shall we, and join the party? Tell me, Mole, do you ever get up to London . . .?'

'It's a terrific bonus,' Miles was saying to Caroline, as they stood together in the hall, refilling their glasses. 'To get a command in Hong Kong is almost too good to be true.'

'I can imagine that you must be pleased.' Caroline watched him as he poured the wine. 'Bit hard on poor old Fliss, though?'

It was a question and Miles pursed his lips, shrugging a little. 'Oh, let's not make too much of it, shall we?' He lowered his voice slightly, as if dissociating the two of them from the family. 'She won't be the first to have a baby abroad – and she won't be the last. She's tough, Fliss is. To begin with I thought that she was such a delicate flower. Of course, her appearance suggests that, doesn't it? But underneath she's strong. A chip off the old block, if you ask me.' He patted her arm, intending comfort. 'Fliss'll be OK.'

He smiled confidently, glancing round him, and Caroline watched him thoughtfully.

She thought: How odd it is that I imagined myself in love with him. But he was different then – eager to please us all, longing to be a part of the family. He was dazzled by the Chadwicks, by Fliss especially, but there are no stars in his eyes now.

Aloud she said, 'I'd better just check that the bridge party aren't dying of thirst,' and he nodded, quite happy to be left, to stroll over to Jake, who leaned against the door jamb watching the impromptu dancing in the courtyard.

'That looks fun.' He smiled at Jake. 'So you're Kit's young man.'

It was a statement – but Jake shook his head ruefully.

'That assumption might be going too far,' he murmured.

Sin and Mole had now joined the group around the gramophone and Miles chuckled.

'Unable to choose between them?' he suggested, his eyes on Sin, who had begun to gyrate, encouraging Mole to join her. 'Lucky man.'

Jake smiled to himself. 'If you say so,' he said courteously.

Maria stepped between them. 'Any offers?' she asked. Her voice was brittle and, glancing at her, Jake thought that she looked near to tears. He bowed to her and swept her out into the dancers.

Unaware that they had been seen, Hal and Fliss still stood, confronting each other at the back of the hall. They'd bumped into each other, Fliss coming from the kitchen with fresh supplies, Hal going to fetch some more ice. He'd jumped back, opening the door for her and then stopped. Her fair hair was coiled high on her small head, corn-coloured wisps escaping about her face. She wore a long dress in soft sprigged cotton, gathered high under her breasts, and she looked delicate and frail and very sweet. He stared at her, frowning, holding the door but blocking her way. She stood quite still, grasping the tray tightly, gazing up at him.

'Oh, Flissy,' he said at last. 'Darling Flissy, you look so lovely.'

'Thanks,' she said quickly. 'You're looking pretty good yourself. And Maria, of course. I love her dress . . .'

'Don't,' he said. 'Don't do that.'

'Do what?'

'Be . . . well, kind of distant, as if we're strangers.'

He moved towards her and she clutched the tray more firmly, so that it pressed into his chest. He covered her hands with his own.

'You'll be all right, won't you?' he murmured. 'Going so far away. I shall miss you . . .'

He made it sound as if he'd just discovered the fact and her eyes filled with tears. His hands clasped hers more tightly.

'Don't,' she whispered. 'Please, Hal. It's not fair.'

He released her then, and stepped back a little. 'But I shall,' he said quietly. 'Take care of yourself, Fliss.'

Caroline came into the hall from the drawing room and

they moved apart, he onwards to the back of the house, Fliss towards the long table which had been set up to hold the drinks and sustaining snacks.

'There you are,' said Kit, appearing from the courtyard. 'Come on out and dance. Actually, we need more men – but then is there ever a moment when one doesn't need more men? Are you OK, little coz? You need another drink by the look of it. Here we are. Let me fill up this glass for you. Now. Come on, honey, we might have to dance together just like we did when we were small . . .'

Chapter Ten

Kit woke early the next morning. She lay quite still for a few moments, her eyes shut, listening to the birds and the rustling of leaves. Presently she would go down to the kitchen and talk to Ellen whilst she made Fox's early morning tea. Kit knew that Fox's aching joints kept him awake for most of the night and that he greeted dawn with relief. She also knew that however early he arrived in the kitchen Ellen would be there before him, raking out the Aga, the kettle boiling on the hotplate. They were like an old married couple together and she could hardly imagine one without the other. How odd – and terrible – it would be if one of them were to die . . .

She stirred restlessly, unwilling to think about The Keep without its full complement of present inhabitants. Indeed, it was quite impossible to think of it at all without her grandmother in control, without Uncle Theo pottering about his quarters in the east wing on the first floor, or without Fox and Ellen – and Caroline, of course – keeping the place running smoothly. Fond though she was of her brother, the thought of him and Maria established at The Keep was too awful to contemplate. Now, if it had been Hal and Fliss . . .

95

Kit pushed back the bedclothes and swung her feet to the floor. Did she dislike Maria because she had displaced Fliss or was it simply a natural antipathy? There might be some other Freudian explanation, Hal being her brother, but Kit shrugged that off. After all, she would have been more than content to see Hal and Fliss married, to have Fliss as chatelaine of The Keep. That would have been right, somehow. Hal and Fliss belonged together – and to The Keep – in some indefinable way; like Ellen and Fox, for instance, or Grandmother and Uncle Theo. She suddenly realised that she had mentally named two couples who were not married . . .

Kit thought: How odd. Yet they are so *right* together. Or is it because they're *not* married that they are so content?

Confused and faintly depressed, she wandered over to the window and stared out at the familiar scene. Her bedroom was in the west wing, directly beneath Susanna's, looking out over the lawn with its long herbaceous border beneath the high wall. Behind the fuchsia hedge at the end of the lawn was the orchard with its bent and twisted fruit trees whose twiggy branches were covered with a silvery, crumbly lichen. Tall rhododendron bushes, whose scarlet and mauve glory was over now, hid the kitchen garden away to the right, and at the furthest point of the boundary stood Susanna's three tall fir trees. Kit had looked upon this scene in spring, when the fruit trees were washed over in a huge wave of blossom and drifts of daffodils grew in the grass beneath the rhododendrons, and in winter when the exposed bones of the garden lay still and silent, sealed beneath frost. Now, the summer was beginning to fade; fruit was setting on the ancient trees and Michaelmas daisies and tall Japanese anemones bloomed in the border, which was edged with a brilliant riot of nasturtiums.

Kit was hardly aware of them; she was thinking of Fliss and the conversation she'd had with her the night before. Both of them had had quite a lot to drink and they'd sat together on the wooden seat in the courtyard, watching the dancers and talking.

'I *do* love him,' Kit had said of Jake. 'I *do*. But is it the real thing, little coz? How am I to know? How awful if I married him and then fell madly in love with someone else.'

'Oh, Kit,' Fliss had said, 'it's a terrible decision to take. If you have any doubts at all then don't do it.'

Her voice had been grave and, looking at her profile in the dim light, Kit had seen the delicate features set in severe lines. For a moment she'd seen the resemblance to their grandmother and felt strangely frightened.

'Don't look so serious,' she'd said, almost childishly, shaking Fliss's arm. 'Don't, Fliss. What's the matter?'

'But it *is* serious, Kit,' Fliss had answered. 'Marrying the wrong person is . . . Well, it's a life sentence.'

She'd been staring straight before her, at the group around the gramophone, and Kit followed her gaze. Mole was dancing now with Janie, Miles with Sin. Jake was partnering Susanna but Hal and Maria stood apart, clearly outlined in the light which poured out from the hall. It was clear from their posture and gestures that they were arguing: Maria's arms were crossed tightly over her breast in utter rejection but, as they watched, Hal extended both his hands to her and then thrust them angrily through his hair when she shook her head.

'Aah,' Kit had murmured thoughtfully – and glancing

again at Fliss was shocked by her expression. 'Oh, Flissy. Is it as bad as all that?'

For one brief moment Fliss stared back at her, jaw clenched in misery, a tiny frown between the fair feathery brows, her eyes clouded and distant. It had taken a moment or two for Kit's question to penetrate her thoughts and, as it did so, her face changed and lightened. She'd raised her eyebrows questioningly, swallowed some more wine and taken a deep breath.

'As bad as what?' she'd asked lightly. 'Oh, good heavens. I'm not talking about me, you twit. It's Hal and Maria I'm worried about. I've seen some of these problems in the Navy now, that's all. There's so much pressure, with all the separation and moving about, and Maria's not cut out to be a naval wife. She misses Hal so much.' She'd smiled then, dismissing Hal and Maria. 'And as for *you*, well, I think Jake is simply lovely, I adore him, but marriage is something else again. Just don't do anything unless you're absolutely certain, Kit, it's not worth it.'

Jake and Susanna had jigged over to them then and there had been no more private talk. The four of them had danced in a little group until Hal had joined them, saying that Maria had a bit of a headache and had decided to go to bed. '*I'll* dance with you,' Susanna had said cheerfully. 'Come on, Hal . . .'

Now, as she turned back into the room, Kit felt unsettled, anxious about Fliss, still undecided about Jake. There was only one place to go: down to the kitchen to Ellen and Fox. She would curl up in the huge dog basket with Perks and pretend that she was a child again, with no cares and no worries. She would put her cheek against Perks's warm hair and snuff up the lovely smell of warm, happy dog. Ellen and Fox would bicker, as they had done all down the years, and their voices would form a background of familiar sounds with the clinking of china, running water, scraping of chair legs on slate, and she would be able to sink into a kind of timelessness of peace and safety – until Ellen noticed her and there would be the usual exclamations . . .

Kit thought: I'm pathetic, really. Does everyone – even when they're grown up – need a place to go where they feel secure?

She thought about Jake. There was a similar aura about Jake; she tended to gravitate towards him when she felt blue – but was that enough to make her want to marry him? She remembered Fliss's words, '*it's a life sentence*' and shivered a little. She'd looked so . . . Kit cast about for an appropriate word. She hadn't just looked miserable or unhappy or as if she might be about to burst into tears, as she had earlier when Kit had found her in the hall holding the tray. No, it was something more than that. Kit frowned, trying to make her tired, hung-over brain work properly. Yes, that was it: Fliss had looked stern, grim, determined. As if she were coming to terms with something terribly difficult; overcoming something . . .

Kit thought: But it can't still be Hal. Surely she went through all that two years ago? It must be the thought of going out to Hong Kong and the baby. Poor old Flissy. Oh God, I shall miss her terribly.

She pulled on a shirt and her jeans, still brooding on Fliss and their conversation about marriage and remembering what Sin had said some weeks earlier. Fliss and Miles *did* look perfectly happy together but that special ingredient was missing: did it matter? Could one be just as happy without that exciting spark of chemistry? After all, one only had to look about to see that most couples managed without it, but did she, Kit, simply want to 'manage'? Was Sin right and was Fliss simply 'managing' with Miles? Certainly she'd never heard Fliss speak out so vehemently before. Of course, they'd both had rather a lot to drink . . .

The thought of hot black coffee carried Kit out of her room and down to the kitchen. Just outside the half-open door she paused, listening.

'. . . and you know perfectly well that Caroline walks Perks in the morning. There was no call for you to get up early and go hobbling about. The idea! Never mind you taking it slowly. I know all about that. Get those wet boots off.'

'She was up late last night, poor maid. Thought it would be a bit of a help.'

'Of course, *you* weren't kept awake with all that music, I suppose? Dancing in the courtyard till all hours. Whatever next, I wonder.'

'Oh, it weren't so late, maid. Very nice 'twas, too. Gave me a bit of company, like. Dancing, they call it. You and me could've shown them a thing or two, Ellen. Funny kind of dancing, if you ask me.'

'Well, I doubt anyone will be asking your opinion. Dancing at my age! Just you sit down and get this hot tea inside you.'

Kit sighed with pleasure, pushed open the door and went in.

★ ★ ★

By Monday all the guests had gone and only the family remained at The Keep. Kit had driven away on Sunday afternoon after lunch, with her mother beside her to be deposited in Bristol, and Sin and Jake in the back. Julia had left after tea, following Hal's Sprite down the lane, and Fliss and Miles drove off an hour or so later. Janie went home by train next morning.

'She really likes you,' said Susanna, as she and Mole stood on the platform of Totnes station, waving goodbye to Janie.

'Yes,' said Mole thoughtfully. 'I like her, too. She's very nice.'

'I could invite her again, later on in the holidays,' suggested Susanna casually. 'Might be fun.'

'Yes,' said Mole again, thinking not of Janie but of Sin's staggering invitation.

'Kit's going to France with Jake,' Sin had said, watching him, eyes bright, lips curved in a lazy smile. 'The first week in September. Will you still be around? Or will you have gone back to Dartmouth?'

'No,' he'd answered quickly – too quickly. 'Well, not till the eleventh, I think.'

'So,' she'd said, still smiling. 'How about a few days in London? I'm sure there are some things you need. Or some old chums you'd like to look up. Would it be a problem?'

He'd known quite well what it was she was asking. Would his conscience be a problem? After this weekend he suspected that his grandmother was far too astute to view his staying with Sin, unless Kit was around, without a certain wariness. Of course, he had one or two friends who might be prepared to give him an alibi. Either way, it seemed, he would have to lie about it. He needed time to think.

'I'll deal with that,' he'd said shortly, and she'd cast a surprised and delighted look at him.

'I think you will,' she'd agreed. 'So have we a date?'

'I might be going up to London a bit later,' he said now, to Susanna, as he followed her off the platform. 'We'll work out some dates for Janie.'

'OK,' she'd said cheerfully enough. 'Where did we put the shopping list?'

Mole, driving carefully into the town in his grandmother's Anglia estate, thought briefly and longingly of his cousin's little sports car. Maybe, when he passed out from Dartmouth, his grandmother might give *him* such a present.

'It was nothing,' Hal said wearily, for the hundredth time. 'Honestly nothing. Please, darling, can't we just stop this? She was holding the tray and I offered to take it from her. Good manners and all that. Nothing else.'

'You didn't see your face,' she hissed, hating him, loving him, utterly miserable.

Hal gritted his teeth lightly together, wearied by the relentlessness of Maria's jealousy. He knew that she was partly justified. In that strange moment with Fliss in the hall, all his old longings and love for her had come rushing back. In an undefinable way it felt as though she were a part of him; a very dear and necessary part. She'd felt it, too, he'd known it. Afterwards, guilt had assailed him. It was unfair to both Fliss and Maria and he'd cursed himself, especially when he learned that Maria had seen them.

'I'd been drinking.' He'd said this again and again. 'Fliss

is my cousin. I'm very fond of her and she's going a long way away to have her first baby. I suddenly felt a tremendous affection for her. Surely it is not wrong to feel affection for my cousin. I'd feel the same for Susanna. Or Mole.'

In his heart he knew that it wasn't quite true. Fliss was special; damnably special. It was unfair to deny Maria's intuition or to attempt to make her jealousy seem irrational. It would be easy to swing the guilt around, to make love to her, persuade her and so move into that desirable situation where she was apologising for being a cow, asking him to forgive her for her lack of faith in his love. She tried to overcome her jealous nature and he knew that it was only because she loved him so much, was terrified of losing him, that she felt so insecure. It was a rotten thing to do, to try to put her in the wrong. Often, when her reactions were quite unreasonable, her accusations hurtful, he was prepared to take a stand, to justify his behaviour, but this time . . .

'Look,' he said gently, 'I don't know what it looked like but I accept that I'm to blame here. I'd drunk quite a bit and I was in that silly, sentimental stage. It's very difficult for you but you simply have to believe that I love you. We only have one more week of leave left and then I'm going to sea for six weeks. Please don't let's waste any more time. It was lovely having Ma to stay but it's even better to be on our own. This time next week I shall be gone and we'll both be miserable as hell. Can't we enjoy the few days left?'

Maria's felt her misery gather inside her, a tremendous weight in her breast. She knew that what he said was true: in a week's time she would be crying her eyes out, missing him desperately, wishing that they hadn't wasted time rowing. It simply wasn't that easy, however, to forget the quite uncousinly look she'd seen on Hal's face as she'd come out of the drawing room. She sat on the arm of the chair, her arms crossed tightly beneath her breast, head bowed.

'Please?' He touched her shoulder. This time she did not shrug him away and he took courage. 'Honestly,' he said, kneeling on the seat beside her, putting his arm round her, 'I only want you, Maria. Please believe me. If I'd really wanted Fliss, I'd have been with her now, wouldn't I? But I'm here with you because I want to be. It'll be easier here, I promise you. I know lots of people and you'll be able to make some friends with wives of your own age. We'll find a nicer place to live and the family's just up the road when I'm away. I'm sure we'll have a baby soon. And you don't have to worry about Fliss. She won't even be around for two years. Please, Maria, I hate it when we're like this. I need you, too, you know . . .'

She turned to him then, balancing on the arm of the chair whilst he kneeled on the seat, and he closed his eyes as he kissed her, so that she wouldn't see the sudden, inexplicable rush of tears which he was unable to prevent.

Chapter Eleven

It was hot; almost too hot to play. In the cool of the drawing room Freddy allowed her fingers to wander haphazardly over the keys of the Bechstein as she sat trying to decide which particular music would suit her mood: the tempestuous sonatas of Beethoven or the sonorous intricacies of Bach's fugues? The problem was that she had no clear idea of her present mood. In an attempt to analyse it she realised that she felt unsettled, faintly irritable, spoiling for an argument. Freddy smiled to herself as she played the opening notes of one of Chopin's studies. No wonder Theo had disappeared so promptly immediately after luncheon. He had gauged her mood with an unerring instinct, developed over years of experience, and made his timely escape. They were all a little jumpy. Fliss was staying for the last time before she flew out to Hong Kong. She'd brought some things to be stored, Miles having agreed to let the house in Above Town to a fellow officer coming to the college for two years.

'He's married,' Fliss had said. 'They're in their thirties but no children. Perfect as far as Miles is concerned.'

There had been something in her voice which had alerted

Freddy, a note which had been almost – almost *bitter*, Freddy decided. When pressed, however, Fliss had been evasive and had deftly turned the subject to Hong Kong; the eighteen-hour flight with the break at Dubai; the flat which had been arranged for them in Mount Austin Mansions on the Peak, overlooking Victoria Harbour.

'Miles has it all planned,' she'd said. This time her voice had been altogether more cheerful but Freddy was not deceived. 'One of his old friends in SOO in HMS *Tamar*. That's the shore establishment. He's organised everything for us. Miles is determined that there won't be a hitch. It's such a relief to be married to someone who's so dependable. He hates inefficiency. It must be hell to have a husband who was doing it all for the first time. So frightening.'

But much more fun. Freddy had not said the words but they had come unbidden to her mind and she'd been confused at her instinctive thought. Surely it was better for Fliss to be going so far away with someone who knew the ropes rather than with some raw beginner? Yet two young people could have such fun discovering things together. It occurred to Freddy that the wives of Miles's fellow officers must be a great deal older than Fliss. Did she have any friends of her own age? She had such good times with Kit and Sin and – in a slightly different way – with Susanna and Mole. Did she miss the companionship of people of her own age?

As Freddy played, her heart grew weighty with anxiety and fear. It had been a relief when Fliss had elected to accept Miles's proposal. Freddy had been glad to think that she would be looked after, protected; but did Fliss need protecting? Through the music, Freddy heard Theo's words, uttered when they'd received the news of Fliss's engagement.

'. . . *a myth has grown up around Fliss because of the way Peter and Jamie died . . . She missed their influence . . . the comfort of having someone older and stronger to rely on and so she turned to Hal . . . Now she has turned to Miles. She is using his strength to help her over this painful time and is committing herself in so doing. I think that she has enough strength of her own to deal with it, if she is given the space to develop it.*'

He had gone on to speak of women who were capable, who had great emotional strength, coming to resent men who refused to allow them to exercise their potential abilities; that, though they might be temporarily seduced by such men's power and instinctively submit to it, there would eventually be a dangerous point of conflict. At the time Freddy had been distracted by their own situation, realising at last why Theo had refused for so long to live permanently at The Keep; that he had feared that he might influence her and that she might come to resent him. When they returned to the subject of Fliss's engagement to Miles he had told her that he was frightened for both of them and counselled that they should wait.

Freddy thought: It was an impossible situation. Without reopening all the old wounds of her love for Hal we could not have discussed it with her.

Once again, she remembered Theo's words. '*I'd rather she was unhappy for a while,*' he'd said, '*than committed to a man she doesn't really love.*'

Her answer had been a realistic one. '*But then we don't know that she doesn't love him, do we? There are other kinds of enduring love than that which is described as love*

107

*at first sight ... Fliss will be happier with an older
man ...'*

That was when Theo had talked about the myth which
had grown up round Fliss after the death of her parents and
brother. Freddy recalled her own frustration at that point,
her anxiety. Yet during these last two years these feelings
had subsided. Fliss had seemed quite content, happier, in
fact, than Hal and Maria. Surely it was simply because Fliss
was expecting a baby and going to Hong Kong that everyone was touchy and on edge? It was so easy to get things
out of proportion when one was anxious.

The knock at the door made her jump and she turned
quickly, calling, 'Come in.' It was Mole.

Watching him approach, Freddy's heart bumped
unevenly as he crossed the carpet towards her. How much
he had grown in this last year – and how extraordinarily like
Theo he was: tall and lean, his thick dark hair flopping
forward, the brown eyes watchful and serious. Fifty years
wavered and dissolved and Freddy felt the pain that she'd
experienced each time she'd seen her brother-in-law and
been unable to tell her love. She saw that his smile, too, was
Theo's smile, crinkling round his eyes but barely touching
his mouth.

She swallowed. 'What d'you want?' she asked hoarsely.

Mole frowned a little, alerted by her tone, surprised. 'I'd
like to talk to you,' he said, 'if it's not inconvenient.'

'Do they call you Sam at Dartmouth?' she asked.

He was caught off guard by this apparently irrelevant
question. 'Yes, they do,' he answered. 'Nobody there knows
my nickname. I made Hal promise he'd never tell.'

Well, that was reasonable enough. Freddy stared at him.

Unforgivably, she wanted to punish him for looking like Theo, for disturbing all the old demons which she'd tried so hard to crush. When had he grown up and become a man?

'Why did Alison call you Sam?' She was thinking aloud.

'Her f-father was called Sam,' Mole told her, still puzzled by his grandmother's behaviour. 'Well, Samuel, actually. But I'm just Sam. When I was first born and she told people my name, they'd say, "Oh Samuel," and she'd say, "No, just Sam," until everyone called me "Just Sam". Well, until I started hiding under things and they nicknamed me Mole. That was Daddy, actually.'

He watched the tears start in her eyes, her hands tremble in her lap, and he went down on his knees beside her and put his arms around her. She turned her face against his broad shoulder and wept; wept for herself and for Theo; for her darling boys, Peter and John; for Alison and Jamie; for Fliss . . . She reached for her handkerchief but he took out his own and gave it to her, watching her as she blotted her eyes and cheeks and blew her nose in the white linen.

'What were you going to say?' she asked in barely more than a whisper, holding him where he was, still kneeling beside her.

'I want to go to London next week,' he said.

'To whom are you going?' she asked – as she had once asked Theo – and waited breathlessly for his answer.

Mole, puzzled as Theo had been at the strange phrasing of her question, stared into her eyes.

'I'm going to Sin,' he answered slowly – and they both were silent as if listening to his words as they hung in the air.

'Yes,' she said at last. 'I'm sure you are.'

He frowned and made to say that this wasn't what he meant – and paused as he realised that it was very nearly true.

'Kit's away,' he said, as if confirming this, and she nodded and looked away from him.

'Why are you telling me?'

He did not reply immediately. 'I didn't know that I was going to,' he said at last. 'Oh, I meant to say that I was going off for a few days, naturally, but I hadn't decided quite what to say about . . . going to stay with Sin.'

Freddy thought: It is quite right for him. She will give him the confidence he needs to approach other girls later. It will be exciting and very educational and fun.

Aloud, she said, 'I don't wish to know anything else.' Her hand held his own tightly as she smiled at him. 'I'm not certain that I am being a responsible grandmother to you, my dear boy.'

He smiled back at her, relief sweeping through him, excitement rising. 'You're being wonderful.' He began to laugh. 'After all, to sin is human, to *forgive* divine. You're being divine, Grandmother. In advance.'

'To *err* is human,' she corrected him sharply – but she still smiled as she released him. 'Go away. And, Mole . . .'

He turned back at the door, grinning at her, eyebrows raised.

A terrible sadness convulsed her so suddenly that she could barely see him. Dark images and shadows surrounded him . . . Death striking suddenly out of a bright day.

'Be careful,' she muttered. 'Please, take care.'

He stood for a moment, puzzled but too elated to be truly anxious.

'Of course I will,' he told her. 'And thank you, Grand-mother.'

She was alone, shaken by this unknown fear. If only she could bind her children to her, to cling on to what was left, she who had lost so much . . .

A hand gripped her shoulder and she turned quickly to see Theo looking down at her.

'I was on the terrace,' he said, as if in answer to a question. 'Be brave. Hold on at least until Fliss has gone.'

She nodded, laying her cheek briefly against his hand. 'I can, if you are here.'

'I am here,' he answered. 'Not much longer now. It's nearly teatime. Half an hour before Fliss comes back from her walk for tea. Play for me, Freddy.'

On the hill behind The Keep, Fliss stood watching a phalanx of geese flying in formation above her. As they flew along the valley they began to lose height, wheeling round to land in the water meadows beside the river. The harsh honking, which had attracted her attention, faded, dying into the heat and silence, and she looked about her, fixing the familiar scene in her mind. It had been a day of goodbyes. This taking of farewells was something she had done ever since she first went away to school but never with such an intensity as today. Here, in the shadow of the high stone wall, it was cool, but beyond its shade the countryside shimmered in the heat. The cattle stood knee-deep in the river, their tails swishing away importunate flies, and on the higher slopes the sheep had long since sought the meagre shade provided by granite boulders and the occasional outcrop of rock.

Perks came wagging up, impatient to be started, looking forward to her walk. Fliss bent to smooth the rust-coloured head and gently pulled a floppy ear.

'Come on, then,' she said. 'Down we go.'

Perks gave a short pleased woof of approval and set off down the track. Watching her busy back view, Fliss smiled a little. Dogs were such a comfort when you were feeling unhappy. They didn't ask questions or sympathise or tell you to pull yourself together, they were just *there*, undemanding and companionable. Miles had vetoed a dog at the house in Above Town.

'Totally impractical, my sweet,' he'd said kindly. 'I don't approve of dogs in towns, anyway, even if the house were suitable, which it isn't. Apart from which, they're a terrible tie.'

This was before she'd told him about the baby. Maybe, once they were tied with the baby, he'd agree to the dog. Fliss laughed at such foolish hopes. She knew he wouldn't. He'd been so relieved to let the house to a suitable couple; people who wouldn't stub out cigarettes on the furniture or spill drinks on the carpets.

Fliss thought: I'm being a cow. I'd hate it, too, if anyone did horrid things in our dear little house.

She forced her mind into more positive channels. It would be very exciting to see Hong Kong and to travel about as Miles had promised they would. It would be fun to meet other naval wives and to be the 'Captain's wife'. Fliss felt a tug of tenderness when she thought of Miles's delight in his new posting and promotion. He was doing his best, given that he did not really want the baby; trying to organise a ground-floor flat, telling her that October and November were the best months to arrive and acclimatise, encouraging her and giving her confidence. It was simply that she did not want to go.

The gorse bush which overhung the path was in brilliant, paint-bright flower, and berries were forming on the branches of the hawthorn tree. Summer was nearly over but this year she would not see an English autumn. Fliss stumbled a little on the dry shaly track and instinctively put her hands across her abdomen, shielding the life within her. The little shock was becoming familiar; the shock that came when she thought of the baby she carried. Excitement and terror in equal parts strove within her.

'I shall be a *proxy* godmother,' Kit had said firmly, 'but we'll all be together for the next one, Flissy.'

Tears filled her eyes. If Miles had his way there would be no more children.

'One is more than enough,' he'd said firmly. 'We can do much more for one. Anyway, there's no room for more.'

He'd talked of the advantages of first-class schools and of university but Fliss had been thinking about all that the child would miss. Of course siblings fought and argued, but underneath was a deep bond which was irreplaceable . . .

Perks was back with a stick which she dropped invitingly at Fliss's feet. Head cocked, eyes bright, tail gently waving, she looked from the stick to Fliss and back again.

Smiling, Fliss bent to pick up the stick and, taking careful aim, flung it far down the hill. With a scrabble of paws, barking excitedly, Perks was off in pursuit. Fliss followed her. Of course, the baby would have cousins in plenty if all the younger members of the family married and had children. Kit would probably marry Jake and start producing, and she was certain that Susanna would have a whole tribe of babies. Mole might take a little longer to get to the starting post but Hal and Maria . . .

The tears came quite suddenly. She'd been holding them back all day, determined that no one should be upset at this last meeting. She'd managed to be cheerful and positive but now, with the sun beating down upon her head and Perks barking somewhere further on, there was no need for restraint. She stumbled on, weeping, wiping at her cheeks with the hem of her long cotton skirt, too miserable to care about anything except the need to find some shade.

The spinney was dark and cool, an oasis in the bright, relentless heat. She stood looking up at the trees, drying her eyes, remembering . . . Presently she felt calm; her courage had returned and with it some measure of acceptance. Two years was not so very long, after all. She would soon be home again, with her child, back at The Keep. There would be so much to show him – or her – so much to share, so much fun ahead. If only she could be absolutely certain that when she returned everything would be the same; everyone in their appointed place.

A thought was forming in her head. Running round the spinney had been a kind of test, a challenge. Later, it had become a symbol of achievement. There was something mysterious about the trees, the dense shadows, the silence.

Fliss thought: If I run round the spinney I shall come back safely with my baby and they will all still be there, Grandmother and Uncle Theo and the others.

She laughed at herself. It was simply superstition. There was no real test here for her – yet there was a compulsion to do it, as if it would be a kind of completion of something and a gesture of hope to the future. The three of them were setting out again. Not from Kenya, this time, to live with their grandmother but out into the world: Susanna to university; Mole to sea; she, Fliss, to Hong Kong. It would be a symbolic act performed for the three of them, setting out on the next stage of the journey.

Fliss touched the trunk of the tall beech, took one last glance at the high walls on the hill above her and, with her hands about her baby, she began to jog gently round the spinney. Perks dashed out of the trees, skittering in her wake, and somewhere high above her a lark began to sing.

Book Two
Autumn 1976

Chapter Twelve

The moon was rising; apricot-coloured, immense, it hung just above the horizon, lending its reflected light to the patchwork of fields so that the pale stubble glowed warm within its fretwork of inky hedgerows. It was early yet, barely eight o'clock, but the September evenings were drawing in, misty and cool, and already memories of the long, blazing summer were receding before the expectations of autumn.

Leaning from the nursery bathroom window, a towel wrapped turban-like around her newly washed hair, Susanna held her breath. It was a magical scene made more poignant because she knew that, after today, nothing could ever be quite the same again. Tonight was her last night at The Keep and tomorrow everything would change. She might lean from this window in the years to come but it would be different because *she* would be different. Excitement and apprehension churned in her stomach and she reached for her dressing gown, dragging it on as she hurried across the landing to her own room.

Tying the belt firmly about her waist, she went to kneel on the window seat. From this window she could no longer see the moon but the western sky was not yet dark. The tall fir trees stood motionless, clear-cut, black against the greeny-gold afterglow of sunset. A thrush – Fox called it a stormcock – was singing in the orchard and there were rabbits feeding at the far end of the lawn. White scuts flashed and bobbed, disappearing into the chrysanthemums and dahlias whose colours were barely visible in the gathering twilight. This familiar scene calmed her and she smiled a little at her earlier attack of self-dramatisation. Perhaps nobody ever really changed. Whatever might happen to her, perhaps the core of her would remain the same; perhaps she would always carry with her the small Susanna who had kneeled on the window seat each morning to wave to her guardians, standing tall at the end of the orchard. She would bring her own children here and tell them the story of the three fir trees . . .

At the thought of these children, Susanna sat down abruptly on the wide seat, feet drawn up, arms hugging her knees, her eyes still fixed on the scene below. Briefly she tried to imagine her grandmother as a small child. No, it was impossible. Surely her grandmother had always been utterly adult, tall, imposing, all-seeing, confident. Uncle Theo, then. That was more likely simply because she merely translated him down in age to the younger Mole – and she could easily remember Mole as a boy. Anyone could see how like his great-uncle Mole was and, anyway, there was also something – Susanna frowned thoughtfully, childlike wasn't the right word – something young at heart about Uncle Theo. He was wise but he never felt it necessary to instruct people. The word 'humility' hovered about in her mind but confusing it with humble – the Uriah

Heep-like meaning of the word – she dismissed it. There was a quality about Uncle Theo which held him apart; he was never judgemental, yet it would be terrible to know that she had disappointed him. More terrible, oddly, than upsetting Grandmother and, goodness knows, she was strict enough and very ready to deliver a good old-fashioned telling-off if she thought it necessary. Susanna sighed. It was all rather confusing. She'd heard someone say, 'Age is relative,' but relative to what? To her, Hal, Kit, Fliss and Mole seemed quite unchanged, yet they were all growing older.

Susanna thought: I am twenty-one. *Twenty-one.* I'm old. Grown up. And tomorrow is my wedding day.

She turned her head so that she might see her dress hanging on the cupboard door. Luminous in the growing gloom, the heavy ivory silk fell long and slender from a lined bodice of delicate lace, the sleeves gathered into narrow cuffs. When she'd first tried it on, she'd been unable to believe the sight of herself in the mirror. She'd been transformed: ethereal, beautiful . . . Turning to look wonderingly at her sister she'd been unsurprised to see tears pouring down Fliss's cheeks. It was a tiny, amazing miracle. She, too, would have found it terribly easy to cry, there was something so poignantly unreal, so fairytale about her, quite unlike her ordinary everyday self. It had been almost a relief to change back into her jeans.

Gus had laughed when she'd told him how beautiful she'd looked. 'You are always beautiful,' he'd said. 'But I can quite see that there might be something frightening about it. My knees shake at the mere thought of it all. Have you quite set your mind against elopement?'

She'd hugged him happily, knowing how lucky she was to find him.

'You're like us,' she'd said to him once. 'You're weird, too.'

He'd frowned cautiously. 'Until I know your definition of "weird",' he'd said, 'I reserve the right to react indignantly to that statement.'

Susanna knew exactly what she meant. Her years at college had shown her that her family was unusual to say the least. 'You're an anachronism,' a college friend had said after a weekend at The Keep. 'That Victorian grandmother of yours! What a matriarch. And the old retainers in the kitchen. It's pre-war.' Susanna had felt very hurt and secretly alarmed. After a great deal of thought she'd decided that children simply accepted that how they grew up was the norm. Away at school it hadn't seemed a difficulty but, once out in the world, she could see that the seclusion of The Keep and the old-fashioned attitudes of its occupants were not in keeping with the ways of most other families she met.

'You had a generation missing,' Aunt Prue had explained after this particular weekend when she'd returned to Bristol, hurt and made anxious by her friend's observations. 'Apart from me popping in and out, you've been surrounded by old people. Your grandmother, Theo, Ellen and Fox, they were all middle-aged by the time you came back from Kenya. There was no social life at The Keep, no friends dropping in. It's bound to show. But does it matter?'

'We had Caroline,' Susanna had said, rather defensively. 'She wasn't all that old. I don't think I want to be an anachronism.'

122

Aunt Prue had smiled. 'Perhaps your friend might be jealous?' she'd suggested. 'I think what you've got is rather special. Don't knock it, as Kit would say.'

'Are Hal and Kit different from us?' she'd asked, still worrying at it. 'We all seem the same to me.'

'They spent quite a lot of time at The Keep, too,' Aunt Prue had answered. 'And they had no father, which makes a difference. I wasn't what you'd call a model mother either but they've survived. Hal's doing well. Of course, the Navy is still a place where an unusual background might be an advantage – it's a world of its own. And as for Kit . . . well, Kit isn't exactly what you might call an ordinary girl.'

'She's got Sin and Jake,' Susanna had said thoughtfully.

'Quite. Like calls to like. The thing is to find your own kind of people. Janie doesn't think you're an anachronism, does she?'

Susanna had felt a touch of comfort here. This was the secret then: to find like-minded people with whom to work and live. Later she'd mentioned it to Uncle Theo.

'Being true to yourself is what matters,' he'd answered. 'Otherwise you will become as unsteady as a weathercock, trying to be all things to all men.' She might have answered that she did not yet quite know herself but instinctively she understood what he was telling her. She could grow, adapt, develop, but she need not jettison the past which had moulded her, nor deny the teachings which informed her thoughts and reactions.

She'd met Gus when two years later, she'd answered an advertisement in the *Western Morning News*: a graphic artist in Totnes required an experienced assistant for the Easter holidays. She'd found him hidden away in a small court near the castle, living over the shop. Having let herself in through the gate in the wall, she'd stood for a moment, looking round the sunny little courtyard in delight, before approaching the open door. Inside, someone was whistling and humming and occasionally bursting into song: a setting of one of Housman's poems, 'Bredon Hill.'

'Hello,' she'd said, during a pause. 'It's me, Susanna Chadwick. I've called about the job.'

He'd come towards her from amongst the clutter of drawing boards and long trestle tables, peering at her over the top of the reading spectacles which slid down his nose.

'Thank goodness,' he'd said, removing them and holding out his hand. 'I didn't quite believe my luck when you answered my ad. The truth is, I'm terribly behind and I'm getting in a muddle.' He'd smiled then, still holding her hand. 'Hello, Susanna Chadwick. I'm Augustus Mallory, commonly called Gus.'

It was as simple as that. From that moment she'd known that Gus was her person and that she belonged to him; that the crowded office and the cosy flat above it were to become her world.

'My father is a parson,' he'd told her, 'and I'm the youngest of six children. By the time they got to me my parents had practically given up the battle. I was allowed to choose my own career and drawing is the only thing I can do reasonably well apart from singing. I have a passable baritone voice of which you will become extremely tired. Feel free to shut me up whenever you please.'

He talked endlessly, which delighted her. There was no subject in which she could not interest him and they chattered for hours; learning each other, she called it. He was fascinated by stories of The Keep and her family and, in return, he told her about his own upbringing in a Somersetshire parsonage on the edge of Exmoor.

'My parents named us all after saints,' he said cheerfully. 'Wishful thinking no doubt. My sisters came off best. Anne and Theresa. But with us boys they became more adventurous: Barnabas, George, Crispin and me. It should have been Augustine but my godmother intervened, bless her. You'd like my godmother.'

At the end of the holiday she could hardly bear to leave him. They'd both been rather quiet on her last day. He'd hummed beneath his breath, a sure sign that he was thinking something through, and she'd felt that she might burst with misery and the longing that he would say something to her which would show that he felt as she did. How could she go back to Bristol without some sign that he cared for her, that he would miss their growing companionship?

'I've been thinking,' he'd said, as she'd brought them both mugs of coffee from the small kitchen, 'that I might take on a full-time assistant. The work's pouring in at the moment. I've really captured the hotel trade and I've got hundreds of brochures to do . . . but it might not appeal. I imagine you have your sights fixed on London at the end of the term?'

For the first time he'd found it impossible to look at her and she'd known an unfamiliar surge of triumph: a strange mix of power and tenderness. His grey eyes had looked rather sad as he'd sat hunched on his stool, his shoulders uncharacteristically bowed, turning a pencil in his long fingers. She'd remained silent for a moment, deciding what to say, and he'd sighed, shrugging a little, anticipating her refusal.

'It's only to be expected,' he'd said. 'I wouldn't be able to pay very much and you wouldn't meet lots of exciting people. It's a terrific cheek to ask, really. Why on earth would a beautiful, talented girl like you want to bury herself in a little studio in Totnes?'

'Because I love you.' She'd answered his question truthfully and accurately and he'd turned quickly, dropping his pencil, standing up.

'Oh, Sooz. Do you? Honestly? I love you too. Only I didn't think I'd have a hope. Oh, dearest, darling Sooz . . .' He'd stretched out his arms for her – and knocked over the coffee, spilling it all over his drawings . . .

Now, still sitting on the window seat, hugging her knees, Susanna chuckled. They'd had to do the drawings all over again and Gus had sung loudly the whole time, punctuating the work with quick hugs and rather longer kisses.

Beneath her a window opened and light streamed suddenly across the terrace.

The thrush which had been singing in the orchard had long since flown away and the garden lay deserted and silent below her. Susanna jumped up and went across to the cupboard, bending down to root about for her hair dryer. Fliss had promised to come up for a chat before supper and here she was with her hair still dripping. She rubbed her head furiously with the towel and reached for her brush. She hadn't wanted a hairdresser fiddling with her hair although she'd had a trim the week before. Now it was slightly longer than jaw length and she planned to sweep it back above her ears with two clips and place the simple veil with its circlet of flowers on the top. It was lovely to think that she would look beautiful for Gus but she needed to feel that she was truly herself, too. Marrying Gus wasn't a fairy tale sustained by promises of a happy ending. It was real: real as the busy office in the funny old cottage, real as the panics about clients paying their bills and the monthly anguish of finding the rent.

Susanna plugged in the hair dryer and perched on the end of her bed. She brushed the thick dark hair away from her face, lips curved in a tiny, unconscious smile. It was going to be such a lovely day with all her dearest people about her: dear old Mole giving her away and Fliss's darling twinnies following her up the aisle. Gus's ten-year-old niece was to be in charge of them and his two nephews were to be ushers, under the watchful eye of Hal. She'd been oddly relieved that Hal's children were far too young to take a leading role in the ceremony. There seemed to be a kind of strain when Maria was with her children at The Keep; a kind of contest as to which children were the most admired, most valued by their relatives. Everyone adored all the children equally and in their different ways: Grandmother affectionately; Uncle Theo cautiously; Fox lovingly: Caroline warmly but sensibly . . .

If only Ellen had been here to see her married. It was the single dark shadow cast across the brightness of her happiness. During Fliss's second year in Hong Kong, Ellen had slipped on a patch of ice and broken her hip. Pneumonia set in and she had died quickly and without regaining consciousness. The shock to the family had been numbing, their grieving long, relieved only by the arrival of news and photographs of Fliss's twinnies; and even this had carried the pain of knowing that Ellen would never see the children . . .

Susanna wiped away the tears, imagining she could hear Ellen's voice from the shadows. 'Crying on your wedding eve. Whatever next, I wonder . . .' Surely Ellen was still here with them, knit into the very fabric of The Keep.

'She'll be there,' Gus had said confidently. 'No need to worry about that. The vital part of Ellen can't be contained by the earth.'

Now she thought of it, Gus was rather like Uncle Theo: a strange blend of toughness and compassion; of love and unyielding strength. Joy flooded back into her heart, driving out sorrow. Tomorrow they would be married, setting out on the rest of their life together. Wielding her brush in one hand and the hair dryer in the other, Susanna began to sing.

Chapter Thirteen

Freddy, flanked by Theo and Fliss, sat in the Chadwick pew and looked about her. Caroline had done wonders with the flowers despite the unrewarding material with which she'd had to work. Single-stemmed coral chrysanthemums, green hydrangeas and autumn berries glowed against the ancient grey stone. Kit had brought roses down from London; long red ones for the church and house, tiny buds for the posies. Autumn was not the best time for a wedding but it had been a question of getting Hal, Miles and Mole all together at the same time. 'Anyway,' Susanna had said, 'I don't want all those fancy hothouse flowers. I want it to be simple. A country wedding, not some grand London affair.'

The organ was competing with the murmur and quiet bustle in the church behind her: '*Jesu, Joy of Man's Desiring*'. Freddy listened carefully, approving the organist's abilities, although the piece was not a favourite. She was aware of Gus and his best man in the pew across the aisle, of Theo's reassuring presence and of Fliss's anxiety. Freddy knew very well that Fliss was living in terror that the twinnies might be overwhelmed by the occasion and so ruin Susanna's day. She put her gloved hand lightly on Fliss's clenched ones and

watched the thin fingers relax. Glancing sideways she saw
Fliss smile, roll her eyes comically, nod gratefully. Removing
her hand, Freddy straightened her shoulders, wondering, as
she so often did now, how much Fliss was suffering. She had
returned from Hong Kong with two enchanting blonde moppets, Elizabeth and Jamie, and several new lines etched about
her eyes and mouth. More than ever now she looked like her
mother: the tiny frown perpetually clouding her brow, her face
stern in repose.

Freddy thought: She is coping with the knowledge that
Miles is not interested in his children. Oh, he puts on a bit
of a show for us all, pretends he adores them, but you can
see from their attitude to him that it is not the way he
usually behaves to them. Poor darling Fliss. For her, of all
people, it is such a tragedy. Poor Miles, too. He should have
remained a widower or probably never married in the first
place. He's a good man – strong, determined, dependable,
successful – but he's not a family man. I should have seen
that all those years ago but he was so in love it was almost
painful to see him. He'd been so faithful, so patient . . .

Fliss glanced quickly over her shoulder and Hal, catching
her sudden movement, smiled reassuringly and put up his
thumbs, jerking his head towards the door. So the bride's
attendants had arrived and were safely in the porch. She
sighed with relief, caught Gus's eye and nodded encouragingly. He grinned, pretending faintness, and she grinned
too, her anxiety evaporating in the face of his happiness.
She was aware of his family filling the pews directly behind
him. His father was assisting at the service but his mother,
sitting amongst Gus's assorted siblings and their offspring,

smiled placidly at her youngest son as he turned once more to glance hopefully down the aisle.

Fliss thought: What a lovely family they are. How lucky Susanna is. I really don't think Grandmother need worry about her.

She knew that her grandmother was concerned by Gus's lack of material substance and she hid another grin as she recalled Gus's description of the interview.

'It only needed a raised lorgnette to complete the scene,' he'd told her. 'She terrifies me. I explained about the business and so on and she listened very patiently and then said, "But on what do you intend to *live*?" clearly dismissing my work as an adequate means of support. I said, "Well, actually, not that much, to be honest." She looked at me, very *grande dame*, obviously contemplating some utterly devastating remark, but your Uncle Theo leaned forward and said, "Shall you mind if Susanna talks to strangers on trains?" I was a bit thrown, I have to say. I thought it was a kind of test question and that my future happiness depended on getting the answer right. I was so nervous I said what came into my head first. "Why on earth should I?" I said. "I've met some terrific people on trains." He looked at your grandmother and said, "It is clear to me that Gus and Susanna were meant for each other." Well, she snorted in a disdainful kind of way but let the financial aspect drop. I was jolly relieved, I can tell you. I don't know where the train bit came in but I think your Uncle Theo's a great guy.'

Someone from the back of the church had given a sign and the organist was moving smoothly from the voluntary to the introit, playing loudly now. The congregation rose to its feet and turned expectantly, Gus included. Catching sight of his face, Theo experienced a stab of pure envy. How glorious to have the right to express your joy and love quite openly like that! Unconscious of anyone else, Gus was watching Susanna come up the aisle on her brother's arm. Tall, dark, elegant in his naval uniform, Mole made a perfect foil to Susanna's pale cloudy beauty. Traditionally, her face was covered with a single floating layer of her veil and her posy of tiny yellow rosebuds matched the circlet on her head.

Watching her, Freddy found herself remembering the little group waiting on Staverton station nineteen years before: Mole clinging to Fliss, the small Susanna gazing up at her unknown grandmother with round brown eyes, her rag dolly clutched to her smocked dress. Freddy had bent down to pick her up, her heart full of fear, wondering how on earth she would manage with these three small orphans . . . Now, as she drew level, Susanna leaned forward to smile at them, at her grandmother and Uncle Theo and her sister, and Mole, aware of the pressure on his arm, paused, so that the two of them were held motionless for one moment in time and space before they passed on. Tears slid down Freddy's cheeks, though she stared straight ahead, chin lifted, daring either of her supporters to notice. Theo, head bent, was silently concentrating on willing her his love as he had done so many times in the past.

Fliss swallowed her tears and smiled down at the two small persons who were now standing on a level with her in the aisle. Excited by the occasion, delighted by their part in it, they beamed up at her proudly. Bess's dress of blue velvet matched Jamie's shorts, and her small posy of pink and white rosebuds had been brought with the others from London by Kit. Jamie's fair hair stood up in spikes, witness to earlier anxious twiddling, but Bess's still retained its blue velvet hair ribbon, tied demurely on one side of the bright little face.

Fliss thought: How odd it is that my twinnies are older than Susanna was when we arrived back from Kenya. Where have all the years gone?

Now she understood in part the terror her grandmother must have felt, being confronted with three children who were utterly dependent on her. It was this reliance – their helplessness and utter trust – which was so frightening. Supposing she should fail them? She knew that Miles, who had been helping Hal with the seating of the guests, was sitting somewhere behind her, leaving space for Mole to slip in beside her when he'd given Susanna away. She remembered their own wedding, a very quiet affair, in this church six years before and wondered if he were thinking of it, too. Cautiously she turned to locate him, reminding him of their bond, but he was studying his service sheet and didn't see her.

The familiar words were spoken, the opening bars of the hymn, '*Love Divine, all loves excelling*', were played, the sun broke through the clouds and filled the church with warm, golden light. Theo went out to the lectern to read the lesson: I Corinthians Chapter 13. '*Though I speak with the tongues of men and of angels, and have not charity, I am become as sounding brass, or a tinkling cymbal . . .*'

The Keep was *en fête*. According to Susanna's wishes everything had been done simply but effectively. She had rejected Fliss's suggestion that a marquee should be erected on the lawn, protesting that she wanted the house itself to be host. Caroline and Fliss, consulting together, agreed that with the number of guests – fewer than sixty – it should be possible to arrange it as she wished by using most of the ground floor and having the speeches in the hall, some of the guests standing on the stairs if necessary. The day before the wedding the hall was cleared of its furniture and Caroline and Fliss decorated it with sprays of eucalyptus leaves, tall red roses and trailing ivy, and the red and yellow berries of the cotoneaster. The huge fireplace was swept and the fire laid tidily with the biggest logs; chairs were placed discreetly for the infirm and elderly. Early on the morning of the wedding, the caterers arrived and took possession of the kitchen. Now, all was ready.

'It's too bad,' said Kit sadly, drinking champagne with Sin. 'These mere children getting married. I think I feel old.'

'You've had your chance,' said Sin unsympathetically. 'Don't come to me when you realise what a mistake you've made. I see that Jake is chatting up Gus's pretty sister.'

'You can't love people to order,' protested Kit, watching him. 'Or *not* love them. As *you* should know.'

Sin grimaced. 'I shouldn't have come,' she admitted. 'Weddings are too utterly depressing. Yet I can't resist. It's like worrying at a painful tooth.'

'We're masochists,' said Kit gloomily. 'Oh hell, Ma's coming over. I know just what she's going to say. "You'll be next," she'll say, and she'll attempt to comfort me. Go and deflect her. Talk to her about my nephews. It always works.'

'She'll say it to *me*, too,' protested the departing Sin, 'and I might break down and tell her that I have loved not wisely but too well.'

'Don't you dare,' said Kit. 'And don't be long. I'll go and find some more champagne.'

'Quite charming,' Maria was agreeing to a remark made by one of Gus's friends regarding the floral decorations, 'but I prefer something a little more formal myself. Of course, these county families are so old-fashioned.'

She hitched the small Jolyon higher on to her hip and glanced about for Hal, hoping that he would notice her flirting lightly with this rather good-looking young man. He'd already made several flattering remarks about her being too young to have two children. Maria was far too insecure ever to take such polite social comments at their true value. She always treasured them up to tell Hal later on, hoping that they would unsettle him.

'It's a lovely house,' Gus's friend was saying. 'Wonderful position.'

'It is nice, isn't it?' said Maria casually. 'Of course, it will be Hal's one day. Quite soon, I suspect. Mrs Chadwick is getting very frail.'

She sipped at her champagne and jiggled her small son a little, knowing that they made a charming picture. Jolyon's face crumpled and he began to whimper.

'Oh dear,' said her companion. 'Getting tired, is he?'

'Shush, darling, shush.' Maria looked about her again, hoping that Hal was near at hand; he was so good with the children when they were fractious. 'Be a good boy, now.'

Jolyon's cries grew louder and, smiling a farewell at the

young man, Maria began to move away through the guests. Jolyon needed his afternoon sleep but she felt faintly irritated at being the one who had to leave the jollity. Trust Hal to be busy elsewhere when the children played up. The baby had been fed on their return from the church and tucked up in the cot which had been erected in their bedroom.

Hal, now a Lieutenant Commander, was First Lieutenant of HMS *Diomede*, based in Portsmouth, and he and his family were staying at The Keep for a week. As she climbed the stairs, looking back over the crowd below, Maria was thinking how much she would enjoy a quiet stay with only the older members of the family present. She was rather tired of the wedding scene. There had been nothing else talked about for months. Of course, it had been a problem getting all the men together. This was the earliest date that could be managed; Miles was on Cincfleet's staff at Northwood, Hal was just beginning two weeks' leave and Mole, having finished his nuclear training, was about to join HMS *Warspite* as its navigational officer. Everyone kept their fingers crossed that no international incident should spoil the day and prayed that nothing should rock the boat. 'An apt phrase,' Hal had remarked at the time.

Maria gently opened the bedroom door and slipped quietly inside. She wanted to talk to Hal very seriously but had decided to let it wait until after the wedding. As she removed Jolyon's shoes, murmuring to him, lulling him into sleep, she was planning what she should say to him.

Fox had been at the church but he was sitting unobtrusively in a corner of the breakfast room when Kit arrived in search of liquid support. One glance at his disconsolate form showed what he was thinking. Caroline shot her a speaking glance as she passed her in the doorway and Kit paused beside him, slipping an arm about his shoulder, resting her cheek against his grizzled head. He leaned into her, recognising and accepting her affection and sympathy.

'If she could have just seen the two little tackers,' he said, by way of explanation. 'She knew all along, that's what gets me. She was that unhappy about it. 'Tis a downright pity, maid, that's what.'

'Oh, Fox,' said Kit sadly. 'It is. It's beastly rotten luck. Don't sit here alone, though. Ellen wouldn't want that. Come and talk to people. You must protect me from tactless friends who keep asking me why I'm not married or I shall have to escape into the garden to eat worms.'

He chuckled a little, despite his grief. 'At least you won't be getting in the old dog basket,' he said with an attempt at cheerfulness. 'Not in that smart get-up.'

'Too true, I fear,' agreed Kit, thinking with longing of the basket and Perks's recumbent form, peacefully asleep, exuding comfort. 'Though I can't tell you how tempting it is. I do hope that frighteningly efficient girl from the caterers is being kind to our Perks. Come along. We can't skulk here. Up you come. But you mustn't leave me. I'm counting on you, remember.'

Mole was watching Sin talking to Gus's father.

'I simply cannot resist men of the cloth,' she'd told him, during one of their brief uninterrupted moments. 'Oh, Mole, you both looked so beautiful coming up the aisle together. I cried buckets.'

There was an unspoken agreement between them which forbade any serious discussions regarding marriage. Perhaps, if it had been the other way round, the eight year gap would not have mattered so much but Sin clearly shrank from the thought of being the wife of a so much younger man; not that Mole had ever proposed to her. From the beginning she had kept the relationship on a very light footing. Mole knew how lucky he was. Once or twice he'd attempted to explain his feelings but she'd shut him up at once with jokes about her unrequited love for Uncle Theo and her unbridled passion for gorgeous young men. Mole was relieved to have the subject deflected. He did not quite know exactly what it was he felt for Sin but he suspected that it would be immature and gauche to profess undying love or to insist that their relationship should be made respectable and official. She was so sophisticated that he was afraid of committing some awful gaffe, or appearing raw and inexperienced.

Mole thought: She's given me so much. Perhaps it's as well that I'm at sea most of the time. It keeps it all very casual. Anyway, I expect she has other lovers.

Part of him felt guilty that he took what she offered so readily but he suspected that there was nothing he could do about that except stop seeing her. It was she who made the moves, suggesting when he should come, staying in touch, yet resisting any serious approach, and he was content to allow the relationship to continue along its easy, satisfying path.

'Looking forward to going nuclear?' Hal materialised beside him.

'It'll certainly be good to get the smell of diesel out of

my clothes,' Mole answered. 'Although I can't quite get used to the idea of having showers on board. These hunter killers are quite different from the conventional boats. Positively luxurious. Of course, you skimmers are used to soft living and pampering yourselves. A clean shirt every day and changing for dinner.'

'That'll do,' said Hal, too full of food and champagne to feel able to hold his own during the usual banter. 'No cheek from you, young Mole.'

'Enjoying being back at sea?'

Hal glanced about instinctively to see if Maria were at hand. 'It was good to be at Dartmouth,' he said. 'Specially with the sprogs arriving and so on. Just the right timing. But it's good news being Jimmy. We're off to Gibraltar in a couple of weeks. That was a very good speech you made, by the way.'

'Oh, it was nothing much,' Mole shrugged off his cousin's praise, and glanced upwards as Susanna appeared on the stairs, changed into her casual going-away clothes, ready for the trip to Cornwall.

There was an appreciative cheer as Janie caught her little posy and then they all followed the newly married couple out of the door and across the courtyard, hugging, kissing, shouting farewells. She and Gus climbed into his battered Citroën Dyane and they drove out of the gate and down the drive, an arm waving wildly from each of the two front windows, until they disappeared from view.

It was much later that they found the envelope, propped on the piano in the drawing room. Freddy opened it whilst Theo, Mole and Fliss crowded closer, trying to see over her shoulder. Susanna and Gus had made the card together. The Keep was drawn in section: Fox and Ellen could be seen in the kitchen with all three dogs; Caroline was upstairs in the nursery; Freddy was playing the piano in the drawing room; Theo was at his desk in his study. Inside the card was a drawing of the hall. Before the fire stood three children: Fliss was holding Susanna's hand, her arm round Mole, and all three were smiling happily. Underneath, Susanna had written:

> *My love and thanks to every one of you.*
> *It's all been perfect.*

Presently, Mole bent to pick up the folded sheet of paper which had fluttered to the floor.

'What does it say?' Fliss broke the long emotional silence, suppressing her desire to weep unrestrainedly.

He looked round at them, blinking back his own tears, smiling a little.

'It's a thank you letter from Gus,' he said. 'He's added a postscript. It says, "How on earth do I follow twenty-one years of perfection?" '

Chapter Fourteen

The car stood waiting just inside the gates. Caroline had already backed it out of the garage and was now placing the hamper in the back with a rug, two folding chairs and various waterproofs, whilst Perks watched wistfully, knowing that she was too old for such jaunts. Theo smiled to himself as he glanced from his first-floor window. He knew that Caroline did not trust him when it came to negotiating the new Escort estate out of the converted store room built into the thickness of the gatehouse wall. He had a marked tendency to graze the shiny new paint on the front wing or to churn up the grass. He'd never managed the trick of turning it on the flagstones as the other members of his family did. He accepted his shortcomings as a driver placidly now. In earlier years, Freddy's efficient driving skills had made him feel inadequate but it was rather too late in the day to worry about such things. As he watched Caroline – who now appeared to be checking the petrol gauge – Fox came hobbling into the courtyard from the garden room, leaning heavily on his stick. Theo hastened to gather up his belongings; he knew from experience that Fox would stand patiently beside the car, deeming it to be too forward to climb in first.

141

These outings had begun nearly two years ago, quite by chance, but Theo, pocketing his loose change and rummaging in his drawer for a clean handkerchief, even now felt a twinge of something akin to remorse. It was Caroline who had asked if he would drive Fox to his appointment at the surgery. Some crisis had occurred so that she was unable to take him and she was afraid that he might insist that he could manage alone. Remembering, Theo smiled wryly to himself as he hastened downstairs. It must have been quite an emergency for her to suggest that *he* go with Fox. He had never amounted to much as a driver, and he was rarely allowed behind the wheel. He'd managed the journey to Totnes very well, however, and, when Fox was once more seated beside him, suggested that they might take the opportunity to go for a little drive. It had been spring and the bluebells were just coming into their full glory. The lanes were vivid with freshly minted colours: pinky-red campion, bright yellow celandine and white ramsons. They'd paused to watch a dipper, bobbing on his rock in a tumbling, rushing stream, and listened to the yaffingale, laughing in a distant wooded valley. They were enjoying themselves so much that Theo had ventured onwards, through Ashburton and up on to the moors. He'd stopped the car at a high point on the narrow white road and smiled with pleasure at the scene before them.

'Glorious, isn't it?' he'd asked, indicating the sweep of country across to the impressive granite outcrop of Haytor rocks and far beyond the patchwork of fields and woods to the sea, glittering in the pale spring sunshine. 'I love this bit. It encapsulates all of Devon for me. Moor and sea. Woods and valleys, farmlands and villages. It's all here. Glorious Devon. Got a favourite view?'

There was no answer and he'd turned to look at Fox, surprised at his silence. He'd been staring out over the moor, a rapt expression on his seamed, weather-beaten face, his eyes dazed. He'd shaken his head at last.

''Tis beyond anything,' he'd said simply. 'I've never been this far from home, sir, and I'd no idea of it, if you take my meaning. Beats our old hill into a cocked hat, this does.'

Theo had sat for some moments, shocked and ashamed. 'My dear fellow,' he'd said. 'Do you mean to tell me that this is the first time you've been on Dartmoor?'

'It is indeed,' Fox had said. 'There's been no call, you see. Mrs Chadwick always liked to drive herself, and then Caroline took over the ferrying of the children to and fro. Had my old bike, of course, for getting round the lanes and I've been to Totnes many times.'

'As a boy?' Theo had ventured. 'Did you get about much?'

'Born and brought up in Devonport, I was,' Fox had answered cheerfully. 'No money, nor no transport for getting about in those days. Joined the Navy when I was fourteen and I was twenty-two when war broke out. Since the first war finished I've been at The Keep.'

This morning, as he came through the hall, Theo still felt an echo of the shock he'd felt at that moment: eighty-two years old and Fox had hardly been further afield than the grounds of The Keep. It was quite clear that he felt no resentment, quite the contrary. It had never occurred to him that the Chadwicks might have given him the opportunity to go to the moors or to the coast. His humility had touched Theo's heart and so it was that the outings had become a regular occurrence. Not so regular as to become a habit – he'd known instinctively that Fox wouldn't have liked that – but as a delightful treat on sunny days.

'Fancy a spin?' Theo would put his head round the kitchen door, eyebrows raised, and Fox's face would dissolve into a hundred creases as he smiled joyfully back at him. He'd guessed the reason for Theo's kindness. With Ellen gone the time lay heavy on his hands, although Caroline did everything she could to mitigate his loss. Freddy had been faintly surprised at Theo's philanthropy but understood that Fox, more than any of them, must be suffering terribly without Ellen. They'd been close companions for nearly sixty years and it was inevitable that he must be lonely and lost without her. It would not have occurred to Freddy to take her servants on outings and Theo knew this and accepted it. Yet she was quite ready to approve anything which should lessen Fox's grief and help him to come to terms with it, even if it meant trusting Theo with the car.

'Just don't kill yourself doing it,' she'd said tartly. 'It would rather destroy the object of the exercise.'

Theo grinned to himself as he took his stick from the brass container by the front door and waved it cheerfully to the patiently waiting Fox. Caroline hurried out behind him to give him the car keys and to remind him to stop for the coffee which was made up in a flask in the hamper, and Freddy came to the door of the garden room to wave them off.

'So,' said Theo, easing himself behind the wheel. 'Where shall we go today?'

'I wondered whether it wouldn't be a right day for the moor, sir,' answered Fox rather shyly. He still wasn't used to having his preferences so readily consulted. 'But wherever you fancy will do me. Can't go wrong on a day like this.'

'The moor it is, then,' said Theo cheerfully, crashing the gears woefully, and juddering the car between the gatehouses. 'We'll go out through Ashburton and have our coffee by the bridge below Rushlade Common.'

Fox sighed with deep contentment as they passed down the lane. Any strain between the two of them during these outings had long since passed. In the early days at The Keep, Fox had called the young Theo 'Padre', later he had become 'Mr Theo' but now he simply called him 'sir'. He had gently but firmly resisted Theo's request to drop the formality when they were alone together, and Theo had respected his need to retain it.

Once through Ashburton, always a rather breathtaking business with Theo at the wheel, they turned right at Ausewell Cross and drove out on to the moor. Beyond the cattle grid, a shaggy, heavy-headed pony stood immobile in the road and Theo edged cautiously round him, narrowly missing the sheep that were grazing at the verge. Fox smiled to himself as he leaned from the window to pat the pony's rump, wishing that Ellen was still alive that he might regale her with his adventures on his return. On the other hand, if Ellen were still alive there would have been no adventures, nothing to tell . . .

The car swung right at Cold East Cross and, having pulled in by the stream, Theo switched off the engine with a sigh of relief. They sat for a moment or two in companionable silence, listening to the gentle splashing of the water and the outpourings of a skylark somewhere above them.

The bracken was just beginning to turn to fiery rust: rowan berries gleamed brightly crimson amongst the yellowing leaves. High cirrus formed whorls and streaks of white against the chalky blue sky whilst, lower down, cushiony creamy clouds tumbled and bumped along before the strong west wind. It was sheltered here, by the stream, and Fox sat quite still, his eyes bright and wondering as he surveyed the scene before him with delight.

'Coffee,' said Theo, getting out and going round to open Fox's door, lending him tactful assistance to swing his legs out of the confined space. 'Sit there for a moment in the sun while I get organised. What d'you say to going over to have a look at Jay's grave later? Or we could go round by Trendlebeare Down.' He opened the tailgate and reached for the hamper. 'Now let's see what Caroline has given us today.'

'An odd alliance,' murmured Freddy, listening to the sound of the engine dying away and returning to the garden room where she kept her tools and the rest of the paraphernalia necessary to her gardening activities. It was many years now since Fox had plumbed in the cold water tap to the small sink and built shelves round the walls to hold vases and bowls and her reference books. The walls were white-washed and, above a row of gumboots and overshoes, old coats hung from a line of wooden pegs. Today she was transferring the bedding varieties of her fuchsias into pots and the big deal table was covered with plants and earth. It was a pleasant sunny place to be on such a morning, with its warm pungent smell and the door standing open to the courtyard.

Caroline left her amongst her plants and went back to the kitchen, the portly Perks waddling faithfully behind her. She thought it was good for both Theo and Fox to have these times together but secretly she rather envied them. She, too, would like to drive off in the car, to spend the morning pottering about the moor or along the coast. It had taken her a week or two to recover from the wedding but now the house was quiet again and she could afford to relax a little; a little but not too much. There was a great deal of work to do even though they were such a small household now. She sometimes wondered how on earth they had managed when the children were small. Of course, they'd been much younger, capable of so much more. And they'd had Ellen. Nevertheless, even with Josh working most days in the grounds she wondered if they could cope without the property deteriorating, becoming neglected.

She pushed the kettle on to the hotplate of the Aga and stood looking at the breakfast washing-up and the pile of ironing. Which should she tackle first? How she missed Ellen, who'd managed an enormous workload without whining or making a fuss. Perks climbed into the dog basket, turned round a few times on the old blanket and settled with a thump and a deep sigh. Caroline reached for a mug – with a mental apology to Ellen, who would have despised such a drop in standards – and spooned in coffee, brooding on various people's attitudes to the daily round.

She'd been rather surprised at Maria's lack of stamina during the week she and Hal had spent at The Keep after the wedding. The trouble was that Maria assumed that Caroline was there to wait on her and her children. Now that the honeymoon – as it were – was over and she was a well-established member of the family, she made it clear that she expected Caroline to be at her beck and call. She did it very nicely, very polite and charming, but there was an air of expectancy that was often extraordinarily irksome.

Caroline thought: After all, I am a servant, if it comes to that. Why should I resent it?

She made the coffee and sat down at the table, ignoring washing-up and ironing alike, frowning thoughtfully. None of the children behaved like that. When they were at home they pulled their weight. Mole was willing but had to be supervised, Susanna was a reliable, cheerful worker but one who preferred company, Kit was liable to be easily distracted – by a novel idea or the dog doing something amusing – and forget what it was she was supposed to be achieving, Hal liked to be in charge, disliking menial tasks and being rather too ready to delegate, but was first-rate in a crisis, and as for Fliss . . . well, Fliss was the best if you needed simple efficiency. She just got on with it, requiring neither direction nor praise nor company; having Fliss about seemed natural, somehow. Of course this was her home, she knew where everything belonged, the small routines, the way the place was run. She had been a tower of strength during the weeks preceding the wedding and a tremendous help at clearing up afterwards. As for those twinnies . . .

Caroline laughed aloud at the memory of Bess and Jamie perched on cushions placed on kitchen chairs, wrapped in enormous aprons, sorting out the silver: spoons in one lined drawer, forks in another and so on. How careful they had been, how proud of the responsibility entrusted to them. Coming into the kitchen to fetch some milk for Jolyon,

Maria had looked faintly put out to see them so employed. Fliss had smiled at her but Maria had barely responded, pouring the milk into Jolyon's drinking cup and hurrying away again with a waiting pile of newly washed and aired, fluffy white napkins. The little Baby Belling boiler had been in continuous use since her arrival and Maria had been outspoken in her amazement and disdain that there should be no washing machine at The Keep.

There'd been a little silence once she'd gone.

'Jolyon's too young to help,' Jamie said to his sister.

'He can't do knives,' agreed Bess. 'He'd cut his little self.'

Her tone unconsciously reflected Maria's; she was always on guard lest the twinnies should perpetuate some horror against the twenty-month-old Jolyon, always explaining why he could not join in their games or be held or taken for a walk in the courtyard.

'He's just a baby,' agreed Jamie, with all the complacency of someone who was three and three-quarters.

It had seemed odd when Fliss and the twinnies had gone back to Northwood. During the long hot summer, Miles had sent them down to The Keep, to the country. Fliss told Caroline that she'd been only too ready to be packed off. The married quarter in Capella Road, just outside the base, had been stifling, the tiny garden baking in the relentless glare of the sun. The cool spaciousness of The Keep and the shady garden and orchard had been a welcome relief. It was lovely to have the twinnies about, and Caroline and Fliss had spent many happy hours together while the children played near at hand; almost like old times.

For some reason, however, it had not been at all the same with Hal's family for the week after the wedding. Maria rarely came near the kitchen, although she was always ready to give time to Mrs Chadwick or Theo. It was rather as if she used the place as a hotel, leaving Edward's nappies to be boiled up, requesting picnics when she and Hal and the children went off to the beach, arriving back in time for tea in the hall.

Caroline thought: Perhaps it was because Hal was with her. She might have been different if she'd been on her own. And after all, this is Fliss's home. She's bound to behave differently.

As she finished her coffee it occurred to her that, when Mrs Chadwick died, it would almost certainly be Hal and Maria who would be living here at The Keep, not Fliss and Miles. Caroline frowned at this unwelcome thought. Hal, yes; she could imagine Hal here and, no doubt, his children, too, but the idea of Maria as mistress of The Keep was a distressing one.

Feeling suddenly depressed Caroline stood her empty mug with the rest of the dirty dishes, rolled up her sleeves and prepared to do the washing-up.

Chapter Fifteen

The detached house, with its large private garden, was not very far from the cottage which Hal and Maria had rented four years ago in Boarhunt but it was worlds away from the cottage's tiny old-fashioned simplicity. Streamlined, modern, smart, this well-appointed house had been built in the highly desirable Meon Valley, close enough to Winchester for Maria to do her shopping in that charming town, driving herself in the large Citroën GS X whilst Hal used his Sprite to get himself to and from the dockyard.

With Hal's rise in salary since his promotion, added to the allowance from his family and the generous assistance which her parents bestowed upon their adored daughter, Maria could now afford to have someone to help with the housework and the children. Hal protested that they could manage the garden between them but, each time the ship sailed, Maria called in an elderly odd-jobman from Southwick to help her with any heavy work. The other naval wives, managing simply on their husband's salaries, envied her the large house and her 'help'. Maria gloried in her superiority; these were the things that gave her confidence amongst her peers. She liked to talk about Hal's 'place' down in Devon which he would inherit shortly and to which she and the children would move, no longer having to follow from port to port or live in married quarters. Some of their friends were already scraping money together to buy their own homes and Hal had suggested that he and Maria should do the same. She'd been taken quite by surprise.

'But why on earth should we?' she'd asked.

He'd shrugged, clearly thrown a little by her reaction. 'I know how you hate quarters,' he'd answered. 'I thought you might prefer a place of your own. Of course it'll always be in the wrong place. If we buy here I'll be posted to Devonport and vice versa. Or I'll be given a desk job at MOD. But at least you could settle down, sort out schools and so on. I'd get home as much as I could, of course, and we might be lucky and get a home posting.'

'But we shall have The Keep,' she'd replied, frowning. 'It's a waste of money, surely, to buy a house of our own.'

Hal had been silent for a moment. 'Well,' he'd said at last, 'it was just a thought.'

This evening the rain clouds were dark, purplish-grey, swollen and heavy. The highly polished laurel leaves clattered in a sudden gust of wind as Maria snatched the last of the washing from the line, thrusting it down into the basket, making a dash for the kitchen before the rain came. She dropped it on the floor and darted out again to fetch Jolyon's wooden push-along tricycle. He watched her from his high chair at the big pine table.

'Wet,' he said cheerfully. 'Bike's all wet.'

Maria wiped it over with a towel and smiled at him. 'Not any more,' she said. 'Have you finished your soldiers?'

Jolyon carefully picked up a Marmite-spread strip from

the plate on his tray and showed it to her. 'Sholder,' he said carefully.

Maria sat opposite him, recognising Hal in the small face with its mop of blond hair. 'S-s-s-ssoldier.' He had difficulty with his speech and it worried her. 'Say it, darling. S-s-s-ssoldier.'

'S-s-s,' hissed Jolyon happily, 'sholder.'

Maria got up, hiding an impatient sigh. Small children could be extraordinarily tiresome and she'd had a long day. She needed Hal to come home, to pour her a drink, massage her neck, listen to her list of grievances. He would cheer her up, make her laugh, give her the courage to go forward.

'For heaven's sake,' another naval wife – one whom she had counted her friend – had said. 'Whatever have *you* got to grumble about? You don't know you're born, stuck up here with all the commanders and captains and someone to do all your work. As for Hal being at sea, of *course*, he's at sea. He's a bloody *sailor*, for God's sake.'

Maria hadn't spoken to her since. She'd felt the usual mixture of hurt and inadequacy. No one appreciated how much more difficult it was for her than it was for the other wives. They'd been brought up in the bustle of siblings and busy family life, living away from home later on whilst they trained as nurses or teachers. Naturally, they were more able to deal with the loneliness and difficulties, to manage without a husband around. She, on the other hand, had been cosseted and protected; nothing had been required of her except that she should look pretty and be a delightful daughter until she married.

'You were spoiled rotten,' Hal had once said out-spokenly – and, though he'd laughed as he'd said it, she'd never forgiven him for it. Surely it was what he'd first loved in her – her feminine ways and clinging adoration. It was unfair to expect her suddenly to become efficient, strong, independent.

She looked at herself in the mirror which hung over the double drainer stainless-steel sink. In a little bag on the windowsill she kept a comb, powder compact and lipstick so that, should anyone ring unexpectedly at the doorbell, she could check that she was looking her best. Now, she performed the familiar little rite – touching her nose with the powder puff, stretching lips as she outlined them, pulling the comb through the long dark hair – wishing she still had time to bathe and change as she had in the old days, before the children came along.

Jolyon watched her, interested. Once he'd tried the same operation on himself, dragging the chair across to the sink, climbing up and trying to peer in the mirror in order to investigate the results. He'd toppled over, all amongst the washing-up, and smashed a glass. Mummy had just started cleaning him up when Daddy arrived home. She'd been cross, lips all tight, eyes small, and he'd been frightened until Daddy had come in, taken one look and laughed his big growly, roaring laugh which came from right deep inside him, taking him from Mummy's quick, hard hands and swinging him up high, telling him how pretty he looked.

Remembering, Jolyon began to laugh too and Maria peered at him through the mirror.

'Daddy's home,' he said, in explanation, hopefully.

'Not yet,' said Maria, glancing at the mahogany-framed clock on the kitchen wall. She went through to the big playroom where Edward had fallen asleep on the big sofa. The wretched child *would* do this, refusing to sleep until late in the afternoon and then being wide awake all evening when she wanted to be alone with Hal.

'Stop fussing,' he'd say easily, taking Edward in his arms, pressing his cheek against the downy head. 'I hardly see him. I'll have him on my lap while we eat. He's no trouble.'

The irritating thing was that this was quite true. Edward *was* no trouble with Hal; he lay quietly crooning to himself whilst Hal forked up his food, smiling at his father, happily content, which made it difficult to explain just how exhausting a day she'd had and how trying the children could be. She moved Edward slightly, hoping that he'd wake, taking his thumb from his mouth, readjusting his coverlet, but he continued to sleep and she went back to the kitchen to check the dinner. As she stirred the cassoulet in its brown earthenware pot, turning the beans so that they should all be crustily browned, Maria rehearsed today's tiny grievances: Jolyon had dropped his Peter Rabbit mug, which was now in two halves; the iron had sizzled violently, frighteningly, before dying; the dog had been sick . . .

The dog was a serious grievance. It was Maria who had demanded that they should have a dog, simply so as to complete her mental picture of them as a family: the slim, pretty, charming mother, the tall, handsome, naval officer father and the two adorable blond babies. Only a dog was needed, sitting in the back of the estate car, behind the two boys in their car seats, walking beside the pushchair. Hal had been cautious, pointing out that she appeared to have quite enough on her hands as it was, underlining the problems a dog could cause. Maria had stood firm. A puppy would be such fun and, when it grew up, it would be company and protection for her when Hal was at sea. She'd never been allowed a dog and she was quite sure that it was good for children to have animals about them.

Finally, Hal had given in. He'd checked with another naval family who had a golden retriever and then took Maria to meet the breeder. It was Hal who'd made the good impression, chatting knowledgeably with the breeder, utterly at ease with the big dogs, discussing diet and exercise. Maria, playing charmingly with the puppies, had protested at the suggestion that her boys might tease their own puppy, solemnly declared her passion for animals, and had eventually chosen a jolly fellow, to be collected in three weeks' time when he would be old enough to leave his mother.

That was three months ago and Maria was at her wits' end. To begin with, Rex chewed anything that was left in range, did antisocial things on the kitchen floor and dug holes in the lawn. Now, thanks to Hal's training during a fortnight's leave, Rex was settling down but there were still accidents and naughtiness with which to contend, and she could see that exercising him was going to be an utter bore. It had been such bliss to leave him with a friend when they went down to The Keep for the wedding. Maria's heart bumped nervously. She had decided that this was the evening to talk to Hal seriously so perhaps it would be unwise to begin with a recital of the hardships of her day. They'd been back for a fortnight and no moment had presented itself: it simply must be this evening. As she hung up the tea towel, he came into the kitchen.

'There's a real old storm brewing,' he said, brushing

drops of rain from his jersey. 'Hello, darling. Something smells good.'

She returned his hug, wishing that the Navy had not introduced the jersey in place of the jacket. Even with his gold epaulettes on each shoulder there was a casual look about him of which she disapproved. This was not the moment to say so, however.

'It's me or the cassoulet,' she said teasingly. 'Take your pick. Knowing you, it's the cassoulet that's caught your attention.'

'You always smell delicious,' he said – and bent to kiss his son.

Jolyon raised his arms and Hal swung him up and out of his chair whilst Maria hastened to fetch a cloth to wipe Jolyon's sticky hands and mouth.

'Where's Edward?' Hal sat down at the table with Jolyon on his lap. 'And Rex?'

'Rex is in the garage,' Jolyon told him, his face serious. 'He eatened something bad and he was sick.'

'Ah.' Hal looked apprehensively at his wife. This was usually a cue for an outpouring of woes. This evening, however, she merely shrugged and even smiled a little.

'The wretched animal's such a pig,' she said with an unusual indifference. 'Goodness knows what he's picked up this time. We went for a walk in Hundred Acre so it might have been anything. I thought it best to confine him for a bit. It's not so bad if he throws up on the concrete floor out there.'

Hal glanced about him. There was a large circular damp patch on the corded carpet which bore witness to Rex's earlier excesses.

'I eatened up all my sholders,' said Jolyon – 'Ate,' corrected Maria automatically. 'Sssoldiers.' – anxious that his father should receive some good news. 'And we watched *The Clangers.'*

'Blue string soup,' said Hal at once. 'How would you like blue string soup for tea?'

Jolyon made suitable noises of disgust but Hal laughed at him, jogging him up and down on his knee. They began to sing together.

'To market, to market, to buy a fat pig,
Home again, home again, jiggety-jig.'

'You sound happy.' Maria had poured him a gin and tonic, which she stood on the table, close enough for him to reach but beyond the range of Jolyon's flailing arms. 'Good day?'

'Oh, the usual kind of day.' Hal rarely discussed his job with Maria. He knew now that she was only interested in his relationship with his senior officers and his chances of promotion. Her own friendships were confined to one or two of the wives who, like her, were preoccupied with their families and kept their social lives at the coffee morning level. He was sorry that she took none of the opportunities to develop other acquaintances but she seemed more content since the children had come along and she loved this big house, although he was faintly embarrassed by such opulence. His oppos were still at the cottage stage, babies crammed into tiny bedrooms the size of large cupboards, bigger children stacked on bunk beds. Of course, these were the families who were buying their own places . . .

Hal removed his wristwatch and passed it to his son –
a ritual which delighted Jolyon who immediately held it
to his ear – and reached for his gin. It still puzzled him
that Maria had so flatly refused to consider buying. Was it
because she knew they couldn't afford such a place as
this?

'It's a nice kitchen.' He spoke aloud, looking round the
big bright room which contained every modern conven-
ience known to man. He'd been about to add that it could
be made much more cosy, much less clinical, but Maria,
who had been weighing the rice to be cooked presently,
turned quickly.

'Isn't it?' she said eagerly. 'I really love it. I've been
thinking, Hal. We could do something like this at The
Keep.'

'At The Keep?' He repeated the words, puzzled. 'How
d'you mean?'

'Well, take out that filthy old Aga for a start. All that ash
and coal dust is lethal in a kitchen. Strip out the sink and
build in a whole new double drainer and lovely pine units.
Paint the dresser or, better still, have one built in with the
units. Clear out the tatty old rugs and lay a proper carpet.
You can buy ones like this, industrial stuff that's really
hardwearing, and you can scrub if you need to. You'd be
surprised how big and light that room could look if it was
modernised. Of course, that goes for the rest of the house.
Still, we'll get it right in time.'

'Hang on a sec.' Hal was trying to laugh but he felt
strangely anxious. 'Aren't we looking a bit far ahead? It
might be years before we move to The Keep and even
then—'

'But that's what I wanted to talk to you about.' She perched opposite him, her own drink clutched in her fingers. 'Don't you think it's a bit selfish for your grandmother to go on living in that big place? Just her and Theo? It's a family house. Don't you think that it's time that she abdicated,' she laughed a little at the word, 'in favour of you? We've got a growing family and we need the space—'

'Wait,' Hal interrupted. 'Hold it. I think you've got the wrong idea somewhere along the line. The Keep is my grandmother's home. We're not talking about some entailed property or primogeniture inheritance here. She might have decided to leave it to us but it's still her home. Hers and Uncle Theo's. You wouldn't expect *your* parents to move out of their nice big house just for us, would you?'

'It's not the same at all,' cried Maria impatiently, too intent on putting her point to listen to reason. 'My parents are barely in their fifties. It's crazy that two such aged old dears should take up so much space.'

'Are you suggesting that we should move in with them?'

'Of course not.' Maria had earmarked Freddy's spacious south-facing central rooms for her own use, whilst Theo's wing would be perfect for the children whilst they were small. She had no intention of putting them up on the second floor where there was no heating and the plumbing was antique. 'But don't you honestly think that they'd be happier in something smaller and more convenient? A nice modern bungalow, for instance?'

Hal tried to imagine his grandmother in a nice modern bungalow and failed utterly.

'Grandmother belongs at The Keep,' he said positively. 'It's her place. She'd hate anything else. I'm sorry, Maria, but this is quite ridiculous. You must have realised that I would never attempt to turn Grandmother and Uncle Theo out of The Keep just so that we could live there. Even if I had the power I wouldn't do it. It's their home, dammit. And even when we do move in one day, it won't be solely ours. It belongs to all of us. That's the agreement. You see how everyone comes and goes. That's how it's always been and how it must stay. The family must be able to come whenever they want, just as they do now.'

Maria was silent but, watching her sullen face, Hal suddenly knew exactly what was in her mind.

He thought: But they won't want to come when Maria is mistress of The Keep. Everything will be changed and they will no longer feel welcome and she will encourage the feeling so that finally it will be just ours.

For a brief moment he had an inward vision of Fliss and her children as he remembered them from a brief spell during the hot summer when the ship had been in at Devonport for some urgent repair. His captain had given him a few days' leave – provided he stayed locally – and he'd spent them at The Keep. Now, suddenly, he had a mental picture of the twinnies sitting together on one of the sofas in the hall after tea, leaning drowsily together whilst Fliss read quietly to them; he saw them squashed together on the swing, shouting with excitement as she pushed them higher and higher; playing ball in the courtyard; out on the hill with old Perks and Caroline. They'd worn canvas sandals and floppy sunhats, their smooth limbs tanned a honey brown, and he'd given them piggybacks up the hill when their legs got tired. He and Fliss had taken them to Totnes, with only just enough room on the narrow pavement for the double pushchair which they'd pushed together up Fore Street. He'd bought them ice creams at The Brioche whilst he and Fliss drank iced orange juice. Soon, no doubt, Susanna's children would become part of The Keep's landscape, and perhaps Mole's and Kit's. It was not to be jealously guarded simply for his own sons . . .

Maria was watching him across the table. 'What are you thinking about?' she asked sharply.

'Nothing.' He moved Jolyon, easing his languid weight into the crook of his arm. 'I know you think it's a silly arrangement, Maria, but that's the way it is.'

'It's quite ludicrous,' she said angrily. 'Why should we be obliged to run a kind of hotel for the rest of your family? It's stupid and it isn't fair.'

Hal swallowed back his irritation with difficulty. 'It's unusual, I grant you,' he said, 'and it might not work once the old people have gone. It's an ideal, if you like. An ideal that we could all pull together, share the place and stay close as a family.'

'It sounds like something out of Walt Disney,' answered Maria scornfully. 'And *we* foot the bill, no doubt, for this – this commune?'

'I don't know,' he said wearily. 'That remains to be seen. The trust pays for the upkeep. At the moment it's academic. I hope that Grandmother lives for another ten years, which is why I suggest that we get on with our lives and buy our own place.'

They stared antagonistically at each other across the table but, before she could reply, Edward woke and began to cry and Maria slammed back her chair and strode towards the playroom. Jolyon, who had been half asleep, jumped violently and Hal held him close, murmuring soothingly, but his heart was heavy in his breast as he surveyed the wreck of the approaching evening and the recriminations and arguments which would follow.

Chapter Sixteen

Fliss let herself into the house in Above Town and stood for a moment just inside the door. There was a chill, empty feel about the place and she shivered a little, glad of the guernsey she'd snatched up at the last moment and now wore over her shirt. The tenants had left suddenly, pleading an unexpected posting, and she'd driven down from Northwood to check the place out, hoping that no damage had been done. The house had been let ever since she and Miles had gone to Hong Kong and so far they'd been lucky with their tenants. It was long since she'd tried to persuade him to sell it and she had decided to let the matter drop. She suspected that Miles was hoping to hold on to the house until the twinnies went away to school, when it would be quite reasonable for him and Fliss to move back to it. Meanwhile it could be rented to selected candidates whilst they continued to live in larger quarters.

At least the twinnies weren't ruining his precious furniture. Fliss shook her head at this cynical thought as she went into the kitchen and dropped her bag on the breakfast bar. Did he seriously imagine this small house would contain Bess and Jamie as they grew bigger, along with all the paraphernalia of going off to school or having friends to stay?

She looked critically about the kitchen and sighed with relief to see the sink gleaming, the floor clean, no greasy corners. The kitchen and bathroom were always the vulnerable spots but it looked as if their luck was holding. Now there would be all the trouble of finding new tenants, responsible people with no children and too old to want to give rowdy parties, but Miles always attended to that side of things. She'd quickly learned that it was best to pass the reins back to him on his return from sea, to keep explicit records and explain her reasons for any change in the normal running of the household. He checked everything, queried each decision, allowed her little room for manoeuvre. Some wives resented this behaviour. If they were to be left in charge then they reserved the right to do what they felt was best at the time without criticism. It was an area of naval life which was fraught with difficulties but Fliss had learned to keep her head down, to do that which was essential and nothing more. Only where the children were concerned did she insist on complete autonomy. Miles granted her that readily. He had no particular desire to be embroiled in their lives.

Fliss climbed the stairs to the drawing room. She'd left the twinnies at The Keep in Caroline's care and was hoping to be home in time for lunch. Susanna and Gus were coming over and it would be such fun to see them again. She opened the door and looked in at the long room. Impersonal without their small, portable belongings, the drawing room was as spotless as the kitchen. Having heard many horror stories from other naval families who had let their homes, Fliss heaved another relieved sigh. Miles certainly knew how to pick his tenants. They'd been friends of friends so far, naval people with good references and a sense of responsibility. He would be pleased to hear that all was well. She continued her tour of the house, finishing in the living room opposite the kitchen. Only here was she assailed by memories: of long chats with Mole and tea parties with Susanna; of late-night sessions with Kit and conversations with Maria when she'd come to stay all those years ago. In this room, Fliss had put her Chinese lamps and her big ginger jar. Somehow they didn't quite fit in with the décor upstairs, although the smaller jars were quite at home in the kitchen. The little amah, Remy, had given her the large pot as a farewell present but she'd bought the smaller set and the lamps in China Products, the department store in Central. The jar Remy had given her was much older, not tourist stuff but probably bought in the crowded, jam-packed markets of Wan Chai; or maybe it had belonged to her family. Fliss picked it up, trying to remember the story the figures described, remembering her sadness at the final farewells with Remy at Kai Tak airport. The twinnies – it was Remy who had so christened them – had been inconsolable . . .

The jar was broken. It had been professionally repaired but her fingers could trace the cracks that ran jaggedly through the frieze of characters and she could see the crazing of the pink and blue glazing. As she held it in her hands, other images formed in her mind: the green and white Star ferries scuttling like water beetles between Kowloon and the Island; the shock of the noisy streets, always full of bustling, pushing crowds, and the dazzlingly bright confusion of the neon lights and the advertising banners which hung down so that it was impossible to see more than a few feet ahead; the branches of delicate pink almond blossom that decorated the vestibules of banks and hotels during the Chinese New Year. She remembered standing at her window high on The Peak watching the harbour below crowded with junks and sampans and ferries, hardly daring to look as she saw HMS *Yarnton*, returning from her weekly patrol, weaving her way through the busy waters. Surely Miles must mow down those frail craft that sailed practically beneath his bows? Some days the thick swirling mists would obscure this view from her eyrie until suddenly, inexplicably, a gap, round as a porthole, would be torn in the dense curtain and she would see the tall skyscrapers of Central, rearing up below her. Miles had been determined to make the most of his posting. She could recall the delight with which he'd bargained with an old woman for a trip on her sampan round Aberdeen Harbour where the Chinese lived on these strange crafts with all their belongings piled on board, even their chickens, swinging in cages up in the sterns of the sampans. They'd driven through New Territories and seen the duck farms, which she'd mistaken at first for paddy fields, and once they'd visited the Po Lin Monastery, richly ornamented in golds and reds, set amongst the peaks of Lantau Island.

Still holding the jar Fliss thought of Remy, the little Filipino amah who had been so good with her 'twinnies', sleeping in the cold but spotless little bedroom off the kitchen. She'd been quite content to leave them with Remy whilst she went shopping at the Welcome supermarket or caught the Peak Tram to the base to wander round China

Products, buying souvenirs, such as the two lamps and the ginger jar. When the twinnies were older she and Remy had taken them by ferry to the beach at Cheung Chau. So many memories: old men hurrying through the crowded streets carrying birds in cages; red kites soaring and circling below her as she stood watching from the sitting-room window; the pattering of Mah Jong tiles and the fragrant smell of root ginger and garlic being stir-fried; the feeling of absolute safety and the bright red taxis . . .

Gently Fliss replaced the ginger jar on top of the bookcase. The more valuable items had been taken with them or stored at The Keep but they'd decided to leave one or two things so as to give the house a homely feel. It was reasonable that, when speaking of value, Miles had been talking in financial terms. Remembering Remy's faithfulness, her love for 'my twinnies', the tears which had poured down her cheeks as she waved them off, Fliss let her own tears fall. How could she have been so careless as to risk her ginger jar to strangers? Blowing her nose, she gave one last glance round and let herself out into the rain.

By evening the rain had settled into a steady downpour. Prue stared out at it disconsolately. She was well aware that just lately she was doing an awful lot of staring out of windows; moving from one room to another; upstairs then downstairs; tidying unnecessarily, straightening ornaments, plumping up cushions. The blues, that was what Kit called this terrible depression that assailed her. Watching the rain bouncing on the pavement, running down the gutter, dripping from the railings, Prue fought the now familiar desire for oblivion. The well-known negative sensations were weighing down her heart, numbing her brain; her existence seemed utterly pointless, her past a wasteland, her future bleak. She struggled with this nihilistic demon, reciting to herself the blessings she enjoyed, but she knew that eventually the demon would drag her into submission unless she took drastic steps. At this time of the day her usual means of defence was the telephone but already this week she'd exhausted the list of friends who might reasonably be expected to enjoy a bit of a chat. One or two of these were suffering in the same way – 'The change, dear,' one of them had said. 'Who'd be a woman?' – and they generally managed to cheer each other up and make a bit of a joke of it.

Tonight, however, the hours stretched endlessly till bedtime. It was easier during the day. Determined not to give in to self-pity she'd flung herself into a certain amount of good works, visiting the housebound, doing their shopping and collecting library books. The toughness of mind of some of these indomitable and courageous elderly people strengthened her own resolve and she enjoyed her time with them, spending much longer than was necessary with them, cooking them little treats, always willing to listen to their stories regarding their children and the children's offspring. Prue would proudly show photographs of Kit, or Hal and Maria with the children, basking in the ready praise and interest. What with this and her small circle of friends, most days were bearable. Evenings, however, were something else again – and especially wet evenings such as this. Her heart weighed even heavier at the thought of the approaching winter. She tried to jolly herself with the thought of the plan she'd made with Kit, to stay with her in London and do a few shows and some shopping. She loved the Christmas lights and decorations, and Kit and Sin were so easy to be with and made her so welcome.

Prue thought: But why doesn't Kit marry? What is it that holds her back?

She'd broken the cardinal rule and spoken directly of it to Jake at Susanna's wedding.

'Why is it,' she'd asked, making a joke of it, 'that no one wants to marry my Kit? Don't you think she's rather nice?'

His reply had been equally direct. 'I think she's gorgeous,' he'd said, 'and I'd marry her like a shot but she won't have me. I've asked her a dozen times but she rejects me each time.'

'She must be mad,' Prue had answered feelingly, looking up at him appreciatively, tall and dark, handsome in his morning suit. 'Quite mad.'

He'd grinned, bowing his thanks to her, and she'd laughed too, wishing that Kit would settle for this delightful man.

'Why ever not?' she'd demanded of her daughter later. 'He is simply delicious. I wish *I* were twenty years younger.'

'I'm sure you do, honey,' said Kit patiently. 'And I don't know why, except that I've known him for so long. He *is* gorgeous, I admit, and I adore him but he's so ... oh, I don't know, familiar, I suppose. I long for romance and excitement.'

'Well, don't wait too long,' she'd answered tartly. 'You might just live to regret it.'

Later Prue had felt remorseful for her sharp words but Kit bore no malice and they'd planned the trip to London

171

quite happily together. After all, she could hardly blame Kit for this longing for romance and passion; she'd been exactly the same herself and it had been very evident in Hal's earlier feelings for Maria.

Prue frowned out at the rain, thinking about her son and his family. Maria had changed now that the children had finally come along; the clinging adoration was hardening into a kind of possessive selfishness. She still seemed quite unable to come to terms with the separations and other problems which beset the naval wife and she was determined that Hal should take an active part when he was at home. Well, there was nothing wrong with that. Hal clearly took pleasure in his small sons and was perfectly happy to assume the role of family man when he came home from sea. Maria was a good mother, if slightly overprotective, and the house was always spotless, the garden tidy and well-kept. There was, however, a kind of joylessness in her approach, a tendency to make the daily round a martyrdom. Prue was rarely invited these days, and then generally only as company when Hal was at sea, but her offer to look after the boys so that Maria and Hal could go away for a week of his leave had been gratefully received and Prue was looking forward to it. The responsibility was faintly awesome but she knew that Maria would leave lists of instructions, contact telephone numbers and plenty of prepared food in the brand-new freezer, and it would be such fun to have the darling children all to herself . . .

Prue thought: I have so much to look forward to. The trip to London and the week in Hampshire.

The depression was not so easily dismissed, however, and she turned back into the room and went to the drinks cupboard. A good stiff gin and tonic was a tried-and-trusted way of shifting the blues, and afterwards she would try to think up a special treat for supper. After that she might have to resort to the television; perhaps it was the night for *The Avengers*, which would be fun. Kit had recently gone to Molton Brown's for a 'Purdey' cut and, although her hair wasn't quite so thick and blonde as Joanna Lumley's, it suited her very well.

Prue thought: Oh, if only she would marry Jake. He is so absolutely right for her, I know he is. I shall work on it when I go to London.

She carried her glass through to the kitchen and took out her favourite cookery book. Food could be such a comfort.

Chapter Seventeen

'Do you think it's a sign of approaching age,' asked Kit idly, 'when neither of us leaps to answer the telephone any more? We sit here saying, you go, no, it's your turn, no it isn't, I got it last time and so on. Until the caller hangs up.'

'And the really terrible thing is,' agreed Sin, 'that we don't even care who it is. Remember those nail-chewing moments wondering if it was the gorgeous chap we'd met at some party and whether or not he'd bother to ring again?'

'Only to find, after nights of waiting in, that it was Ma phoning to ask if I'd forgotten Uncle Theo's birthday or something really riveting.' Kit sighed heavily. 'Was it *ever* the gorgeous chap we'd met at some party?'

'Perhaps,' said Sin glumly, 'the real sign of approaching age is that, even at thirty-two, I can't ever remember *meeting* a gorgeous chap at *any*one's bloody party. If you're getting up, put the Carly Simon on, would you? I want to hear "You're so Vain". It makes me think of Martin and then I feel superior.'

'I'm not getting up,' said Kit, who lay stretched out flat on the sofa. 'Do it yourself.'

'Yes you are,' insisted Sin. 'You're getting up to make the

lunch. I did breakfast. Jump to it, you idle wench.'

'Breakfast,' scoffed Kit. 'Is that what you call it? Two mugs of black coffee?'

'What I call it doesn't matter. It was a deal. Go on. I'm starving. And don't forget to put that record on.'

Grumbling, Kit hauled herself upright, pausing by the record player to extract the LP from its sleeve.

'I have to keep this hidden from Jake, I'll have you know,' she said, studying the picture of Carly Simon, who clearly wore no bra under her long-sleeved T-shirt. 'It's quite shocking. I found him leafing through the pile the other night, looking for it.'

'Poor old Jake,' yawned Sin. 'What d'you expect if you keep him on stoppage? And all for that weed Mark Thing.'

'Mark Thompsett has given me a terrific opportunity,' said Kit with dignity. 'I am now a freelance art dealer. I supply top hotels with paintings and *objets d'art*. No more boring old gallery for me. He's got masses of contacts.'

'So you keep telling me,' said Sin. 'But he's not a patch on Jake.'

'You could be right,' conceded Kit. 'He is a bit . . . well, a bit . . .'

'Conceited?' suggested Sin. 'Big-headed? Self-opinionated? A know-all and a bore to boot? All of the above but not necessarily in that order?'

'He doesn't wear well,' admitted Kit, 'but he's pretty stunning, you must agree. I was a bit knocked off my feet at first. I thought, Wow! This is it! But now I'm not so sure.'

'You're a fool, Kit Chadwick.' Sin pushed aside the mass of Sunday newspapers and twisted round to look at her. 'I wish Jake fancied *me*. I'd be up the aisle with him quicker than you could shake a hairy stick.'

'And what about all those high-minded declarations of undying love for Uncle Theo? *What*, if it comes to that,' Kit shook the record cover at her and then dropped it on the floor, 'what about Mole?'

'I'm in love with Mole,' said Sin flatly.

There was a deep silence. Rain beat against the windows and gurgled in the guttering. Out in the hall the telephone began to ring again. Kit and Sin stared at each other.

'Oh, honey,' said Kit at last. 'Oh, I did wonder and then I thought you couldn't possibly be. He's so much . . .'

'So much younger,' finished Sin. She drew her legs up beneath her and rested her head against the back of the chair. 'I know he is. That's why I can't do anything. It's best not to think about it. Only I can't help it. I just love him.'

Kit sat down on the arm of the chair opposite and looked at her compassionately. The telephone cut off sharply and there was another silence.

'I thought to begin with it was because he looks so much like Uncle Theo,' said Kit gently. 'I thought it was a bit of a . . . well, not quite a joke but . . . you know?'

'Yes, I know,' said Sin wearily. 'Perhaps it was, to begin with. But not any more. He's special, Mole is.'

'Oh hell,' said Kit. 'Oh *hell*. But he *is* too young. He's twenty-four in a few weeks' time and I shall be thirty-three so that means—'

'I've done the sums. I know I'm eight years older than he is. Eight years and five months, if it makes a difference.'

'It would be later when it would really matter,' said Kit after a moment. 'When you're forty-two and he's only thirty-five. It would be ghastly. You'd fear every younger woman and all those pretty girls. Oh, *why* is it that men of fifty are distinguished and women of fifty are old bags?'

'I'd risk it,' said Sin, 'if Mole really loved me and really wanted to, I couldn't resist him. But he doesn't. Oh, he's made chivalrous, well-bred noises but he's been relieved when I've shut him up. Don't look so shocked. What d'you expect from a young chap just starting out on life? At least, he was when we began all this. I think I'm just a habit now and he's too kind to give me the push.'

'This is awful,' said Kit. 'It must be perfectly wretched for you. I had no idea.'

'Why should you?' Sin shrugged. 'He's away at sea most of the time anyway. It's just I can't get him out of my system. Bit like poor old Jake and you. Perhaps Jake and I should get together. At least we could comfort each other.'

In one short moment Kit realised that she would hate Jake to be comforted by Sin. They'd joked about it many times but this time, after such a serious confession, Kit felt a strange anxiety. Was it possible that Jake and Sin might ultimately turn to each other?

'What about Martin?' she asked, attempting to hide her panic. 'I thought you had something going with him?'

'Oh, Martin's OK,' said Sin. 'He's a bit like Mark Thing. Rather too full of himself. It's being a barrister does it. Earning a fortune for wearing a wig and showing off in public. It gave him a bit of a shock when I told him that I was an archivist at the BM. Didn't know I had a brain under my Afro hairdo. Shut him up for a full two minutes and forty-four seconds. That's a record, that is. I rubbed it in by telling him about my first from London University. He's a Cambridge man, of course, but he was impressed.'

Kit began to laugh. It was ridiculous to imagine that dear old Jake would ever abandon her. Perhaps she might telephone him later and go over for supper; she'd neglected him a bit lately for Mark, but he always kept in touch. It might even be he that had telephoned . . .

The telephone began to ring again and she raced out into the hall. Sin raised her eyebrows at such a precipitate departure. One thing was sure: it wasn't Mole. *Warspite* was at sea and wouldn't be back for another eight weeks. He might send her a postcard but he'd never written her a letter. His instinct for self-preservation ran very deep, hand in hand with his fear of commitment. It would have to be a very special girl who could capture Mole.

Sin thought: How terrible that moment will be. I shall hate her. How kind he will be to me. Oh God, I can't bear it . . .

Kit was standing in the doorway looking disgruntled.

'So?' asked Sin. 'Who has been desirous to have speech with us? Do I gather from your expression that it wasn't that gorgeous chap we met at someone's party?'

'It was Ma,' answered Kit crossly, 'ringing for the third time to remind me that the Birthday is approaching and what am I going to buy Grandmother and please make an effort to go down for the weekend because Mole and Hal are at sea so it will only be me and Grandmother celebrating.'

'I shall come with you,' announced Sin, getting out of her chair. 'We shall go together to swell the ranks. How about it?'

'Why not?' agreed Kit thoughtfully. 'And I'll ask Jake to come.' She brightened visibly. 'That's a brilliant idea. We'll all go. I might just give him a buzz to make sure he's free.

Be a duck and start the lunch, would you? It seems like years since breakfast and I'm starving.'

Now, with the autumn drawing on, the studio courtyard was at its best first thing in the morning. Hart's-tongue fern grew at the base of the wall alongside the clump of montbretia with its sword-like leaves and yellow and orange flowers. These were nearly over now but the leaves of the Virginia creeper were turning crimson and scarlet and gold, and a tiny wren hopped amongst the bright berries of the cotoneaster. At the top of the steps which climbed up to the first floor a wooden tub full of winter-flowering pansies made a glorious splash of colour against the grey stone, and there were still red and purple bells on the sturdy standard fuchsia which stood in its pot by the studio door.

'It can be a bit dank in the winter when we lose the sun,' Gus had said, 'but it's amazing how quickly it picks up when the spring comes.'

Susanna liked to sit outside on the top stone step beside the pansies, cradling a mug of coffee in her hands, looking over the wall to the huddled roofs of the houses below the castle. Now, in early October, the morning sunshine was still warm, glinting off the slate rooftops, lingering on the colour-washed creams and pinks of cottage walls, touching the castle ramparts and turning them to rose.

Soon Gus would finish in the tiny bathroom, which was only big enough to contain a shower, a small basin and a lavatory, and she would join him for breakfast in the huge room which was sitting room, dining room and kitchen. This was a very jolly place; the kitchen, at one end, was hidden by tall rattan screens and the dining room part was made up of an oak gate-leg table set under the window which looked over the courtyard. The sitting room, at the other end, consisted of several big and ancient armchairs tactfully covered with tartan rugs and grouped round a pretty Victorian fireplace. The walls were lined with book-shelves which held not only a great number of books but also Gus's collection of records, sheet music and scores.

The other room, which was their bedroom, held the big, sagging bed, a walk-in cupboard containing their clothes, two small rickety bamboo tables, one each side of the bed, and a pine chest of drawers. On the uneven walls, which were painted cream, Gus had hung some Victorian cartoon prints to which Susanna had added some of her brightly coloured posters advertising various strange and long out-dated products.

Their wedding presents had done much to add character to the flat. Fliss and Miles had given them a big patchwork quilt, which lent the aged bed a touch of class, whilst Mole had found several big square Persian rugs to add warmth to the well-worn drugget which covered the top floor of the cottage. Susanna and Gus, used to draughty nursery quar-ters, large unheated houses and the privations of boarding school, felt themselves to be surrounded by luxury. Uncle Theo and Grandmother had given a joint present, a most sophisticated radio – they both still called it a wireless – which quite overwhelmed Gus with its range and quality of sound and which had pride of place in the sitting room on its own special little oak table, given by Caroline and Fox.

Hal, clubbing together with Kit, Sin and Jake, had given them a year's supply of wine, delivered monthly by the Wine Society, whilst Maria, disapproving of this reckless gesture, had presented them more formally with a Royal Doulton dinner service, white with gold-leaf edging. Gus's family had sensibly supplied bed linen and kitchen utensils, and Janie's present of six sturdy coffee mugs, hanging on hooks from a shelf in the kitchen, completed the picture of homely comfort.

Sitting on the step, Susanna stretched luxuriously. Presently the busy day would begin; there were the negs to be delivered to the printer and a new client was coming to see them to discuss ideas for his restaurant. She had some typesetting to do and after lunch some proofs had to be taken to a customer over at Broadhempston . . .

She loved the studio almost as much as she loved the upstairs flat. In the studio itself were two long trestle tables which held their drawing boards and at which they worked, opposite to one another. The light box stood in the corner, at one side of the door to the kitchen and store room, and the typesetter stood at the other. At the bottom of the stairs was the light trap at the entrance to the dark room, which contained the enlarger, process camera and processing trays. It was all very compact, with its flavour of bustle and efficiency, but there was a very friendly atmosphere, too. Gus's old transistor radio stood on the windowsill pouring out music and there was always a mug of coffee for any client who dropped in unexpectedly.

Friends had warned that working together might put a strain on their marriage but Susanna could not imagine this to be a problem. On the contrary, being together in the studio, discussing prospective work, alternatively cursing and joking about difficult clients, snatching a hurried sandwich at lunchtime, seemed to be strengthening the bond between them. Everything was shared. Of course, it might be different when the babies came along. It would be impossible to have small children in this working environment – although she could come back to it once they started school – and there was little room for them in the flat, but at the moment the question didn't arise. The business was doing well but not well enough yet to move to a bigger place so as to start a family; that must wait for a year or two. It was something to look forward to, to plan for, and meanwhile she and Gus were terribly happy.

Strains of 'O ruddier than the cherry' grew louder as Gus emerged from the bathroom, towelling his hair vigorously, and passed into the bedroom. Presently the bedroom door slammed and he came into the living room behind her and, standing up, she went in to him.

Chapter Eighteen

The seas, lashed by the south-westerly gale, piled into the shore in mountainous heaps, thundering over the smooth sand, crashing against the craggy rocks, creaming in across the beach. Salty foaming spray, glittering diamond-like in the bright sunlight, was flung far up the cliffs almost obliterating Burgh Island, which looked perilously isolated, cut off from the mainland, as the waters raged about it.

' "*They that go down to the sea in ships: and occupy their business in great waters; These men see the works of the Lord: and his wonders in the deep.*" That's the Bible, isn't it, sir?'

Theo stirred in his seat. The car was parked in the deserted car park above the beach at Bigbury and both men had been silent for some time, awed by the magnificent spectacle being enacted before them.

'It's a psalm,' he answered. 'Often used in services at sea. Wonderful imagery. You like the psalms?'

'I don't be a great one for reading,' admitted Fox cautiously. 'I be too slow, if you take my meaning, but I like the . . . the imagery, if that's what you call it. Makes me feel things inside and then I think that there's much

185

more to it all if only I could go beyond.'

'Beyond what?' asked Theo, when it seemed that Fox had finished speaking.

'Beyond me,' answered Fox promptly. 'If I could just let go of something, all the things that tie me down, then I could enter in.'

'In?'

'Into what's beyond,' explained Fox patiently. 'That's what it's all about, isn't it, sir?'

'Yes,' said Theo at last. 'Yes it is. It's forgetting ourselves and opening up to God. Waiting in silence upon him.'

His natural diffidence and conviction of his inadequacies made him dread any conversation regarding religious beliefs, especially with the members of his own family. It had been so much simpler within the framework of the Navy; facing a chapel full of sailors held no fears for him. They accepted him for what he was and expected certain patterns of behaviour. He'd been very happy as a naval padre but he suspected, looking back, that he should have chosen the contemplative life . . .

'It was the collects that Ellen loved,' Fox was saying. 'Knew 'em by heart, she did. She had her favourites. One about casting away the works of darkness and putting on the armour of light. And another one about evil thoughts assaulting the soul.' He sighed and shook his head. 'How I do miss her,' he murmured. 'She's read 'em to me of an evening and I went off to bed the better for it.'

' "*Almighty God, Who seest that we have no power of ourselves to help ourselves; Keep us both outwardly in our bodies, and inwardly in our souls; that we may be defended from all adversities which may happen to the body, and from all evil thoughts which may assault and hurt the soul; through Jesus Christ our Lord. Amen.*" Is that the one?'

'It is indeed.' Fox looked pleased. 'Fancy you knowing it off pat like that. I've got her Prayer Book, you know. Caroline gave it to me, said that Ellen would like me to have it and I felt that she was right. Keeping me on the straight and narrow, she'd've said, but I can't never find what I'm looking for.'

'I could mark them for you,' offered Theo tentatively. 'That collect is for the second Sunday in Lent and the first one you spoke of is the collect for Advent.'

'What a memory you've got,' said Fox admiringly. 'Now if only I had something useful in my head . . .'

'Nonsense, my dear fellow,' said Theo impatiently. 'It is my *work*. I know nothing of runner beans or marrows or when to plant seed potatoes' – ('Best to get 'em in before Good Friday' murmured Fox, deprecatingly) – 'but it's a poor priest who doesn't know his Bible or the Prayer Book. I suspect that you've been far more useful during your life than I have.'

There was a silence. Fox was rather shocked at such a suggestion but could think of no suitable rejoinder and Theo was lost once again in the contemplation of the seascape before him. Seagulls rode the billowing waves and wheeled, screaming, in the turbulent air, their wings a dazzling white against the azure sky. Cliffs stretched away on either side, the trees, continually tormented and shaped by the prevailing winds, bending low beneath the force of the gale.

'I think that it would be unwise to venture out for the hamper,' said Theo thoughtfully. 'Perhaps we should drive on to a quieter, more sheltered spot.'

Fox beamed at him. 'Don't want to go calling out the coastguard,' he agreed. 'Be blown straight over the edge, I reckon.'

'On we go then,' said Theo cheerfully, switching on the engine and grinding the gears about. 'And don't forget what I said about Ellen's Prayer Book. Let me have it and I'll put some markers in it. There are one or two passages I think you might enjoy.'

'I'll do that, sir,' promised Fox, sending up a prayer of grateful thanks that Theo had chosen the correct gear and was backing away from the edge of the cliff. He'd had a vision of them both sailing straight out into the teeth of the storm. He bit back a chuckle that was part hysteria; put your life in his hands sometimes and that was a fact . . .

Fox thought: But there's no one's hands I'd rather be in than Mr Theo's. Hope he sees me out . . .

The car jolted out of the car park and down into the deep narrow lane where the wind swirled through gateways, roaring tumultuously above the hedgerows where the briony berries burned like ruby fire amongst the dry brown leaves and faded grasses.

In the drawing room, Freddy was playing Schumann's *Davidsbündlertänze*, shutting out the sounds of the wind keening round the house, rattling at the windows, howling in the chimney. Once she had loved the noise that the elements made: rain beating on the roof, thunder rolling in the distance, the south-westerly gales roaring in the trees. It pleased her that these forces of nature defeated man's puny attempts to restrain them; she delighted in their mighty power and lofty indifference. Lately she was less hardy; she was increasingly aware of her mortality and of her own impotence in the face of old age.

It was Ellen who had really shown up this weakness. Her passing had been the first breach in the bulwarks and now they all faced the implacable advance of the rising tide. Theo, as usual, laughed at her fears but then he had his faith to sustain him whilst she fought against his comfort, refusing to accept his beliefs. Sometimes she wondered if it were sheer childish petulance on her part; a kind of foolish pride; a refusal to acknowledge a God who would allow such terrible cruelties as the loss of loved ones. Theo might talk about freedom of choice, about love, but was it possible to love that much?

'You must find God first,' he'd replied. 'The love follows afterwards. But you must really want Him, more than anything else in the world.'

He'd told her the story of the novice who felt that he was well on the path to sainthood. His teacher had taken him down to the lake and held his head under the water until he'd nearly drowned. When he finally released him he told him, 'My son, when you want God as much as a moment ago you wanted air, then you will be ready to begin your journey.'

Freddy shook her head. How could you want something you didn't understand? Yet it was Theo himself who made it impossible quite to reject it all. There was something about him, some serenity, a detachment; yet he had a compassion which encompassed anyone who crossed his path. Sometimes this had roused all her worst instincts. Why should he waste his time and money and care upon strangers? She'd raged pointlessly whilst he smiled, turning away her wrath, gently showing her the baseness of her jealousy, whilst holding her firmly in his love. How empty her life would have been without him ... and now he risked himself, driving Fox about the countryside, tootling about like a couple of adolescents ...

Freddy took her hands from the keys and glanced at her wristwatch. Today they had taken a picnic lunch but Theo had promised to be home in time for tea.

'Do you think it's wise?' she'd pleaded with him. 'The weather forecast is terrible. A tree might come down on top of you, anything might happen in this wind. Gales are forecast.'

His eyes had smiled at her fear, making light of her terrors.

'Are you certain the word hurricane wasn't mentioned?' he'd asked. 'Or even a tornado?'

She'd glared at him, hating him because she needed him so much, because he risked himself.

'Must you go?' She'd sunk her pride. 'Can't it wait for another day?'

'Are you sure there will be another day?' His words had struck terror into her heart and, seeing this, he'd tried to soften the blow. 'Do you know that the dear fellow has never been to Bigbury? Yet the children have gone there so often that he longs to see it. I think we must seize this opportunity. The sun is still warm and the sea should be magnificent today.'

'Wait until the spring,' she'd pleaded – and he'd looked at her strangely, as if he wasn't seeing her.

'Fox might not be able to wait that long,' he'd said gently. Her hand had fallen from his arm and he'd bent to kiss her, promising to be back for tea – and now it was nearly half-past three. She turned round on the stool, her heart weighty with a formless dread, her hands icy cold.

There was a light tap at the door and Caroline's rumpled grey head appeared. Freddy stared at her. Had Caroline received some message? Surely she would have heard the telephone?

'Sorry to interrupt. It's such a horrid day that I decided to light the hall fire. It's rather a solemn thought, isn't it? First fire of the winter and all that, but I thought we needed it. It's turned cold and I thought it might cheer us all up.'

Freddy stood up and walked towards her, assisted by the chair backs. She felt weak and old. Caroline watched her, holding the door open so that she might pass through into the hall.

'Thank you,' she said, pausing beside her. 'It was exactly what was needed. I suppose I must wait a little longer for my tea. Theo said that they would be home by four o'clock.'

'They were rather late setting out,' Caroline explained, 'but I'm sure they'll be here at any moment. Come and get comfortable and then I'll go and put the kettle on.'

Freddy sat down at the end of the sofa nearest to the leaping flames, ignoring *The Times*, which lay folded as usual on the long low table. Theo read her snippets at breakfast but just lately she did not peruse the newspaper at teatime. The news was too depressing, filled with horrors. Why did she have to have two grandsons in the Navy when the world stood continually on the brink of nuclear war? How could Mole, with all his private terrors, go to sea in a submarine, moving stealthily in deep waters, hunted and hunter? Was it out of bravado that he pushed himself to the edge of such danger? If he were to be given command of a Polaris submarine, might he really be capable of pressing the button that would release warheads capable of laying waste to vast areas of the earth?

'It is a deterrent,' he'd told her. 'The whole point is that the results are so horrific that no one will ever use them. There will never be a nuclear war, Grandmother.'

He had looked almost prophetic, serious yet grim, and she'd felt another surge of fear for him, some terrible premonition.

'How would you know?' she'd said angrily. 'Supposing some madman should get hold of one? Those unstable eastern countries, for instance, or the Chinese, who can't agree among themselves.'

He'd remained unshaken by her vehemence and had even laughed a little, saying that he'd only become a submariner because a submarine was the safest place to be if the worst should happen. He'd reminded her so much of Theo that she'd been obliged to leave him, pleading a headache, going to her room. The question of Sin had never been raised again but it was clear that he had not lost his heart to her, although she suspected that he still went to see her. She hoped that Sin had remained unscathed, too . . .

Her thoughts wandered on, considering her other grand-children and all those little ones that were beginning to grow up, to be worried about in their turn. How quickly the years rushed past. In a week or two she would be eighty-two years old. It would be a quiet Birthday this year. Mole and Hal were at sea so there would be only Kit to share the celebrations although some of the family were coming to toast them; Prue was coming and Fliss and Miles and the twinnies. Maria had decided that she couldn't manage on her own with the babies and the dog, but Gus and Susanna would certainly be over. There would be quite a gathering at teatime. She wondered what delight Theo would choose for her this year – and glanced anxiously at her watch, her fear flooding back.

As she did so, she heard the car bumping in between the gatehouses and she was swamped by relief; all was well. He was home. She saw Fox hobbling in through the garden room, round to the kitchen and, as the front door opened, Caroline came in with the tray. Theo stood his stick in the brass container and beamed upon them both.

'What excellent timing,' he said. 'We rather misjudged the depth of the water on the tidal road at Aveton Gifford but all's well that ends well. Your picnic was superb, Caroline. Every crumb eaten and enjoyed. A delightful day on all counts but I'm certainly ready for some tea. That cake looks delicious.'

'If you've eaten all the lunch Caroline packed,' said Freddy acidly, hiding her joy at the sight of him, illogically wishing to punish him now that she knew he was safe, 'I'm surprised that you can manage anything at all.'

'Fox was starving, poor fellow,' said Theo, shaking his head. 'I've never seen a chap put it away so fast. I hardly had a mouthful.'

'Sit down,' said Freddy resignedly as Caroline disappeared, grinning. 'I don't believe a word of it. Fox's manners are far too good. But you shall have some cake. There. Now, take your tea and tell me where you went and what you've seen and omit nothing, not even the tidal road at Aveton Gifford. Now that you're safely back I can cope with anything.'

193

Chapter Nineteen

It was two o'clock in the morning; the middle watch. In the dimmed red lighting, Mole leaned on the chart table, sorting out the harbour entry plans requested earlier by the Captain and feeling all the responsibility of being the Navigation Officer. He was sharing the watch with the SD Supply Officer, Trevor Lukes, a kindly easy-going man, and a very comforting person to have with you when you were still new and unsure of yourself. Mole's sense of anxiety was heightened by the knowledge that they were covertly tracking a cargo vessel out of Libya, suspected of gun-running for the IRA. It seemed to be nothing out of the ordinary to the experienced men about him but he had a sense of unreality that he should be a part of this small drama and felt the familiar churning of the stomach, a sensation usually associated with the idea of the unknown assassin, blank-eyed, closed lips smiling: an image which had haunted him since the murder and ambush of his parents and brother. He knew that those closest to him considered it odd, given these private terrors, that he should have chosen the branch of the Navy that was most fully engaged in the silent, secret war against the Russians, where there was the most danger and the most risk. He could hardly explain it to himself; how the attraction of secrecy and silence had drawn him since his earliest days in Kenya when he had crawled beneath tables or under chairs and concealed himself with rugs and cushions; the overwhelming relief that he was secure, safe from discovery. Had the translation from his safe English nursery to the long, low African bungalow been such a great trauma to his year-old self?

As he sorted through the charts he was thinking about the familygram he'd received the day before, full of news, recounting the twinnies' latest escapades, keeping him up to date with the gossip and reporting the welfare of the elder members of his family. As usual, it was Fliss who made certain he was abreast of the family's affairs, although he knew that if any real disaster happened he would know nothing about it. This was his own choice. He could decide whether he should be told if the members of his family were ill, dying even, knowing, however, that there was nothing he could do about it; or he could choose to remain ignorant until the submarine docked. He had chosen the latter, suspecting himself to be incapable of remaining efficient once he knew that any of his loved ones was in danger. He'd heard of a case where one of the crew arrived home to find his youngest child dead and buried. The shock must have been unbearable. Mole wondered how the man's wife had coped through the long, lonely weeks without support or comfort. He understood the Navy's position; it was unrealistic to expect the men to be flown out the moment a serious problem occurred at home – and especially in this area of defence where the submarine was a secret weapon – nevertheless it was a harsh and frightening world. It made him more determined in his resolve never to marry or have children of his own. The enormity of such a responsibility was terrifying; suppose he should be unable to protect them? It was impossible to legislate for every eventuality and the attempt to do so would drive him distracted. Imagine going home, anticipating the happy cheerful scene, only to find that your youngest child – hardly more than a baby – was not simply dangerously ill but already dead, buried in the cold earth? Sudden death striking out of a bright sunny day . . .

He thrust away such morbid thoughts and glanced about him. Over on the starboard side, seated between and slightly behind the two planesman who monitored the steering and balance – the trim – of the boat, Trevor was talking quietly about his retirement plans which centred round the running of a restaurant in Rosyth. The low murmur of his voice blended with the atmosphere of relaxed, hushed weariness, adding to the intimacy of the control room at night when the submarine was at three hundred feet and very, very quiet. Mole got on well with Trevor, who liked a run ashore and engendered confidence. He was glad that he was there, seeing him through these first early weeks. He bent to look at the computer screen, checking the progress of the cargo vessel, listening to the conversation between the two sailors monitoring its progress as they talked to the sonar team.

'A submarine is a blind man with big ears,' Trevor had once said to Mole.

Mole had a momentary vision of the submarine gliding silently through the water, guided purely by a tiny dot on the screen and the ping of the sonar. He knew how the atmosphere could change instantly at the least irregularity; how quickly the tension could increase.

'Coffee, sir?'

'Oh, thanks, chief.' He smiled gratefully at the steward and returned to his charts. Planning the approach was not so simple as it sounded and he was determined to get it as right as he could. One of the planesman was pleading for a cigarette – 'Oh, come on, sir. I'm gasping for a fag' – and others were adding their pleas to his. If they'd been at periscope depth there would be no chance but, 'OK. Just one all round,' Trevor agreed, and there was a general easing and stretching, a lightening of the mood.

The chef put his head in, announcing that he was about to start baking the bread for breakfast, and the engineer officer of the watch, just out of his pit and wanting a report for his team in the manoeuvring room, paused on his way aft.

He and Mole murmured together. '. . . We're just here . . . Bay of Biscay . . . still tracking . . . have to break off in a couple of days. Got to be back in Devonport . . . heading towards southern Ireland . . . might alter course up the west coast . . . southern Irish port . . . doing about twelve knots . . . another three days.'

He went away, yawning widely, and Mole finished his coffee. Once the cargo vessel was safe inside territorial waters a report could be sent back to HQ, the intelligence services alerted . . . Mole was yawning too, longing for some sleep. Up there, three hundred feet above the submarine, the moonlight was probably reflecting on the water, the stars beginning to fade as the dawn approached. In his mind's eye he saw an image of The Keep, a small stronghold in the silence of the surrounding countryside, slumbering until early morning light. He yawned again, glancing at his watch and, with a small internal shock, remembered that today was his birthday.

Later that day, travelling west for the Birthday weekend, Fliss was thinking about Mole.

'It's a pity he'll miss the celebrations,' she said. 'Hal, too. At least Kit's coming down. Poor old Mole. He does enjoy a family get-together.'

'He's a big boy now,' said Miles. 'I expect he'll be able to live with it.'

'I expect he will,' agreed Fliss, crushing down a surge of irritation. Miles was always so relentlessly adult but, if she were honest with herself, she knew quite well that this was what had attracted her to him. After the devastating news of Hal's engagement Miles's competence, his self-assurance, his readiness to take control had been the qualities against which she had rested. She had been driven by two needs: the first was the compulsion to eschew any thought or memory of Hal and the second had been a desire to show herself unaffected by his engagement to Maria. This combination of weakness and pride had delivered her into Miles's keeping.

Fliss thought: But he is a good man. It isn't fair to condemn him now for the very qualities I needed then.

Resolutely she turned her mind away from the next involuntary thought: *'If only I had waited . . .'* This recurring reflection, an insidious destroyer of peace, had to be kept in its place; logic firmly applied. Even if she had known that she would continue to love Hal would she have acted differently? Would she never have married? Never have had the twinnies? Fliss turned to glance at them, sitting in their car seats behind her. Jamie's thumb was in his mouth, his fingers twiddling up his hair as he listened to Bess's tiny murmuring voice reading to him.

' "Suddenly round a corner she met Babbitty Bumble – 'Zizz, Bizz, Bizz!' said the bumble bee . . ." '

She couldn't really read yet, of course, but she could memorise some of the words which went with the pictures and Jamie was perfectly happy with her rendition of their favourite story. Fliss's heart went out to them. How could she contemplate with any pleasure a situation in which the twinnies might not exist? Turning back, she touched Miles's knee and he smiled at her, unaware of the guilt from which the gesture sprang.

'I'm glad you could get the day off,' she said. 'It makes such a difference travelling first thing on a Friday.'

'Wait until the M5 is open all the way down to Exeter,' he promised her. 'Shan't know we're born. Wish I had a crystal ball, though. I'd like to know what posting I shall get next. I'm beginning to wonder if we shall ever get back to Dartmouth. Perhaps I should have taken your advice and sold the place when we went to Hong Kong.'

She looked at him, surprised. It was the first time she'd heard him express doubts at keeping the house in Above Town.

'But I thought you wanted to retire to it,' she said, 'and, anyway, we might get a West Country posting next.'

'Mmm.' He pursed his lips doubtfully but shrugged. 'We'll see how this next lot of tenants do. Of course, we might get abroad again if we're lucky. An attaché post or NATO, perhaps.'

Fliss remained silent. She knew that it was foolish of her to be so attached to her own country, to prefer to be in easy reach of her family. It had been terrible to know that Ellen had died so far away, without being able to see her once more or to say goodbye. As a naval wife she should be prepared for these hardships, even to look forward positively to foreign postings. She supposed that she'd always been a bit of a chicken. She'd hated leaving grandmother and Uncle Theo and Aunt Prue and the twins when her parents had decided to go out to Kenya. She'd felt uprooted, vulnerable, alien. It was her big brother, Jamie, who had helped her to endure the rupture; entering into their new life so enthusiastically, turning it into an adventure. How she'd envied him when he'd returned to England to school, when she'd known he was spending his excats at The Keep with Grandmother and Ellen and Fox.

'I heard from Richard Maybrick yesterday,' Miles was saying. 'He's over for a few weeks. Some relative or other has died and he's got some property to sort out. He's asking if he can come and stay for a day or two. Mary's not with him, apparently.'

'Of course he must come,' Fliss answered mechanically but without a great deal of enthusiasm. Richard was in shipping and had become great chums with Miles out in Hong Kong. She did not care much for him – he was an aggressive, noisy man – but his wife had been a tremendous help, especially when the twins were about to arrive. She was a quiet, motherly woman, unobtrusive but effective.

Miles glanced sideways at Fliss, looking her over, summing her up. He sometimes wished she'd make a little more effort with her appearance. Her fair hair was bundled back into a long plait and her small face was devoid of make-up. She wore her usual uniform of navy Levi cords and a guernsey over one of his old shirts, and the whole effect made her look about twenty. Yet there was something formidable about Fliss; some quality which she'd inherited from that old grandmother of hers; something steely and – and what? The word incorruptible occurred to him but it sounded rather too fancy. He had learned, however, never to dissemble with her. It was better to keep his own counsel rather than take her fully into his confidence and risk her disconcertingly direct – and occasionally crushing – observations. Yet there was that other vulnerable side. If he had known how maternal she was, might he have married her? Looking back, he could never quite remember what had driven him to propose. Sometimes he wondered now if it had been merely a desire to recreate his youth. He'd been approaching middle age and he'd needed to know that life hadn't quite passed him by. The Chadwicks had been such a merry group, so full of life, such fun.

Miles thought: I think I was in love with the whole damned lot of them. Fliss was the embodiment. She was so sweet.

What might his life have been like if she had not telephoned him that day, quite out of the blue, lonely and miserable? How triumphant he had been, how determined to seize his chance . . . He sometimes missed his freedom, his bachelor ways, but he always crushed down such disloyal thoughts and remembered the fun they'd had together – and would have again when the children were older and off to boarding school. At least Fliss had no qualms about sending them away. They were to go to

Herongate House, where Mole and Susanna had been so happy. He knew that Fliss thought that eleven would be a good age but he was hoping to bring her round to the idea of sending them at eight. After all, Susanna had gone at eight and one couldn't wish to meet a more sensible and balanced girl than Sooz. Once they were settled life would become a little more flexible and he could begin to carry out his plans for their future. Perhaps, however, it would be wise to keep them under his hat for a while longer. An idea occurred to him . . .

He reached out and held Fliss's hand for a moment and she returned the pressure unaware of the guilt from which the gesture sprang.

'I was thinking,' he said. 'Why don't you spend a few extra days down at The Keep? I can fetch you back when you've had enough. Didn't you say *Warspite* was in at the end of the week? Why not stay and see that brother of yours?'

'I'd love to,' she answered, surprised but delighted. 'Are you sure? You know I hate leaving you on your own.'

'Oh, nonsense,' he said cheerfully. 'I'll do a few extra duties and eat in the Mess. It's not a problem.'

She was filled with gratitude – an emotion easily mistaken for love – and remorse for her earlier mental criticism. He was so kind, so generous . . .

'It would be simply lovely,' she said warmly. 'Thank you, darling. Oh hell, if only we'd thought of it earlier I'd have put more clothes in for the twinnies . . .'

Chapter Twenty

Maria was barely inside the house, Edward still in his carrycot, Jolyon having his coat removed whilst trying to unwrap his new Dinky toy, when the doorbell rang.

'Damn,' she muttered. 'Blast.' She'd learned to be fairly restrained with Jolyon growing so quickly, copying everything she said. 'Who can that be? Wait, darling, please. Just *wait*. I'll open it for you in a sec.'

With Jolyon trailing her, still carrying the toy enclosed in its plastic bubble, she went out into the hall and opened the front door. A man in his early forties, broad-shouldered and with a rather nice smile, stood looking at her hopefully. She recognised him vaguely and instinctively she responded, smoothing out the worry lines, pulling in her stomach, raising her eyebrows interrogatively.

'I'm frightfully sorry to trouble you,' he said, 'but I've got a bit of a problem. The telephone's gone dead and my car simply will not start. Do you think I could possibly use your telephone? If yours is not on the blink, too. I'm not an absolute stranger. I live just along the road half a mile or so. We've seen each other driving to and fro. Well, I've noticed *you*, of course. *You* might not have noticed *me*.'

She was already laughing at his air of distraction which, combined with his barely disguised admiration, was rather engaging.

'Of course I recognise you,' she said. 'Sounds like you're having a bad day. Come on in. I'm Maria Chadwick and this is Jolyon.'

'How do you do? My name's Keith Graves.' He was following her into the hall. 'This is really very kind of you. I see your husband going off some mornings while I'm walking the dog.'

'Don't talk about dogs,' said Maria ruefully. 'For one glorious moment I'd forgotten mine. The wretched animal's been locked in all morning and will now go utterly berserk. I must let him out. The telephone's just there. Is it working? Oh, great. Do you need the book?'

'No, no. Got the number with me. Thanks.'

'Come through when you've finished,' she said cheerfully. 'I'll put the kettle on. Come along, Jolyon. No, he can see your tractor later. Come on.'

Strangely elated by the diversion she went to let Rex out of the garage, shut the kitchen door firmly upon his joyful greeting and began to deal with Jolyon's new toy. Edward was still lying placidly in the carrycot and she decided to leave him whilst she made the coffee, hoping that he wouldn't begin to grizzle. She swung Jolyon into his high chair, placed the red tractor on the tray before him and went to switch on the kettle.

There were a few discreet taps on the door and Keith put his head in, smiling now and looking decidedly relieved.

'All done?' she asked.

'All done,' he echoed. 'Thanks, yes, I'd love a cup if

you're quite sure. This is very neighbourly of you.'

'Nonsense.' Maria smiled at him. She was suddenly glad that she was wearing her new Donegal tweed flares with the short matching blouson – not that it mattered a bit, really. 'You know I think I've met your wife at a fund-raising coffee morning somewhere.' She frowned, trying to jog her memory, remembering a fair, smart, pretty woman with a decided manner and very positive views. She'd made Maria feel just the least bit mumsy. 'The Dysons' was it? I hope she's OK?'

'Yes . . . Well, no. Oh dear.' He grimaced, looking uncomfortable. 'I was determined not to burden you with my problems, apart from using your phone, that is . . .'

He hesitated awkwardly as Maria passed him a mug of coffee, all her curiosity aroused, determined to offer feminine assistance and consolation should it prove necessary.

'I'm so sorry, I didn't mean to pry or anything,' she assured him, quite untruthfully. 'I just wondered if she might be ill or something but, honestly, it's none of my business.'

'If only it were that simple,' he said rather bitterly. 'Her being ill, I mean. Oh well, why not? Everyone will know sooner or later. The truth is she's left me. She's gone off with her boss, quite out of the blue. I simply had no idea anything was going on.' He bit his lip and turned away, smiling down at Jolyon. 'I say. That's a very smart tractor.'

Jolyon smiled back but was suddenly overcome with a fit of shyness. He lowered his head, driving the tractor round the tray, making quiet brmmm-ing noises to himself, and Keith reached out and lightly ruffled his blond hair.

'I'm so terribly sorry,' said Maria, after a moment or two

of startled silence. 'I had simply no idea, of course.' She shook her head helplessly.

'Why should you?' He shrugged. 'It's come as such a shock, that's the problem. I don't quite know how to deal with it. They always say the husband – or the wife – is the last to know but I hadn't the least suspicion. Talk about naïve. Apart from anything else, I feel such a fool. How could I have been so gullible? All that business about working late and things. I work from home, you see. Bit of a role reversal, isn't it . . .? Sorry, I'm going on, aren't I? Forgive me. It's just such a relief to have someone to talk to, I suppose.'

'Of *course* you must talk,' cried Maria, all womanly sympathy and enjoying every moment of it. 'It's the most frightful thing to happen. Look, sit down properly. Don't just stand there propped against the sink. You can say anything you like and I promise I shan't say a word to a soul. Honestly.'

He looked so pathetically grateful, so crushed – in a handsome, gentlemanly sort of way – that she could have almost hugged him, just to comfort him, naturally. He swallowed, trying to smile, and she took his arm gently and led him over to the table in a pseudo-motherly manner.

'Sit!' she said, as she might have to Rex, making a joke of it. 'Stay!' and he laughed then, looking at her gratefully, appreciatively.

'You're very sweet,' he said – and she patted his arm almost affectionately.

'Nonsense,' she said. 'Just drink your coffee and relax. You don't have to talk about it if you don't want to. Anyway, it's nice for me to have some adult company, you know. My husband is away at sea for weeks on end and it gets a bit lonely. Weekends are the worst. Everyone else is being a family and it's pretty miserable on my own, even with the boys.'

Even as she spoke the words she knew that some message was being given and understood; a very tiny signal, but a terribly important one, and she fiddled about with the shopping – putting it away, busying herself – so as to hide her confusion.

'Well, if I had a wife like you I'm damned if I'd go away for five minutes.'

He'd said it and she felt that she'd almost willed him, pushed him into it. She felt guilty, slightly ashamed, but oddly excited.

'Not that I can say anything about that, can I?' he was asking bitterly. 'Clearly I haven't made much of a success at being a husband so I'm a fine one to talk.'

'Don't be silly,' she said lightly, pulling herself together, fluffing up her long thick hair. She'd refused to have her hair chopped off like Kit – or frizzed like Sin – nor would she wear it dragged back as Fliss did in that childish plait. It was cut carefully, very regularly, and she wore it layered and curled in a glossy mane. Aware of his eyes upon her she moved lightly, consciously, about the kitchen; the silence lengthened so that it became charged with meaning . . .

Edward woke, whimpered briefly and began to wail. She hurried to him, grateful for the release from the strange tension that had been building. She picked him up, crooning to him, holding him so that her cheek rested against his head; aware of the maternal picture they were making, mother and child. She saw that Jolyon was watching impassively, almost critically, and she felt another hot wash of embarrassment.

'Do you have children?' she asked Keith impulsively, ready to sympathise with this added dilemma, but he shook his head. The expression in his eyes made her feel excited again, rather daring, and she pushed down the guilt. Why shouldn't she enjoy his company? No doubt Hal was being asked to parties, having fun, each time the ship touched shore. He wasn't left alone, dealing with the dreary round of dogs and children. It would do her good to relax, to behave as he did; it might make her more tolerant, less jealous. After all, he was always telling her that she was too strait-laced, that she took things to heart, that there was nothing to get upset about . . .

'If you can bear it,' she said, still cuddling Edward, using him as a shield, almost as a warning, 'you're very welcome to stay for a bite of lunch. Very simple stuff. Some soup and cheese and things. But you've probably got to get back?'

'That's the nicest offer I've had since I can't remember when,' he said warmly, pushing back his chair, half rising. 'I should love it. If you're really sure? Look. Let me hold him, shall I? I'm an uncle so I know how it's done. Or shall I do something else to help?'

'Sit down,' she said, laughing. 'Stop fussing. OK, you have Edward, if you feel you must be useful but he's probably horridly soggy. No, not too bad. Now then, let's see what we've got. I've got a rather nice Brie here somewhere. So tell me, what are your plans? You poor thing. Honestly, I really feel for you . . .'

★ ★ ★

'You've been away for ages,' grumbled Kit. 'Missing the Birthday, no one knowing quite where you were. All this secrecy and silence business. So tell me all.'

She was not feeling quite so light-hearted as she sounded. Ever since her conversation with Sin about Mole, Kit had been growing steadily more certain that Jake might be the love of her life after all. She'd worked herself up to this meeting, praying that he'd bring up the subject, as he usually did, proposing to her – even in a jokey kind of way – so that she could explain these new feelings to him. She had no anxieties about his reaction but she felt rather foolish, annoyed with herself for taking so long to realise that what she wanted most had been under her nose for the last twelve years. How patient he'd been, how understanding and comforting. No, she simply couldn't imagine life without Jake.

She regarded him, now, looking at him properly for the first time since she'd arrived at the flat earlier that evening. He looked tired, preoccupied. She knew that he'd been back in France on family business; his matriarchal paternal grandmother had died suddenly and there had been lots to sort out, loose ends to tie up. His father was dead and a great deal was now falling on Jake's shoulders. The Villons were a clannish family, staunch Roman Catholics, and even Jake had been under his grandmother's thumb. He'd also been extraordinarily fond of her.

'Was it hell?' Kit asked sympathetically. She'd met Jake's grandmother once – Jake had felt that he and Kit had much in common on the family front – but it had not proved an overwhelming success. 'I'm so sorry, honey. You'll miss her, won't you? She reminded me a bit of Grandmother. Very austere and tough as old boots.'

Jake nodded, made an attempt to smile and sighed instead, pushing his hands through his hair. Kit saw that there were streaks of grey in the black and felt a twinge of terror. The years had fled so fast and she'd wasted so many of them. She opened her mouth to tell him so but he was already speaking.

'I'm moving to Paris,' he was saying abruptly. 'I've arranged a transfer with the bank. It's not a problem, apparently. There's so much to look after and Uncle Jean-Claude is too old to take it all on.'

She stared at him. In his dark city suit, white shirt, sober tie, he looked frighteningly adult; not the familiar Jake of student days but a mature man with responsibilities and worries.

Kit thought: He's not far off forty. Nearly middle-aged. Thank God I realised before it was too late. Paris will be fun. I'll learn the language properly, settle down, have darling French babies. He's hating the thought of leaving, I can see that. Oh, Jake . . .

Aloud she said, 'Well I can understand that. You're the only male of your generation, aren't you? You can't just abandon them.'

He looked at her then, eyebrows lifted quizzically, and she guessed that he was surprised that she should respond in such a calm manner. With an inner twist of bitterness, she realised that he would expect her to be far less adult; to protest or make light of it, refusing to take it seriously. Her heart gave a twinge of compassion, imagining his feelings at the thought of the separation which surely lay ahead.

'No, I can't just abandon them,' he agreed heavily, turning away, dragging off his jacket. 'But it'll be a hell of a wrench.'

She guessed at the reason for his misery; she had refused him so often that it was unlikely she would change her mind now that he was returning permanently to France. Her calm manner could also have been interpreted as indifference.

'Oh, Jake,' she said quickly, 'it will be, I can see that. You'll be leaving so many friends and memories here. But do you think that I could come with you?'

She waited for his look of joy, the straightening of his shoulders, the outstretched arms, knowing he would not misunderstand or play games with her. This was far too important . . . He was staring at her in disbelief.

'I love you, you see,' she said, rushing on, determined that he would understand, trying to remove all the past pain of rejection. 'I realised when you were away. I always have, I can see that now. It's taken me too long to grow up. Oh, honey, I missed you so much.'

Jake sat down abruptly on the arm of the sofa, fists between his knees. He closed his eyes for a moment and she came to kneel behind him on the cushions, her cheek against his shoulder.

'I can't believe this,' he said quietly. 'No. Wait. It's no good, Kit. It's too late.'

She kneeled up abruptly, fear in her heart. 'What d'you mean? Oh, Jake, it doesn't matter about going back to France. I don't mind. It'll be fun—'

'Wait!' he shouted. 'Shut up, Kit! It's too late. I told you. I'm engaged to be married. She a cousin of mine, Madeleine . . .'

In the silence that followed, the name seemed to drift, echoing on the air. He'd said it in the French way, with the middle vowel ignored, lyrical, romantic. In Kit's mind an image rose: a young girl with a sweet, gentle face and long red-brown hair, smiling adoringly at Jake. She'd been charming to Kit, the guest in her grandmother's house, but her attention had been all for Jake . . . Kit straightened up, still kneeling on the sofa, her brain too stupid, too shocked to take it in properly.

'I remember her,' she murmured – and her heart ached in her breast.

'She's loved me ever since she was a child.' He was speaking rapidly, his back still turned to her. 'Her parents have been dead for years and Gran'mère took her in. She always wanted us to marry. Madeleine's father was a second cousin to my father and they were great friends. But there was always you, Kit, until the last time. Not now, for the funeral, but back in the summer. You remember you didn't want to come? You were too busy with Mark and your new job.' He shrugged. 'I felt we'd come to the end somehow, that you were in love with him. You were moving on. I was pretty low and Madeleine was so sweet, so loving. Can you imagine how comforting that was? How boosting to the ego? Pathetic, isn't it?' he said savagely. 'Well, she was there and I took full advantage of her.' He put his head in his hands. 'I am very fond of her,' he muttered desperately.

Kit swallowed, still kneeling up, hands clenched together. 'But does that mean that you have to marry her?' She tried to keep her voice level, despite her very real terror. 'I can understand everything you've said. But to marry her, Jake? Is it fair, anyway, if you don't truly love her? I don't mean to sound so prosy but—'

'She's pregnant,' he said flatly. 'Three months. She wasn't going to tell me but after the funeral it was all too emotional for words and she wasn't very well, poor child. I think I guessed, anyway. She was so nervous and brittle, so unlike her usual self. She admitted it in the end and . . . it didn't seem to matter too much, after all. I never guessed that you'd . . .' He raised his joined fists and drove them down on the arm of the chair. 'For Christ's *sake*, Kit!' he shouted. 'Why now? Why bloody *now*? When it's too late. Twelve years, Kit. Twelve bloody years and you're three months too late.'

He turned to her, tears streaming down his thin cheeks. Snatching off his spectacles he swiped at his face with his wrist and she reached out to him, holding him.

As she let herself in, the sitting room door opened and Sin came out into the hall.

'Jake telephoned,' she said without preamble. 'He was worried about you.'

Kit stared at her, barely seeing her. Every movement was an effort; the pain in her breast intolerable. 'I was too late,' she said, almost conversationally. 'You were right about that, anyway. Oh, Sin, I've lost him,' and as she stumbled forward Sin reached out for her, putting her arms about her as she began to weep.

Chapter Twenty-one

The sun rose late now, swinging up above the distant heights in showers of rose and gold, washing the bleached stubbly fields with warmth, lending colour and depth to the monochrome world. Grey, dew-heavy swags of cobwebs, stretched hammock-like across the hedge-tops, sparkled into jewelled fragility. In the lane a pheasant chirred, running stiff-legged, neck stretched, across the path of the milk van, whose driver leaned to watch the flash of glossy feathers as it scrambled to safety in the hedge.

Two young rooks bickered raucously in the hawthorn below Theo's open window and he drew back, realising that he was chilled, too bewitched by the miracle of sunrise to be conscious, until now, of the freezing air. As he closed his window, his eyes still drawn to the scene beyond it, he saw the rooks circling below him, heading for the stand of elms where they built each spring. The rookery had been their home for the last hundred years; this hill was their territory, fought for and defended season after season. As other rooks rose from the trees, flying to meet them, he found that he was thinking of Fox, uprooted at last from his own small territory within the gatehouse walls.

It was Caroline who had insisted that Fox should take up residence within the house. He was too crippled now to build up his fire, even if she made certain that he had fuel at hand, and she knew that his quarters were damp and not properly aired. He'd fought every inch of the way.

'It's like winkling a snail out of its shell,' Caroline had said despairingly, 'but I'm sure it's the right thing to do. I've thought it through very carefully.'

Theo had no doubts on that score. Caroline had always known the importance of balancing physical needs with mental and spiritual requirements. This instinctive wisdom had been her great strength, informing her decisions regarding the children, and she was now applying it to Fox. She was weighing his need for privacy and independence against his physical welfare and, as so often is the case, had been obliged to settle for a compromise.

'But where shall we put him?' Freddy had asked, puzzled by the idea of Fox wandering the corridors of The Keep in his dressing gown. 'Of course, if his quarters are uninhabitable . . .'

Caroline had exchanged a quick glance with Theo, aware that Freddy was remonstrating privately with herself that the thought had never occurred to her. Fox had lived in the gatehouse cottage for nearly sixty years; it was where he belonged. She would never have presumed to intrude on him there, nor question what he did within his own walls. Now she was castigating herself for neglect.

'It's simply that he can't keep himself warm,' Caroline had said gently. 'These old places are fine if we keep the fires going and open the windows regularly to maintain a flow of air. But poor old Fox can't keep his fire in, you see.

He can't manage a shovel with coal on it, and even small logs are difficult for him. The result is that the place is getting colder and damper. It's all he can do to open the windows and the struggle to shut them is often so great that he leaves them open and then it's really bitterly cold in there. We must do something before winter arrives.'

'I quite see that.' Shame had made Freddy's voice sharp. 'But where is he to go? I assume he finds stairs difficult? Not that he has any in his cottage, of course.'

'I've got it all planned out.'

Now, remembering Caroline, hands eloquent, rough grey curls on end, Theo smiled to himself. So she had been down the years, making her point, eagerly defending the children, intent on their welfare, parrying Freddy's criticisms. On this occasion Freddy had smiled, too. Perhaps she was also recalling a younger Caroline. 'I'm sure you have,' she'd said drily.

The answer had been simple enough. Fox was to have the living room off the kitchen as a bedsitting room. He could wash in the scullery, and the lavatory was just along the passage. By day, weather permitting, he could potter in his workroom but it was to be hoped that he'd stay in the warm areas of the kitchen quarters.

'But what will you use as a sitting room?' Freddy had asked, concerned. Caroline's rooms were still on the nursery floor and the living room had made a pleasant rest area for the three of them in the past. They had a television and some comfortable chairs there, and it was a very cosy place to be when the coal fire was burning in the small Victorian grate.

Caroline had shrugged away Freddy's anxiety. 'With Ellen gone I hardly bother to use it except in the evening to

219

watch television, and I'm sure Fox will be very happy to have some company,' she'd said. 'I tend to stay in the kitchen. Fox spends a lot of his time there as it is and it's so simple to hop in and keep the fire stoked up if it's really cold. We must simply do it. Move his things and tell him afterwards. That's if you agree?'

'You must do whatever is right,' Freddy had said. She'd looked weary, suddenly, with a kind of resigned patience, accepting the fact that she could no longer control events, and Caroline, with another anxious glance at Theo, had vanished away, her mission accomplished.

She and Josh had moved Fox's bed and other small items of furniture whilst he and Theo were out on one of their jaunts, hurrying to make it as comfortable as they could before their return. Theo, fully briefed, had taken the puzzled Fox to see his new quarters. As they'd stood at the door of the room Theo, firmly grasping Fox's elbow, had been aware that his arm was trembling as he stared about him, bewildered. Caroline had made it quite delightful: a small fire burning in the green-tiled grate; his bed made with fresh linen, covered with one of Ellen's quilts; his few books in a small bookshelf; a lamp on a table by the bed. The television still stood in the corner beside the fire, comfortable chairs at the ready, and his few clothes were contained in a chest of drawers beneath the window. A cupboard in the passage outside was available for coats and boots.

'My dear fellow, this is charming,' Theo had said, his hold tightening on Fox's arm. 'You'll be warm and comfortable here. I shall expect you to invite me in for a cup of tea when you're settled.'

There'd been a silence whilst he'd waited breathlessly for Fox's reaction.

'Don't seem right,' Fox had cried piteously at last, 'being in the house. 'Tisn't what I'm used to, sir. I can't do it.'

Theo had been conscious of Caroline, hovering anxiously behind them, and he'd moved further into the room, propelling Fox along with him, aware that he might have a real battle on his hands.

'Nonsense, man,' he'd said sternly ('I used my officer's voice,' he told Freddy later somewhat anxiously). 'Times change and we all have to be prepared to change with them, you know. What's the problem exactly?'

Fox had looked about the room, his knotted hands working together, his expression distraught, but he'd tried to collect his thoughts and express himself properly.

''Tisn't mine, if you take my meaning, sir. Sixty years I've been in the gatehouse cottage and it's my home. It's all I've got that's mine. I know where to lay my hand to any little thing, you see. This, well, it's right smart and cosy, but it isn't *mine*.'

This last had come out in a kind of wail, and Theo had felt Caroline's distress emanating from the doorway behind him. He'd emptied his mind and waited for assistance. It came swiftly.

'I quite understand, my dear fellow,' he'd said compassionately but firmly, 'but we must do what is best for you and for others, too. We care about you, you see. You must allow us to look after you as best we can. Poor Caroline can't be expected to do that properly if you stay in the gatehouse. Remember when we moved Ellen down from the nursery wing to the first floor? It was exactly the same thing. She was getting too old to be toiling up and down two flights of stairs and three small children were simply too much for her. Poor Ellen felt not only displaced by Caroline but also as if she were intruding into the family's private quarters. To begin with she was very upset by it all but she was sensible enough to know that it was best for her and for the rest of the family. Sometimes one person must give way before the needs of the whole community. Remember how quickly she adapted? She soon felt quite at home. I am quite certain that you will feel just the same if you will only give it a try. Will you do that for me? Give it a try? If it doesn't work you shall go back to the gatehouse cottage. You have my word. What do you say?'

Whilst he was talking he'd felt a stiffening of Fox's spine, a strengthening of will, and he'd turned to smile reassuringly at Caroline.

'Whatever would she be thinking of me?' exclaimed Fox remorsefully. 'Making a fuss like I was no bigger than they twinnies. And this room got up so nice and Caroline ready to give it up. Proper ungrateful I be . . .'

'She'd've said, "Stay in that damp old cottage when you can be in this warm room? Whatever next, I wonder."' Caroline had come forward and was standing beside him, pretending not to see the tears on his cheeks. 'Mind you, we haven't got all your bits and pieces over yet. I thought you'd want to arrange those yourself. We could hang that nice framed photograph Mole gave you of his submarine on the wall. I hope you'll let me spend the evenings here with you as usual. Think what fun it'll be watching television by the fire and not having to go out in the cold and dark afterwards. And you can make yourself a cup of tea in the kitchen when you can't sleep, and chat to Perks.'

'You do have a point there, maid,' Fox had agreed, rather struck by the thought of such riotous and luxurious living. 'And my mum's old chest'd fit a treat at the bottom of the bed . . .'

Theo had gone quietly away, leaving them discussing the final domestic details together.

Now, as he prepared to go down to breakfast, he wondered what they would have done without Caroline's good sense and capacity for hard work, her loyalty and love. As he passed his desk, on his way out, a piece of paper drifted to the floor and he bent to pick it up. Looking at his small clear writing he remembered that he'd copied the prayer out for Fox but had not yet given it to him, although he could not now recall why he'd thought it might be of benefit to him. It was part of one of the Sayings of St John of the Cross: a prayer of a soul in love.

Who can free himself from his meanness and limitations,
If you do not lift him to yourself, my God, in purity of love?
How will a person
brought to birth and nurtured in a world of small horizons,
rise up to you Lord,
if you do not raise him by your hand which made him? . . .
so I shall rejoice:
you will not delay, if I do not fail to hope.

Theo read it, moved as he always was by the yearning and the promise. Why had he decided to write it out for Fox? He shook his head; it was not important. If it were meant for him then the appropriate moment would arise. Tucking the paper into his Bible, Theo left his rooms and went downstairs to breakfast, still thinking about Fox.

'He's happy as a sandboy,' Caroline told Fliss a week or so later. 'Luckily, he hasn't much in the way of belongings – quite spartan he is – so we were able to fit in all his treasures. We've left the cottage looking neat and tidy, though, so it doesn't depress him when he pops over. He still uses his workshop although he can do so little now. His poor old hands . . .'

She shook her head sadly. Fliss, sitting opposite at the kitchen table, was remembering all the toys which Fox had mended and made in the past; the bicycles oiled and polished.

'He says he's making a bird table for Susanna,' she said doubtfully.

'Oh, he is,' Caroline assured her. 'Very, very slowly and with rather a lot of assistance from Josh.' She grimaced. 'And that's another story.'

'Why? What's the matter with Josh?' Fliss settled herself more comfortably, glancing at her watch. The twinnies were in with Fox, watching *Play School*, whilst she and Caroline had some coffee and a gossip. She enjoyed these moments, catching up with the life of The Keep, shedding the odd sense of isolation that she felt when she was away from it.

'You remember he married a local girl a year or two ago?' Caroline frowned, racking her memory. 'He always calls her "the missis" and I never can recall her name. Anyway, he's been making noises lately along the lines that he needs more money. I let it go for a bit, trying to decide what might be best before worrying Mrs Chadwick, but when we cleared out the gatehouse cottage that day I had a brainwave and asked Josh what he'd say to living there rent free in return for full-time employment.' She paused, anxious lest Fliss thought that she'd taken rather too much on herself. 'I was just testing the water,' she explained. 'Just getting an idea of what he might be prepared to do.'

'What did he say?' asked Fliss curiously. 'I can't imagine Josh in the gatehouse cottage somehow.'

'Neither could Josh,' said Caroline drily. 'He laughed and laughed. "I can just see my missis giving up her nice council house to live in this damp old place," he said. And went on to tell me that he was definitely putting his rates up. There's a baby on the way, I gather.'

'So what now?'

Caroline shrugged. 'He'll give us two days a week for the same pay as four,' she said. ' "That's some increase!" I told him, but he doesn't care. He's got lots of people after him and I have the feeling that Mrs Josh rides him a bit hard.'

'But how will you manage?' asked Fliss, concerned. 'You do far too much as it is. Can't we afford to have him more often?'

Caroline shrugged. 'I haven't spoken to Mrs Chadwick yet. Of course there's a terrific difference in having someone who lives in. Fox never stuck to an eight-hour day. He was always about, carrying out some work or other from the moment he got up until he went to bed. Not just gardening but all the maintenance as well. Josh won't do all the things that Fox did. Look, I'm not saying that Fox was exploited. He loved it. This was his home. He took pride in its upkeep and you were his family. But I'm afraid things aren't like that any more.'

'You must speak to Grandmother,' insisted Fliss. 'You

simply mustn't take on any more yourself. You do far too much as it is.'

Caroline smiled at her. 'I'm like Fox,' she said. 'This is my home, too, and you're my family. And speaking of family, have you spoken to Kit lately?'

Fliss was distracted from the worries of running The Keep by the mention of her cousin. 'Not for any length. Not since she came to stay with me for a few days,' she said. 'She talked about coming down . . .?'

Caroline nodded, rightly interpreting Fliss's hesitation. 'Yes, she came for the weekend. I'm glad you warned us about Jake. She's lost weight and there was something different about her. She was so quiet, really subdued. Poor Kit. She didn't get in the dog basket once.'

Neither of them smiled at this statement; both were silent, thinking about Kit.

'Why did I take so long to grow up?' she'd asked Fliss miserably. 'God, I've been such a fool . . .'

'Is there no chance he might change his mind?' Caroline was asking. 'He's loved her for so long.'

'The girl, Madeleine, is having his child,' explained Fliss. 'He feels he can't simply abandon her. The family is very keen on the match, you know, so he's under a lot of pressure. She's quite a lot younger than he is and he feels terribly guilty about it all. Of course they're both Roman Catholics so there's no question of an abortion.'

'Of course not,' said Caroline quickly. 'No, I was simply thinking that there might be some other relative who would bring up the child. He's taking such a risk, marrying a young girl when he's in love with someone else. Does she know about Kit?'

'She's met her.' Fliss's sympathies disloyally reached out to the little French girl who'd loved her big cousin for so long, who'd given him comfort and was now carrying his child. 'The French aren't so strait-laced about cousins marrying,' Kit had told her. 'Pity you and Hal weren't French, little coz . . .' Fliss swallowed the last of her coffee and pushed back her chair.

'Poor child.' Caroline remained sitting at the table whilst Fliss washed out her mug and set it on the draining board. 'And poor Kit. Oh, why must life be so complicated?'

Before Fliss could answer, however, the door opened and the twinnies came in, followed more slowly by Fox, and Caroline's question remained unanswered.

Chapter Twenty-two

'Oh, what shall we do?' cried Prue, tucking her feet under her and settling into the corner of the sofa. 'She's so thin and she looks so . . . oh, I don't know, gaunt and hollow-eyed. How can life be so cruel?'

'Terribly easily,' answered Sin, pouring drinks. 'It's had so much practice, hasn't it?'

Prue accepted her glass gratefully but she still frowned. 'It's her own fault, that's the problem. Whatever we do or say she's going to kick herself for the rest of her life. After all, he waited long enough for her. Oh, I can't believe it.'

'The timing is horrendous,' agreed Sin. 'Poor Kit is trying to put a brave face on it but she's devastated. It's not just that she's realised that she's in love with him. He's also been her best friend for twelve years. She's losing that, too.'

'What can we do?' asked Prue for the tenth time. 'I can't bear to see her so unhappy. She says she won't come to The Keep for Christmas. Do you think she'd like to come to me in Bristol?'

Sin sat down at the other end of the sofa. 'Look,' she said. 'I hope you won't be upset but I think it's best if she gets right away. It'll be hell for her with everyone feeling sorry for her and being tactful and things. So I'm taking her to Spain, just over the French border in the foothills of the Pyrenees. I've got friends there who will be delighted to have us and I think it'll be better for Kit. It's quite a big house party, lots of jolly people. It'll be snowy and cold and fun. Do you mind?'

'Dear Sin,' said Prue, tears threatening. 'How on earth could I mind? You've been such a chum. Talk about Jake being her best friend . . .'

'Well,' Sin shrugged away her thanks, 'it'll be a change for me, too. I'm not sure that The Keep would be quite right for either of us at the moment. How's Hal?'

'Funny you should mention Hal,' said Prue, distracted just as Sin had intended. 'There was the oddest atmosphere when I was there last. The boys are simply heaven, of course, but Maria was in a very strange mood. Almost snappy, even to me.'

'Pregnant again?' enquired Sin.

Prue looked thoughtful, wrinkled her nose, pursed her lips and finally shook her head. 'Could be. But she wasn't like that either time before. They didn't say anything to me about it, of course, but I could see that Hal was edgy. Such a pity. I did hope that their holiday would do them good but all I can say is that Maria seemed terribly pleased to be home again.'

'Perhaps she missed the boys?' hazarded Sin.

'Perhaps.' Prue reached for her bag and pulled out her cigarettes. 'I must say that she was most unsympathetic about Kit. She said that she'd asked for it and that it was time she grew up a bit and thought about the future.' Prue blew smoke in the air and balanced an ashtray on the arm of the chair. 'Hal said something about Kit always living in the present and Maria snapped that she should take a lesson from the story about the wise and foolish virgins with their oil and so on.'

'How extraordinarily smug,' remarked Sin. 'And what then?'

Prue began to chuckle. 'Hal was a bit cross at her attitude and said that any man in his right mind would much prefer to be out in the dark with the ten foolish virgins, and Maria flounced off in a temper.'

Sin laughed. 'So they won't be going to The Keep either for Christmas?'

Prue shook her head. 'Hal's Captain lives in Kent and he's going home, which means that the First Lieutenant has to stay within half an hour of the ship in case there's an emergency. So they'll be spending Christmas at home, which is no bad thing. I think that small children should be in their own homes for Christmas. It was only as the twins grew older and needed company of their own age that I started to go to The Keep. Although we always went each summer.'

'So where shall you spend the festive season? With Hal and Maria?'

Prue sipped at her gin thoughtfully. 'Apparently not.'

'Didn't they ask you?'

'Oh, Hal made noises,' said Prue lightly, 'but he was rather embarrassed about it and looked distinctly relieved when I told him that I'd made other arrangements.'

'And have you?' asked Sin after a moment.

'Well, no. I wondered whether you'd both be going to Devon, you see, but now that I know you aren't . . .'

'Oh hell,' said Sin remorsefully. 'I'm really sorry. I was thinking about Kit, you see. Look, how would you like to come to Viella with us? I'm sure my friends would be delighted.'

'My dear girl,' said Prue, puffing cheerfully on her cigarette. 'I wouldn't dream of such a thing. No, I shall go to The Keep. As long as you're all settled and don't need me I shall be perfectly happy down in Devon. Now don't give it another thought. Truly.'

'If you're sure.' Sin still sounded anxious. 'But you'll be weighed down with gifts for the family, I warn you. Kit has bought her goddaughter the most divine teddy bear. Well, she bought one for each of them actually but their jackets are different colours and I've noticed that Bess's is now wearing a rather lovely little silver necklace.'

Prue shook her head. 'She loves to spoil them, especially Bess. I think that Miles is faintly miffed that "Bess" has taken over almost completely from "Elizabeth". Well, except for Freddy and Theo, of course, who are still rather formal. I remember that Freddy clung to "Henry" and "Katherine" long after we'd shortened them to Hal and Kit and the same with "Felicia". In fact it was Kit who shortened it to Fliss. She couldn't manage Felicia when she was tiny. Anyway, I like the name Bess. We all do.'

Sin grinned. 'Kit is delighted. She was determined to think up a name for her goddaughter and Bess suits her, don't you think? There's something very regal about her, isn't there? Surprising in one so small. Good Queen Bess.' Sin chuckled. 'Jamie loves it. He's the one who really adopted it but then Elizabeth *is* a bit of a mouthful when you're very small. It was Miles's mother's name, I understand.'

'So I believe. But I was rather surprised that Fliss called Jamie after her brother,' admitted Prue. 'How she adored him. He was so like Hal, you know. You might have taken them for twins.' She was silent, remembering the scene in the courtyard, years ago, when Mole had first seen Hal and thought it was Jamie back from the dead. 'Oh, Sin. Life can be so cruel.'

'This is where we came in, if I remember rightly,' said Sin, getting up and reaching for the bottle. 'Kit'll be back in a moment and we mustn't be miserable. Don't you think we were clever, getting tickets for *La Fille Mal Gardée*? And we're taking you to a very special little Italian place afterwards. So what are you going to wear? Kit tells me she chose you something very daring in Harvey Nicks yesterday which you're keeping from me. Go on. Go and get it while I pour us another tiny one and then we'll start casting lots for the bathroom.'

Maria drove slowly, feeling as though her guilt was weighing down her limbs, making it impossible to press more firmly on the accelerator. Events had swung out of control and she felt rather frightened and ashamed. Yet a kind of nervous excitement pushed her onwards making it impossible to refuse to see Keith or to stop this foolish behaviour, which must surely lead to disaster. She'd told Hal that she was going to have her hair done – and so she was – but first she was going to meet Keith in a pub called The Cricketers which he'd assured her was in the middle of nowhere.

'I can't,' she'd protested, clutching the telephone, turning her back on Jolyon who had come to see what she was doing. 'Honestly, Keith. There's so much Navy round here. I daren't—'

His voice had been passionate and needy, telling her of his love for her, how he couldn't live without her, how beautiful she was. Hal never talked to her like this, as if she were a precious, highly desirable treasure, and she found it intoxicating. It wasn't as if Keith were trying to force her into bed with him – although it was perfectly clear that he'd like to – no, it was her company for which he craved, and her longing to see that look of adoration and hear his words of love was quite irresistible.

For those remaining weeks whilst Hal was at sea he had come round every day. Once he knew their routine he'd appear when the boys were having a nap or later in the evening when Jolyon at least was in bed. They both knew that Jolyon was old enough to spill the beans, albeit innocently, and they both pretended that it was quite by chance that, most of the times when Keith popped in for a chat and a cup of coffee or a drink, the boys were well out of the way.

When Hal returned from sea everything changed. Reality crowded in, bringing guilt with it. He had two weeks' leave due, one of which they had spent away together quite disastrously. She simply couldn't handle this strange mixture of guilt and resentment. The guilt made her want to be nice to him but at the same time she resented the fact that he didn't treat her as Keith did. She loved Hal, of course she did, but it was as though he had ruined a game which she was enjoying without quite making compensation for missing the fun. Of course, the rot had started earlier than her meeting with Keith; it had begun with all those rows about The Keep. Hal was so cagey about the details, refusing to discuss it properly, insisting that the other members of the family had just as many rights as he did. This was nonsense. Mrs Chadwick had always made it clear that Hal was her favourite. He was her executor and he had power of attorney as well as being the eldest of the grandchildren. One day, she was fond of saying, he would be an admiral like his great-grandfather.

Maria peered at the directions scribbled hastily on the piece of paper beside her on the passenger seat, and swung the car left into a narrow lane. She tapped her fingers irritably on the wheel. The idea of Hal as an admiral and *in situ* at The Keep was a very encouraging scenario which carried a great deal of weight when, during wild flights of fancy, she imagined herself giving in to Keith's impassioned proposals. Once Keith had gone home, however, and reason returned, she knew that she would never seriously consider giving up all that she had, and would have, with Hal. Keith might seem to be doing very nicely as an accountant working from home but when the divorce proceedings started it was likely that he would have to sell up his nice big house and settle for something smaller. His social life seemed nonexistent and Maria knew her status would drop considerably if she ceased to be Mrs Chadwick and became Mrs Graves.

Apart from anything else, she had the boys to think about; they needed their father; they adored him and he was so good with them. She didn't have the excuse that he ignored them or was disinterested in them as Miles was with the twinnies. She felt a momentary pang of sympathy for Fliss. It was clear that Miles, kind though he was, was

235

simply not father material although he would probably be fine once they were older. It was not terribly unusual for a man to be bored by small children and Miles was a bit of a bachelor at heart. It must have been difficult changing his ways to accommodate a wife and children. So many people commented on Hal's involvement with his boys, that he was a lovely daddy and so on. Of course she agreed with them but she longed to tell them – and occasionally did – that he was not so attentive to his wife.

Once, not so long ago, his presence, his love, his attention were all she had sought, all she had desired. Now, Keith had shown her what it was like to have a devoted adoring man ready to put the beloved before everything. To Keith nothing mattered but Maria; her welfare, her happiness, her hopes, her fears were paramount. It was a heady experience and she found it impossible to resist his importuning. She longed to see his adoring expression, to feel his arms about her as he gave her a quick hug, but she did not require much more than that. As she turned into the deserted pub car park and saw him waiting, her guilt returned, however, making her irritable and brittle; cross with him for putting her in this awkward situation.

He was opening her door, helping her out and she had a brief desire to scream at him, to tell him to leave her alone, that it wasn't fair to pursue her and make her life so difficult. Yet, in the next moment, as he slid his arm about her shoulder and kissed her tenderly, she felt the familiar excitement rising along with her new sense of power.

'I shouldn't have come,' she said coolly, glancing about her. 'It's too risky. Supposing someone recognises me? Hal knows so many people.'

'Oh, darling Maria. I simply had to see you.' He held her close to his side, pleading with her as they crossed the car park, protecting her from the cold wind. 'This place is always empty on a Saturday morning, I promise you. We used to live just round the corner so I know. You shall have some nice hot coffee. Don't worry. No one will see you.'

He shielded her with his body as they went inside and he hastened to install her beside a roaring fire, screened from the bar by the back of a high settle. She relaxed a little, holding her hands to the blaze, trying to analyse her confused emotions. Keith had nothing of Hal's vital, charming confidence, yet he seemed able to sap her of her will and dominate her with his sheer determination to love her. His care for her was like a warm, soft blanket into which she might sink. She would never have to be jealous or miserable again; she would never be left alone to cope, frightened and tired. Oddly, however, this possessiveness was beginning to pall; she felt smothered by his obsessive passion but she was enjoying her first taste of power. The French have a saying; in any relationship there is one who kisses and one who extends the cheek. After years of being the one who kissed she was now thoroughly enjoying being the one who extended the cheek. She knew that she was taking tremendous risks but it was irresistible.

Maria thought: I can stop this any time I like, and if Hal finds out it might teach him a lesson. It's just a harmless flirtation, that's all. Why shouldn't I have some fun?

Now, in this strange little pub, on neutral ground, she began to feel more like the young Maria: beautiful, desirable, provocative. She pulled the fur collar of her leather coat high round her face, knowing how flattering it was, smiling at Keith as he put the coffee on the table beside her.

'Just as you like it,' he said. 'Black, no sugar. Yes?'

'Yes,' she said, flattered as usual by his remembering. 'Thanks.'

'So.' He slid in beside her, putting a pint of beer down beside her cup but ignoring it to look at her, touching her cheek. 'Oh, Maria, I've missed you so much. I don't think I can go on like this.'

'Shush,' she said, enjoying his patent need. 'You said you'd be good if I met you here.'

'But that was on the end of the telephone,' he murmured, finding her hand and holding it tightly. 'I couldn't see you then. Or smell you. What is it?'

'Givenchy,' she said. 'Hal brought it back for me. It's his favourite. He says it's the only thing he likes me to wear in bed.' It gave her a tiny cruel pleasure to speak lightly about Hal, underlining his rights and privileges. She saw the pain in Keith's eyes and delighted in the power she had over him. For a brief moment she realised that she had given Hal such power, handed him such weapons, yet he had never once consciously used them, never deliberately made her suffer. Maria pushed the thought aside. She liked to inflict these tiny hurts on Keith, to test this power and bask in her new-found strength.

'You said you liked Chanel,' he was saying. 'I've bought you some for Christmas. Promise you'll use it when we're together?'

'I might.' She lifted her cup, eyes sparkling at him over the rim. 'We'll have to see.'

He tried to smile back, to enter into her light-heartedness, but he took a pull at his pint instead to hide his misery and frustration. Taking pity on him she moved closer, snuggling against him, throwing her scruples to the wind; she simply couldn't resist it.

'So tell me how much you've missed me,' she said. 'Every detail. Don't leave anything out.'

Chapter Twenty-three

The market was crowded on this cold, bright Friday morning. Totnes housewives jostled with farmers' wives in from the surrounding villages, and there was the usual sprinkling of the colourful, Bohemian community which had developed alongside the artistic culture of nearby Dartington Hall. Racks of Indian cotton skirts and dresses, hanging alongside the second-hand stalls, bore witness to this influence and, on this chilly morning, a stallholder selling hand-knitted Peruvian jerseys and shawls was doing a brisk trade. Susanna's basket was already full of local produce: delicious bread, crisp vegetables, free-range eggs. She paused by the second-hand bookstall hoping, as usual, for a miracle. Mole had inherited his brother's collection of Kipling's books of which he was very proud. Only one was missing – *Captains Courageous* – and she always hoped that one day she'd come across a copy bound in the same pinky-red cover. She'd only ever seen it as part of a set but she continued to hope. As her eyes scanned the titles of the books set out on the long trestle table, she tried to imagine the brother who had written his name in full – James Peter Chadwick – in each of those books, but her image of him became muddled with her earliest memories of Hal and it was quite impossible to separate them.

She changed the heavy basket into her left hand and reached for an Elizabeth Goudge. It was *The Rosemary Tree*, a book which Caroline took out of the library at regular intervals because it was such a favourite. Susanna had already found her the Eliot trilogy and Caroline had evinced such delight that she felt quite certain that she would be pleased to have this one on her shelf, too. It would make an extra present to go with the hanks of cream Aran wool which had been for sale at half price a few weeks before. Caroline loved knitting and Susanna knew that she was planning warm winter jerseys for the twinnies. She passed over a fifty pence piece, glowing with pleasure at the thought of the pile of goodies mounting up in the bedroom cupboard ready to be packed up in Christmas paper. The market had proved an excellent source for the purchasing of gifts and she'd hardly needed to go elsewhere.

The woman selling pots of hyacinths smiled as Susanna approached and immediately bent to forage amongst her selection, holding up a green bowl with three sturdy plants not yet in flower.

'Blue,' she said triumphantly. 'That's what you wanted, wasn't it, my lover?'

Susanna beamed back at her. 'Blue,' she agreed. 'My grandmother's favourite colour.'

'Keep 'em in the warm for a week and they'll just about be blooming on Christmas Day.' The woman watched, blowing on her cold mittened fingers as Susanna flung back the alpaca poncho to rummage in the purse she wore on a leather thong round her neck.

'My favourite colour's pink,' Susanna told her as she passed over a five-pound note. 'If I've got any money left over I might buy some for myself. The scent is so heavenly. You'll be here next Friday?'

'Christmas Eve.' The woman nodded vigorously as she sorted out her change. 'Us'll be here. Do a good trade on Christmas Eve.'

'I'll keep my fingers crossed that you have some left.'

The woman watched her, carefully carrying her parcels across the High Street, and smiled to herself. Her young man had already been over much earlier and paid for a bowl of pink hyacinths to be brought to the market on Christmas Eve.

'There's simply no place to hide them in our little flat,' he'd said. 'You won't forget, will you?'

She knew him by sight, a nice young man, she'd decided; not handsome or dashing, just nice, anxious that his pretty wife should have her Christmas hyacinths. 'The dear of 'im,' she murmured, and turned to serve another customer as Susanna passed out of sight.

'Goodies!' she announced triumphantly as she came into the studio. 'Grandmother's hyacinths. They've got to be kept in the warm for this next week so that they'll just be flowering for Christmas Day.'

'Airing cupboard,' said Gus promptly, removing his reading spectacles so as to see the bowl of bulbs more clearly. 'It's the warmest place in the whole house.'

'True.' Susanna paused for a quick kiss as she passed through to the tiny kitchen. 'I'll take it all up in a minute. Coffee?'

'You say the nicest things,' murmured Gus. 'Did you remember the Letraset?'

'I did.' He heard the rush of water, the click of the switch and she was back in the doorway, struggling out of her poncho. 'I shall have to pack the presents this weekend. Fliss is coming down with the twinnies on Monday and she's bound to be over. Those twinnies will be into everything. I've bought some smashing paper this morning, really cheap.'

'Isn't Miles coming down?' Gus left his paste-ups and began to search through the contents of the basket for the Letraset. 'Surely Fliss isn't leaving him on his own for Christmas?'

'Course not,' said Susanna scornfully. 'He's coming down by train on Christmas Eve. He can't get away until then and he thinks it best for them to come on ahead when the roads are a bit emptier. They're stopping off in Bristol to pick up Aunt Prue.'

'Are you absolutely certain you don't want to stay at The Keep?' Gus had found the Harberton Art Workshop bag containing the Letraset. 'I know we're going for Christmas Day but won't you miss all the fun of Christmas Eve and all the traditional things? I'm quite happy to go, you know.'

'I know you are.' Susanna sat down in the big Windsor chair that was kept for clients and visitors. She pushed her dark hair behind her ears and drew her feet up onto the chair seat, hugging her knees with arms. 'It's just that I think it's important that we do our own things, too. People talk about traditions but they all have to start somewhere, don't they? You can't hang on to other people's for ever. The Keep has its own traditions now, but if Grandmother had kept going back to her parents then it wouldn't have them, would it? She made her own for her own family and then we came and added to them. I know we haven't got children yet but we've got to make a start somewhere, haven't we?'

He smiled a little at her earnestness as he put the Letraset in its drawer. 'I see exactly what you mean. I suppose I'm just a shade nervous at measuring up to the great Chadwick traditions.'

'It'll be easy.' She grinned at him. 'It'll change a bit when the babies come, of course, but I've been thinking about it and I've got it all planned. We shall go to the market on Christmas Eve morning and listen to the carols and do last-minute shopping. Lunch, then tidy up in here and do all the fiddly little jobs. Have supper at The Kingsbridge Inn and go to the midnight service at St Mary's. Walk home, have hot coffee and mince pies and go to bed in our nice big saggy bed together. When we wake up we'll open our own presents and then we'll go over to The Keep for lunch and the great present-opening tree ceremony at teatime. Back home for a bite of supper. What do you say?'

'It sounds great so far.' Gus couldn't think why he felt strangely weepy. Susanna often had this effect upon him although she was actually a most prosaic person. 'I specially like the bit about our nice big saggy bed.'

'Thought you would.' She beamed happily. 'I like that bit, too. That's settled then. Now, I'll make the coffee and then I'll show you what I've bought.'

'So you have a Christmas tree,' said Kit, taking off her sheepskin coat and picking up Bess to give her a hug. 'I wondered if you would, since you're off to The Keep on Monday. Isn't it pretty? Hello, gorgeous one. Hello, Jamie. Gosh, you've grown.'

She hoisted him into her other arm and they laughed at their mother as they clasped an arm each about Kit's neck.

'You're both much too heavy,' Fliss told them. 'Poor Kit. You'll break her.'

Kit let them slide down and collapsed on to the sofa so that they could scramble up beside her instead.

'What a lot of presents,' she said, eyeing the pile beneath the green, tinsel-laden branches. 'I can see that you won't need mine.'

'These are for the children on the married patch,' Fliss told her. 'We're having our own Christmas here before we go to Devon. Bess and Jamie have lots of friends and they're all coming to a party tomorrow afternoon. It's going to be great fun.'

Kit looked at the twinnies. Bess wore scarlet woollen tights and a jersey under her navy cord pinafore; Jamie was dressed in dungarees. Their faces were bright with the pleasure of seeing her. Jamie shouldered in under her arm, thumb in mouth; Bess kneeled beside her, leaning against her. How lucky Fliss was to have these two moppets to hug and cherish. She swallowed back the tears which had hovered near the surface ever since she'd said a final goodbye to Jake the week before.

He'd looked so drawn and grim she'd hardly recognised him. Even now she could hardly believe that she'd thrown away so much. How could she possibly have had him so close for so long and then lost him? She had been too complacent; so convinced that he would always be there, taking him utterly for granted. She'd hurt him badly with the way she'd behaved with Mark, she knew that now, neglecting Jake for this newer fancy, wondering if he were to be the great love she'd always believed would come along. It was just like those awful fairy stories in which the prince went out searching for his heart's desire which was always back at home . . .

'Would you like your present now?' asked Fliss, hating to see the bleakness in Kit's eyes. 'I was wondering earlier why we shouldn't have our own private Christmas. Just the four of us. There will be so many other presents to open on Christmas Day. Why shouldn't we open just one or two now?'

The twinnies were gazing at her, eyes wide with amazement. They'd been told – on the pain of Father Christmas leaving them off his calling list – that none of the family presents must be touched before Christmas Day, and they were shocked by this subversive suggestion. Jamie took his thumb out of his mouth and they both stared up hopefully at Kit, holding their respective breaths, waiting for her reaction, fearing that she too might be horrified at such heresy.

'It's a great idea.' Kit smiled at Fliss, whilst the twinnies heaved huge sighs of relief. They bounced with excitement, squeaking with glee.

'Hang on,' said Fliss, as they tumbled off the sofa and began to crawl about under the tree. 'Not those presents. We shall only open ours from Kit and she will open hers from us. That's fair, isn't it?'

'Yours are still out in Eppyjay,' said Kit. 'I was going to smuggle them in later so that these two young thugs didn't get their mitts on them.'

'Bring them in while we fetch yours from upstairs. They're on my bed all ready and waiting.' In the hall Fliss took Kit's arm, holding her back whilst the twinnies raced ahead up the stairs. 'Are you OK? Silly question. Of course you aren't. Oh, Kit.'

Kit shook her head. Her heart felt so heavy that she was obliged to let out huge sighs from time to time, otherwise she felt it might simply break from its sheer weighty burden of misery. She bit her lip and Fliss put her arms about her and hugged her tightly.

'I miss him so,' she mumbled into Fliss's shoulder. 'He's always been there. He was a part of me. I feel maimed, wounded. Oh God . . .'

'He was like the dog basket, wasn't he?' murmured Fliss. 'Somewhere to go when you were lonely and frightened and feeling very small.'

She felt the hot tears soaking into her shoulder and prayed that the twinnies wouldn't come back, wondering how she could comfort Kit, knowing that she couldn't.

'Sorry.' Kit raised her head, trying to smile. 'Remember that Christmas when I thought I was pregnant and my period started on Christmas Eve? I cried and cried for joy. Why do I have to be such a fool?'

'You're not a fool,' Fliss said gently. 'You weren't sure, that's all. It's so easy to make a mistake. It was a pity that you met him when you were just starting out and there was so much happening. He became part of the scenery before you were old enough to make a proper judgement.'

Kit blotted at her eyes, blew her nose and turned away as the twinnies appeared at the top of the stairs clutching various brightly coloured packages, chattering excitedly.

'Just a sec,' said Fliss, releasing Kit and running up the stairs. 'Let me see what you've got there . . .'

Kit escaped out into the cold air of Capella Road and unlocked Eppyjay.

'Shall we stay in touch?' she'd asked Jake tremblingly. 'Just . . . just letters now and then?'

He'd held her hands tightly, reaching across the little table in the coffee bar where they'd arranged to meet. She'd been unaware of her surroundings, unable to take in the terrible truth that she might never see him again. The door swung open from the kitchen and the music from the radio became clearer. Roberta Flack was singing 'Killing me Softly with his Song'. At the sound of it scalding tears had slipped from her eyes and he'd lifted her hands, holding them against his mouth.

'Oh, Kit,' he'd said sadly. 'How can we? You know how dangerous it would be.'

'I can't bear it,' she'd gasped. 'I'd no idea how much I needed you, Jake. How can you leave me now?'

'*Please*,' he'd whispered fiercely. 'For God's sake, Kit.'

The waitress had dumped the coffee down, forcing them to draw apart, and Kit had stared round her in the gloom, wiping her eyes.

'Why did we have to meet here?' she'd asked, trying to sound normal. 'It's a dump. I could have come to your flat.'

'Coming to my flat doesn't work any more,' he'd answered grimly. 'We always end up in the same place and it leads on to one more meeting. I'm flying over to Paris tomorrow, Kit.'

She'd stared at him, watching his long-fingered hand holding the spoon, stirring the black liquid round and round and round.

She'd thought: I know now why people talk of dying of a

broken heart. Mine is so heavy it could easily break. If only it would. Whatever is the point of life without him?

'I've got to try,' he'd said. 'You must see that. I made this muddle. It's not Madeleine's fault. She's the victim of our muddle. I owe it to her to give it everything I've got. It would be wrong to try to hold on to you, too. We had our chance and we blew it.'

She'd shut her eyes. It was as though he had struck her, brutally emphasising all that she'd had within her grasp – and lost. She'd picked up her cup and gulped at the hot bitter coffee, burning her mouth.

He'd watched her, seeing her anguish, making up his mind. 'I have something for you,' he said at last, reaching into his jacket.

'You said "no presents".' Her mind had been already leaping to and fro, trying to think what she might give him, wishing she'd brought him some keepsake.

'I can't take anything from you now,' he'd said. 'I want nothing I might have to hide or explain away. Women can be very astute about noticing such things.'

'But you have a whole past behind you.' She'd been unable to hide her pain. 'Are you going to throw away all the presents you've ever had?'

'No,' he'd said impatiently. 'Naturally not. But I have no guilt about anything in my past. It is only from now forwards things must change. Anything you gave me now would be charged with emotion and memories. I couldn't bear it. I know I'm cheating with this but you're not going to be married. Not yet anyway, and then this will belong to your past. It belonged to my mother. She gave it to me on my twenty-first birthday and told me that I should give it to the woman to whom I gave my heart. I remember that she said that this might not be the woman I married and I thought that it was quite a sophisticated viewpoint – for an old-fashioned Englishwoman.' He smiled bleakly. 'I always hoped that it would be my morning gift to you but now I see that she was right . . .'

Now, as she reached into the car, Kit automatically felt for the heavily chased silver locket which she'd worn round her neck from that moment. She held it in her hand for a second before lifting the presents out, relocking the car and going back up the path to the house where the twinnies waited expectantly.

'Binker,' repeated Bess, hugging her teddy tightly. 'Binker and Pudgie. Aren't they funny names, Mummy? It's what she called her pretend friends when she was small like us.'

'Yes,' said Fliss, swallowing back tears as the three of them stood out in the road, waving after Eppyjay. 'Yes, I know.'

At the turning the Morris convertible paused. The twins held up Binker and Pudgie, waving their velvety paws, so that she might see them, and for a moment they saw the silk holly-red scarf, chosen so carefully by all three of them, waved furiously out of the window in response. Fliss discovered that she could no longer see the car properly and she closed her eyes for a moment.

She thought: Oh, Kit. I do love you so much. Please be safe.

She turned away, following the twinnies into the house, clutching the little leather folding case which contained two photographs taken at Susanna's wedding; one of Kit and

Hal, joshing together, and one of Mole and Susanna, smiling out happily at the world.

'I had them done specially for you,' Kit had said as they'd hugged goodbye. 'Your special people. Well, some of them.'

'I love it,' said Fliss. 'It's just perfect. Have a good Christmas, Kit. Love to Sin. And don't forget, I'm always here. Wherever we are, there's a place for you with us.'

'There'd better be. I'm counting on it from now on.' She'd given Fliss one last squeeze before she climbed into the car. 'Happy Christmas, little coz. Happy Christmas, twinnies. Happy New Year. And as darling Uncle Theo would say, God bless us everyone.'

Book Three
Winter 1980

Chapter Twenty-four

Freddy stood at her window, staring down into the court-yard. The January afternoon, misty and dank, was fading into an early dusk as the rain swept in from the west. It pattered against the window, gurgling in the drainpipes and soaking the flagstones so that they gleamed in the light which shone out from the hall below her. She was accustomed now to the gatehouse cottage being in darkness. Three years since Fox had moved over to the house; three years since a friendly light had streamed from the cottage window, an indication that he was pottering about his small domain. Poor Fox; he had only enjoyed his new quarters for one winter, dying before the spring came ... Freddy pressed her thin hand to her breast in an attempt to subdue the pain. Fox gone, Ellen gone, even Perks was gone. It seemed fitting somehow that Mrs Pooter's line should die out with Fox. It was he who had brought home Mrs Pooter as a puppy – to assuage the grief Freddy was suffering at the death of her beloved cairn, Kips – and Mugwump and Perks had followed after her. Now they were all gone. Only she and Theo and Caroline remained, the rest of the family scattered about the country.

With an effort Freddy reached up and drew the curtains against the encroaching dark. This room had always been her private sanctuary and she stood for a moment, looking about her, thanking heaven that at the time The Keep had been built it was quite usual to have fireplaces in the bedrooms. Now that she kept so much to her two rooms it was such a comfort to see the flames leaping in the grate, to hear the crackling and shifting of the coal. She lowered herself into her comfortable armchair, drawing the tartan rug about her legs. Even with the fire burning so cheerfully she was chilled and she felt for the hot-water bottle which Caroline tucked behind the cushions. The bottle was barely warm and she let it drop to the floor. Theo would be here presently and he would refill it from the hot tap in her bathroom.

She remembered how anxiously she had consulted him, years ago, about that bathroom; requiring the assurance that it was not purely a luxurious whim to install a second one on this first floor. How glad she was that he had encouraged her to go ahead. The little suite of rooms was so right for her, now that she was no longer very mobile. Everything was at hand for her comfort; all her treasures about her. In the corner cupboard her special pieces of glass and china, collected down the years, were displayed. The bow-fronted bureau held her papers; a tall glass-fronted bookcase was full of her favourite books; Widgerys hung on the pale walls. Her newest acquisition, however, stood on a low table next to her chair. For Christmas, the children had clubbed together and bought her a most wonderful piece of equipment; it was a radio which not only had a turntable for records but also boasted a cassette player. These new advances of technology were quite extraordinary to her mind and it had taken some time for her to master the technique required to operate its component parts. Now that she was too weak to play her beloved Bechstein this gift was doubly precious, helping to assuage her loss, for the rest of this same present had been a collection of these cassettes. This selection had been carefully chosen and, even now, used as she was to hearing concerts on the Third programme – now called Radio Three for some obscure reason – she was amazed by the clarity and sheer beauty of the recordings of her favourite works. When the pain was intolerable she only had to reach out her hand to be transported to another plane where she might forget her diseased flesh and move beyond this world to glory.

Who can free himself from his meanness and limitations, if you *do not lift him to yourself, my God, in purity of love?*

These words, now so familiar to her, had become important although she did not quite understand why. The paper had fallen, one day, from Theo's Bible, and she had picked it up intending to return it to him. She had never done so. Gradually these lines written in Theo's small clear hand had imprinted themselves in her mind, bringing a kind of comfort. She knew that during her life she had rarely attempted to free herself from meanness and limitation; she had liked to be in control and was, certainly where Theo was concerned, frequently jealous. Music, however, always had the power to free her, releasing her from the world of small horizons, raising her to that other, different plane.

How will a person
brought to birth and nurtured in a world of small horizons,
rise up to you Lord,
if you do not raise him by your hand which made him?

With an effort, Freddy leaned to press the catch on the radio – she still referred to it as a wireless – which would expel the cassette. At this moment, she had neither the strength nor the will to choose a different one. This one, already to hand, must do. She reversed it, pushed it into place and clicked the 'play' button. It was Barenboim playing Beethoven. The dramatic introductory *Grave* of the *Pathétique* had the power to relax her and she sank back against the cushions, breathing deeply, willing down the pain. As the music took hold of her she allowed her mind to open up, letting images come and go, entering into a kind of meditation. It was only lately that she had been able to achieve this state of quiet grace. She did not quite understand it but was grateful for its peace, holding the words of the prayer faintly in her consciousness.

so I shall rejoice:
you will not delay, if I do not fail to hope.

As the effect of the pills, swallowed earlier, eased her, subduing the pain, Freddy breathed more deeply. The rain streamed down the window, dripping from the sturdy branches of the wisteria, puddling in the irregular hollows of the flagstones; the coals rustled, falling together, settling to feathery, ashy embers in the grate. The music filled the room, sustaining her, enfolding her, and presently she slept.

★ ★ ★

In the kitchen, Caroline put aside her knitting and glanced at her watch. Lately, since Mrs Chadwick rarely moved from her rooms, meals had become rather patchy affairs. The tiny amounts which she picked at were carried up to her on a tray and, since she now preferred to struggle with the exhausting business of eating unobserved, Theo had begun to eat in the kitchen. Caroline was glad of his company. With Fox gone there was a subtle difference in the atmosphere. The kitchen quarters seemed larger and emptier without his presence and she'd begun to feel lonely for the first time since she'd arrived at The Keep. Slowly she had become accustomed to being without him; no Fox in the rocking chair by the Aga, no Fox with whom to watch the television, no Fox to share with her in the progress and achievements – and disasters – of the family. When Perks died only days after Fox's funeral, it did indeed seem as if a whole part of her life had come to an end. It had been difficult enough to lose Ellen but after Fox's death her usual common sense had deserted her and the future had seemed bleak indeed without her old friend's gentle, undemanding company, his humour and his courage. She'd been grateful that Susanna and Gus lived near at hand. They had comforted and encouraged her, mourned with her and reminisced with her, until she was able to pick up the pieces again and carry on with her tasks. Now, three years on, the loss was easier to bear but she often looked back longingly to those early happy days when she'd first arrived at The Keep nearly twenty-five years before.

Caroline thought: It was twenty-two years ago last summer. Twenty-two years . . . After a moment she took Fliss's letter from the various papers scattered on the kitchen table and re-read it. For the last eighteen months Miles had been the Commanding Officer at HMS *Royal Arthur* in Corsham but now there was a talk of a NATO posting, and Fliss was anxious at the thought of leaving the country whilst her grandmother was so near the end of her life.

'. . . *I thought we might come down for the twinnies' birthday,*' she'd written. '*Luckily it's a weekend, so no school. Miles can't get away but is quite happy for us to come. Let me know if it would be too much for you . . .*'

There was no question of that. The twinnies knew that they must be quiet when they were near their great-grandmother's rooms and Fliss was always such a tower of strength. It would be lovely to see them all, to have some company. Prue had been down for Christmas, staying over the New Year and into January, and The Keep seemed so strange and quiet once she'd gone back to Bristol. The silly thing was that she had no desire to go back to her empty little mews house, it was simply that she felt that she was outstaying her welcome.

'I've never been Freddy's favourite person,' she'd said to Caroline, 'and she's always been just the least bit cross with Theo for bailing me out so many times. I'd hate her to think I'm taking advantage of her now, muscling in when she hasn't got the strength to throw me out. She's so thin, isn't she? The pain must be awful but she's so brave . . .'

Caroline had attempted to reason with Prue, to tell her that it wasn't like that, but Prue held firm. Strict and formal though she might be, her mother-in-law had always played fair with her and she was determined not to cause her any twinge of irritation now that she was helpless and weak. She'd promised to come back again soon – or at any time she was needed – but she'd stuck to her guns. They'd hugged goodbye on Totnes station, closer than they'd ever been after those two weeks, both feeling better for the shared friendship. They'd had lots of chuckles together, despite the sombre atmosphere of the house, sympathising over the horrors of middle age, reminiscing about the past. They'd gone shopping in Totnes, walked round the gardens at Dartington, had coffee in the Royal Castle at Dartmouth.

'Imagine,' Prue had said suddenly that morning, as they'd approached the car parked by the boatfloat. 'We've known each other for thirty-five years,' and they'd stared at each other, awestruck, across the roof of the car.

Picking up her knitting again, Caroline wondered where those years had gone. They had been busy, happy years but how was it possible that so great a span of time should pass so quickly? Yet she felt content, grateful that she'd been in the right place at the right time for her own transitory passage through life; unworried by regrets. She knew that she was one of the lucky ones but it occurred to her to wonder how it might be in the future. It would be a natural progression for Hal to become master at The Keep. She knew that Fliss would continue to move with Miles and she couldn't quite see Susanna and Gus *in situ*. No, it seemed much more likely that Maria would move here with the boys, and Hal would hope for postings to Devonport, meanwhile weekending whenever possible. Caroline knew that this was what his grandmother had always envisaged although she thought that it was rather early for Maria and the children to settle down, leaving Hal to live in the Mess when the ship was alongside. The boys needed their father around . . .

Theo's entry disturbed these musings and she smiled at him, delighted to see him, putting her knitting to one side. These days she found herself scrutinising him closely lest he, too, should be showing signs of some inward disorder, but he looked as usual and his presence calmed her. It wasn't that he was unmoved or indifferent to pain or suffering but he had the detachment of one who looks beyond these things; who sees the possibilities for growth contained within them.

'She is quite warm and comfortable,' he said, sitting down opposite. 'She thinks she might rest for a while. I've made up the fire and refilled her hot-water bottle.'

'Her wortle.' Caroline laughed as she tidied away her knitting into the large tapestry bag. 'It was Jamie who was responsible for that one. He could never get his tongue round "hot-water bottle". He got as far as "wortle botter" and then gave up. It's odd, isn't it, how these words filter into a family's vocabulary?'

'It's rather nice,' said Theo, 'although I imagine that it might be irritating for outsiders. Do I see a letter from Fliss?'

'You do indeed. She's coming down next weekend. Isn't that good news? It's the twinnies' birthday so it's extra nice.' She hesitated. 'There's no reason why she shouldn't come, is there?'

'None that I can see,' he answered at once. 'It will do us all good to see them. How is she?'

'Read it.' Caroline pushed the sheets towards him. 'Apparently Miles won't be coming . . .'

She fell silent as Theo began to read, moving about the kitchen, preparing the supper which they would presently share. It was months since Theo abandoned the formal evening meal, sitting solitarily in the breakfast room, and now they dined lightly on soup or eggs in the kitchen. At bedtime she made them a hot drink which they had with biscuits or a piece of cake each. Now that Freddy no longer played the piano after dinner the drawing-room fire was rarely lit, and Caroline had got into the habit of keeping the hall fire made up. It was cosier to sit there during the evening than to move into a chilly room simply because of habit and, though she might have felt a little out of place in the drawing room, she was quite comfortable sitting in the hall with Theo.

'I see she writes about a foreign posting.' Theo folded the sheets and put them back into the envelope. 'She doesn't seem to be looking forward to the idea.'

'The last time we spoke she told me that Miles was suggesting that the twinnies should be sent off to boarding school if the posting comes off.' Caroline pushed the pan of soup on to the hotplate and gave the contents a stir. 'Fliss isn't at all happy about that. They are only seven next weekend and she feels that it's far too young to send them off, especially if she and Miles are going to be out of the country. I must say that I agree with her but I think she may have a bit of a battle on her hands.'

'Is there any real reason why the twinnies shouldn't accompany them abroad?'

Caroline shrugged. 'I don't think so. Schooling might prove a bit of a problem but Fliss says there are usually English-speaking schools, and she feels that it would be quite an education for them. She's also worried about Mrs Chadwick, of course.'

Theo was silent. Caroline put some rolls to warm in the oven and went to fetch the cheese. Neither of them was prepared to discuss this subject although they both knew that the end could be only a matter of a few months away.

'What a blessing music is to her.' Theo suppressed a sigh, watching Caroline as she set out plates and knives and spoons. The knowledge that he would never hear Freddy play again filled him with a terrible sense of loss. 'What a miracle it is. To hear such wonderful quality of playing merely by pressing a button or two. We take so much for granted in this modern age.'

Caroline's mind was running on ahead, planning for the weekend. They would give a little party for the twinnies and she would ask Gus and Susanna to come over. It might distract them all from their present anxiety – yet it seemed so heartless to be thinking of birthday parties when Mrs Chadwick was so ill. She frowned, feeling guilty and confused . . . Theo was smiling at her.

' "*To every thing there is a season, and a time to every purpose under the heavens:*" ' he quoted. ' "*A time to be born and a time to die; . . . A time to weep, and a time to laugh; a time to mourn, and a time to dance;*". The twinnies' birthday should be a time for laughter.'

Caroline smiled back at him gratefully. 'I'll make a list,' she said. 'And we'll have to think about presents. Perhaps I'll have a word with Fliss first. After supper I'll get down to it . . .'

Chapter Twenty-five

Fliss, setting out from Corsham, was struggling with mixed emotions. She was trying to decide why, when on the few occasions she was the victor of a battle of wills, she rarely felt a sense of triumph. Instead she was a prey to doubt and guilt, and knew an overwhelming and pathetic urge to back down and apologise. It really was irritating that Miles was generally right on a moral front – but that still left many grey areas which, though open to debate, were fraught with danger.

Although he had been perfectly happy for Fliss to take the twinnies down to Devon for the weekend, he was absolutely against the suggestion that they should be allowed to take the Friday off school.

'It makes travelling so much easier,' she'd explained – almost pleaded. 'Saturday is such a busy day for local traffic.'

'If you would only drive across to Bristol and join the M5,' he'd said impatiently, 'you'd have no problem. It will be practically empty. You will insist on going on the old roads.'

'I like the old roads,' she'd answered stubbornly. 'Much

nicer than those horrid motorways, and we can go to the little cafés we know, like the one in Honiton.'

He'd shaken his head, as if unable to accept or understand such foolishness. 'I don't like the children missing school. You know that. There's no good reason for it and it sets precedents. They will grow up believing that they can do as they please. It's bad for discipline, surely you can see that? You were a teacher yourself, for goodness' sake.'

'They're not even seven years old yet,' she'd protested. 'And Miss Andrews is quite happy about it.'

'You're missing the point,' Miles had said dismissively. 'I'm not interested in what Miss Andrews is prepared to allow. You know very well that you can twist her round your little finger just because you go in to help out whenever there's a problem. The children are preparing for boarding school and they'll find it a very different proposition to a small village school. They will be expected to be part of a team, to develop a sense of responsibility. If you allow them to think that they can be granted privileges for something as unimportant as a birthday they'll find it that much more difficult when they go to prep school. You went away to school so you should know that they'll be exposed to a stringent discipline.'

It was when he became so didactic that she found it difficult to see the familiar Miles; found it impossible to appeal to the human, kindly side of his character.

'It's just this once,' she'd said, trying not to sound as if she were wheedling. 'I discussed it with Miss Andrews who agreed that they would be missing nothing important. And, after all, it's not just the travelling. I want them to spend some time with grandmother before she becomes—'

She had bit her lip, frowning, but Miles had given a short laugh and shrugged helplessly.

'My dear Fliss, that's no sort of argument, is it? Taken to its logical conclusion it means that the children would be off school until your grandmother dies.'

He'd seen her face, then, and immediately tried to make amends; taking her in his arms, attempting comfort. She hadn't rejected him, although part of her longed to push him away. She hated – no, it was not too strong a word – she *hated* the insensitivity which sometimes clouded his whole personality. As he grew older it was a trait which seemed to be growing and she felt afraid. She knew that he was impatient for Bess and Jamie – he never referred to them as the twinnies – to go off to school; knew that he thought that he and Fliss would be able to re-enter the private world they'd shared before the children were born. Her fear was that it already might be too late. It was as if he had put their own life together on hold whilst the twinnies grew up and she sometimes felt that she was living with a stranger.

'But they're barely seven years old,' she'd said persuasively, taking advantage of his gentler mood, returning his embrace, 'and they won't be going away for a few years yet. Eleven is a good age for Herongate. It's not the usual run of prep school, as you know. All that sailing on the lake and the drama and music. Eleven will be quite soon enough. Taking a day off school won't ruin their characters, I'm sure.'

She'd known that she was risking another confrontation. Miles had hinted very strongly that, should he be offered a foreign posting, it would be sensible to send the twinnies off to school. At present he had not come right out into the open but she had already made her position clear: she was not prepared to go abroad without them whilst they were still so young. Fliss knew that Miles was biding his time, waiting for confirmation of the post.

'It's your decision,' he'd said heavily, releasing her and turning away. 'You know my views.'

She'd gone on with her preparations cheerfully, as though she were unaware of his weighty disapproval, packing clothes, putting the presents into the back of the estate car and covering them with old blankets. Having learned to ride Fliss's old bicycle at The Keep, the twinnies were being given their own new ones.

'They could have them early,' Fliss had suggested, hoping to thaw the frost a little. 'Wouldn't you like to see their faces when they realise what we've bought them?'

Miles had smiled at her. 'I think they're having quite enough rules bent for them as it is,' he'd said, 'without getting their presents early. I expect I'll manage to live without the excitement of it.'

He'd seen the disappointment in her eyes and had patted her shoulder.

'Come on, darling,' he'd said gently. 'Can't have it both ways. I don't mind you going down to Devon for the children's birthday, you know I don't, so you mustn't get upset if I'm not bothered about seeing them open their presents.'

'Surely it wouldn't hurt,' she'd begun – but seeing the irritation rise she'd backed off. No doubt the idea of the twinnies having two birthday celebrations would be another dereliction of discipline.

Now, as she drove towards Honiton, her spirits began to

rise a little. She'd made the decision and stuck to it; no point in souring the occasion with guilt. To begin with it had seemed such a good plan; an attempt to alleviate the desolation of her grandmother's dying with the acknowledgement that there was the promise of the future in the shape of Bess and Jamie. Celebrating their birthday at The Keep with their grandmother had, at the time, seemed an important, positive thing to do. Briefly, Miles had shaken her belief but as she drew closer to her old home her confidence began to re-assert itself.

She looked in the driving mirror, seeing the two blond heads close together, smiling as she listened to them singing through their repertoire. Their small voices rose together and she began to sing with them.

'I had a dog and the dog pleased me,
I fed my dog by yonder tree.
Dog goes Bow-wow, Cat goes fiddle-I-fee.'

Rather later on the same day, Susanna was riding her old, sit-up-and-beg bicycle out of Totnes. Once through Dartington she turned off the road and bumped along a cart track which led to the partially converted barn that stood at the end of it. It was quite a big L-shaped building, although only one storey high, standing end-on to the road and looking across the fields to the hills beyond. The roof was newly slated but the window frames and doors, reclaimed from dumps and second-hand shops, gave the old stone building a mellow look. Susanna leaned her bike against the wall and, taking a key from her pocket, opened one of the two big central doors which led into the long part of the L.

She stood quite still for a moment, looking about her. The hollow shell was full of light. The original high-vaulted roof beams were exposed and the huge opening at the west end had made the perfect opportunity for a picture window. The shorter leg of the L contained the bedrooms, a bathroom and a lavatory, and a utility room with an outside door. The rest of the building was one enormous living space. Gus had nicknamed it the atrium and they had ignored the gloomy warnings of those who said that it was too large to heat, that they would regret not having separate rooms, that cooking smells would fill the whole area. Gus and Susanna listened politely, agreed with everything and continued with their own plans.

The kitchen was situated at the bedroom end and already contained an oil-fired Esse range, some built-in cupboards, the Welsh dresser, which had been such a bargain, and other essentials, including a long quarry-tiled working surface whose high carved wooden back – an abandoned rood screen from a derelict church – would divide the kitchen from the atrium.

The central area was to be the busy, active living space. An enormous refectory table flanked by various sizes and shapes of chairs, unearthed gradually during the last two years, would stand between the two big, partially glazed doors and the long back windows which looked north. A deep, comfortable four-seater sofa would be set beneath these windows on a raised step so that it was possible to see through the long panes of the upper part of the front doors whilst actually sitting down. At the west end the floor level was already raised and three long, shallow steps led up to the snug. A fireplace with a brass hood had been built into the wall and a fire basket already stood on the big slate square beneath it. Armchairs would be placed here, alongside shelves for books and music, and clever lighting would make it cosy and intimate.

As she stared into the huge light shell, Susanna could visualise it quite clearly. She knew exactly where each lovingly restored piece, at present carefully stored in the gatehouse at The Keep, would stand. She imagined the long, rich blue, heavy velvet curtains, made with Caroline's help on the old Singer sewing machine in the nursery along with the striped ticking cover for the sofa, and could almost feel the warmth of the log fire. Leaving the door open behind her, she wandered around the atrium. Bars of sunlight lay across the wooden floor which would presently be covered with warm, thick rugs, and she paused at the west window to look out to the moors, indigo and purple and gold, as the cloud shadows raced across the craggy slopes.

It was odd that she'd needed to come here when the news was confirmed; that she felt that this was the place in which she now belonged. She'd always thought that she'd hate to leave the flat where she and Gus had been so happy but during those joyful years their plans and dreams for this place had slowly become a reality and she was quite ready now for the move. After all, it was not as though they were leaving the flat. They were continuing to rent it along with the studio and had various ideas for extending the business. She would still want to sit on the steps in the courtyard, smelling the honeysuckle and watching the birds on the table which Fox had so painstakingly built . . .

Susanna moved back from the long wide window, folding her arms beneath her breast. How terrible and cruel life could be. Ellen and Fox gone and now Grandmother was dying. She moved to the edge of the snug and sat down on the top of the shallow steps. Grandmother was dying and would not see the baby which she carried within her. For the first time she realised how important it was that her grandmother should know her, Susanna's, baby. That her child should grow up without that tremendous sustaining love was a sudden, terrible shock. Whom did she know who could possibly replace her? For the first time in twenty-three years Susanna yearned for her unknown mother; how wonderful it would be to share this tremendous news with her. How would she have reacted? Susanna, closed her eyes, straining to remember something, anything, about her long-dead mother. Her mind remained empty. Of course, there was Gus's mother, but she already had numerous grandchildren and, although she would be delighted at the news of the baby, it wouldn't quite be the same.

She could understand now a little of what Fliss must have felt when she'd discovered that she would have to give birth to her first baby out in Hong Kong, so far from home. She'd had Miles with her but even so . . .

Susanna thought: She must have been so lonely. At least I shall have her with me. And Caroline and Uncle Theo.

She'd taken so much for granted during those careless, happy years of childhood. How could she be certain that she would be able to give her own child such emotional security? Memories came flooding back; games in the orchard with Mole; walks on the hill with Fox; trips to the beach and to the moors with Caroline; tea in the hall with Ellen's delicious scones; her grandmother reading to her at bedtime, listening to her prayers, kissing her goodnight . . .

Susanna bent her head until her forehead touched her knees.

'Don't die,' she begged. 'Please don't die.'

She didn't hear the car's engine and Gus was already in the doorway before she realised that he'd arrived.

'What is it?' He was kneeling beside her, his face tense with alarm. 'Is it . . .? Are you . . .?'

'We're pregnant,' she told him, tears still streaming down her cheeks. 'Nearly two months, she thinks. But it won't be in time . . .'

She stared at him, eyes tragic, mouth trembling, and he gathered her into his arms, understanding at once.

'But she'll know anyway,' he murmured. 'You know that, Sooz. She'll still be around, with Ellen and Fox. Closer than you could be to her now.'

'I sort of know it.' Susanna scrubbed at her face. 'But it's not the *same*. I want to *see* her seeing my baby.'

'We don't absolutely know that she won't,' he told her comfortingly. 'Shall we wait and see? Let's not start like this, Sooz. Let's be happy about it. It's so fantastic. Listen.' He sat beside her, an arm about her, and looked around. 'I've got an idea about how she can see all this at least. I know she's too frail to come out here but we can do her a drawing like the one we did of The Keep so she can see where everything will be.'

'Oh yes.' Susanna sat up straighter. 'Oh, Gus, that would be great. Let's do it today and take it over later when Fliss has arrived and tell them all the news.'

'Come on, then.' He stood up and pulled her to her feet. 'Goodness, your hands are freezing. Too cold for cycling. We'll have to put the bike in the woodshed and collect it later. Oh, Sooz, isn't it just amazing?'

She grinned at him, lips pressed tightly together, and he grabbed her and they hugged furiously before going out together into the sunshine, locking the door behind them.

Chapter Twenty-six

Hal straightened his back and stared up at the sky. There was a new sharpness in the fitful gusts of wind. In the tall surrounding hedge the laurel leaves shivered and a blackbird's stuttering cry broke the silence as it swooped low across the damp lawn.

Rex, who had been foraging at the far end of the garden in the shrubbery, gave up his search and returned, tongue lolling, tail wagging. He lived in eternal expectation of catching one of the squirrels which swung in the branches of the trees and scampered over the lawn.

'A triumph of hope over experience, old chap,' murmured Hal, shrugging himself into his jersey. He was cold now that he'd finished chopping the firewood but he viewed his efforts with satisfaction. A good pile of kindling was ready to be stacked and the wheelbarrow was full of logs with which to fill the two big baskets. Away in London at staff college all week, he made certain each weekend that Maria and the boys should not be cold. She'd refused to consider the possibility of living in London and had decided to remain here in the same house, continuing to rent it for another two years, so Hal drove himself to Greenwich each

Monday morning and returned each Friday evening in the MG which had replaced his Sprite.

As he began to tidy the sticks of kindling into a pile, Hal wondered if he'd been right in agreeing to let them all stay in Hampshire knowing, as he did then, that she'd been having some kind of a relationship with Keith Graves. He would never have believed it if he hadn't come home unexpectedly – the ship had sailed, discovered an engine fault and put straight back into harbour – and found them in the kitchen together. Their expressions, the silence, the tension, all these things had told him just as much as if they'd been upstairs in bed. It had been an ugly little scene. Graves had blustered, defending himself by accusing; his accusations were ludicrous. Whilst he had charged Hal with neglect, womanising, indifference and selfishness, Hal had leaned against the sink, arms folded, ankles crossed, watching Maria. Her face had flamed beneath his steady watchful stare, hardening from embarrassment and humiliation into a stony sullenness. He'd seen quite clearly the emotions which assailed her; he knew she was deciding which way to jump. Should she ally herself with Graves or appeal to her husband's loyalty?

When Graves had run out of breath, Hal had stirred, standing upright. He'd been ashamed that he was pleased to find that he overtopped him by several inches.

'If you've quite finished,' he'd said coolly, 'I should be pleased if you'd leave me alone with my wife.'

Graves had looked pleadingly at Maria, spoken her name, begged her to leave with him. Maria had remained unresponsive, back turned, head averted, picking at a garment which lay on the working surface.

'Please, my darling,' he'd entreated. 'For God's sake, after all you've said . . .'

'Get out.' Hal had taken him by the shoulder, whirled him round, opened the back door and thrust him through it. He'd shut the door and turned to look at his wife. It was odd that the sensation uppermost in his mind was one of pity. He'd known instinctively that Graves had not been her lover, knew that it was not in Maria's character to be either promiscuous or even simply generous. He'd thought that he could now understand her recent touchiness and he'd felt an overwhelming sadness. Knowing of her frustration at being denied The Keep, of her inadequacies as a naval wife, of her jealousy and loneliness, it was not terribly surprising that she'd reacted in this way to the first man who had fallen in love with her.

'Where are the boys?' His question had had the effect of shaming her further, implying failure as a mother.

'Jolyon's with a friend. Edward's upstairs having his sleep.' It was hateful that he might think that she was entertaining her lover whilst her baby slept upstairs. 'It's not how you think,' she'd muttered.

'I hope it's exactly how I think,' he'd said easily. 'Graves looks a bit of a wanker, if you ask me. Must have been one hell of a boost to his morale to come here and have your company. Get out of hand, did it?'

He'd seen her swallow and had guessed at her dilemma. Part of her longed to attack his confidence and arouse his jealousy by admitting her temptation to Graves's proposals; part of her knew that she was being offered an honourable way out. His certainty that she had not been unfaithful was almost insulting but he had no intention of degrading either of them with uncivilised scenes.

He'd waited. She'd bitten her lips, fingers busy shredding and pulling at the small garment, shoulders hunched, unable to respond. Fearing an impasse, Hal had willed her to turn round. He had not wished to get up and go to her, to force her physically to answer or look at him. The silence lengthened.

'Perhaps I've got it wrong,' he'd said at last. 'Perhaps it's arrogant of me to imagine that you're not having an affair with him. Perhaps you'd like to go with him . . .?'

The telephone had shrilled into life, making Maria jump, demanding attention.

'Maybe that's him.' Hal hadn't moved. 'Better make up your mind, hadn't you?'

She'd looked at him then, a question in her eyes, and he'd shrugged, opening his hands wide, letting them fall, showing a hint of indifference.

'It wasn't my fault,' she'd said rapidly. 'He kept coming round. I felt sorry for him at first . . . I don't want to speak to him . . .'

Suddenly she'd burst into a fit of violent weeping and Hal had stood up and gone out. When he'd returned she was wiping away her tears with a tea towel and she'd looked at him fearfully.

'It was the ship. We're sailing this evening at twenty hundred hours,' he'd said unemotionally. 'Do we put this right or don't we? Your choice.'

She'd rushed at him then, twining her arms about him, bursting into tears again and he'd held her tightly, comforting her . . .

Hal finished tying the kindling into bundles and put them on top of the logs in the barrow. Rex had found a ragged piece of wood and was chewing at it.

'Drop it, you wretch, you'll get splinters in your tongue.'
Hal made a grab at it and Rex, delighted by the attention,
raced off round the lawn, ears flapping wildly. Mud flew up
about his paws as he skidded to a halt and Hal began to
laugh despite himself. Maria would be cross if Rex got too
muddy and the poor animal would be relegated to the
garage for yet another afternoon.

There had been a honeymoon period after the Graves
affair, helped by the fact that his house had almost
immediately sold and he'd been obliged to move away, but
gradually the old insecurities and tensions crept back and
poor old Rex was usually the chief offender. He'd become
the scapegoat and, just lately, Hal's temper had been
wearing rather thin because of it. The fact that there were
golden hairs everywhere – especially during the moulting
season – that his soft mouth made dribble marks on
clothes, that his feet were invariably muddy, that he made
a mess at his drinking bowl, all these sins were continually
weighed against him. The boys were almost afraid to
touch him lest they made him excited or triggered some
misdemeanour which brought down a new tirade upon his
luckless head – and theirs.

Hal thought: I should have been firmer at the beginning
and refused to have a dog at all. I knew it wouldn't work.

His amusement at Rex's antics shifted to a faint depression. He'd better get the wood in, clear up any mess and
then clean Rex before he could make the kitchen floor dirty.
Hal put away the axe and wheeled the barrow round to the
side door where the log baskets were waiting. It was Jolyon
who defeated his good intentions. Coming to find his father,
he left the kitchen door ajar and Rex sneaked inside,

wandered about for a bit and then shouldered through the door into the hall. Maria found him curled up on the rug before the fire in the sitting room.

Her shouts summoned Hal, who had filled the log baskets and was just putting the kindling away in the big hall cupboard.

'Out! I said out, you bloody animal. Just *look* at the carpet. There's mud everywhere. Who left the door open?'

Hal went swiftly through to the kitchen. Jolyon cowered white-faced by the table whilst Maria dragged Rex by his collar to the door which connected into the garage.

'What the hell . . .?'

'I *told* you not to let him in!' Her face was fierce with anger as she glared at him. 'The bloody animal's got mud everywhere. As if I haven't got enough to do. The back door was wide open.'

Hal glanced at his small son, who turned and, folding his arms on the edge of the table, buried his face in them. The brief glimpse of his expression of unhappy fear made a deep impression on Hal. His heart ached with pain for his son's misery and he felt anger building inside him. Yelping, Rex was pushed and kicked bodily into the garage and Maria slammed the door upon him. Red-faced, breathing quickly, she looked defiantly at Hal.

'Someone's got to discipline him,' she said, 'but I know that I can't rely on you to do it. I've told you that I simply cannot cope with him but you do nothing.'

'You're quite right. But don't worry. I shall deal with him now.'

He knew that the weekend was going to be a washout, another tiny failure, and he was determined to act, to make a gesture, to break the mould of the on-going defeatism which was beginning to ruin their lives and was making his son unhappy. He began to wash his hands with quick sharp movements, holding them under the tap, scraping them dry on the towel.

'What are you going to do?' She watched him warily.

'I'm going to take him down to The Keep. Caroline will look after him,' he crouched beside Jolyon, holding him by the shoulders, smiling at him. 'He'll be quite safe down there and Mummy won't be worried about him any more. You'll see him when we go down to visit Grandmother and Uncle Theo. OK?'

Jolyon nodded, relieved but miserable too. He loved Rex and would miss him terribly but the anger and shoutings were frightening.

'What are you talking about?' Maria was standing above them, hands on hips. 'You can't mean that you're going *now*?'

'Yes.' Hal stood upright. 'Now. Let's deal with this once and for all, shall we?'

'And what about our weekend? I suppose it doesn't mean too much to you that we shall miss our weekend together? I've been on my own all week, remember.'

Hal's jaws clenched, his hands balling into fists. Jolyon moved beside his leg, his small hand reaching for his father's, and Hal relaxed.

'That's too bad, I'm afraid,' he said lightly. 'Best to get it over with so that no more weekends are ruined.' He bent down and touched Jolyon's cheek. 'Like to come, too?' he asked.

The child's face brightened but Maria was too quick for him.

'Of course he can't come,' she said scornfully. 'It's far too late to set out for Devon. No one will be ready for you and the house will be freezing. Try to remember that your grandmother is dying. It's no place for a small child. Don't be so damned selfish.'

The brightness died out of Jolyon's face, fear and anxiety returning. Hal swallowed down his anger, and, picking Jolyon up, he swung him round and gave him a hug.

'Come and talk to me while I get changed,' he said cheerfully. 'I'm all over sawdust' – and they left the kitchen together, leaving Maria seething with fury, mopping the floor.

A short while later Hal returned carrying an overnight bag.

'The boys are watching *Sesame Street*,' he said. 'I'm off. I'll telephone to let you know I've arrived.'

She stared at him unbelievingly. 'You're not serious.'

'Quite serious. I shouldn't have let it go on so long. You'll have to manage with my car, I'm afraid, but I should be back tomorrow afternoon. Don't let Jolyon worry, that's all. I've explained it all carefully and he understands. Just try to keep your temper under control. See you tomorrow.'

He kissed her unresponsive cheek and went out into the cold air, shutting the back door behind him. When he swung open the garage door Rex came tearing out, barking with relief and excitement, and Hal bent to pat him. He backed the car on to the gravel turning circle and climbed out again to pile tins of dog food on to the back seat. He put in the big feeding bowl and bottle of water and, lastly, he flung Rex's bed into the back of the car, watched Rex jump in after it. Then Hal shut the tailgate, climbed back in, settled himself in his seat and drove down the drive and out of the gate.

★ ★ ★

It was dark when he arrived at The Keep but the lights shone out of the hall windows and, as he switched off the engine and climbed out, the door opened and Fliss came down the steps to meet him. He held out his arms and she went into them, slipping her arms around his waist, resting her cheek against his chest.

'Sorry about the telephone call,' he said, 'I must have sounded quite demented. Is it going to be OK?'

'Perfectly OK.'

She leaned back a little so that she could look up at him and it seemed quite natural for him to stoop his head to kiss her. Presently he released her, looking about, still holding her hand.

'Where is everyone?'

'In the hall. The twinnies wanted to come out to see you and Rex but they know they mustn't disturb Grandmother.' She indicated the curtained windows on the first floor. 'She's resting but she knows that you're coming. She's a bit muddled. Thinks it was all arranged and it's all tied up with the twinnies' birthday. I thought it was best to leave it like that.'

Hal grimaced. 'I was probably just a touch high-handed,' he admitted.

'Just a touch,' agreed Fliss, grinning at him. 'But why change the habits of a lifetime?'

He laughed and went to let Rex out. Fliss stroked him, pulling gently at his ears, murmuring to him.

'Will Caroline be able to cope?' asked Hal anxiously. His confidence had diminished somewhat during the long trip. 'Am I being selfish?'

283

'She's thrilled to bits,' Fliss assured him. 'He's just what she needs at the moment. It's a bit lonely for her, you know. Uncle Theo spends so much time with Grandmother, and she still misses Fox and Perks. She says that the kitchen is all wrong without a dog and, let's face it, there's so much space for him here. He won't be any trouble and I can't see Caroline throwing a fit even if he does get his paws muddy. I've told her that we'll have him if there's a real problem. My twinnies would die with joy but Miles wouldn't be too pleased.'

There was a tiny silence whilst Rex sniffed about and then lifted his leg against the gatepost. Both of them could sense the danger; the temptation to draw together as a relief from difficult spouses.

'Let's take him in and introduce him to his new home,' said Fliss quickly – and she crossed the courtyard, calling softly to Rex.

Hal took his bag from the car and, as he followed her into the house, the first flakes of snow began to fall.

Chapter Twenty-seven

The room was filled with a strange luminosity; a ghostly white glow which lent it a dreamlike unfamiliar quality. Jamie pushed himself up on his elbows, the better to check this phenomenon, and suddenly guessed the reason for it.

'Snow,' he murmured. 'So it did settle. Brill.'

He leaned out from his berth on the top of the bunk beds and peered down at Bess, who lay below huddled beneath her quilt and several extra blankets. She seemed so deeply asleep that it was a pity to waken her, even for the excitement of snow. He hung upside down for a minute or two, remembering their birthday. It had been a terrific day. The bicycles had been a wonderful surprise and they'd spent the morning practising on them, round and round the courtyard so that Great-grandmother could watch them from her window. When lunch was over they'd gone up to see her and showed her their other presents but after a while she'd fallen asleep. Then Uncle Theo had come downstairs with them and they'd all played Cluedo until teatime. Hal and Rex arrived not long after their birthday tea party and Hal had to be given some birthday cake; then Rex had to be settled in, by which time it was really snowing, and with so much happening they'd gone to bed much later than usual. Remembering all this, it seemed only fair to let Bess catch up on her sleep. Jamie rolled back into the bunk, dragging his covers up to his chin. His foot touched his wortle and he drew it back quickly from the cold clammy bottle, pulling his knees up, hugging them under the weight of the blankets.

He lay quiet, thinking about things, sifting remarks and filing away his own observations into his memory. He needed to do this. It helped him to get his bearings and supplied the framework to a picture in which he had his own special position. The Keep especially had this effect on him. People and places had to be connected, events put into their proper sequence. Then there were the small day-to-day happenings to be considered; things like the look on Uncle Theo's face when Great-grandmother had fallen asleep in her chair. It was a mixture of things which he had difficulty in sorting out and filing away. Kindness was one of the things but there was more than that. He'd looked a bit like Bess when she wrapped up her Cabbage Patch baby and put her in the little cot and sang to her. Jamie squeezed his eyes shut, trying to think of words that stood for expressions. Gentle was another word which might fit Uncle Theo's look but he knew, deep down, that there was so much more to it than that. Understanding grown-ups' expressions was like playing a game when you didn't know the rules. Quite suddenly he began to chuckle, burying his head under the blankets, remembering Uncle Theo playing Cluedo. They'd had to keep explaining the rules to him and, in the end, he and Bess had cheated so that Uncle Theo could win just one game. Mummy had known and she'd smiled secretly . . .

He stopped laughing and began to frown, thinking about the expression on Mummy's face when she'd come back from the telephone and told them that Hal was on his way with Rex. She'd had a smiley, bright look, although she tried to hide it, and after that she'd been really happy, almost silly-happy, just like he and Bess had been the day before their birthday. Of course, Mummy loved dogs but there'd been that same feeling – that there was something which he couldn't quite understand. She always seemed extra happy here at The Keep and she never tired of telling them about the house and all the family who had lived in it, going back years and years. This room, for instance, had once been Ellen's room and, before that, his grandfather's governess's room. His brow furrowed again as he tried to imagine these people.

Miss Smollett; he mimed the word silently, exaggerating the movement of his mouth to make up for the lack of sound. He liked to do this. Words and phrases fascinated him and, as people talked, tiny pictures formed in his head, rather like cartoons. Miss Smollett had been 'one of the old school', 'a bit of a tartar'. He'd seen a picture of a tartar once, a fierce-looking fellow in baggy trousers and sheep-skin boots, waving something which looked like a scythe; he'd had straggling hair and a savage grin and was astride an even fiercer-looking horse . . . It had been rather difficult to fit Miss Smollett into this image but he'd done his best. He'd been shown a photograph of her since then; a rather short woman, standing between his grandfather and his twin just before they went off to school. They'd worn long woollen stockings and knickerbockers and Miss Smollett had a hand on a shoulder of each of them, as if restraining them. She was smiling, her hair drawn back and up into a hard round lump on her head, not at all straggly, and she didn't look a bit fierce. He'd rather regretted the sheepskin boots and the scythe he'd managed to introduce into his mental picture of her, but he'd been younger then, and he'd let his imagination run away with him . . .

Jamie sighed as he twisted into a different position, humping right under the blankets. He'd discovered that the life that went on in his head was more colourful than the rather dull version outside it and this discovery often got him into trouble at school. He was inclined to daydream, to be distracted by a sentence, and then he'd get into trouble. He wondered if the snow might be so deep that they would be unable to go home today; whether they might have to stay at The Keep and so miss a few days of school.

'Miss school? Whatever next, I wonder.'

The words seem to come from nowhere but he knew at once who'd spoken them. Ellen. Mummy had told them so much about Ellen that he felt as if he'd known her too. This had been her room after the twins had gone to school and Miss Smollett had moved on to another family. She'd helped Grandmother to bring up the twins and, later, she did all the cooking, and when Mummy and Mole and Susanna had come back from Africa she'd looked after them, too. He didn't know whether the words were so clear in his head because Ellen's ghost was here or simply because Mummy had said them so often.

'I know what Ellen would say to you,' she'd say. ' "Don't want your sprouts? Whatever next, I wonder." '

They'd shout the last bit out with her and it had passed into a kind of family-speak along with wortle and one or two other things.

Jamie poked his head out of the blanket, just in case Ellen might be in the room with him. Part of him hoped she would and part felt just a tiny bit jumpy at the thought of it – but there was no one there. He peered again at Bess but there was still no movement. Heaving another sigh, he rolled on to his back and stared up at the white ceiling. After Ellen had moved downstairs, when she'd got old and her legs didn't work too well, Caroline had come to look after Susanna and Mole when they were very small and she'd been here ever since. Her bedroom was next door although just for now she'd moved downstairs where Ellen used to be so that she could be near Great-grandmother in the night. This room, however, and Susanna's old bedroom were kept now for visiting children. Susanna had been really envious of their bunk beds.

'I wish Mole and I could have had them when we were little,' she'd said. 'We'd've had such fun.'

Susanna didn't feel or look like an aunt, not like Aunt Prue, who was kind and gentle and was really good if you felt miserable. Susanna was young and funny and sometimes Mummy told her off just as though she were only seven, too. 'Oh, Sooz,' she'd say. 'Honestly, you are a twit.' It was the same with Mole, even if he did go to sea in his submarine. He wasn't an uncle like Uncle Theo. It was more as if Sooz and Mole – and Hal and Kit, too – were like very big brothers and sisters. There were lots of photographs of Mole and Susanna when they were small and he loved to look at them. It was odd that these small people should be grown up now; that they'd turned into his uncle and aunt. He'd spent a whole afternoon on board Mole's submarine and been allowed to look through the periscope and pretended to sleep in one of the bunks, hardly bigger than the one he was in now. He'd loved it. Mole was not just his uncle and godfather – he was Jamie's 'best person'. They both had a best person. Bess's was Kit. These two were the best after Mummy – and Daddy, of course.

He wriggled awkwardly as he always did when his thoughts got difficult, almost as though he were trying to escape from them. Daddy was a tricky person to put in his filing compartment. He was more like a strict schoolteacher than a daddy, which was a silly thing to say because Mummy actually *was* a schoolteacher . . . He frowned again, trying to work it out. Hal was a different sort of daddy; he hugged Jolyon and Edward a lot, gave them piggybacks and played with them. Mummy had explained that Daddy was rather a lot older than Hal so it was bound to be a bit different. Jamie sighed. He liked Hal's sort of daddy better than his own and it made him feel wrong inside. It had been great when Hal had come in last night with Rex. It sounded so funny when Hal said to Rex, 'You are a *dog*, sir,' as if Rex were really a person and Hal was being rude to him . . .

At the thought of Rex, downstairs in the dog basket in the kitchen, Jamie's whole inside turned over with excitement. He simply couldn't wait another minute. Carefully he pushed back the covers, carefully he turned round so as to climb down the ladder. As he reached the floor, Bess emerged from her blankets and stared out at him.

'It's morning,' he said quickly, almost defensively. 'It's been snowing and everything's gone white. Look.'

He ran to the window, dragging back the curtains, showing the snow piled up on the windowsill obscuring most of the glass. Bess sat up quickly, trying to see out and shivering.

'Gosh, it's cold.'

'It must be morning,' he told her. 'You see, it's quite light. I'm going down to see Rex.'

'Rex.' They gazed at each other, relishing the treat in store. 'Put your dressing gown on,' she said. 'Where are your slippers?'

'I can't find them,' he said, going down on his hands and knees, peering under the chair, his dressing gown flapping round him. 'I don't care. It's not that cold.'

She kneeled up, making big eyes, pursing her lips. 'Go downstairs in bare feet?' she exclaimed in her 'Ellen' voice. 'Whatever next, I wonder.'

They shouted it together – but quietly – so as not to wake Mummy across the passage, and Bess dragged out the slippers which had been kicked under the bed. Slippers on, dressing gowns bundled round them, they went out quietly and crept downstairs together.

'Thank goodness for the Aga,' said Caroline as she and Fliss washed up the breakfast things together. 'The electricity was off when I came down so there must have been a power cut in the night. Telephone's OK.'

'I'll have to try to get back,' said Fliss. 'It's times like these when I wish that the twinnies were still really small. It was so nice not having to bother about school. They're having such fun out there with Hal and Rex.'

'I must say that it'll be wonderful to have a dog again.' Caroline tipped the water out of the bowl and wiped it round. 'I still miss them. Silly, isn't it?'

'Not really.' Fliss hung the tea cloth to dry over the Aga rail. 'Even now, it seems really odd to go for a walk all by myself, I'd got so used to having the twinnies along all the time. Yet I used to walk alone an awful lot when I was first married. Remember when I used to come up on the river-boat from Dartmouth and you'd meet me in Totnes for a quick cup of coffee or some tea, depending on the tides?'

Caroline shook her head. 'How long ago it seems. Of course, Ellen was still here, then, so I could snatch a few hours.'

'Ten years ago,' mused Fliss. 'What an amazing thought. Do I hear voices? Let's get the kettle on. They'll be freezing.'

The twinnies looked anything but freezing; their cheeks were poppy red, eyes sparkling.

'Rex slid on the ice and Hal threw a snowball at him,' they chorused, 'and Rex tried to catch it and eat it. Hal says there's an old sledge somewhere that Fox made for Uncle John and Grandfather.'

Fliss thought: How odd it is to hear them call Daddy 'Grandfather'. Oh, if only he could see them . . .

Hal was smiling at her across the kitchen. His thick fair hair was crushed beneath an old moleskin cap and his jersey was covered with lumps of icy snow which were now beginning to melt. She felt that he had guessed her thoughts and she smiled back at him, feeling a wealth of kinship and affection flowing between them.

'How is it in the lane?' she asked him. 'I suppose we have to fight our way back home?'

'I shall certainly have to,' he answered, casting the cap on to the table. 'I'm in the middle of writing a paper which I left up at Greenwich. It's a project which I have to get in this week. Never mind. It's really not too bad at all out there. A tractor's been along and I'm sure the main roads will be cleared. It looks worse than it is because it's drifted from the north-east. It'll be good out on the hill, though, especially if we can find that sledge.'

The twins flung themselves upon him, begging him to search for the sledge, pleading with him not to go back.

'What!' he cried dramatically. 'Would you keep me from my duty? Down, down, I say!'

Rex began to bark, jumping up at them, tail wagging furiously.

'Down! All of you!' cried Caroline. 'Let's have some organisation here. First of all, Hal, when will you go?'

'After lunch.' He sat down at the table, allowing the twinnies to climb on to him, one on each knee. 'That should give us plenty of time to find the sledge and have a few runs.'

'We'll go about the same time,' said Fliss. 'I'd like to be home before it starts to freeze, and if you're sure the roads will be clear . . .?'

'We shall drive in tandem.' Hal joggled his Jamie knee up and down, seeing Jamie's long face, guessing at his disappointment. 'It'll probably be even worse further upcountry. Schools closed for weeks and so on.'

Jamie looked up at him, hope rising, cheerfulness restored, and Hal gave him a little private wink. He grinned back and then slid down and went to crouch by Rex who had been coaxed by Caroline into the dog basket and was now drying off on the big tartan rug. He licked Jamie's cheek and sighed contentedly as Jamie sat beside him, stroking his ears. Rex dropped his big head across the boy's knees and relaxed.

'Mrs Pooter, Mugwump, Perks and now Rex,' murmured Jamie, so that the dog might feel his special place in the natural order of things.

'Your boys are going to miss him,' said Caroline, making coffee whilst Fliss poured milk for the twins.

'Possibly.' Hal's face closed, precluding any discussion. He'd explained it all last night and he didn't want to think about it again. Time enough for that when he started the long drive home. 'They'll see him when they come down to visit.'

Caroline opened her mouth to say that, in that case, it might be some time before Jolyon and Edward saw Rex, and shut it again. She could see that she'd already been quite tactless enough. Her eyes met Fliss's and a tiny message passed between them. Something was not right with Hal and Maria – and it wasn't just Rex – but it was clear that Hal had no intention of discussing it. She put the mugs down on the table and Jamie carefully lifted Rex's head aside and scrambled out of the dog basket.

'What about the sledge?' he asked hopefully, lest it might get forgotten.

'In the workshop,' said Caroline, passing Hal the sugar. 'Hanging up on the wall. I can't remember when it was last used but Fox would have put it away in good condition.'

'Dear old boy,' said Hal. 'How I miss him.'

'Oh, don't,' said Fliss quickly. 'Not . . . not now.'

There was a silence whilst the three adults thought of the elderly woman upstairs. The twinnies finished their milk and looked round at them, surprised by the sudden change in atmosphere. Hal smiled at them reassuringly.

'No, no time now for reminiscing,' he said, 'not if we want to find that sledge. Who's coming with me? OK. Sledge-finding party, muster at the back door in three minutes. Full outdoor rig.'

Jamie, hesitating at the kitchen door and looking back, saw a similar expression on Hal's face to that of Uncle Theo's looking at Great-grandmother – but Hal was looking at Mummy. Jamie struggled briefly with his confused ideas, remembered the sledge and hurried after Bess to find his gumboots.

Chapter Twenty-eight

Although they'd been living in South Hill Park now for nearly three years, Kit still experienced a little thrill of pleasure at the thought of being a resident of Hampstead, delighting in being familiar with its lanes and squares and alleys, enjoying the freedom of the Heath itself and even the busy excitement of the Lower Fair on Bank Holidays.

This morning, looking out from her bedroom window, she saw that the pond was frozen over, the ducks crouching disconsolately on its banks; the trees on the heath beyond were lightly dusted with snow, their bare branches gleaming whitely in the morning sunshine. Kit glanced at her watch, wondering if Sin would be around after her late night out, deciding that she wouldn't. It was not much after ten o'clock and it was unlikely that, on a Sunday morning, she would surface much before midday. Kit wondered whether she, too, might be able to go back to sleep but decided that she was not in the mood. She felt quite wide-awake, rather restless, on the edge of a Sunday depression, but she already knew what she would do. She would go up to the top flat and talk to Clarrie whilst he pottered in his eyrie which smelled so deliciously of pipe tobacco and coffee. He was always ready for a good gossip and they would laugh together about 'the memsahib', his cousin Andrew's domineering wife, who lived in Wiltshire, ran a donkey sanctuary and rarely had the time to come up to town.

Andrew owned the tall house in South Hill Park, keeping the ground-floor flat for himself and any member of his family who might be passing through or need a bolthole. He was a passionate lover of opera, and came up to town regularly to sit on the four different boards of which he was a director. Clarence was his second cousin and was almost ten years older than Andrew. It was through Clarrie that they'd heard of the flat three years before . . .

Kit had come home one spring evening to find Sin in the kitchen, opening a bottle of wine which she brandished at Kit triumphantly.

'Behold,' she cried, 'I bring you tidings of great joy.'

'Oh yes?' said Kit wearily, who'd had a difficult day with a client who wished her to find paintings for his new fifteen-bedroom hotel. 'Don't tell me. We've won the pools. I'm perfectly prepared to share it fairly down the middle with you as long as it's not less than a tenner. Do we *do* the pools?'

'Certainly not,' said Sin, pouring wine, 'and do try to raise your mind above the sordid subject of money. What have we been saying to each other this last few months? What do we long for more than anything else in the world?'

Kit yawned widely, frowned deeply and took the proffered glass.

'A part in Robert Redford's new film?' she suggested. 'A cook? A new electric blanket? Give me a clue.'

'I can see that you are in one of your tiresome moods,' said Sin severely. 'Have we not agreed that we are bored and require pastures new? Have we not longed for change? What do you say to Hampstead?'

'Is this a joke?' demanded Kit. 'One of those knock, knock things? What do you say to an old boot? Put a sock in it and so on?'

'Sit down,' said Sin, 'and I will tell you all. That's it, there's your glass on the table. Now, are you sitting comfortably? Then I'll begin. You know Clarrie?'

Kit closed her eyes. 'Possibly,' she murmured. 'Probably. Animal, vegetable or mineral? Look, could we stop the twenty questions bit? Just tell me. Words of one syllable and keep your voice down. My head is splitting and I am nigh unto death.'

'Clarrie is an accountant at the BM,' began Sin, 'and he is an absolute sweetie. Cudgel the brain. You met him at a party and just loved him. Remember? He was in India in the war and then stayed on for a bit. His wife and child died out there so he came back and got the job at the British Museum and moved into a flat in a house in Hampstead that belongs to his family. It actually overlooks the heath – from the back, anyway. They keep the ground floor for themselves and Clarrie's up on the top floor. Follow me so far?' Kit nodded, eyes still closed. 'Now pin back your ears. Clarrie is retiring next week and we were having a farewell lunchtime drink together yesterday and he told me that the nice big first-floor flat is up for grabs for the first time for hundreds of years.'

She paused and after a moment Kit cautiously opened her eyes. 'Are we at the good bit yet?' she asked. 'I mean is that it?'

'You're being deliberately difficult,' Sin said crossly. 'Haven't we always talked about living in Hampstead? Walking on the heath and going to the fair, and hobnobbing in the lovely pubs and things?'

'Certainly we have. We have also talked about meeting Paul Newman unexpectedly in Harvey Nicks and having him fall suddenly and passionately in love with us,' observed Kit. 'I should think the odds are about the same. Have you any idea what the rents must be like in Hampstead, especially for nice big first-floor flats that overlook the heath?'

'Aha!' said Sin excitedly. 'A*ha*!'

'Oh God.' Kit closed her eyes again. 'You're sounding just like Rabbit when he was planning to kidnap Roo. It all ended in tears if I remember rightly.'

'Just shut up.' Sin swallowed back her wine and set her glass down with a click. Kit winced and sighed heavily. 'The thing is that his cousin prefers to let the flat to people he knows, friend-of-a-friend stuff. See? Apparently he might be prepared to adjust the rent if the prospective tenant is someone with whom he feels he would like to share his house but can't quite stretch the budget. Now Clarrie thinks that two charming, quietly behaved, respectable, attractive women would be considered very suitable.'

'So do I,' said Kit, levering herself up a little and reaching for her glass. 'Very suitable. Where does he hope to find such paragons of virtue?'

'You're impossible,' said Sin despairingly. 'And I thought you'd be so pleased. You've been miserable for weeks. Ever since . . . Christmas. And I thought you'd be really thrilled . . .'

'Look,' said Kit, pulling herself together, 'I know I've

been hell since Jake went – oh yes, let's be honest about it, none of this since Christmas stuff – but do you honestly think we can afford Hampstead?'

'Well, that's what I'm trying to tell you. Clarrie went home and gave Andrew – that's his cousin – a glowing report about us, "poor but good" and so on, and he is seriously prepared to drop the rent a bit if he thinks we'll fit in. At least let's give it a chance.'

'Sorry,' said Kit remorsefully. 'Really I am. It sounds so impossibly good to be true that I don't quite want to believe it, just in case it isn't, if you see what I mean. I didn't mean to be a cow.'

'Forget it.' Sin was refilling their glasses. 'We're going to meet him on Saturday and have a look at the flat. Clarrie's described it and it sounds just heaven. He's given us a terrific build-up so we must try to live up to it.'

'I think I do remember him,' said Kit thoughtfully. 'A short round jolly chap with a military moustache and a great sense of humour.'

'That's him,' agreed Sin. 'So let's drink to it, shall we?'

For the first time since Jake's departure, Kit felt the stirrings of excitement, of a new hope.

'Yes,' she said. 'We shall. Here's to Hampstead!'

Now, nearly three years on, she paused once more at the window to look at the familiar, well-loved view, before pulling on a warm jersey above her jeans and pushing her feet into sheepskin-lined slippers. The central heating system was antiquated and, on a morning such as this, barely adequate. Well wrapped up, she let herself out of the flat and started up the staircase that climbed from the back of the hall on the ground floor to the top of the house. There was no question that Clarrie would not be up. He rose early now so as to take his wire-haired dachshund out for his morning walk on the heath. Fritzy – re-named Fozzy by Clarrie who was a devotee of The Muppets – had been recently brought up from the country when the memsahib found that he upset the labradors and chased the hens, and it had been decided that a good home must be found for him elsewhere. Andrew had mentioned Fozzy to Clarrie, telling him how he outwitted the labradors on every front and had compounded his many misdemeanours by digging a very large hole in the memsahib's herbaceous border whilst ostensibly hunting for a rat.

'He's a jolly little chap,' Andrew had said, rather wistfully. 'Only a puppy, of course, but I warned her that she'd find him a bit of a handful. Poor old Margaret. She's got used to labs after all these years. Can't blame her for being unable to cope.'

'Don't see why she had to have him in the first place,' Clarrie had said testily. He found it perfectly easy to blame Margaret for almost everything. He was very fond of his cousin and disliked the way his wife browbeat him, trading shamelessly on his gentle character and sweetness of disposition. 'You can't experiment with dogs. It isn't fair.'

'It wasn't *quite* an experiment,' Andrew, the peacemaker, had replied. 'The breeder's a close friend and was determined that the puppy would make an excellent companion and watchdog now that the labs are getting a bit aged. Poor old Mags found it impossible to say no to her. The breeder would almost certainly have him back but it's a bit embarrassing. Fortunately she lives up in the north so Mags thought she'd try to find Fozzy a really good home and break the news later on.'

'Prevaricating.' Clarrie had sniffed contemptuously. 'Surprised she's being so sensitive about it. Margaret doesn't usually find it so difficult to say no to people. Why can't the poor little feller come here?'

Andrew had looked at him with some surprise. 'Here? Do you think it's fair to have a dog in town?'

'Good grief! We're right on the Heath, man! Bring him up and let's have a look at him. We might as well keep him in the family if we can.'

Now, as Kit beat a tattoo on the door, she was answered by Fozzy's deep-throated bark, out of all proportion to his size though, despite his short legs, he was a very large, sturdy animal. She opened the door, which was rarely locked, and greeted Fozzy who was just inside.

'Hi! It's me!' she called. 'Is it a bad moment?'

'Why ever should it be?' Clarrie bustled out from the kitchen. 'Come on through. We've had our constitutional and it's jolly cold out there, I can tell you. Coffee's hot, so pour yourself some and top mine up for me.'

Even in the kitchen there were books everywhere: leaning together on shelves, piled on the table, spilling off chairs. Clarrie's pipe was resting in an enormous ashtray and he had an encyclopaedia on the table open at a large map.

'Met a chap when we were out just now,' he said, going back to the table. 'He was in Burma in the war and happened to know a friend of mine. Quite extraordinary coincidence. We had a good old chinwag and I was looking up the place where he was based. He's just moved into a little flat in Well Walk so we arranged to have a jar in the Holly Bush at lunchtime. Want to come along?'

'Love to,' said Kit promptly. Clarrie's acquaintances were generally interesting and amusing and could be relied upon to give good entertainment. 'Did Fozzy behave himself?'

'Course he did.' Clarrie snorted. 'Nothing wrong with him, is there old chap? Man's dog, that's what he is. Needs to know who's boss but doesn't need to be squawked at all day long.'

Kit grinned to herself as she took a quick sip of the hot strong coffee. She put Clarrie's mug beside him on the large, shabby pine table and settled opposite.

'I think you only took him in to prove a point,' she said provocatively. 'You wanted to show the memsahib that you could succeed where she failed. Go on, admit it.'

He beamed at her, short white hair on end, eyes twinkling. 'Had too much character for her,' he said triumphantly. 'She can deal with poor old donkeys that are too far over the hill to fight back, and with those fat, unhealthy old labs, but give her something that's got a bit of character and where is she? Making life hell for poor old Andrew. That's where!'

'I must admit that I find her quite terrifying,' admitted Kit. The memsahib had travelled up to London to give Kit and Sin the once-over, and she had proved to be a truly formidable woman: tall, angular, tweeded and with a very sharp tongue. It was clear to see why Andrew made regular sorties to the house in Hampstead, using it as a refuge.

'She was a pretty girl,' said Clarrie reflectively, 'but quite unsuitable for Andrew. She got her hooks into him, though. Saw straight away that she could wind him round her little finger. Didn't have an earthly, poor old boy. Talked to him like a father, tried to make him see the light. Terrible mistake. Brought out the chivalrous streak in him and we very nearly fell out.'

'I can't imagine Andrew falling out with anyone,' murmured Kit. 'He's so incredibly nice.'

'Good job he's got this bolthole.' Clarrie closed the book and picked up his pipe. 'He'd have gone mad long since.'

'It's a pity there are no children.' Kit bent to stroke Fozzy, who had curled into a ball beside her chair. 'He'd have been a lovely father.'

'Don't think he was allowed to try.' Clarrie grinned evilly. 'Doesn't like that sort of thing, the memsahib. Nasty, messy business. Andrew told me as much when we talked about children once. Discreetly, of course. Quite understood, must make allowances, and all that guff. No wonder she looks such a dried-up old stick.'

'Honestly!' Kit began to chuckle. 'I don't believe a word of it.'

'Truth,' declared Clarrie. 'Don't you say anything now. So he was out with Sin last night, was he?'

'The opera. Wagner, I think. It's no good, Clarrie. I think we have to give up hoping that Andrew is going to suddenly have a rush of blood to the head and elope with Sin. He's one of the most married men I've ever met.'

'Too honourable,' said Clarrie gloomily. 'Here he is with you two gorgeous creatures and all he can think of is Wagner. Now if I were only twenty years younger . . .'

'That's just your excuse.' Kit lounged on the table and made big eyes at him. 'Here we are, languishing after you, following you about . . .'

'Silence, wench. Tempt me not. Had breakfast? I thought not. Brunch. That's what we need. Something inside us before we go to the pub. I'll see what I've got and you can sit there and tell me all the gossip. What's the latest news from Devon? How's Fliss and those twins of hers? Nice girl, your Fliss. And how's your grandmother?'

Kit settled into the corner, kicked off a slipper, and rested her foot on Fozzy's warm, rough back. At moments like these, she could almost imagine herself in the kitchen at The Keep in the old days of Ellen and Fox and the dogs. She sighed with pleasure, picked up her coffee and prepared to regale Clarrie with all her news.

Chapter Twenty-nine

The room was very quiet. The cassette had stopped playing long since but Theo was reluctant to move lest he disturb Freddy, who was sleeping in her chair. Although she spent a great deal of the time asleep she refused to stay in bed. He knew that it was her final struggle, her last act of independence, against the disease which was slowly but implacably defeating her. She rose late and went to bed early but during those hours in between she got herself dressed with Caroline's aid and spent the time in her sitting room. Perhaps it was a blessing that every physical act took so much time to accomplish. It was nearly mid-morning by the time her breakfast was over and he arrived to keep her company. It was important that the day had a series of small events to which she could look forward; small goals to be attained; little treats to savour. Breakfast over, Theo would arrive with *The Times* from which he would read carefully edited portions of the daily news. It was clear that it was an effort for her to keep pace with the world beyond The Keep, nevertheless he never let her guess that he knew it. When they'd finished with the newspaper and selected some music – which was another very time-consuming occupation, looking through her growing library of cassettes, discussing the relative virtues of various pieces – it would be time for coffee, despite the fact that by now it was much nearer to lunchtime. Not that time mattered any longer; the former routine had become flexible; each meal a movable feast.

Freddy breathed regularly, face turned into her cushion, but Theo tried not to look at her; he knew she would hate it, that to Freddy it would be a violation of her privacy.

He thought: The sleeping are so vulnerable, so frighteningly unprotected. It isn't fair to take advantage of their helplessness.

He looked down at the book which he had been reading aloud when she had drifted into sleep: *Mansfield Park.* Her attention span was very limited, partly caused by the medicine on which she relied to keep the pain at bay, but she loved him to read to her. He tried to see it as some kind of recompense for all those years in which she had played to him, although it could not possibly give her the joy with which her playing had filled him. These last years had been blessed by a deep contentment and he gave thanks daily that he had never submitted to the temptation of admitting his love. It would have destroyed at one stroke the quiet, strong affection and invaluable friendship which had informed their relationship. Even if she had reciprocated his love it was likely that passion, jealousy, misunderstandings would have clouded that deeper understanding which had drawn them so close in these last fifteen years and enabled them to provide a strong, secure framework for the children.

Soon she would be gone from them. Theo closed the book upon the bookmark and stared into the fire. Although his own beliefs gave him spiritual comfort, his human heart could not so easily come to terms with a future without Freddy. She was his friend, his companion, the one person who had been a constant in his life. He had never known his mother. His father and brother had died whilst he was still very young, Freddy had been there for more than sixty years and it was impossible to imagine The Keep without her. Yet it sometimes seemed that they had been imprisoned in these two rooms for ever. How strange time was; sometimes the distant past felt closer than yesterday; sometimes events and people merged together in the memory.

He'd stood with Freddy at the window, watching the twinnies riding their new bicycles round the courtyard, just as he and Bertie had ridden theirs when they were children. He remembered Freddy's boys, Peter and John, doing the same thing, and, later, Fliss and Mole and Susanna. At that moment, the twinnies had represented all the children who had ever lived at The Keep, stretching back into the past, going on into the future. He'd glanced quickly at Freddy, wondering if she might be sharing his vision, and seen the tears on her cheeks. He knew that she was facing the harsh truth that she would see no more children riding round the courtyard and, although she had waved cheerfully to the twinnies, smiling down at them, once she'd turned back into the room where they could no longer see her she had collapsed into his arms and wept.

He'd held her as he had done before, down all the years; when she'd heard that Bertie had been killed at Jutland; when the telegram had come to tell them that John had died on convoy duty; when the letter describing the deaths of Peter and Alison and Jamie had arrived. More recently there had been Ellen, her friend Julia Blakiston, and then Fox to mourn, and now she was facing the approach of her own death. He'd held her closely, aware of his own inadequacies, saddened that he had never been able to bring her spiritual comfort or any conviction of the possibility of a oneness with God. In this respect he had totally failed her but he had no intention of insulting her now, in this weakened state, by offering her placebos; of talking of a storybook heaven or promising a benevolent God with the limited stature of a deity out of some Greek myth.

He had merely continued to hold her, willing her his strength, and presently she had straightened up and smiled at him. By the time the twinnies had come up to see her she was composed, ready to listen to the recital of their achievements, to share in the joy of their presents and accept their hugs and kisses with dignity and pleasure. She had been slightly confused at, if delighted by, Hal's later arrival and he'd spent some time alone with her before he'd driven away in convoy with Fliss on the Sunday afternoon. Since then Theo thought that he'd detected a new element of peace, a kind of detachment which also meant a relinquishing of what remained of her control.

A coal shifted, settled precariously and then rolled into the grate. Freddy startled into wakefulness but Theo was already standing beside the fire, tongs in hand, placing the coal back amongst the flames. She pulled herself into a more upright position, collecting her thoughts, smiling at him.

'I think I nodded off,' she said ruefully.

'For a few minutes.' He shrugged it off, resuming his own seat, picking up the book again. 'It's nearly lunchtime but I think we've just time to finish the chapter. Now where were we . . .?'

★ ★ ★

The cold spell had been a brief one. After a few days, the wind backed round to the west and rain swept in, thawing the snow and bringing mild weather. After lunch, when Theo had returned to Mrs Chadwick's room, Caroline finished the washing up, picked up the tea cloth and glanced at the expectant Rex. Since his arrival she'd fallen into the habit of taking him out for a walk after lunch. These days, by the time tea was over it was practically dark and it seemed sensible to get some fresh air whilst she could. Rex, whose walks had hitherto been brief and infrequent, could hardly believe his luck. He missed his own people, especially his master, but his new mistress seemed to have been perfectly trained. She talked to him, allowed him to live with her in the large, warm kitchen, fed him regularly and took him for wonderful forays into new and unexplored countryside. She never shouted at him nor struck him with his lead – in fact, his lead had not appeared yet – nor berated him for being muddy and overfriendly. Nevertheless, he deemed it wise to take nothing for granted. He hauled himself into a sitting position and waited hopefully, ears pricked as the now-familiar after-lunch acts were performed. When she uttered the words, '*Right. That's that then,*' which were accompanied by strange ritualistic acts to which humans seemed subject, he would know that his moment was at hand.

'Right,' said Caroline, putting away the last of the plates and hanging the wet tea cloth on the Aga rail. She topped up the kettle with cold water from a jug, replaced the kettle's lid and put the jug away. 'That's that then.' She reached for the jar of Cremolia, rubbed some cream into her hands and

311

smiled at Rex. 'How about a walk?'

At the one word he truly recognised he stood up and came wagging out of his basket. She bent to stroke him, smoothing his head and ears while he waited quietly, aware of the tension which was running out of her, down through her arms and hands and into his own body. She sighed, relaxed now, fears and anxieties suspended, and he tensed expectantly.

'Come on then,' she said. 'Just let me put my boots on.'

Outside on the hill, Caroline paused beside the wall where the dogs were buried, paying them a brief homage, remembering past walks and excursions, whilst Rex raced ahead. A congregation of rooks wheeled overhead where ragged clouds drifted slowly, grey on white, with occasional patches of inky black. The breeze was soft against her cheeks and she breathed deeply, thrusting her hands into her pockets, her spirits rising. The darkness of the short winter days, combined with the hushed atmosphere of The Keep, could easily depress her and she was glad of a good reason to be out of doors. She'd fully expected Maria to ask for Rex's return, to say that were all missing him much more than they'd imagined, but the weeks had passed and no word had been said, apart from Hal telephoning from Greenwich to ask how Rex was settling in and to check once or twice since that she was able to cope with him.

Following the well-worn sheep tracks down the hill, Caroline found it difficult to understand how they had been able to part with him. Of course, she did not have two small children to deal with and there was plenty of space at The Keep, but Rex was such a charming fellow. Jolyon and Edward must be missing him terribly. As yet she hadn't taken him beyond the immediate vicinity of The Keep but she was rather looking forward to putting him in the car and taking him to the beach. She was deeply grateful for his company, glad to have him to talk to and to have the small necessary routines of feeding and grooming him. Theo was spending more and more time now with Mrs Chadwick and Rex had brought a purpose to Caroline's life, something to brighten the lonely days.

She skirted the spinney, heading down to the river where early catkins hung and snowdrops grew in the shelter of the bank. It seemed unlikely that Mrs Chadwick would venture outside the house ever again and Caroline was hoping to take some evidence of the coming spring back to her. It was still nearly two months until Easter but there were signs that the worst of the winter might be behind them. The gorse was in blossom and the willow bushes were tipped with fluffy white down.

Rex was already paddling. He loved the water although he rarely showed any tendency to go in further than the shallows where he waded to and fro, dipping his muzzle into the cold water and then shaking his head furiously, so that the glinting drops flew wide.

'I think you were a water buffalo in an earlier existence,' she told him – and he flattened his ears at her, tongue lolling out so that he seemed to be laughing. When she bent to gather some of the delicate, drooping snowdrops with their fragile, white, green-veined blossoms, he came out of the water, padding along the bank to see what she was doing and sniffing inquisitively at the snowdrops.

'Great elephant!' she murmured to him. 'Get your huge feet off those poor little flowers.'

He licked her cheek and she pushed him away, wiping her face with her sleeve, pretending to tussle with him. He barged about, in and out of the slowly flowing water and back up the bank, and presently found a stick for her to throw. She placed the small posy carefully in a bag and put it into her largest pocket before picking up the stick and hurling it further along the bank, beneath the trees where the few early catkins hung. He raced after it, the shingly earth spraying up behind him, his feathery tail describing great circular sweeps. Taking the secateurs from her pocket, Caroline cut a few sprays and put them into the bag with the snowdrops. Once more she threw Rex's stick, this time aiming it back the way they had come, and then followed him, climbing slowly, pausing to look out across to the dun-coloured hills.

Her mind was full of the past: of Fox and Ellen and other dogs; of the children, Fliss, Mole and Susanna. It was difficult, with Mrs Chadwick so near the end of her life, to feel anything but melancholy. The landscape matched her mood – the chalky colours of grey and brown; the sensation of being held helplessly immobile in this wintry, drab existence. The twinnies' birthday weekend had been a glowing moment in the midst of the gloom and the sight of their bright faces and happy laughter had shown her that there was a future, that Mrs Chadwick's death would not be the end of everything. The glow had remained for a while but, during the last week or so, there had been a further deterioration in the old lady's health, and Caroline's depression had returned.

She thought: I love her. We have cared for the children together for nearly twenty-three years, been through so many ups and downs, so many terrors and joys. How will it be without her?

Memories crowded into her mind: standing beside the car watching Mrs Chadwick saying goodbye to Fliss on her first day at boarding school and then coming back to the car muttering fiercely, 'Get in quickly and drive. *Quickly*,' and seeing the tears falling as they passed out of the gate; sitting beside her as they drove anxiously to Exeter to meet Mole and Susanna from the train after their first journey home from school alone. 'I'll drive,' she'd said. 'I shall be happier if I'm doing something,' her hands clenched on the steering wheel, knuckles white; the fierce pride on her face when they'd heard that Mole had passed his AIB; the expression of joy and tenderness when she saw the first photograph of the twinnies . . .

The misery pushed up, making a lump in Caroline's throat and she swallowed once or twice before it dissolved into tears. Standing there on the hillside she cried out her unhappiness, the tears mingling with the rain on her cheeks as she held both hands against the terrible pain in her heart.

Rex came back to her, pushing against her leg, and she crouched beside him, an arm about his shaggy neck. He stood firm, puzzled but steady, licking her face from time to time, tasting the salt.

Presently the sobbing ceased and she rubbed her face against his warm ear, straightening up, feeling for her handkerchief. He wagged his tail tentatively, encouragingly, and she smiled waveringly, grateful for his company as they set off together; going back to tea, going back to give Mrs Chadwick the first fruits of a spring which she would never see.

Chapter Thirty

'I'm doing that terrible sighing thing,' said Prue anxiously, on the telephone to Caroline. 'You know, like old ladies do, with their mouths tucked down and never looking at you properly. My mother used to do it to make my father feel guilty. I only remembered that recently. Isn't it strange that I should think of that after all these years?'

'It's to do with feeling miserable,' said Caroline. 'As if your heart is terribly heavy.'

'But why should I be miserable all the time? I'm fed up with these awful depressions and coming over all hot. It's so embarrassing. I'm in the middle of buying something and I have to rush out of the shop. That or strip all my clothes off. I feel such a fool.'

'The thing is to try not to panic.'

'I *do* try not to panic. It comes on so quickly when I'm not ready for it. I *wake up* panicking although there's nothing to panic about at all. Do you think I'm going mad?'

'Of course you're not going mad. It's just middle age. We're all the same.'

'Other women don't seem so bad – well, I've got one or two friends who understand – but I'm so unbalanced. One of my old ladies died the other day and I cried for hours, couldn't stop, and then there's Freddy . . .'

'It's because you're alone too much. I wish you'd come down, Prue. You can't imagine how much it would mean to me. I'm going through this middle-age thing, too, you know, and it's awfully depressing here knowing that . . . well, you know.'

'Oh, I can imagine. It must be terrible for you and poor Theo. And Freddy, of course, that goes without saying. It's simply that I don't feel I can just turn up without Freddy approving. I know it's silly.'

'Supposing I have a word with her and she invites you, would that do?'

'Well, if she does it of her own free will. Don't coerce her or anything.'

'Don't be an idiot. You've got over sensitive about it. We'd all love to see you.'

'Oh, Caroline, I'd love it, too. I could give you a hand and keep you company, and I'd so much like to see Freddy. We were never terribly close but she was very fair always and I have an enormous respect for her.'

'I'll have a word with her and I promise not to prompt her. How's the family?'

'Oh, I don't know. That's another thing. I'd love to go and see Maria and Hal and the children but I know how precious weekends are when your husband's away all week and Maria doesn't sound terribly enthusiastic about my going for a couple of days midweek. We used to be so close, too.'

'You're sighing again, I can hear it. Now don't get in a state about Hal and Maria. Hal was in great form that

318

weekend he brought Rex down. Oh, Prue, I can't tell you what a comfort Rex is. He's just about saved my life. Look, you simply must come. It would do you so much good to get out on proper country walks and we could have good old chinwags. How's Kit?'

'Kit never changes. It really worries me, actually. I wonder if she'll ever marry now. At thirty-six she's just the same as when she was twenty. I wonder if it was not having a father. She's a sort of Peter Pan. That darling old Clarrie keeps an eye on her and she simply adores him, but she and Sin go on much as they ever did. I'm sure that Kit still hasn't got over Jake, you know. So tragic but I warned her often enough. As for Sin, she jokes about an unrequited passion so much that I'm beginning to believe it might be true, but they both seem happy enough.'

'Well, that's something. At least they're all fit and healthy.'

'That's true. How's Susanna?'

'She's fine. She and Gus come over regularly, bless them, and they cheer us all up and make us laugh. Their barn is coming on and they hope it'll be ready to move into in time for the baby.'

'Darling Sooz. It seems quite impossible to imagine her as a mother. How's she coping with Freddy?'

'She's very upset that her grandmother won't see her baby but she's dealing with it very well and Gus is an absolute tower of strength. Perhaps it's to do with being a parson's son but he has that same kind of serenity that Theo has, which is such a comfort.'

'I don't think I would ever have survived without Theo. He's a kind of living example of all he believes in but he never goes on about it. I think about him when I'm in a muddle or feeling bitchy and just the thought of him makes me want to be better. Funny, isn't it?'

'I know exactly what you mean. He keeps me going and yet he must be feeling so desperate inside. They've been together for so long.'

'Oh, don't, Caroline. I simply cannot bear it. It won't be The Keep without Freddy, will it?'

'It will certainly be different. I don't want to think about that just yet. Look, I'll have a talk with Mrs Chadwick later on when she goes to bed and I'll phone you back. About nine? OK? And, Prue. No more sighing!'

'It's the indignity of it all,' whispered Freddy. 'My dear Caroline, how often I've had cause to be grateful to you – but I didn't think that it would come to this.'

With an effort she held out her arms and Caroline deftly dropped the nightgown over her head, placed the shawl around the thin shoulders and lifted the long legs into the bed, freshly made with clean linen. Firelight danced across the walls and the bedside light was shaded to a soft glow so that the room had an intimate restful quality. Caroline checked that there was fresh water in the glass and tablets within reach, and smiled down into the sunken eyes.

'Perhaps it's being a nanny,' she said gently, 'but I've never found caring for people, whatever age, to be undignified. Dignity comes from inside, nobody can take it from you.'

Freddy lay back against the pillows and Caroline took her hand, as she always did now at the end of the day. Freddy knew that it was a kind of farewell, just in case she, Freddy, died in the night, and she held it as tightly as she could in her enfeebled state.

'Thank you, Caroline,' she murmured.

'God bless.'

They remained for a few seconds longer until Freddy's grip loosened.

'Tell Prue that I should like to see her.'

'I'll tell her. Sleep well. Theo will be in later to say good night as usual.'

Freddy nodded, eyes closing, and Caroline went out, gently shutting the door behind her. The clock ticked quietly but steadily, measuring the minutes, and the flames whispered in the grate. There was a gathering silence in the house about her and darkness pressed against the windows.

Who can free himself from his meanness and limitations, if you do not lift him to yourself, my God, in purity of love?

Ah, but you had to want to be lifted; want it more than life itself. You had to truly want to step free of your pettiness, your love of self, to long for the freedom.

Her thin hands clasped together as she felt the great wash of thankfulness which accompanied the knowledge that she had never told her love. How undignified it would have been, even if Theo had returned it, to admit her passion for her husband's younger brother. Would she have ever known the peace she possessed now or had the comfort of their deep friendship? She knew herself too well now. She would have resented any interference and been even more jealous than she'd been when she had no rights over him. In some obscure way she had been saved from herself and it was her

321

greatest fear that in one of those moments of morphia-induced rambling confusion she might speak of it to him. It was her one last prayer that she might not weaken.

> *How will a person*
> *brought to birth and nurtured in a world of small horizons,*
> *rise up to you Lord,*
> *if* you *do not raise him by your hand which made him?*

If only this detachment, this gentle inflowing of some kind of healing peace, had come to her earlier.

Freddy thought: But I did not want it earlier. I fought against it all my life lest it interfered with what I wanted. Just as I fought Theo . . .

How could she go, leaving Theo behind her? She had talked long with Hal, charging him to care for the family as a whole, passing to him the responsibility of its welfare, insisting that The Keep must be kept as a refuge for anyone of the family who might need it. He had promised, calmly assuring her that her wishes would be followed, giving her absolute confidence in his integrity. The relief had been tremendous, as if some weight had passed from her feeble frame to his strong, broad shoulders. For a brief, confused moment she'd imagined that it was darling John sitting beside her, holding her hand, giving his word; John who had died so young, leaving Prue with her small twins, just as she, Freddy had been left; Prue, whom she felt had never been good enough for her son, whom Theo had championed . . .

Freddy stirred restlessly. Theo had always been fond of Prue, taking her part, helping her out, protecting her from

Freddy's wrath. How jealous she had often been of Prue. Yet it was Prue who had brought them Caroline.

In the early days of her illness, it had irked her to know that Prue and Caroline and Theo were together downstairs whilst she was confined, irritated that Theo was enjoying Prue's company whilst she lay upstairs, alone and weak . . .

Who can free himself from his meanness and limitations, if you do not lift him to yourself, my God, in purity of love?

As she lay alone, fretting and cross, these words had come into her mind and she'd found the piece of paper in the drawer of her bedside table and re-read them. Why had Theo written it down? She'd never asked him but the words had remained with her, like some insistent Questioner in her head. *In purity of love?* Might it be remotely possible that she could at last lift her love for Theo absolutely into that sphere? Might she finally free herself of her meanness and limitations, at least within this relationship which had become so precious?

Freddy turned her head on the pillow, wondering if she had the strength to reach for the glass which Caroline had left close beside her. Dear Caroline . . . Her thoughts drifted, forming and re-forming. Caroline had asked if Prue might come for a few days. She had telephoned for a chat, miserable and rather lonely and longing to see them all, but insisting that she didn't wish to be a nuisance . . . Silently Freddy acknowledged Prue's delicacy, clearly recognising her sensitivity; admitting her own selfishness and prejudice. Was it because John had defied her, choosing Prue in the face of her own disapproval, holding to his love for her despite his mother's opposition? After his death, she had given Prue all that she needed but never once had she generously extended her hand in love.

She thought: Oh, Prue. You shouldn't have had to ask. I have failed to make The Keep a refuge if it is necessary for you to ask my permission to visit, especially now when you are lonely. You of all people should have a special place here. John's wife, his widow and the mother of his children, and you are left all alone in that little house. Forgive me, Prue . . .

It would be good for them all to have Prue with them – company for Caroline and someone to make Theo laugh again. He and Prue had always been so close . . . The familiar green-eyed monster muscled in, briefly showing his teeth, shaking her resolve, reminding her of past grievances. It had always hurt her when Theo had taken Prue's part against her . . .

How could she go, leaving Theo behind her? He and Caroline rubbed along together very well but it would have been good to know that there would be someone to fill in the terrible gap; someone for whom he cared. Of course, Hal and Maria and the children would probably move in before too long but it would be hard for Theo, used to her own constant companionship, her love . . .

How will a person
brought to birth and nurtured in a world of small horizons,
rise up to you Lord . . .

The Questioner was pressing her, indicating the way, offering her an opportunity. The battle was short but painful.

Approaching death brought along with it the awareness of one's unimportance. It was terrible to know that soon, very soon, her power and influence would be gone, that laughter and happiness and life itself would go on without her. Yet she still held some tiny measure of that power. Theo, like Hal, would consider himself morally bound by her last wishes; a few words would make the difference, one way or the other. There was the usual choice: self – or sacrifice of pride; stepping free of meanness and limitations in purity of love – or holding on to power which might extend beyond the grave. It had always been so important to know that she came first with Theo . . . She opened her eyes to find him bending over her.

'How are you feeling?' he asked.

'Theo.' She reached out and grasped his wrist. 'Will you do something for me?'

'Anything.' He covered her hand with his own and sat down in the chair beside her. 'What is it?'

'It's Prue.' She was too tired to prevaricate. Time was too precious. 'Caroline's inviting her down.' Did she see a familiar shadow of anxiety in his eyes? Shame for the past seized her afresh. 'Theo, I want you to ask her to consider making her home here. I think she's lonely all by herself in Bristol and the children can come here to see her just as easily. Promise you'll ask her with my blessing? Please?'

'My dear Freddy . . .' Her hand clutched his briefly and he lifted it to his lips and saluted her.

'She will be good for all of us and she deserves . . . so much.'

She relaxed on to the pillows, exhausted, and he sat for some moments in silence. Presently she opened her eyes and smiled at him. They looked at one another with deep understanding and she nodded, acknowledging, accepting, confirming.

'Go and do it now,' he could barely hear her, 'and come back after you've talked to her. After your supper. Remember, Theo, *with my blessing.*'

He nodded, pressing her hand, going quietly away. Darkness pressed in but Freddy was no longer aware of the shadows. She lay in silent contemplation, lost in the quiet radiant joy of surrender . . .

so I shall rejoice:
you will not delay, if I do not fail to hope.

Chapter Thirty-one

Coming home with the boys across the frosty field, Hal turned to watch a flock of lapwings circling in ragged formation above the quiet landscape. The mist was rising and the low line of distant hills appeared to be mysteriously receding into the approaching twilight. The boys' breath made vaporous clouds in the freezing air as they shouted to each other, running zigzag towards the gate which opened on to the lane.

They came galloping up to him as he reached the gate, knowing that they must not run out into the lane, each seizing a hand. Looking down into their glowing faces, Hal felt a sharp sense of fear, of terrifying responsibility. Their dependence on him, their confidence in him, was awe-inspiring. It should be much more difficult to have children; adults should be made to pass some sort of test to prove that they were ready for it. No other undertakings of such magnitude were entered upon with such indifference . . .

'Carry!' cried three-year-old Edward, whose short legs were feeling the strain. He flung his arms about Hal's knees and his father bent and hoisted him on to his hip, straightening his woolly bobble hat, which was decorated with a series of Snoopies.

'You're too big to carry,' he told him – but Edward merely beamed at him and leaned to look down upon Jolyon with a certain satisfaction.

'I can walk,' Jolyon told his father seriously. 'You don't have to worry about me.'

'I know that, old son,' said Hal, wishing it were true. He held the small gloved hand tightly. 'You're a big boy, now.'

'I miss Rex.' Jolyon swung his father's hand to and fro and then carried it around his small shoulders. 'Walks are different without him. I wish we could have managed him.'

'I wish we could, too.' Hal searched about for comforting words which were in no way disloyal to Maria. 'The trouble is a huge chap like Rex needs lots of room. He's very happy at The Keep, you know.'

Jolyon looked up at him. 'Certain sure?'

'Certain sure. I promised I'd keep an eye on him, didn't I?'

'Mmm.' Jolyon nodded, face slanted downwards. 'But I miss him.'

'I'm hungry.' Edward buffeted Hal's cold cheek with a mittened fist, demanding his share of attention.

'So am I.' Hal was glad to change the subject. 'Home for tea, then?'

'Mummy and Grandma are making chocolate cake.' Jolyon gave a tiny skip, Rex momentarily forgotten. 'It's my very favourite in all the world.'

'And mine,' piped Edward. He bounced up and down,

trying to make Hal hurry and began to sing in a small breathless voice. Jolyon joined in, jumping along at Hal's side.

> *'To market, to market, to buy a fat pig,*
> *Home again, home again, jiggety-jig;'*

Singing with them, Hal's thoughts were occupied elsewhere. A visit from his mother-in-law, Elaine, was not an unusual occurrence, nevertheless he suspected that there was some significance on this particular occasion which had not yet been made clear. She had already made several pointed remarks about his grandmother's approaching end, voicing vague suppositions as to what would happen to The Keep. It seemed that both she and Maria were only interested in its future and he was sad that Maria refused to take the boys down to see his grandmother before she died. His wife stood firm, however: the boys were far too young to understand about death; they would be frightened to see their great-grandmother looking so ill and confined to bed; it simply wasn't fair – and so on. It was clear that she had primed the boys, Jolyon in particular, who declared anxiously that he didn't want to go down to The Keep but, when Hal tried to reason with him gently, Jolyon had shaken his head, retreating from him, and Hal wondered exactly what it was that Maria had told him. When he broached the subject she'd denied frightening Jolyon but she was clearly embarrassed by Hal's direct approach, taking an indignant stance, surprised that he should want to expose such small boys to the gloomy atmosphere or fill their minds with the images of death.

Elaine underlined Maria's beliefs. She'd gently pointed

out that Mrs Chadwick was only the boys' *great-*grandmother, a very old lady whom they hardly knew. They had two quite young and lively grandmothers, she'd reminded him archly, with whom they had very happy relationships, so it was surely unnecessary to worry them with morbid thoughts? Hal pointed out that Fliss's twinnies had formed a very strong attachment to their great-grandmother but she'd hastened to draw his attention to the fact that Mrs Chadwick had brought Fliss up, taking the place of her mother, so in her case this was quite reasonable, especially as, since Miles's parents were also dead, the twins had no other grandparents at all. She'd added that the twins, being two years older than Jolyon, were able to remember Mrs Chadwick when she'd still been fit. Poor little Edward, she'd said reproachfully, had no memory of her other than as an invalid.

Hal had backed off at this point although, later, he'd suggested to Maria that the two of them might go down together leaving the boys with her mother. She'd behaved more like the old Maria then, pouting and hunching as a child might, and saying that she couldn't bear sick people, that illness gave her the creeps . . . It was odd, Hal had reflected, that what could be appealing in a twenty-one-year-old was simply irritating ten years on.

In an effort to subdue this irritation he'd deliberately brought to mind his grandmother's words spoken during their last talk on that snowy Sunday morning. She'd talked about her hopes for the future of The Keep, putting the responsibility into his hands, advising him, warning him, extracting promises. She'd been weak but alert and he'd made no attempt to dissemble – though he was rather surprised – when finally she asked him if he were happy with Maria.

'As happy as most couples are,' he'd answered rather shortly.

Her next remark had thrown him. 'I often think that I was wrong about you and Fliss,' she'd said reflectively. 'I was afraid that it was a silly infatuation on her part and a protective instinct on yours but I think I misjudged both of you. Am I right?'

His long silence had answered her question and she'd smiled so sadly that he'd felt compelled to comfort her.

'It was impossible for any of us to be certain at the time,' he'd said quickly. 'Fliss was so young and we'd got used to each other. I could have stood firm, you know.'

She'd shaken her head. 'There was too much pressure from your mother and me,' she'd said, 'and there was also the question of your fathers being twins and the effect on any babies you might have. You were too young to stand up against it all. Now, I wonder if it mattered, after all.'

He'd laughed a little bitterly. 'Rather too late to be wondering.'

She'd watched him, lightly touching his clasped hands, thinking things through. 'Maria is the mother of your children,' she'd said finally. 'Promise me you'll do your best to make a happy home for the three of them.'

'I have no intention of leaving her,' he'd answered drily.

'Perhaps not,' she said with some of her old sharpness, 'but there is a difference between merely doing your duty and investing your actions with a positive attempt at love.'

'Is that what you believe?' he'd asked curiously. 'That I am merely doing my duty?'

'I know how much you love your boys,' she'd assured him, 'but children are very sensitive to atmosphere. You must be wholehearted. You chose Maria, it was your decision, and you should always try to see things through.'

'And supposing,' he'd said, after another silence, 'that despite my best – my wholehearted – effects she decides that *she's* made a mistake and leaves *me*?'

'In that case you are absolved,' his grandmother had replied, 'and you have the freedom to make your own happiness, assuming that it is not at the expense of *any—*' she'd stressed that word – 'of the children.'

'Thank you,' he'd said with his former dryness. 'I'll bear that in mind.'

'Oh, Hal,' she'd reached for his hand, 'I only ever wanted what was best for you. The problem is that the old always think that they know what that is. Forgive me if I have done you harm.'

He'd put his arms about her then, holding her frail body close.

'There is nothing to forgive,' he told her. 'Don't worry. All will be well, you have my word.'

'I entrust it all to you, my dear boy,' she'd said, 'with my blessing. Dear Hal, your father would have been proud of you . . .'

As they turned in through the gate, Hal found that he was subconsciously bracing himself and, as he removed the boys' gumboots and unwound their scarves, he knew with a strange certainty that some kind of confrontation was imminent. They went into the kitchen where the table was already laid for tea and Maria and Elaine were waiting for them. Elaine remained sitting by the table but Maria hurried the protesting boys away to the small cloakroom to wash their hands. Hal smiled quickly at his mother-in-law as he washed his own hands at the sink.

'The boys have been talking about that cake all the way home,' he said cheerfully. 'I'm looking forward to a piece myself.'

Her answering smile was distracted, a gesture at good manners, and his heart sank even further.

'If I could have a quick word, Hal . . .'

He noticed that Maria had closed the kitchen door behind her and he knew with absolute certainty that she and her mother had set this up between them.

'No need to make it a quick one, Elaine.' He tried not to make too much of a point of it. 'I have a feeling that Maria won't be back for a minute or two.'

Her glance was sharp, suspecting him, but he raised his eyebrows as if surprised by her suspicion and she nodded, as though accepting an invitation.

'It's simply that Maria's father and I have been wondering about the future.' Elaine moved one or two knives. 'You know, we both believed that The Keep would be yours when your grandmother died but Maria tells me that this isn't so.'

Hal dried his hands on the roller towel behind the door and leaned against the sink, folding his arms across his chest. His silence unnerved Elaine and she looked away from his steady gaze for a moment as she marshalled her argument. He looked at her dispassionately, noticing that the short, well-cut hair was still a determined brown, her face carefully made up.

'The thing is, Hal, and this is what concerns Frank and

myself, Maria says that you are reluctant to explain exactly what the situation is. Now, I don't want you to think that Maria is telling tales out of school.' She laughed lightly at such a foolish idea. 'No, indeed. We have asked her what the situation is, it's only natural that we are concerned for her welfare, and she is so muddled that Frank and I discussed it and decided to ask you outright.'

His gaze did not waver. 'Ask me what, Elaine?'

She bit her lip. 'I think it is only right that we know your plans for the future,' she said sharply. 'Maria is our daughter, after all.'

'I thought that you already knew our plans for the future,' he answered mildly. 'In so far as I know them myself. I shall finish the staff course, get my promotion to Commander – I don't think there's too much doubt about that – and either be given a sea-going command or perhaps get a desk job at the Ministry of Defence before I go back to sea. Maria seems to be reluctant to move from this house, although I've suggested that we should buy one, so we must hope that we can continue to rent it. The owner lives in Hong Kong so I think we're safe for a while. I don't think you and Frank need to worry about us.'

Elaine was sitting very still, her eyes narrowed, lips compressed, as she watched him and he saw quite clearly exactly how Maria would look when she was in her fifties. The thought depressed him.

'I think you are deliberately misunderstanding me,' she said icily. 'I'm talking about the future of The Keep.'

'The Keep is my grandmother's home, Elaine.' He spoke gently. 'Maria and I don't discuss what we might do with your house. Why should we discuss The Keep?'

Her cheeks brightened but her eyes were cold. 'You gave us to understand that you were your grandmother's heir.'

'I might have said that she was leaving The Keep in my care,' he replied quickly. 'She thinks that I would be the one of her grandchildren most likely to live in it but I have always told Maria that she also intended it to be used for the benefit of the entire family.'

'It is a ridiculous plan,' she snapped. 'Once she is gone that kind of setup simply won't work. It needs a matriarch at the head of a large family to keep the other members in their place. You are not old enough for such a role and Maria would hate it. It is the end of an era and one must face up to it.'

'What do you suggest?' he asked with deceptive meekness, as one seeking advice.

She was too angry to notice the set of his jaw. 'You should explain to your grandmother that it is unfair for her to burden the next generation with her obsolete ideas. You must have permission to move in on your own terms, even sell it if you should wish to do so.'

'Assuming that my grandmother is no longer with us, what do you suggest happens to the other people who live there and whose home it has been for more than twenty years?'

Her eyes slid away from his then, but she was not prepared to back down.

'If The Keep was sold, no doubt there would be money to house them elsewhere,' she muttered. 'Or, even if you felt strongly enough to let them stay, at least this plan that it should be some kind of hotel for the rest of the family should certainly be discounted. In all fairness The Keep

335

should be left solely to the eldest son and his descendants and I think that you should try to carry this point with your grandmother before it is too late.'

'Well, I can try.' Hal shrugged. 'But even if I were to succeed in overturning the Trust nothing would change. Fliss would certainly continue to run The Keep along the lines my grandmother has laid down.'

'Fliss . . .?' She goggled at him. 'What . . .?'

'My father and hers were twins,' he told her, 'but her father, Peter, was older than mine by some twenty minutes. Fliss is his oldest surviving child and, given your reasoning, would inherit The Keep. She holds the same views as our grandmother and would want to see The Keep kept as a refuge for the family.'

They stared at each other. 'I think you have deliberately misled us,' she said angrily.

He frowned a little. 'Are you saying that you would have refused to allow Maria to marry me if you hadn't believed that I was my grandmother's sole heir?' he asked.

She swallowed, sensing the trap, and he smiled.

'Let's forget it, shall we?' he asked. 'My grandmother will leave plenty enough funds for the upkeep of the house and grounds. Maria won't be out of pocket, I promise you. Is that what's worrying you and Frank? No need. We can go on exactly as we are now or we can buy our own house. She need not live at The Keep at all. Susanna and Gus would probably be perfectly happy to live there. Or even Fliss and Miles. If Maria finds the idea so awful—'

'Nonsense,' she said quickly. 'Don't be so foolish. I was merely trying to clarify matters. We thought, Frank and I, that it was best to clear up this muddle—'

'I'm sorry that you thought it was a muddle,' he said cheerfully. 'It was always quite clear to me and I thought that Maria understood when I explained it to her. To be honest I don't think it's anyone else's business, certainly not while my grandmother is still alive. I've been led to believe that Maria is your heir but I wouldn't dream of discussing how your house should be utilised whilst you and Frank are alive. The Keep is a family home and I'm sure that there will always be someone ready to live in it if we don't choose to. Maria should have said she didn't understand – or, rather, that you didn't. There was no need for all this. Still, it's always better to clear the air, isn't it? The boys must be dying for that cake. I'll go and tell her that the coast is clear, shall I?'

He went out, swallowing down an odd desire to burst out laughing, and she was left alone, glaring after him.

Chapter Thirty-two

'I'd never have believed it,' said Kit gloomily as she peered into cupboards, banging doors upon their paucity of interesting culinary content, and deciding finally that it must be eggs again for supper, 'that in your declining years you should become an opera buff.' She shook her head in a kind of reproachful despair.

'Hardly a buff,' protested Sin, leaning against the wall of the arch which separated the kitchen itself from the eating area. She smoothed her claret-coloured, crushed velvet dress with a touch that hinted at voluptuousness. 'To be honest, I don't really know my *Tosca* from my *Turandot* but I'm working on it.'

'This is clear,' said Kit severely. 'I've had no sense out of you for weeks. And don't think I haven't seen you boning up on it. *Puccini for Beginners. Wagner in Six Easy Lessons.*'

'Seriously though,' said Sin, sitting down suddenly on the nearest chair at the square oak table. 'I had no idea it was all so wonderful. I cry buckets and Andrew pretends not to notice, just keeps passing me enormous handkerchiefs and ignores my sniffs. The front of my dress gets soaked every time we go—' 'And I thought you'd been spilling your beer,' mused Kit remorsefully – 'and afterwards I have to go to the cloakroom and do my make-up. When I heard Pinkerton shouting, "Butterfly, Butterfly," and she was lying there dead I thought I'd never stop crying.'

'And to think that this was the girl who wanted to strip off with the cast when we went to see *Hair*,' mourned Kit. 'Get a grip before you're completely indoctrinated. Try to remember that you were once a member of that glorious band who didn't think Woodstock was a village just outside Oxford.'

'Andrew's so good about it,' said Sin dreamily, toying with a withered apple in the fruit bowl. 'He just loves sharing it all. He says it's as if he's seeing them again for the first time through my eyes. I think Margaret must be mad. Stuck down in Wiltshire in the mud, all amongst the donkeys, when she could be here with him, going to the opera and having delicious little suppers afterwards and discussing the performance.'

Kit looked at her thoughtfully. 'I suppose she knows all about your latest craze?' she asked casually. 'That Andrew has begun taking you along on his opera evenings?'

'He's told her that he's educating my mind.' Sin beamed at her. 'She doesn't seem the least bit interested.'

'Of course, she doesn't know you well enough to share in the general amazement that he's discovered that you've actually got one,' said Kit tartly. ' "Educating your mind." I can't believe Andrew would be so patronising.'

'He isn't,' Sin assured her. 'We simply decided that it was the best thing to tell her. She simply can't take me seriously so she's quite ready to believe it, which means Andrew doesn't have to lie or make excuses. Naturally he doesn't want to hurt her in any way and he seems quite incapable of lying.' She frowned regretfully at this inconvenient deficiency in his character.

'Well, he could certainly take your correspondence course on that one,' murmured Kit, inspecting a piece of elderly cheese. 'But I do agree that he's almost pathologically honest. Frightening really. Ah. Do I hear someone knocking?'

She watched with a mixture of amusement and anxiety as Sin leaped up and rushed out into the hall. There was a murmur of voices and Andrew, distinguished in his dinner jacket, appeared in the doorway and waved cheerfully at her.

'Ready for another evening of debauchery?' she asked genially. 'What is it this time? *Tristan und Isolde*? Oh, good grief, did nobody ever write a real side-splittingly funny opera? No, I suppose not. Well, I hope your pockets are full of handkerchiefs, Andrew.'

He smiled, indicating that he was well prepared, and turned as Sin came in behind him. 'All ready?'

She nodded, picking up her short fur jacket and giving Kit a private grin. 'Enjoy your egg, dear, and go to bed early.'

Kit waved aside this persiflage. 'I shall be living it up with some rather special Spanish Rioja and my *Saturday Night Fever* tape. *You* might not consider that the Bee Gees are in the same league as Verdi—'

'Oh, shut up,' said Sin. 'Come on, Andrew, She's having one of her moods.'

'I certainly am not,' said Kit indignantly. 'Never forget that once, when I was young and innocent, I sat through the entire Ring Cycle and, let me tell you, I was absolutely sober throughout the entire ordeal. Anyone who has endured twenty hours of Wagner without the numbing benefit of alcohol is entitled to an opinion on opera.'

Sin drew breath to point out that Kit had suffered simply in order to impress her escort with whom she had imagined herself in love – and suddenly decided to remain silent. Kit raised her eyebrows irritatingly in a silent question and Sin glared at her.

'Well,' said Andrew, unaware of any by-play, 'opera does seem to be something one either loves or hates. It's certainly not everybody's passion. Margaret can't stand it. I'm just delighted that Sin is enjoying it. The thing about a passion – whatever it is – is that it's really such a joy to share it.'

'You couldn't speak a truer word,' murmured Kit provocatively, making big eyes at Andrew who began to laugh.

'Hopeless woman,' he said, helping Sin into her jacket. 'Are you ever serious?'

'Don't wait up,' hissed Sin as Andrew led the way into the hall, Kit trailing behind, and Kit shut the front door behind them with rather more force than was absolutely necessary.

She wandered back into the kitchen and stood looking at the solitary egg which had been unearthed earlier during an excavation of the fridge. It was not the first time that she had forgotten to do the weekend shopping, nor would it be the last, and a mood of dejection took possession of her. Sin's evenings out with Andrew were becoming a regular event and for the first time in her life Kit was beginning to imagine what it might be like to live alone.

'Who loves ya, baby?' she asked moodily of the egg and, taking a glass from the draining board she poured herself some wine. Andrew was nothing like many of the married men that she and Sin had fielded in recent years and she had the horrid feeling that when he woke up to the fact that he was falling in love with Sin there would be all sorts of ructions. As for Sin . . . Kit scowled at the unfortunate egg and glanced about her for the bread. It was quite possible that Sin was enjoying her evenings at the opera but it was also clear to anyone who knew her that she was becoming deeply attached to Andrew; and once they both woke up to their other passion, what then?

Kit was very fond of Andrew and would have been delighted to see him rescued from his wife, who clearly had very little time for him, but it would be very odd to lose Sin. Kit sighed as she unwrapped the bread, which had seen happier days. She was pleased that Sin seemed to have at last recovered from her love for Mole. Since he'd been posted to *Osiris* as First Lieutenant, almost a year ago, he had not been to London. True, the submarine was based at Devonport and had been at sea most of the time since he'd joined her, but there seemed to be a tacit understanding between them that he was taking this opportunity to make the break. Even before his posting to Devonport his visits had grown less frequent and Kit knew that Sin was trying to accustom herself to the idea that he no longer needed her.

'It's no good blaming him,' she'd said once. 'I never let him think it was serious. I had too much pride. I couldn't have borne it if one day he'd fallen in love with a girl much younger than me.'

Kit had done what she could to cheer and comfort Sin as

Mole's visits grew further and further apart and they had joked about their joint foolishness where men were concerned; Sin about Mole and Kit about Jake . . .

Unable to give her mind to her supper, Kit pushed the bread aside, drank some more wine and fingered the locket at her throat. Jake had spoiled her for anyone who'd followed afterwards. She could get along fine up to a point but then the structure which she'd been carefully attempting to build would fall apart. He'd been everything, she could see that clearly now that it was too late: friend, lover, confidant. The trouble was, now that she was past the age when hormones and mother nature were cunningly persuading women that they wanted nothing more desperately than to play their part in the reproduction of the species, marriage didn't seem important any more. Perhaps she'd lived alone too long, become too selfish to be ready to give up her way of life for any man who was unable to sweep her absolutely off her feet. He would have to be someone very special indeed to make the sacrifices worth it. You only had to look at Hal and Maria or Fliss and Miles to see that marriage was no easy option; on the other hand, of course, Susanna and Gus were blissfully happy, which did something to restore the balance . . .

There was a loud hammering at the door accompanied by deep, throaty barking and Kit ran out into the hall, hope rising, her depression evaporating.

'Clarrie.' She flung the door open and he came in, rosy with cold, preceded by Fozzy. 'I didn't know you were back. I thought you weren't due home till Wednesday. How was the old school chum? Didn't it work out now he's married again?'

'Couldn't bear it another moment, could we, old man?' He followed her into the kitchen, struggling out of his shabby British Warm, and subsided on to a chair, unwinding a scarlet woollen muffler from about his neck. His tweed jacket was comfortably worn, patched with leather and carried the familiar scent of tobacco and coffee. 'Poor old Basil. Another good man gone west, that's all I can say. Wretched old haybag nagging him morning, noon and night. It was more than flesh and blood could stand. He'd said I could bring Fozzy and then the wretched woman wouldn't have him in the house. Fozzy, I mean, not Basil. Terribly embarrassing for everyone, especially Basil. I *told* him he was too old to go through it again but he wouldn't have it. Happy first time round, you see, so he thought it was going to be the same all over again. Dear, oh dear, oh dear.' He pursed his lips and blew gustily into his short white moustache.

'How ghastly.' Kit poured wine into another glass. 'Did you get any time alone together?'

'Hardly any.' He raised his glass appreciatively. 'Took him to the pub but he had one eye on the clock the whole time. She didn't want to hear any of the old stories, naturally not, since he didn't know her then. Sort of woman who can't bear for a man to have a past. Took against me from the word go.'

'Did you wind her up?' Kit encouraged Fozzy on to the old sofa and sat beside him. 'Bet you did.'

'Me?' Clarrie opened his eyes innocently. 'I might have made the odd remark but the poor old chap was so distraught that I hadn't the heart. Cat on a hot tin roof the whole time.'

'I think it's terrifying.' Kit shuddered, clasping the obliging Fozzy to her breast. 'It's such a terrible risk, isn't it? I was just thinking that when you arrived. Sin and Andrew are out again, *Tristan und Isolde* this time, and I'm beginning to think that there might be trouble ahead. I've had this terrible presentiment here . . .' She pressed her hand to her heart dramatically.

'Not surprised,' said Clarrie, looking with revulsion at the solitary egg and the heel of aged bread. 'Indigestion, I shouldn't wonder. I can't believe you've never learned to cook properly. You're the most hopeless pair of females I've ever chanced upon in a long and ill-spent life. Look, I've got nothing in yet so what d'you say we go out and forage? Have some supper at the pub?'

Kit kissed the top of Fozzy's rough head. 'I love him,' she told him soulfully. 'And there was I thinking that I should never love again.'

Fozzy sighed, glad of affection after three days banished to a strange, unfriendly garden shed. He regarded Kit, who lay about with him in chairs or on the floor, as a kind of honorary dog and was very ready to tolerate her more unfortunate human habits.

'Poor old fellow,' said Clarrie, ignoring Kit's protestations of affection. 'It's been hell for him. Frightful female squawked every time he put a paw inside the door and she insisted that he was fed outside in the rain. Didn't care that poor old Basil was being shown up and humiliated. Even worse than the memsahib, and I never thought I'd hear myself say that, I can tell you.'

'Poor Fozzy,' murmured Kit, and he sighed even more deeply, rolling a grateful eye, as he stretched out luxuriously across her lap.

'Got his own back,' said Clarrie with a grin of satisfaction. 'Squeezed out of the shed and dug a hole on the lawn. Ye Gods! Could that woman shriek. Sounded like all the furies of hell. Told Basil she could have made her fortune in the war doubling for the all-clear. Lost his sense of humour, poor chap, so I thought it was time to make tracks and we came home. Just in time by the look of it.' He gave Kit's prospective supper another appalled glance and heaved himself out of his chair. 'I'll give him a tin of something while you get yourself ready. Come on, old chap . . .'

'I *do* love him,' Kit told the egg. 'I wonder if my father would've been like Clarrie? Perhaps he and Ma ought to get together. She's really lonely these days . . .'

She murmured on whilst she tidied up a little and finished her wine but presently, finding the egg an indifferent conversationalist, Kit threw the bread in the bin, picked up her bag and went to fetch her coat.

Chapter Thirty-three

'I wish we lived near a beach,' said Jamie, 'and then we could do it properly but we'll just have to make do. We can pretend that the field is the fjord so that we'll see the Germans landing from the lane. Then we can spy on them and when we see they're coming ashore we have to get on our bikes and dash back to our HQ.'

'Is that when we find out that one of our resistance members is a traitor?' asked Bess, pushing her arms into a camouflage jacket – part of an outfit which she'd had for her birthday.

'A quisling.' Jamie rolled the word around his tongue.

Bess thought: It's as if he's tasting it, like something nice to eat.

Jamie was enjoying this new game. It was funny that he liked watching the old war films better than things like *Dr Who* or *The Six Million Dollar Man*. Somehow the films weren't so frightening and he wondered if it might be because they weren't in colour. Daddy loved the new colour television but it made things terribly real sometimes. The black-and-white films were like old photographs; they belonged to another, long-past world where everything was that strange browny-grey colour. The Daleks with their grating, shouting voices terrified him and he knew that Bess didn't like them either. Daddy laughed at them and called them babies so it was good to be able to sit with him to watch the films and not be frightened. Daddy would explain things to him and then he felt grown up; strong and brave. When he grew up he was going into the Army and he wished that he could go away with Daddy on expeds. He was away this weekend in the Brecon Beacons with a group of the men. Because he was the CO he didn't have to go but he thought it was important every now and again. Jamie said that he'd go every time if he were the CO but Daddy said it wouldn't be right because the men would think you didn't trust them.

He watched Bess getting herself dressed for the part, remembering how Ricky's mother – they weren't a naval family – had been rather shocked to see Bess in her camouflage outfit which was exactly like his own. She'd said that she didn't approve of such small children being encouraged to play war games.

'I don't encourage them,' Mummy had answered. 'It seems to come quite naturally. Best to let them get it out of their systems while they're small. Don't you think that forbidding things merely makes them more desirable?'

Ricky wasn't allowed to have toy guns but he was always making pretend ones out of sticks and when he came to play he was the roughest of all their friends. He and Bess didn't like him very much. He'd twisted Bess's arm and so Jamie had hit him and then Ricky had run to his mother and blubbed.

'That's what happens when you encourage small children

to be violent,' she'd said, her face all pinched up and cross, and Mummy had looked anxious, but when Jamie had tried to explain she'd shushed him and told him to say he was sorry. Afterwards, when he'd explained it all, Mummy said perhaps Ricky needn't come round very often. Bess hadn't cried, even when Ricky was hurting her, but seeing her face all crumpled up with pain had made him want to hurt Ricky really badly.

'That's the trouble,' Mummy had said when he'd told her this afterwards. 'It's not playing games about the Resistance that's dangerous in itself, it's because violence breeds violence. If someone hurts you or someone you love, you want to hurt them in return and once it starts it's difficult to stop. When you play your games all your enemies are imaginary so no one gets hurt but in real life it's rather different.'

'Ready?' Bess was watching him.

He nodded, excitement returning. 'I wish we could speak Norwegian,' he said wistfully.

'We'll make up our own words,' she told him. 'Go on. You go first.'

Watching them from her bedroom window, Fliss felt a familiar sense of anguish. Below her on the lawn the two small figures were busy; conferring together, wheeling their bicycles out of the shed, pausing for some more discussion. Jamie had his plastic machine gun strapped across his chest. In a naval environment it was impossible to protect them from the military influence – and anyway would it be right to do so? Miles had no time for the anti-nuclear lobby or the pacifists but Fliss was always confused by this question of defence.

'Would it have been better to allow Hitler to dominate the world?' he'd asked her when she'd attempted to talk through her reservations. 'Should we have refused to oppose him? Refused to fight when he invaded Poland? Do you think he would have stopped at the Jews?'

Was it right that Jamie should stand by whilst Ricky bullied Bess?

Fliss thought: I shall ask Uncle Theo. He'll know the answer.

She felt a sudden longing to be at The Keep; to be with them especially now. It was impossible, of course. She couldn't simply leave the twinnies and Miles. She was pleased to think that Mole would be home soon on leave at The Keep, and Susanna had promised to keep her fully informed about Grandmother's condition on a day-to-day basis. Kit was going down next weekend, picking up Aunt Prue on the way, and Fliss felt a foolish exclusion, as if she were being left out. The problem was that her strong sense of family – Chadwick family – merely underlined the loneliness within her own marriage. As the twinnies grew older so relationships eased slightly between them and Miles but there was none of that normal happy family banter and argument and sharing that she had known until she was ten. Even at The Keep there had been a closeness between them all, despite the age differences, which had included Ellen and Fox and Caroline. In Africa they had a saying: It takes a village to bring up a child. Looking back, she suspected that she had done better as an orphan at The Keep than the twinnies were doing with both their parents.

Bess and Jamie had disappeared now and Fliss turned back into the room. The married hiring was pleasant enough but she was suddenly overwhelmed by a passionate desire for her own home; somewhere she could put down roots and build for the future. Of course, there was the house in Dartmouth . . . Miles was talking again about selling the house in Above Town and she'd wondered if he might be considering buying a family house where they could be together comfortably at last. There was still occasional mention of a foreign posting but since she had finally refused point-blank to put the twinnies into boarding school discussions had rather come to a halt. Fliss wished that she could be much stronger with Miles; question him, demand to know exactly what was going on. He still had the tendency to pat her on the head and say absently that it was all on a 'need-to-know' basis, that he'd explain when he could, and so on.

She was certain now that once the twinnies were born Miles had put their own life together on hold until they could be alone together again. He couldn't see that they had grown slowly but steadily apart during the last seven years and that it would be quite impossible to wave a magic wand and magically be restored to the people they had once been. Perhaps he thought that in five years' time, when he retired and the twinnies were settled into boarding school, they would begin a whole new life together but surely he must see that she would never consider any way of life which excluded the twinnies. The danger was clear: at some point she might be obliged to make a choice.

Fliss thought: I simply mustn't let it come to that. Things are a little better now that Bess and Jamie are growing up. We simply must hold on . . .

The simple problem at the moment was that she wanted to be at The Keep with her family. If only Miles were sympathetic towards this point of view he would be more than capable of dealing with Jamie and Bess in her absence but knowing that he disapproved made it difficult for her to consign them with confidence to his care. He would not be unkind, of course, but he would be indifferent, and she could not decide where her responsibility lay. If only the twinnies had been smaller and she could have bundled them into the car and driven down to Devon, she would have risked Miles's disapproval . . . But perhaps she was, after all, overreacting. Susanna had promised . . . and she could be at The Keep in three hours . . . but supposing Grandmother were to deteriorate and die suddenly. Swallowing back tears of loneliness and fear, Fliss made an uncharacteristically impulsive gesture. She took up the address book and, lifting the telephone receiver, dialled Hal's number.

'Chadwick.' He sounded preoccupied, almost bored.

'Hal, it's Fliss.'

'He-*llo*!' The change of tone, the warmth and undisguised delight filled her with a breathless joy. 'And how are you, Fliss?'

'In a do,' she answered, trying to laugh it off. 'Isn't it silly? Miles has got an exped weekend and I've let myself get worked up about Grandmother. I don't know whether I should be there or not. Miles thinks I'm overdramatising the situation and perhaps I am . . .'

Her voice tailed off as she wondered whether he might sympathise with Miles. The Navy was a tough school and she knew that however loyal and discreet he was, Hal was often irritated by Maria's inability to cope or take decisions.

'. . . but it's only that she might die suddenly,' she went

354

on quickly. 'I take his point that I could be there indefinitely and I can't keep the twinnies off school.'

'Can't Miles manage the twinnies?' Hal's voice was blessedly calm, reassuring, familiar. 'I should have thought that at a time like this he could handle it with a bit of local co-operation from schoolfriends.'

She realised that she was trembling; her teeth were chattering with suppressed excitement and happiness. It was so good just to talk to him, to know that he was thinking about her, concentrating on her anxieties.

'Only,' she explained, 'that it's impossible to make concrete plans. It might happen at any moment or take some weeks and he feels it's a bit . . . well, tricky. He doesn't quite understand the family bit.' She stopped, suspecting that she was being disloyal, knowing quite surely deep inside that she *was* being disloyal. 'And, after all, I can be there in three hours.' Suddenly it was important to be as fair as she could be.

'I don't think that's quite the point, is it? Still, if that's how he feels . . . OK. Decide on a date and go down to The Keep on that day. Make arrangements with the twinnies' friends, have a good rota of mums to meet them from school and so on and tell Miles that from then on you'll be with Grandmother. It simply can't be that long now, Flissy.'

'Oh, Hal.' She pressed her lips together, her happiness giving way before the grim implication of his words.

'Oh, darling, don't do that crying thing,' he said quietly. 'Not when you're such a long way off.'

The hot tears trickled down her cold cheeks. 'I'm OK really. Honestly.' She tried to inject a smile into her words. 'You're quite right. It's best to make a date and stick to it. I'll get organised.'

There was a tiny silence.

'Where are the twinnies?'

She laughed quite naturally then. 'Playing war games,' she told him. 'They were watching one of those old black-and-white movies on the television about the Germans invading Norway so we've been Norwegians for the last week. They've got an arms cache hidden in the old pigsty and they're about to unmask an informer . . . Oh, Hal, is it wrong for them to play these games?'

He made an impatient noise. 'How do you propose to stop them? The world is a violent place and I think it's better to train man's naturally violent impulses towards defence of the weak than to send them underground and thwart or deform them. Then you've really got problems. Easier said than done, of course. Anyway, I hardly think that Jamie and Bess are future Stalins.'

'I know that really. I told you I'm having a daft moment . . . It's good to talk to you. Are you all OK?'

'Elaine's here for the weekend. Anxious about my inheritance,' he said laconically. 'She and Maria have conspired together but we've sorted it out. The boys are fine. They've all gone out to tea with a schoolfriend so I've got an hour or so to myself . . . What are you wearing?'

She was shocked into a momentary silence by the intimacy of the question.

'Cords,' she said at last. 'My old navy cords and a guernsey.' She attempted a chuckle. 'You know me. Always the height of fashion.'

'Yes, I know you. Fliss—'

'Don't,' she said quickly. 'We mustn't. I shouldn't have telephoned but . . . I needed you. I need my family. I keep thinking about Grandmother and . . . I feel so helpless and lonely.'

'I'm glad you telephoned. Don't worry, I know we shall both feel guilty about it but I need you, too. It sounds silly to say that, doesn't it? We need each other so that we can carry on without each other. Well, we've said it now. Make that date and stick to it, my darling, and I shall see you down at The Keep. Don't worry. I shall be there when you need me. Always.'

The line went dead and Fliss replaced the receiver, tears streaming down, leaking into her mouth, soaking her chin. She went into the kitchen, turned on the cold tap and began to splash her face with icy water.

'We were going to have tea at HQ,' said Bess from behind her, 'but it's a bit cold after all. So we've come back.'

'What a good idea.' Fliss buried her face in the kitchen towel. 'We'll all have tea together, then.'

'What are you doing?' asked Jamie, divesting himself of various weapons. He looked at her curiously. 'What's wrong?'

'Got something in my eye,' she said cheerfully. 'It was really painful. Made me cry but it's OK now. Tea's what we need. So what's been happening? Are you going to brief me?'

'I've got to write my report,' said Jamie repressively. 'Haven't had time yet.'

'Right,' said Fliss. 'In that case I'll get the kettle on.'

As she filled the kettle she tested herself. There was guilt and elation in equal parts but it was odd that, although she and Hal both knew that they could never be together, the feeling of loneliness and isolation had utterly evaporated. She knew now that she could make plans to go to The Keep, to do what was necessary, that she could continue to hold on.

Chapter Thirty-four

It was not until Hal had left for Greenwich the next morning that the two women could speak openly. With the boys settled on the playroom floor surrounded by their Fisher Price toys, Maria and her mother were able to have a private talk over the coffee cups. Elaine opened with a barely disguised salvo.

'I must say, darling,' she began, with only a faint attempt to hide her hostility towards her son-in-law, 'I do think that Hal is getting rather arrogant. He's changed, hasn't he?'

Maria, who had been quite ready to enter into a discussion about the Chadwicks, felt irritation rising at this critical approach. Had her mother started on a more sympathetic note she too could have enjoyed slagging Hal off, revelling in a good bout of character assassination. As it was, however, she suddenly resented her mother's interference in her marriage.

'I thought you rather approved of his self-confidence,' she said sulkily. 'You were always saying that he'd go far, if I remember rightly. Ten minutes after he met him Daddy was prophesying that he'd make admiral.'

Elaine shifted on her chair. She had no wish to antagonise her daughter but she was still smarting from Hal's sharp words.

'I think we always valued his good points but I was surprised at the way he took me up yesterday afternoon. Good as told me to mind my own business.'

For a brief moment Maria aligned herself with Hal but remembered in time that it was at her own wish that her mother had confronted him.

'He always gets very defensive about anything to do with his damned family,' she observed, reaching for her handbag which hung by its strap on the chair back and rooting in it for her cigarettes. Elaine watched her disapprovingly.

'I wish you hadn't started up that awful habit again, darling,' she complained. 'You were so good giving it up as soon as you were pregnant. It's such a pity to start all over again.'

Maria lit her cigarette, pulled the ashtray closer and stared narrowly at her mother through the plume of smoke.

'It helps me relax,' she said shortly.

'Well, I can quite understand that.' Her mother assumed a self-righteous expression. 'I think you have quite enough to cope with, I must say. Thank God, at least, that the wretched dog has gone.'

Maria cast a quick look through the open door to the playroom. The boys were murmuring together, immersed in their game, oblivious of their elders.

'Don't speak too loud,' warned Maria. 'Jolyon really misses him. Edward's a bit too young to understand but it's been really tricky explaining it to Jolyon.'

'Well, it's not as if you had him put down or anything.' Elaine shrugged the matter aside. 'He's still in the family. Jolyon will see him again before too long.'

'Of course it's another good mark for The Keep,' said

Maria bitterly, tapping ash from her cigarette. 'Naturally, the wonderful Caroline can deal with him. Apparently Hal had a brilliant weekend. Fliss was there for the twins' birthday and a good time was had by all.'

There was a silence. Elaine studied her daughter covertly, making up her mind to speak.

'Do you really want to live there, darling?' Her voice now was soothing and gentle, and Maria visibly relaxed a little. 'We've simply got to decide what's best for you, haven't we? We can't let you be swept along by the Chadwicks. You have your own life to consider. If The Keep is to be left under those conditions perhaps we should have a rethink. Hal tells me that even if he overturned the Trust it wouldn't help either of you. Apparently it was Fliss's father who was the eldest and she would then inherit. Really,' she shook her head, 'I've never heard of such a stupid thing.'

'Well, I can tell you one thing. I'm not being an hotel-keeper. If Hal thinks I'm going to move in and be an unpaid housekeeper to his family he can think again.'

Elaine took a deep breath. Her eyes were thoughtful as she weighed the facts and looked ahead to the future.

'I have to say that your father and I would be most unhappy to think that all our . . .' She hesitated a little as she fumbled for the right expression and then changed direction slightly. 'You know that everything we have is yours, Maria. We don't want it to disappear into some melting pot for the benefit of the Chadwick family,' she said at last.

Maria stared at her. 'Nor do I,' she said with a certain amount of aggression. 'No way.'

'It might prove difficult to prevent it.' Her mother, now certain that Maria was in full sympathy with her own views, sighed deeply and then smiled, as though recalling happier times. 'Oh dear. I can't help wishing that you'd married Adam Wishart after all. He's done so well, junior partner now, you know, and Daddy's all set to pass the practice over to him when the time comes.'

'Yes, well that's fine,' said Maria crossly, 'but you weren't quite so keen at the time, were you? Not when he was just starting his pupillage and neither of you were too sure how he might turn out. If I remember you were terribly pleased when Hal turned up on the scene and put Adam's nose out of joint.'

Elaine was silenced, biting her lip, cudgelling her brain. It was quite true that she and Frank had considered Hal to be the better proposition at the time and had done everything they could to encourage him.

'I can't deny it,' she said regretfully at last, 'but I think we misjudged Adam. And you did rather fall for Hal, darling, you must admit. It wasn't as if we had to force you into it.'

'I know, I know,' said Maria impatiently. 'Don't rub it in. The trouble was that Hal was so much more sophisticated. He made Adam look so . . . well, *raw* beside him. He was that much older, too.'

'At that age it makes such a difference,' agreed Elaine. 'Adam is only a year older than you, isn't he? You were both still children but at twenty-six Hal was already an adult, taking command, making decisions. The Navy does rather grow them up quick. Now, of course, there's nothing to choose between them, is there? I thought you were getting on so well together when you were home last. Quite like old times.'

There was another silence whilst Maria remembered the dinner party at her parents' home with Adam Wishart seated beside her. She'd enjoyed flirting with him despite – or perhaps because of – the presence of his wife further down the table. Of course, Hal had been away . . .

'He was saying that he's never got over you.' Her mother was watching her. 'His marriage isn't happy, you know. She's a rather trying girl, very prickly, I always find, and not particularly friendly. I think it's true that he still has a *tendresse* for you so it probably accounts for her attitude towards us, although when I think how much your father has done for Adam I think she could be a little more grateful.'

'Well, I don't see that it's going to do any of us much good.' Maria stubbed out her cigarette and swallowed the last of her coffee. 'It doesn't really get us any further, does it?'

'If The Keep can never be yours and Hal's then I don't see much point in your living in it. I agree with you there.' Elaine decided to make her point. 'Why should you run a family hotel? On the other hand, it might be sensible for you and Hal to buy a house instead of renting one. It would be wise to have something behind you of your own, if you see what I mean?'

Mother and daughter looked at one another for a long moment.

'You mean in case . . .?' Maria hesitated.

'Things can change,' said Elaine, deliberately vague, 'when children grow up. I've seen it happen so many times. One should always be prepared.'

'Perhaps you're right,' said Maria thoughtfully.

'Think it over,' advised her mother, finishing her coffee. 'How about a little jaunt into Winchester?' She laughed a little, as if she were about to make a joke. 'Perhaps we should have a look in at some of the estate agents so as to give us an idea of what's on the market. Just for a bit of fun, of course.'

'Yes,' said Maria slowly. 'Why not? I think that's a brilliant idea. Come on. Let's get the boys organised and we might just make it in time for some lunch.'

The studio was in its usual pleasant state of busy, friendly activity. Gus was hunched in a chair talking to a client on the telephone about a brochure; Susanna was standing at the light box 'spotting' negatives. They both looked up as Mole came in. Gus raised a hand, gesturing at the telephone, making faces at him. Susanna laid down her brush, carefully put the lid back on the spotting medium and beamed at him cheerfully.

'We'll go up and have coffee,' she told him. 'Gus has a client coming so we'll be in the way down here. He's got a mug just made so he's OK.'

Mole followed his sister up the stairs to the flat. He looked about appreciatively as she disappeared behind the rattan screens to fill the kettle. All of their earnings had gone into the barn out at Dartington and the flat had remained in much the same state for the three and a half years that they'd been married.

'You'll miss this,' he told her, bending to read the title on the musical score lying on the low table beside one of the saggy armchairs. 'You won't know what to do with all that space at the barn.' He saw that the fire had been kept in –

probably in his honour – which accounted for the warm cosiness. 'Are you allowed to sublet it?' It was rather horrid to think of a stranger in this homely place amongst their things, although their special belongings would be going off to the barn with them. Even so . . .

'Something rather good has happened.' Susanna's voice floated out above the tall screens. 'Well, it's partly good and partly rather sad, actually. Janie's split up with her boy-friend and she's feeling pretty miserable so I've suggested to Gus that she comes down here and works with him when the baby comes. I shall still be able to do a bit but it won't be terribly easy once the baby's mobile. There are too many dangerous things in the studio to be able to have a baby about.'

'It would be nicer if it's someone you know,' agreed Mole, wandering back towards the kitchen end of the big room. 'Is she experienced enough to be useful?'

'Oh, yes. We trained together and she's often been down to stay and given us a hand.' Susanna appeared with the coffee and put the tray down on the gate-leg table under the window. 'Then she could live here, you see. It would be perfect. I've got to check with the landlord but I don't think there will be a problem. Poor old Janie. She's really fed up.'

Mole sat in one of the chairs at the table and looked down into the courtyard. It was still very cold but the wallflower plants in their wooden tub were green and flourishing, and the yellow flowers of the winter jasmine made a cheerful splash of colour against the grey stone walls. He felt a sudden terrible sadness at the thought of this little haven being passed even to Janie. Susanna and Gus had made it so much their own, imprinted their personalities so strongly upon it. Behind the courtyard walls there was the same feeling of safety which defined The Keep. The Barn, open to the surrounding countryside, seemed vulnerable compared to this small haven. He would have been happier knowing that Susanna was safe here when the baby came, assuming that she survived the ordeal. The old childish terror gripped him; the fear that something might happen to her, this very dear companion of his youth . . .

She was watching him, gauging his mood, guessing at his thoughts, aware of his fears. So it had been through all their lives together. She instinctively knew of his ongoing nightmare vision: sudden death striking out of a bright day; the utter finality of such a loss; the frustrating impotence of being unable to prevent it.

'I can't tell you how I long for the barn,' she said, ladling sugar into her coffee. 'This has been perfect until now but it will be heaven to have more space and I'm looking forward to being all on one level. I'm so clumsy going up and down steps, you know, and it will be worse as I get bigger. And then again, the barn will be so much safer for a baby.'

He looked at her quickly. 'Will it?'

'Oh yes. Imagine this place when he starts crawling. Open fire. Screens to be pulled down. Stone steps outside the door and the stairs down to the studio. I shouldn't have a moment's peace.'

She saw that he was taking it all in. 'But the barn is very open,' he ventured at last. 'Won't you miss the privacy of the courtyard?'

Susanna chuckled. 'If you call it privacy when every client walks through it, not to mention passing friends. Gus is going to make me a courtyard at the barn, at the L-shaped end where we've already got the two walls for it. It's a really good idea and it'll be properly private. I'll show you his drawing for it. It'll be just as good as this when we've finished it.'

'That's OK then.' Mole sipped his coffee, wondering whether it had been worse worrying about Fliss so far away in Hong Kong or having Susanna close at hand. He'd been almost relieved that Miles had been so against having any more children. Each time he saw the twinnies or Hal's boys his heart contracted at their weakness and vulnerability and although he adored these small people he was quite glad to see them growing stronger and larger. He had a suspicion that Susanna and Gus might decide to have a huge family . . .

'It would be nice to have Janie here,' she was saying idly – but her eyes were bright.

He grinned at her, his fears receding somewhat, well aware of the implications. 'Very nice,' he agreed amiably. 'Sweet girl, Janie.'

'She's still got a thing about you,' pronounced Susanna.

'So you say.' Mole was unmoved by this recurring theme. 'And I've got a thing about her. A thing that tells me that we're not cut out to be man and wife.'

'You're a misogynist,' she grumbled.

'I certainly am not,' he protested indignantly. 'I love women. Some more than others. I simply don't want to be committed to just one of them, that's all.'

'You sound like Sin,' she observed.

'Do I?' He poured himself some more coffee and refilled her cup. 'Well, she and Kit are agreed on that subject, anyway.'

She was silent, wondering as she often did, whether he had a private passion for Sin, hoping he hadn't. She suspected that he spoke the truth when he talked about commitment, knowing how hard it would be for someone with his ingrained fears to leave a deeply loved wife and children to fend for themselves whilst he was at sea.

'How's Grandmother today?' She changed the subject and saw his brow contract.

'Not too good. She barely leaves her bed these days.'

Susanna thought: At least he has had time to prepare himself for her death and she is very old. He will be able to cope with this.

She said aloud, 'Perhaps I'll come back with you this afternoon and see her. We'll stop off at the barn and I'll show you the latest progress. You're staying to lunch, aren't you?'

'I'd like that,' he said. 'Yes, come back for tea and I'll run you back in to Totnes later. That's if Gus can spare you for that long.'

'I expect he can. So.' She put her elbows on the table. 'How's the Senior Service then? It's great that you've got some leave, isn't it? We'll think of things to do.'

She sounded like the small Susanna then, making plans for the long summer holidays, and Mole felt a sudden pang of nostalgia; a piercing longing for those past days of the childhood which they had shared so happily together.

Chapter Thirty-five

'I shan't really mind anything,' murmured Freddy, 'as long as I don't have Crimond.'

Kneeling beside her, swallowing back his tears, Theo made an effort to smile just as she intended that he should. Planning Freddy's funeral was the hardest thing he'd ever had to do.

'It's no good pretending,' she'd said to him earlier. 'It's the last thing I'm ever likely to organise and I want to get it right. What about hymns? I don't want "Abide with me". Too dreary for words.'

She'd taken him by surprise and he'd found it difficult to respond. Her matter-of-fact approach helped him to keep control of his own emotions but it underlined that terrible finality of it all. He'd been reading to her – they'd moved on to *Emma* now, 'much more entertaining than that boring Fanny,' she'd said – and he'd thought she'd fallen asleep. He'd quietly put the book aside and entered into his own thoughts, brooding on the days ahead, reflecting on the immediate past. It had been a busy week but Freddy had stood up to it well, especially well considering that it was clear that she knew that she was taking a final farewell, one by one, of the members of her family.

Kit had been the first to arrive with Prue, whom she had collected on her way from London, detouring through Bristol. It was plain that they'd had a good talk during the remainder of the drive together.

'I don't know what to do, Theo,' Prue had said, as she'd done so many times across the years. 'Can Freddy be serious? And even if she is, I'm not certain that I ought to just sell the house and move down, although the temptation is enormous, I must admit.'

'Then why not?' he'd asked, amused as always by her intensity. 'You know how much we'd love to have you here.'

'Darling Theo.' She'd put her arms about him and hugged him tightly. 'You've always been so good to me.'

'I'm simply being selfish,' he'd told her, touching the short feathery hair which was now more ash than fair. 'Caroline is lonely without Ellen or Fox and you get on so well together.'

'Well we do,' Prue had said firmly. 'That's quite true. But, oh, Theo,' the smoky blue eyes – Kit's eyes – had been round with anxiety, 'it's such a big step, isn't it?'

'My dear girl,' he'd said gently, 'you don't have to commit yourself to anything. Stay for six months or so and see how you like it. What does Kit say?'

'Kit thinks it's a great idea.' Prue had smiled, as if remembering some pleasing conversation. 'She and Hal worry about me, bless them, and I think they'd be happy to know that I was here with you. As Kit said, instead of just visiting me she'd be visiting all of you as well.' She'd sighed. 'It's certainly a very tempting thought.'

'Then I don't see what the problem is,' Theo had answered.

'I suppose,' Prue had said slowly, 'it's that I can't quite believe that Freddy means it. It's such a . . . a volte-face, isn't it? I mean, let's face it, Theo, I've never been her favourite person, have I? I want to be certain that she means it and that it wasn't something she said when she was at a low ebb.'

'I'm quite certain that she means it.'

Even as he'd spoken the words, Theo had experienced a shaft of doubt. Was it possible that, when Freddy saw Prue, she might undergo a change of mind? He had been deeply moved by the alteration in Freddy's attitude, not just over the question of Prue but also in a wider sense. There was a tranquillity which had brought him a sense of joy. He had feared the end might be clouded by the old railings against God and fate, or made painful by fear. Instead, she seemed to be uplifted by some inner contentment which he prayed would last. He'd had a momentary terror that Prue's actual presence might shake that peace. He'd waited long enough to see her draw the chair close up to the bed and reach out her hand for Freddy's and then he'd left them.

Sitting in the adjoining room, he'd waited, wrapped in prayer. He could hear their voices murmuring together, rising and falling, heard the chair shift suddenly and the sound of weeping. He'd risen then, going quietly to the door, lest he should be needed. Prue was on her knees beside the bed and the two women were holding tightly, each to the other, Freddy's thin hands clasped across Prue's back. Deeply moved, he'd turned away quickly, going back to his seat, his own cheeks wet with tears. Some time later,

Prue had come in to him, shutting the door behind her whilst Caroline assisted with Freddy's supper.

'I'm going to sell the house in Bristol and move down,' Prue had said, her eyes like stars. 'Oh, Theo, she really wants me to. I can't believe it. I always felt she resented me for marrying Johnny and she said that in a way she did. She said that she's been a very jealous woman . . .' She'd broken off and shaken her head. 'There's a change in her, isn't there? She's still the same old Freddy but there's a . . . a softness. No, that's not quite right. I can't quite put my finger on it . . .'

They'd talked quietly, happily, together and then Prue had slipped away, leaving Theo to send up a prayer of thanksgiving.

Hal had arrived even later that evening, driving down from London alone. He looked tense, preoccupied, but he'd been pleased to see his mother and sister and they'd spent several hours together in the drawing room whilst Theo had gone back upstairs to continue his vigil by Freddy's bedside. Kit had crept in later, kneeling beside the bed, slipping an arm about her grandmother's neck. 'Hello, honey,' he'd heard her whisper, and seen Freddy's answering smile.

It was when Kit had gone that she'd talked about the funeral.

'What is your favourite hymn?' he'd asked, after hearing her scathing opinion of 'Abide with me'.

There was a long silence. When she'd spoken, her voice had been tired and he'd had to bend close to hear the words.

'Drop Thy still dews of quietness,
till all our strivings cease;

Take from our souls the strain and stress,
And let our ordered lives confess
The beauty of Thy peace.

'Which hymn is that, Theo?'

'It's "Dear Lord and Father of mankind",' he'd said after a moment. 'So that is your favourite?'

'One of them,' she'd amended. 'I'd like that one. You'll read the lesson for me, won't you, Theo? You know the one? *"For since by man came death, by man came also the resurrection of the dead. For as in Adam all die, even so in Christ shall all be made alive . . . The last enemy that shall be destroyed is death."* You've read it for so many of my family. For Bertie and for John. And for Ellen and Fox. You'll read it for me, won't you, darling Theo?'

He'd wept silently, his head bowed, the tears soaking the sheet. Her hand had gently stroked his hair, just as if he had been one of the children, as he'd wept out his own pain; the cruel weight of the love he had never shown her; the sense of failure at his inability to give her spiritual comfort; his future loneliness. Yet, even now, when it would have been such an emotional release to pour out his feelings, something had held him back; some strength which had saved him – and her – from such a confession.

Presently, she'd found his hand and held it tightly.

'Let's not talk about it any more,' she'd murmured. 'I didn't mean to upset you. Anyway, I shan't really mind anything as long as I don't have Crimond.'

He'd smiled then, as she'd intended he should, but they'd clung together for some while afterwards, until she'd drifted into sleep.

★ ★ ★

With Hal and Kit's departure Mole had arrived for a few days' leave. The boat was alongside for some minor repairs and he was able to share the long vigils with his great-uncle and with Prue and Caroline.

Freddy grew weaker. Susanna came to her room, kneeling beside her, talking to her, explaining and describing, as if she were giving her grandmother a potted overview of the future. She'd already seen drawings of the barn and now Susanna was telling her the names of her putative family.

'It doesn't matter if this one's a boy or a girl, you see,' she whispered breathlessly, 'because Freddy will do for both and I shall see that they all know everything about you. Everything you did for us when we came back from Kenya and how we all were together, you and Ellen and Fox and Caroline and just how wonderful everything was . . .' and Susanna put her head down and sobbed as if her heart would break.

'Don't cry, my darling. Don't cry.' Freddy pushed back Susanna's dark hair, smiling at her, wiping away her tears. 'We had such fun, didn't we? I shan't be far away, you know. I shall see all your babies . . .'

'It won't be the same,' sobbed Susanna. 'I won't be able to see you doing it.'

'You must be very brave,' said Freddy. 'Think about your baby now and when he arrives you must pass on to him all the love and security that we gave to you. Nothing can truly separate us, my darling, Gus will tell you that.' She nodded to Gus, who was hovering anxiously at the door and he came over, bending to kiss her sunken cheek and then raising Susanna who hugged Freddy tightly before allowing herself to be led away.

So the hours passed. People came and went but Freddy remained sunk in a hazy stupor. Once she opened her eyes to see Fliss sitting beside her. For a moment she was reminded of Alison at about the same age, with the tiny frown between her brows and the firm set of the lips, and then Fliss smiled and she saw herself when young. Her mind wandered, trying to remember what it was that she'd done to Fliss, something wrong . . . As she frowned, her fingers plucking restlessly at the sheets, Hal came quietly in to stand beside Fliss, and she saw him put a hand upon her shoulder, saw her smile up at him, and she realised that it must have been in some dream that she had separated them and made them unhappy.

'Be happy, my darlings,' she mumbled. 'Be happy together,' and drifted away again into her half-world.

When she next woke the sun was shining into the room. She lay for some time trying to remember the events of the last few days. Had she been ill? She felt light and free, young and happy. Something had been weighing her down, something heavy and exacting. She frowned, raising her head a little – and then she saw him, sitting near the window reading. Theo. She remembered now. In her dream she had been forbidden to tell him that she loved him, forbidden to explain that she'd made a mistake about Bertie. There was something that made it wrong. Was it the boys? But Peter and John would learn to love him, too, and anyway, what did anything matter but this great passion? It must be seized with both hands; nothing should be allowed to impede it . . .

Her slight movement had attracted his attention. He was closing his book, smiling at her. For a brief second she wondered what he was doing in her room and then she guessed. Of course! He had dared to come into her bedroom because he could no longer deny his passion for her. He loved her, too. Why ever had she doubted it? She lifted her arms to him and he came to her at once, falling to his knees beside her.

'Darling,' she cried – but oddly her voice was barely more than a whisper. 'Oh darling, I love you so. I've never told you but I love you more than anyone ever . . .' She paused to catch her breath, wondering why she felt so weak. She must have been ill but she could remember nothing. He was smiling down at her and, as she raised her hands to smooth back his dark hair, she saw the wrinkles, the liver-spotted skin. In a flash of horrifying clarity she realised that she had betrayed herself. At this final moment, as she had feared she might, she had thrown away a lifetime of discipline, all her sacrifice had gone for nothing and now it was too late . . .

'I love you, too, Grandmother,' said Mole, gently laying her back on her pillows. 'I've never told you, either. Silly, isn't it? I'm so glad we've done it now. Thank you for saying it first. I've wanted to so much but I suppose I just couldn't quite do it without a bit of encouragement.'

'Mole?' She gazed up at him wonderingly, aware now of her mistake. 'Dear Mole.'

He beamed at her almost shyly and she smiled back at him, her heart so full of thanksgiving that she felt that it was about to burst. Her last most vital prayer was answered; in her moment of weakness she had been protected. Her heart was too full to bear any more joy and, still smiling at Mole, she murmured the words which she believed now at the end of her life to be true.

'*You will not delay, if I do not fail to hope.*'

He was still holding her hand when Theo came swiftly from behind him. Her eyes, though open, no longer saw him and Theo's sudden stillness alerted Mole.

'Is she . . .?'

Theo put an arm about his shoulders whilst Mole stood rigidly, gazing down at the calm face whose eyes gazed as if at someone who was particularly beloved though as yet still some distance away.

'Did she speak?' asked Theo gently.

Mole frowned a little. 'She was very weak but she said that she loved me and I told her that I loved her, too.' Theo's hold tightened a little, guessing that the exchange would have meant a very great deal to Mole. He heard him swallow. 'She looked quite happy,' he said slowly, 'and then she said something like, "You won't delay if I do not fail to hope." Something like that.' He shook his head. 'I didn't understand it. And then she looked past me as you came in. I didn't realise at once that . . .'

'No. Bless you, Mole. You made her happy at the end, you see. Now, do you think you could leave me just for a moment? Perhaps you could tell the others?'

'Yes, of course.' Mole hesitated, bent to kiss his grandmother's cheek and then turned away.

When the door had closed behind him, Theo kneeled down. Very gently he closed Freddy's eyes and took her hand. He'd recognised the line that Mole had quoted and wondered where Freddy had discovered it. As he kneeled there, the whole of the prayer slipped into his mind and he was granted a moment of joyful understanding and blessed relief. Raising her hand briefly to his lips, and then holding it against his heart, he began to pray.

Book Four
Spring 1984

Chapter Thirty-six

Here, in a sheltered corner of the churchyard protected from the chilly, chancy breeze, the early March sun was warm. Kneeling on a folded plastic bag, Fliss arranged the sprays of forsythia and *Garrya elliptica* in the dark blue pottery container and sat back on her heels to view the effect.

'It's too early for the *oderatum*,' she told her grandmother, 'but it won't be long now. And I found a few early daffodils on the bank beneath the rhododendrons but you'll have to share with Ellen.'

She put the buds in but took them out again so as to cut an inch or so off the green, sappy stems with a small pair of secateurs.

'That's better,' she murmured, replacing the daffodils and settling the container carefully beneath the headstone. 'Ellen and Fox have got catkins but I kept the forsythia for you. Young Fred is picking some snowdrops. There's masses still under the wall by the gate.'

She glanced about her but could not see him beyond the angle of the granite buttress of the ancient church. A night of heavy rain had given way to a pure, sparkling, rinsed freshness and there were no clouds in the dome of tender blue that overarched the scene. Rooks were squabbling in the great oak tree in the lane, their twiggy nests clearly visible amongst the network of bare branches, and above her head, in the copper beech, a flock of bramblings and chaffinches swung and fluttered. A blackbird gave a warning cry as it skimmed low across the peaceful grassy mounds and the chaffinches set up their alarm call – 'pink pink pink' – as young Fred appeared, breathing hard, a bunch of snowdrops clutched in his chubby fist. He came towards her, eager and flush-cheeked, beaming with delight.

'Lots,' he told her, laying his offering on the grass beside her. 'Lots and lots of snowdrops.'

Fliss kneeled up so that their faces were on a level and put an arm about him.

'Let's see,' she said. 'Good boy. You remembered to pick the stems very long. Aren't you clever?'

He nodded and let out a great puffing breath. He knew that the task entrusted to him had been important and he felt equal measures of pride and relief.

'Put them in,' he said, crouching to look at the arrangement, poking amongst the sprays with his finger. 'In *here*.'

Carefully the snowdrops were inserted amongst the silken tassles of the *Garrya* and the yellow flowers of the forsythia.

'And some over for Ellen and Fox,' she told him.

'Fox,' he murmured. He'd seen pictures of foxes but he knew this was a different sort of fox. In his mind he pictured a jolly swaggering animal – rather like Mr Tod – with his brushy tail sticking out of his trousers. Fliss was smiling at him, guessing at his thoughts. He would be four years old in August and it was already clear that he was going to be very much like his father. He was a delightful sight: blue dungarees tucked into red gumboots and a yellow woollen jacket with the hood pulled cosily over his silky brown hair. Fliss hugged his bundly, sturdy body.

'Give us a kiss,' she said.

Obediently he pursed his lips and placed them gently against her cheek. He pecked, once, twice, lips still pursed and then looked to see how she was liking it.

'Call that a kiss?' she said, pretending scorn. 'You'll have to do better than that, young man,' and she pulled him down across her knees and blew raspberries into his soft warm neck whilst he chuckled with delight. Presently she released him, picking up the remaining snowdrops and reaching for the watering can.

'You know where this lives don't you?' she asked him. 'By the tap, round on the other side of the church? Could you take it back for me?'

He nodded importantly, seizing it enthusiastically; although nearly empty it barely cleared the ground and he leaned away from it, balancing the weight as he lugged it along. Fliss watched him go. It was wonderful to be home again after two years in Brussels followed by two years in London whilst Miles was at the Ministry of Defence. Now he was about to retire and they had moved back to Dartmouth in time for Christmas. At present he was attending the courses that the Navy supplied for officers about to find new careers in a civilian world but he was playing his cards very close to his chest when it came to discussing the future. Nevertheless, Fliss was delighted that he'd accepted that, even with the twinnies away at school, the house in Above Town was too small for them. At last they could look about for something more suitable. Although, in the end, they'd decided to continue to let the house whilst they were abroad and in London, Miles was now very ready to put it up for sale – but he remained evasive when she talked about finding another house.

'No point,' he'd said, 'not until we know how much this might fetch. No good getting ourselves worked up about a place and then finding we can't afford it or someone else pips us to the post. After all, I'm sure we could stay at The Keep if it comes to it.'

This was perfectly true but Fliss longed to be exploring. She looked in estate agents' windows and drove around on what she called 'outside recces' looking at houses which might be possibilities, spying out the lie of the land. It would be wonderful if she could be within, say, half an hour's drive of The Keep, perhaps somewhere along the corridor of the A38 so that Miles could get to Exeter or Plymouth, or even further afield, as quickly as possible if he needed to in his new career – whatever that might be. Whilst he was away on his courses she pottered about checking out houses and cottages in Ashburton and Bovey Tracey, thinking how lovely it would be to have such ready access to the moor. Sometimes she would leave the details of this property or that lying temptingly about, hoping that Miles would read it and be fired with enthusiasm, but as yet he'd made no comment about any of them.

'Have to go where the work is,' he'd say vaguely and she'd be seized with terror that she might find herself back in London or somewhere in the industrial north, hundreds of miles from the children's school and The Keep.

London had been fun. It was good to have Kit at hand, to

go to the theatre together and to share lunches with Clarrie up in his eyrie. As soon as they'd returned from Brussels and settled in the flat in Chiswick, the twinnies had started at Herongate House School. Fliss had missed them quite dreadfully but she and Kit regularly went down to the New Forest together in Eppyjay to fetch them for exeats or to take them out to tea on Sundays. Kit was a tremendous favourite with Jamie and Bess. She had a genius for finding exactly the right present or discovering special places for outings. When matches were being played or concerts given Kit would be there whenever possible, giving encouragement, and often Hal, bringing Jolyon with him, drove over, to stand on the edge of a muddy rugby pitch cheering Jamie on or to attend the end-of-term play.

As she began to thread the snowdrops amongst the catkins on Ellen's grave, Fliss knew that the most wonderful thing about the twinnies going to Herongate was that Bess's musical talent was being cherished at last. She'd first noticed her aptitude at The Keep when she'd heard Bess picking out a tune on the piano. After that she'd encouraged her, taught her what she could, but she'd been obliged to agree with Miles when he refused to consider the idea of carting a piano about with them.

'When we stop moving about we shall have one,' he promised, 'but until then it simply isn't practical in furnished hirings and quarters.'

It was pointless letting Bess have lessons if she couldn't practise but Fliss was longing for the time when she herself could play again, too; there was something so therapeutic about playing, so comforting. Bess was coming on in leaps and bounds and since their next move would be a whole house move there was no reason why they should not have a piano now in Dartmouth. A piano would be hardly noticed amongst all the rest of the furniture to be moved. She said this to Miles but once again he balked at the suggestion.

'We're cramped enough as it is. It won't be long now, surely you can wait a little longer? Bess gets plenty of practice at school and you can always go over to The Keep and play the piano there.' He'd laughed a little, patting her shoulder, softening the blow. 'Poor Fliss. I had no idea you'd felt so deprived.'

Now, as she gathered up the secateurs and the plastic bag Fliss strove to be fair. After all, she had never made much of her own longing to play and Miles wasn't particularly musical. It was unreasonable to expect him to understand. During the last two years, however, he'd made tremendous efforts to bring their relationship onto a new level. With the twinnies away at school it was as if he were trying to pick up where they'd left off all those years ago when she told him that she was expecting a baby. She had the impression that London was a kind of dress rehearsal for a new life together and, although she'd entered into the spirit of it as best she could, she couldn't help feeling that it was utterly unreal. It was impossible to pretend that ten years could be washed out as if they simply didn't exist or that by sending one's children away to school they didn't exist either.

She'd confided her anxieties to Kit. 'Neither of us is the same person we were ten years ago,' she'd said. 'Even Miles can't turn back the clock although I think that he believes that he can. It's weird. There's something so single-minded about him, so determined.'

'He's certainly determined,' Kit had agreed. 'You've only

got to look at that jaw. He sets his mind on something and simply goes for it. Remember how long he waited for you? Five years, was it? He's that kind of chap.'

'But was he waiting?' Fliss had sounded puzzled. 'I know that he was a good friend to all of us but I never noticed anything more than that.'

Kit's smile had been sad. 'I believe you, honey. You only ever saw Hal.'

Stuffing the secateurs into her pocket, the sun warm on her back, Fliss could remember how the quick, uncontrollable flush had made her face feel hot.

'Oh, hell.' Kit had put an arm about her shoulders. 'You and me both, little coz. We're one man women and we both got it wrong.'

Fliss hadn't bothered to deny it. Since her telephone call to Hal just before Grandmother died there had been some subtle indefinable change. Both had acknowledged that they belonged together; neither was prepared to grasp happiness at the expense of partner or children. Yet the awareness of Hal's love was a sword and a shield and she was more able because of the certainty of it.

She turned away from the graves of Ellen and Fox and paused beside her grandmother's headstone. *Here lies Frederica Elizabeth Chadwick* . . . How strange that she should have said those particular words at the end. '*Be happy, my darlings*,' she'd said. '*Be happy together*,' just as if she knew that their love still survived and approved of it. This was quite impossible, of course, yet it had given some small measure of peace, her final blessing.

When Mole had come into the drawing room and told them that Grandmother had died, she remembered that she'd stood up immediately and then been quite unable to move, muscles locked with shock. Hal had taken her icy hands and then slipped his arms about her, cradling her against his breast. Mole had stood watching them, his face bleak, and Hal had stretched out a hand to him, too, drawing him in so that the three of them stood closer together, sharing their grief.

Later, alone together again, Hal had said, 'Play for me' and Fliss had gone to the Bechstein, turning over her grandmother's music, knowing that she was not up to her standard. Nevertheless she had played to him: Bach, Chopin, Schubert. Silently they mourned together through the music, each absorbed by his or her own memories, facing the inevitability of loss.

Later still, Hal had risen, coming to stand beside and a little behind her. Once again she'd felt his hand on her shoulder, felt his lips touch her hair – and then he'd been gone. She'd remembered a spring fifteen years before when he had stood there beside the piano and told her that because they were cousins, because their fathers were identical twins, they must not love each other. 'It was silly of us to get carried away,' he'd said, 'but we'll go on being close, won't we?' His face had been clenched with misery. 'I love you,' she'd said, puzzled, not believing. 'I love you, too,' he'd said sadly, 'but it's got to be a different kind of love from now on . . .' Fifteen years later, as she'd played, it had seemed that losing Hal was bound up in losing her grandmother, her mother and father, her brother . . . Passion, grief and pain had seemed to pour out from her very soul into the music and when at last she'd ceased, limp and exhausted, turning on the stool she'd seen that Uncle Theo had been sitting behind her, his hands gripped tightly together, his face wet with tears . . .

Here lies Frederica Elizabeth Chadwick.

'I miss you,' Fliss told her silently. 'I miss you terribly. I missed you when Jamie got promoted to the under-twelve rugby fifteen and when Bess passed her Grade One with Honours and I couldn't tell you. I miss seeing you walking in the garden and pouring out the tea in the hall and playing the piano. And I miss you when I see Uncle Theo looking at something I can't see and I know he's thinking of you. And I know it will never stop, just like with Mummy and Daddy and Jamie. I will simply get better at dealing with it . . .'

Young Fred arrived at a trot, out of breath and rather damp about the knees.

'I falled over,' he said cheerfully, 'and all the water came out. Never mind.'

Fliss pressed her lips tightly together, swallowed her tears and smiled down at him. Fred might look like his father but he had his mother's sunny disposition. She blessed Susanna for her generosity in lending young Fred for all sorts of expeditions – to the moor, to the beach, shopping in Totnes – without injunctions or warnings, without any rules or regulations. When his new baby sister arrived Susanna had been delighted that Fred should have his own special privileges as befitted an elder brother and handed him over to Fliss with confidence. He was looking up at her now in hopeful expectation.

'Never mind,' she agreed, taking out her handkerchief and wiping away the worst of the mud. 'Time for a quick walk, would you say? I expect poor old Rex is getting bored in the car.'

Fred pursed up his lips judicially – he liked the way she consulted him, almost as if he were a grown-up person – and nodded. He slipped his hand into hers and they passed together between the marked places of quiet earth, beneath branches beginning to burst with fresh green buds, down the mossy path to the wrought-iron gate.

Chapter Thirty-seven

There had been changes at The Keep since Freddy's death. A certain formality, difficult to define but definitely felt, had vanished with her passing. The disintegration had begun in the final stages of her illness and now, four years on, the process was complete. An era was over. The kitchen, once Fox's and Ellen's domain – a domain which Freddy had rarely visited – had become the hub of the house. Mealtimes were more erratic and there was a certain liveliness which in no way impaired the peaceful qualities of The Keep. Prue could be heard singing in the bathroom, calling down the stairs; Caroline's voice would be raised, imploring someone – anyone – to answer the telephone; Theo, who had inherited Freddy's library of music, had become a little deaf and the strains of Bach or Schumann drifted from behind his door on to the wide landing.

Susanna and the children were regularly in and out, and the small room behind the drawing room had lost its sombre atmosphere in its transition from study to playroom. The two small cream brocade sofas, which stood facing each other on either side of the fireplace, were now covered with warm thick tartan rugs against damage from sandal buckles and sticky fingers; the walnut table was hidden by a brightly checked oilcloth so that paints and crayons might be used with impunity. The long climb to the nursery wing, proving wearisome for young legs and old, had inspired Prue to bring down the children's books and toys so that the next generation could be quietly entertained when it visited. Young Fred adored the marionette Muffin the Mule, whose jointed legs enabled it to sit or kneel or dance as the strings were manipulated, whilst Podger – Alison at the font but renamed by Kit, 'Oh, she's such a *darling* little Podger' – was fascinated by the animals which lived inside the wooden ark with Mr and Mrs Noah. Podger's staggering steps were always directed to the big boat with its two doors which opened to reveal such treasures. The Noahs were a delightful pair: he with his round white patriarchal beard and carved flowing robes, she with her smooth black painted hair and comfortably ample form. Podger liked the assembling of the animals to be accompanied by song. They were an eclectic bunch. Bears and camels were paired alongside ducks and sheep which meant that there was a variety of musical choice. It might be 'The animals went in two by two' or even 'Old MacDonald had a farm' – Podger was not yet a purist and the pair of giraffes might be happily substituted for the pigs or kangaroos in the songs – but her very favourite was the one which her Aunt Fliss knew best. Their voices could often be heard raised in unison – Fliss's contralto, Podger's squeak and Fred's husky roar – as the animals were marched up the ramp into the dark.

'*I had a cat and the cat pleased me,*
I fed my cat by yonder tree,

Cat goes fiddle-i-fee.
I had a cow and the cow pleased me . . .'

The older children had their favourites, too. Edward loved his
grandmother's smart toy soldiers in their castle, whilst Jolyon
never tired of the strange mechanical toys which whirred or
danced once they had been wound up with the large keys
which must always be kept safely in a small linen bag. Bess
loved these, too. There was an ice-cream vendor whose legs
pedalled furiously as he propelled his blue and white container decorated with snow and penguins; there was a brightly
painted and erratically hopping frog, as well as several pecking birds, but she loved best the dancing doll from Russia,
which glided on hidden wheels, gently moving her head from
side to side and occasionally pirouetting as she danced.

With Prue's removal to The Keep the legacies of her own
twins' childhood had also become part of the heritage.
Most of Hal's books and toys had gone to his own home –
his train set and his collection of Dinky and Matchbox cars,
his *Biggles* and *Just William* books – but Kit's sets of *Lone
Pine Five* and *Famous Five* books still kept Bess entertained for hours. Jamie, now eleven, had moved beyond the
pleasure afforded by the toys, although he was always
prepared to play with the younger ones, and now found his
own private pleasure in scanning the bookshelves which
lined the walls where the reading of previous generations of
Chadwicks had accumulated. His warlike phase had passed
– although the military life still fascinated him – and he
was becoming a rather dreamy, imaginative boy, growing
up to look like Miles but with a yearning spiritual capacity
which was quite foreign to his father.

Today, with Susanna and the children over for lunch, the kitchen was a place of bustle and communal activity. Potatoes were cooking preparatory to being mashed with butter and milk, sausages were frying, scrubbed vegetables were waiting to be shovelled into the steamer.

'Children's food is so delicious,' said Prue contentedly as, with Podger astride her hip, she turned the sausages with a fork. 'Simple but so tasty. Jam roly-poly for pudding, darling, what do you think of that?'

Podger sucked her thumb meditatively. Beneath the thick dark fringe her brown eyes were thoughtful. Earlier she had managed to extract one of the small ducks from the ark and had kept it to examine it, turning it carefully in her small fingers, delighting in the yellow beak and legs and the skilful carving of the snowy white feathers. One of Fox's last tasks had been to repaint the Noahs' large family and the colours were as fresh and bright as they had been fifty years earlier. The duck looked rather like Jemima Puddle-Duck, and Podger was enchanted by her. When she heard Aunt Prue coming back along the passage to the playroom – having been called away to the telephone – Podger had secreted the duck in the pocket of her navy-blue corduroy pinafore. Aunt Prue had whisked her up and away to the kitchen where she had managed to crawl under the table so as to spend some more deliciously private moments with this small toy. So entranced had she been, dancing it upon the floor, making it waddle about, that Caroline had nearly trodden on her fingers and once again Aunt Prue had lifted her up, moving her out of the way of busy adult feet. The sudden movement had caused Podger to lose her grip on the duck and it had slid down Aunt Prue's front, between her shirt and her cardigan, and was now well beyond Podger's grasp.

She eyed the loose folds of her great-aunt's blue shetland cardigan, faintly distracted by the smell of the sausages. Podger enjoyed her food. She brought to each mealtime the gourmand's sense of dedication, and the aroma of frying sausage, along with the mental image of jam roly-poly pudding, began to edge the anxiety about the duck out of her mind. She knew that she should not have removed it – the nursery rules were still, on the whole, strictly obeyed – but at least it was quite safe. Podger decided that the matter was now out of her hands. She sighed deeply and smiled seraphically upon her Aunt Prue.

'Thothidge,' she said pleasedly, without removing her thumb.

Prue joggled her, dancing a little to make her chuckle, and Caroline came back from a sortie to the larder and lifted Podger away and into the highchair.

'Fliss and young Fred should be back,' she said, glancing at the mahogany-framed wall clock. 'What can they be up to, I wonder.'

'Plenty of time,' said Prue easily. 'The vegetables aren't quite done yet. Isn't it nice to have Fliss back so close? I do hope Miles doesn't have to take a job a long way off. It will break her heart if she has to move away again.'

'I suppose it depends on what he intends to do.' Caroline removed the saucepan, turned the potatoes into a large bowl which had been warming in the bottom oven, and began to mash them with a practised hand. 'Rather difficult, I should think. The only thing he's really experienced in is man management. Has Fliss told you what his plans are?'

'I don't think Fliss *knows* what his plans are.' Prue pushed the frying pan to the side of the Aga and opened the oven door so as to check on the pudding. 'Just right. I'll take it out so that it can be cooling a little. Jam stays so terribly hot, doesn't it? No, as far as I can gather Miles hasn't decided anything yet.'

'Well there's no great rush,' said Caroline. 'He'll have a good pension. No point in hurrying these things. Will you go and call Theo or shall I?'

From upstairs, Theo was watching Fliss and young Fred disembarking from the car. Fred's gumboots had been removed and transferred to Susanna's car and now his shoes were being put on and laced up whilst Rex gambolled round, his feathery tail waving as he paused to lick Fred's face. Theo looked down upon Fliss's fair head, bent over Fred as he sat sideways on the passenger seat, legs dangling. This was the third generation of children he'd watched from this window but he knew that it must also be the last. He'd suffered an unusually severe bronchitis attack during the winter and there were occasions when he felt alarmingly weak and frail. He missed Freddy painfully but still felt her to be somehow present, half expecting to come upon her, in the hall, at the piano, in the garden. His loneliness was assuaged by the companionship of Prue and Caroline, and he blessed Freddy a hundred times a day for preparing the way for Prue's presence at The Keep. She was the bridge over which he and Caroline might pass so that they were now fused together as a group with no real barriers between any of them.

He almost wished that he could give Caroline an allow-ance instead of paying her a salary, thereby truly making her one of the family but he knew that her sense of what was proper would make it difficult to raise the matter. In any case, Prue had removed any of the remaining awkwardnesses which were already beginning to disappear during Freddy's illness. It had been quite impossible – even if he had wished it – to keep up those barriers whilst he and Caroline shared the burden, each supporting the other, giving and receiving comfort.

He delighted in the almost sisterly relationship which existed between Caroline and Prue, grateful that they included him in their plans and expeditions, welcoming him, loving him. He tried to imagine how he might be managing alone, had he not moved to The Keep, in his rather bleak little flat in Southsea and knew how lucky he was to be a part of this happy, if rather odd, family. Gus and Susanna and their children kept The Keep's occupants young in spirit and the regular visits of the other members of the family gave the place an almost festive atmosphere. One never quite knew when Mole might arrive for a weekend or Kit might telephone to ask if she and Sin could come to breathe the country air. Once, shortly after Freddy's death, Clarrie had accompanied them and Theo had enjoyed his company enormously so that now he too had become a frequent guest.

Everything was as Freddy had hoped and planned for The Keep except for her one central concept: that Hal would move in and take over the reins. No one could quite understand why he had never done so, choosing instead to buy a house in the Meon valley. He and Maria and the boys had lived there for the last four years but now he had been given the command of HMS *Broadsword*, which was based

Marcia Willett

in Devonport, and the rest of the family were waiting to see whether the moment had come for Hal to fulfil his grand-mother's wish and become master of The Keep. Hal himself had always refused to be drawn on the subject, evading it with a smile and a shrug but with a tightening of the lips which warned off the inquisitive. Even Prue, who consid-ered that she had a mother's licence to probe, had extracted no reasons. The only advantage to his staying in Hampshire – as far as she could see – was that he was always at hand for the twinnies at school in the New Forest.

'We have to remember,' Fliss had pointed out, 'that Maria's not far from her own parents there and she and the boys will have made lots of friends. I think it's a bit unreasonable to ask her to lift and shift. She knows no one down here and the boys have settled at school. Just because we love it here doesn't mean it's everyone's idea of bliss. And Hal's been mainly based in Portsmouth or London. We have to remember that, too.'

Theo remembered that Prue had looked almost cross at such a reasonable and balanced view and had made one or two dark remarks about Maria's obduracy. However, Hal and his family had remained in Hampshire – until now. With his first posting to the West Country for eight years it would be interesting to see what would happen.

Interesting, too, to see what Miles was planning. Theo had a strong suspicion that Miles was hatching plans about which Fliss knew nothing. It was something in his manner when he talked about his courses and what type of career he was drawn to which had alerted Theo's interest. There was a kind of suppressed excitement about him just lately which made Theo feel faintly anxious. Miles had always worked

398

on the 'need-to-know' basis with Fliss; there was no real consultation or discussion. He had been too old to change when he married her, convinced that he knew what would be best for them both and acting accordingly. Theo knew that Fliss had been too young and inexperienced to take a stand at the beginning and that she had conducted her marriage on the principle of going along with him as far as was possible, whilst tactfully but firmly holding out for what she felt was right.

Theo thrust his hands into his pockets as he watched Fliss helping Fred down from the seat, pushing Rex out of the way. He was quite certain that she and Hal still loved each other. He had come upon them just after Freddy's death, embracing. Their arms were wrapped tightly about the other, Hal's head lowered to hers with his face turned away, but on her face had been an expression of such peace and happiness that Theo had felt tears pricking at the back of his eyes. He had turned and gone away, unseen.

Theo thought: We should never have parted them.

Neither Maria nor Miles seemed to guess at their spouses' love for each other and – as far as he could judge – it had not been allowed to affect their marriages. Yet there was danger in such love . . . Theo thought of his undeclared love for Freddy and sighed for Hal and Fliss. He gave thanks that he had been given strength to cope with it and hoped that they would be similarly blessed. As he turned from the window there was a knock at the door. It opened and Prue put her head in, smiling at him.

'Lunch,' she said. 'Children's lunch. Sausages and jam roly poly. Are you feeling strong?'

'Sounds wonderful,' he told her. 'Fliss and young Fred have just arrived back,' and they went together downstairs to meet them.

Later, when Prue was getting ready for bed, a small wooden duck fell from nowhere, rolling on the floor beside her slippers. She bent to pick it up, recognising it, frowning as she turned it in her hand.

'How extraordinary,' she murmured. 'How absolutely *extraordinary*!'

Chapter Thirty-eight

Andrew Prior let himself into his flat in the house in Hampstead, dropped his overnight case on the hall chair and drew a breath of pleasure. The brief promise of summer had all too soon given way to a cold wet blustery reminder of winter and he found the country depressing in these conditions. The pervading odour of damp wool and wet dog filled the kitchen, and mud infiltrated even into the drawing room. Margaret, who never felt the cold and had no concept of cosiness, clumped about with an insensitive cheerfulness, talking to the dogs and looking rather contemptuously upon him as he huddled by a smoking fire of damp wood.

'Not that cold, is it, boys?' she'd demand heartily of the dogs – she usually apprised him of her feelings through this medium. 'Should get out more, shouldn't he? Get some fresh air in his lungs. Now where did I put that list? I could have sworn it was in this drawer . . . *No*, Hercules, *not* on the sofa while you're still wet. Oh, well, I suppose there's no real harm. Poor old boy. You're not as young as you were, are you? Ah, *here* it is . . . Damn, it's my week for the church flowers. Now what have I got? Hmm . . . Do you think you could make yourself useful, Andrew? That warm

401

spell has really brought on the daffodils. You know? Down by the paddock? A nice big bunch, please. Cut them long enough, won't you? Don't pick them all. Be intelligent about it . . . What? No, it's hardly raining at all. No, it *can't* wait . . . Oh, all right, I'll do it myself . . .'

Feeling guilty but faintly resentful, he'd dragged himself out into the cold dampness, rain dripping down his neck as he bent over the daffodils, drops of water splashing on to his icy hands from the golden trumpets, his booted feet trampling the muddy grass . . .

Now Andrew sighed again happily as he looked about the clean warm flat where there was no evidence of a drying guernsey nor yet the muddy footprint of a wet dog.

'He's a townie, isn't he, boys? Not a countryman, more's the pity.'

Margaret always managed to imply that there was something lacking in anyone who preferred the town to the country; that they were shallow and light-minded. She certainly thought this about Sin and Kit; she utterly despised them, simply could not take them seriously. Yet when he had attempted to explain the nature of Sin's work as an archivist at the British Museum she'd shrugged it aside, barely waiting to hear him out.

'Can't imagine how anyone can be stuffing inside all day, can we, boys? Wouldn't suit us, would it?'

To be fair, it had been some time before Andrew had seen past the flippant exterior which Kit and Sin invariably presented to the world – and even to each other for much of the time – and had begun to learn more about them. It had taken time. He, too, was a private, cautious man, and he acknowledged and respected similar traits in other people,

but once he and Sin had begun to go together to the opera
the barriers had lowered rather more quickly, and slowly,
very slowly, he had become extraordinarily fond of her.
Margaret knew all about their outings – knew and was
indifferent. She had no fear of someone as flighty and
foolish as Sin. Even her name – 'Yes, I appreciate that it's
her nickname, I'm not *quite* an idiot, am I, boys? But even
so . . .' – was a clear indication to Margaret that here was
someone who was beneath her notice.

As he hung up his coat there was a sound from the flat
above, of something falling, and he glanced towards the
ceiling his face brightening. Was it possible that Sin might
be back from the BM already? He glanced at his watch,
remembering that he'd missed lunch: nearly three o'clock,
surely it was much too early? It could be Kit, of course, but
he had a sudden overwhelming desire to go upstairs and
see. It was odd how much he'd begun to miss Sin – well,
both of them, he hastened to tell himself – during his
sojourns in the country and lately he felt rather like a small
boy going home from school for the holidays when he
returned to London from Wiltshire. As he climbed the stairs
he laughed at himself. He was nearly sixty, after all, and
such comparisons were ludicrous yet his heart was bumping
about quite excitedly. It was fortunate that he was a sensible
and happily married man or it might be quite easy for
friends to misunderstand the way he felt about Sin: the way
he liked to keep looking at her, hearing her drawling,
amused voice and wicked chuckle; the way she took his arm
as they walked to the tube on the way to the opera and said
to him, 'Now explain the plot and don't leave anything out.
I don't want to look a complete fool . . .'; the way she'd

reach up to kiss his cheek to thank him and he'd feel an absurd, heady rush of joy; the way he felt an odd emptiness, loneliness almost, when she was away for any length of time . . .

His steps grew slower, his eyes fixed unseeingly ahead until, at the top of the stairs on the landing outside the front door, Andrew finally stood aghast before the fact of his love for Sin. His immediate reaction, shock and fear, caused him to make the attempt of re-adjusting this revolutionary idea. It simply could not be so. He began to see, however, how his marriage had given him an illusion of safety, of invulnerability, and Margaret's own indifference had underlined his confidence, making him – he'd imagined – impregnable. Had she ever been jealous or suspicious then perhaps his own innocence – until now his protection – might have been damaged and the truth acknowledged much earlier because, now that he could see clearly, he realised that he had loved Sin for a long time. Hard though he tried, and he *did* try, standing there before her door, he could not convince himself any longer that he loved her in a brotherly way – he instinctively shied away from the word 'fatherly' – but with a much more complicated emotion than mere fraternal affection.

He grew slowly aware of music drifting from behind the door; a woman's voice was singing something about being killed softly, which Andrew couldn't understand, but there was something poignant and yearning in the song which spoke directly to his confused feelings and, finding it suddenly quite insupportable to be alone, he hammered on the door.

It was quite some moments before it was opened to reveal Kit in old jeans and a grubby jersey. Her hair was untidy and her face was streaked with tears.

He was still too shocked by his own revelation to realise that her appearance gave him a strange kind of satisfaction. In no fit state to analyse his emotions, he intuitively realised that they were both at this moment in a similar state of distress and he walked past her without a word into the sitting room. She went at once to the radio and switched it off. Roberta Flack was abruptly silenced and Kit looked at Andrew with an expression of despair.

'It's that bloody song.' She took it for granted that he required some kind of explanation. 'It was being played in the coffee bar when Jake chucked me. Whatever it was that someone said about the potency of cheap music is absolutely true. It gets me every time. Sorry.' She rumpled her hair, glancing about her as if some solution might be found in the familiar arrangement of the furniture, gave it up and looked more closely at him. 'So what's your problem?'

'Is Sin here?'

There was a brief surprised silence and then, in a moment of absolute mental clarity, Kit grasped the situation.

'Oh hell,' she said. 'This is all we need.'

He stared at her, still gripped by this sense of shared suffering. 'I'm in love with her.' He sat down on the nearest chair. 'I can't be but I am.'

'Yes,' said Kit. 'Yes, well it was only a matter of time, really, wasn't it? That you should see it for yourself, I mean. The thing was that you were so rooted in your image of yourself as a thoroughly married man that it never occurred to you that it might happen.'

He gazed at her – 'Rather,' as Kit told Fliss later, 'as though I were the oracle at Delphi' – amazed at her perception. She reached into the sleeve of her jersey, took out a handkerchief and blew her nose whilst he adjusted to this latest development.

A new thought occurred to him. 'Does everyone know?' he asked anxiously.

She looked at him consideringly. 'When you say everyone,' she began – and paused. It was clear that since he was in a state of shock she should proceed with caution. Andrew wasn't at all the kind of man who agreed with the modern casual approach to affairs and divorce and his recent revelation was clearly causing him a great deal of distress.

'No,' she said gently. 'Hardly anybody. Sin has been terribly careful . . .'

'Do you mean that Sin *knows*?' He gaped at her incredulously.

Kit groaned quietly. That brief moment of clarity was rapidly blurring over and she felt faintly panicky. How would Sin want her to react to this? 'I meant,' she said cautiously, 'that Sin has been careful about showing her own feelings when you're out together. You know what I mean. After all, you never know who you might bump into and although Margaret knows what's going on—'

'Sin? Can you possibly mean that Sin feels . . .?' He cast about for suitable phrases, this new shock completely unsettling him again. 'Oh, no. I can't believe it. She's so young and so delightful but she couldn't possibly . . .' He shook his head. 'She's been very sweet to me, of course . . .'

'Oh, for goodness' sake,' cried Kit – 'I shouldn't have,' she said later remorsefully to Fliss, 'but I was feeling so absolutely bloody myself just then, thinking about Jake' – 'do stop being so medieval and gentlemanly. She's been in love with you for ages, poor girl, and you rushing back to that tiresome old cow down in Wiltshire just when you've got poor old Sin all worked up again and thinking that you might love her after all.'

She paused to draw breath, glaring at Andrew, who was now on his feet and standing quite still, staring past her at nothing in particular. Clarrie appeared suddenly in the doorway. He was clutching a bottle of port in one hand and the newspaper in the other.

'What the devil's going on?' he demanded testily. 'People roaring and shouting all over the shop. Front door wide open . . .'

His bright eyes darted between them, puzzled and intrigued. His arrival defused the situation and Kit gave a short laugh and touched Andrew lightly on the arm.

'Sorry,' she said. 'Only it's all so crazy.'

'What's crazy?' Clarrie came right into the room, and looked inquisitively at the dazed Andrew. 'What's got into you?'

'He's realised that he's in love with Sin,' said Kit brutally, 'and he's come over all peculiar.'

Clarrie snorted. 'Is that all?' he asked contemptuously. 'Thought it was World War Three starting. Well, it's taken you long enough, old chap. So why the doom and gloom?'

Andrew looked at him with mingled despair and joy. 'It's impossible,' he answered simply.

'I tell you what's impossible,' said Clarrie crossly, shaking the newspaper. 'Feller here says that once you open a bottle of port it must be drunk in eleven hours or it becomes undrinkable. *Eleven hours!*'

'I shouldn't have thought you'd have found that too

difficult,' said Kit tartly. 'I recall that the contents of your last bottle of Scotch vanished in less than eleven minutes.'

'That's *quite* different,' said Clarrie, undisturbed by the intended slur. 'Port isn't my tipple, d'you see, but I do like a drop occasionally. Now this damned feller says I've got to drink it up in eleven hours.' He held the bottle up. 'It's been open since Christmas,' he said plaintively. 'It's ruined.'

'Rubbish,' said Kit briskly. 'It's a lie put about to make everyone drink more port. Tell you what, let's try a glass. Andrew could certainly use it by the look of things and since I merely drink for the after-effect it won't matter what it tastes like. At least that way it won't be utterly wasted.'

She went to fetch some glasses and Clarrie looked curiously at Andrew.

'If you play with fire you get your fingers burned,' he murmured kindly.

Andrew gazed at him blindly, just as Paul after his revelation on the road to Damascus might have gazed unseeingly at some well-meaning chum.

'I've been a fool,' he said with the same devastating simplicity – and sat down again in the middle of the sofa.

'Quite,' said Clarrie, rolling his eyes at Kit, who had returned with three glasses. 'And what is Sin going to say to this?' he muttered as they bent together over the table.

'Shut up,' said Kit briefly. 'I need time to think.' She handed Andrew a generous glassful of fine ruby port. 'Here,' she said. 'Get yourself outside that.'

She and Clarrie sat down on either side of him and raised their glasses.

'I love her,' said Andrew happily, after his third glass.

'Feller's got a point,' said Clarrie, peering gloomily into

his glass. 'Something's gone out of it, no doubt about that.'

'Try some more,' said Kit, struggling with the growing impression that she was presiding over some kind of Mad Hatter's tea party. 'Tastes OK to me. You only think that because of what you've read. Bet you wouldn't have noticed otherwise. Have you had any lunch, Andrew?'

He roused himself, blinking a little, and shook his head. Kit and Clarrie exchanged glances.

'I'll take him down and feed him,' said Clarrie, setting down his glass. 'Get him out of the way. You'll want to think things over. Get yourself prepared for Sin and so on. Come on, old chap. Let's go downstairs. I've got plenty of stuff in for you. You can unpack while I cook you something.'

Kit watched them go and then took their glasses into the kitchen. She was beginning to feel guilty about the way she'd shouted at Andrew and anxious that Sin might not be pleased that her love for Andrew had been so recklessly disclosed.

Kit thought: I was momentarily unhinged. Hearing that wretched song out of nowhere and remembering sitting in that coffee bar with Jake . . .

She felt heavy with loneliness and a terrible depression. Would she never recover from the loss of his love and friendship? Even if he had died he could have hardly become less accessible, yet this was not quite true. There was always the faint possibility that he might one day return to her. She was unwilling to dwell on any of the reasons why this should happen but it was this tiny hope which, on really bad days, made life possible. It was odd that Andrew had in some instinctive way recognised her mood which had enabled him to speak out in an utterly uncharacteristic way. The words had been said, however, and now everything would change. Knowing that Andrew loved her might make the whole situation even more frustrating for Sin – yet surely it must also bring a measure of comfort?

Kit glanced at her watch. It was a while yet before Sin would be home and there was time to bath, put on clean clothes and prepare herself for her arrival. Even if Andrew recovered his senses and never mentioned the subject again it was quite impossible to hope that Clarrie would remain silent so it was important that Sin should be forewarned. Remembering that when Andrew had appeared she'd been tidying the small room which she used as a study, Kit swore beneath her breath. A client was arriving in the morning to discuss furnishing his art gallery and coffee bar, and she was still not quite ready for him. Cursing aloud this time she hurried out of the kitchen, paused in the sitting room to pick up the remaining port and her glass, and went to finish her task.

Chapter Thirty-nine

'I can't get over it,' said Maria for the hundredth time as they sat round the pine refectory table, breakfast nearly over. 'I simply can't. It's just so fantastic.' She fondled the letter which had arrived earlier, turning it over, unfolding it, rereading it. 'To be selected out of so many candidates and then offered a scholarship as well.' She shook her head and smiled mistily at Edward. 'You are a clever little boy.'

Edward, feeling that some response was required, slipped down from his chair and went to lean against her, revelling in his moment of glory, yet a little unnerved by the sudden reality of his new status. In September, it seemed, he would be starting as a very junior chorister at the Cathedral School in Salisbury. His mother and grandmother had been so excited by this prospect, this great hope, that it would have needed a much stronger character than his to find the courage to voice the doubts and fears which had been growing steadily in the last few months. He had several of these, the chief of which was that he would have to leave the small private school where he felt safe and happy and where gradually he had made two or three very good friends. He was not yet eight and his conducted tour of the choir school and the great cathedral had done nothing to allay his private terrors. The boys had all been so busy, so confident, so focused, that he'd felt quite alien.

Later, back at home, he'd tried to explain this to Jolyon, who had attempted to reassure him by explaining that soon he would be exactly the same as the rest of the boys; anyone who had a gift brought that same kind of concentration to it.

'Look at Bess,' Jolyon had said comfortingly. 'Her music means an awful lot to her, doesn't it? It's a gift, see?'

Edward had looked at him quickly. 'I wish you'd come, too,' he said. 'If I have to go, that is . . .'

'I can't sing a note,' Jolyon had said cheerfully, 'but we'll all come to listen to you.'

'I don't want to go,' his brother had insisted miserably – and Jolyon had sat down beside him on the bed.

'You'd have to change schools sooner or later,' he'd pointed out. 'I shall have to go somewhere else when I'm eleven. I'm hoping that it's a place in Winchester where all my friends will be going. That's the trouble with life really, nothing ever stays the same. Look at Daddy. He's always having to go somewhere different.'

'But I don't want to live away from home.' Tears had threatened, and Jolyon had cast about him for some distraction.

'Maybe they won't take you,' he'd said. 'They've only got room for a few. Look, it's nearly time for the *Pink Panther*. Let's go down and watch. You can play with my Bond car if you like . . .'

Now, on this Saturday morning, Edward looked across the table at Jolyon, who was still finishing his toast. He was

spreading marmalade slowly and carefully, his fair head
bent, and Edward felt another twinge of anxiety as he
imagined school life without the presence of his big brother.
They might argue and fight but let an outsider become in
the least way aggressive and the ranks closed. Jolyon had
sorted out many a small problem for him in the past but
now, with his place a reality, he began to feel seriously
frightened.

'I don't want to be away from home,' he said tremulously.
'I just don't want to.'

He felt his mother's arm go round him, pressing him
against her, and he smelled the delicious smell that was so
much part of her. He turned and put his arms about her
neck. He wanted to please her, to accept the place he knew
was so important to her, but he simply couldn't bear the
thought of not coming back each day to his own things, to
his own home . . .

'You don't have to,' she said, 'not if you really don't want
to. I'm sure we can sort it all out. There will be a way, don't
worry.'

He was aware of a strange kind of silence and twisted his
head to look at his father who smiled at him.

'It's a long way off,' he said comfortingly. 'No need to
worry about it yet. It's a tremendous achievement, Edward.
How would you like to celebrate your success?'

Edward's clasp on his mother loosened, though he
continued to loll against her, and some of his previous
excitement returned. September was a long way away and
anything might happen in that time. Meanwhile everyone
was very pleased with him and he could see that there was
much to be said for this state of affairs. Grandma had

413

promised him great things, should he be successful. His mother let him go, laughing a little.

'Quite right,' she said. 'A celebration is definitely in order. What's it to be?'

Jolyon was still silent, eating his toast and Edward was seized with a heady sense of triumph, even superiority. He might be a year and a half younger than his brother but at last he'd done something Jolyon couldn't. This feeling of consequence lasted for as long as it took him to remember how Jolyon had comforted him when he'd come back from that first visit to Salisbury.

'What shall we do, Jo?' he asked casually – 'Don't call him, Jo,' his mother said, though less irritably than usual – and grinned when Jolyon lifted his head to look at him.

'It's *your* treat,' his mother reminded him before his brother could answer. 'Not Jolyon's. But it's very nice of you to include him. Do hurry up and finish that toast, Jolyon, and then go upstairs and clean your teeth. You, too, Edward, and you can be thinking about this celebration.'

Jolyon finished his toast, pushed back his chair and the boys went out together. There was another silence. Hal poured himself some more coffee.

'Can I assume from this sudden turn of events,' he asked, 'that you won't be coming down to Devon when I join *Broadsword*?'

Maria stood up and began piling plates together. 'I don't think I actually said that I would come,' she said defensively. 'I certainly don't want to live at The Keep. I've told you before that I have no intention of being a cross between a hotel-keeper and an unpaid nurse to a group of geriatrics. I haven't changed my mind.'

'Yes, you've made that very clear during the last few years.'

Hal watched her as she piled dishes into the sink. It occurred to him that Maria was constantly reinventing herself. She used clothes and hairstyles to create new images and he wondered rather sadly whether the original Maria still existed. Today she was wearing a wide-shouldered turquoise shirt over tight jeans, which were tucked into Western-style leather boots, a gilt chain belt slung about her hips; her hair was carefully layered and casually arranged like the girl's whose name he could never remember in the television programme *Dallas*.

'Well then.' Maria shrugged as she turned on the tap. Hot water poured into the bowl causing the soapsuds to rise in a frothy mounds which covered the china. 'I simply must phone Mum and tell her the good news. She'll be over the moon.'

'I'm sure she will,' he said mildly, 'but you haven't answered my question. We don't have to live at The Keep. There are other houses in Devon.'

'Yes, I know that.' Her voice was irritable. She had no wish to be distracted from this moment of pleasure. 'But you must see that this changes things.'

'Quite. I think that's what I said to begin with, wasn't it?'

'Oh, don't talk in that sarky way to me,' she said impatiently, plunging her rubber-gloved hands into the steaming soapsuds and pausing to add some more cold water. 'I'm not some kind of stupid sailor. OK, yes, it does change things and no, I won't be coming to Devon. Edward's much too young to send away to boarding school. I know he'll be eight soon but he's very young for his age. I shall have to stay here.'

Hal set down his cup. 'Are you seriously contemplating driving him to and from Salisbury every day from here? For heaven's sake . . .'

'Oh, don't be so daft. Of course I'm not. We shall have to move to Salisbury.'

In the pause that followed, the pile on the draining board grew, spoons and knives clattering down beside the plates as she wielded the soft cotton mop.

'And what about Jolyon?' asked Hal at last. 'I thought we'd decided on the day school in Winchester for him.'

'I've been thinking about that.' Maria stripped off the gloves and reached for the tea cloth. 'You know I think it would be best, after all, if Jolyon were to go to boarding school. It would be simpler all round.'

'Simpler for whom?' asked Hal after a moment. His voice was cool and Maria turned her back on him and began to dry the breakfast things. 'You were quite emphatic that you wanted the boys at home. You said that you didn't want them to go away and that not moving around would give them a sense of security. One of the reasons you didn't want to come to Devon was that you said that Jolyon was so happy at school and that he could go on with all his friends when he was eleven.'

'I know I said that,' said Maria rapidly, still not looking at him. 'But you must see how this changes things. It's a wonderful opportunity for Edward. We can't possibly refuse it.'

'I'm not suggesting that we should refuse it.' Hal stood up. 'If you don't want him to board he could live with your mother. She lives minutes out of Salisbury. He could get home here often and I'm sure your mother would be delighted to do her bit. She's talked about nothing else since his interview.'

'And why shouldn't she?' She turned quickly, angrily. 'We happen to be proud of him, even if you're not.'

'I'm very proud of him. But he's not the only member of this family. We have to think about Jolyon, too.'

'I'm afraid that gifted children take preference in any family,' she said firmly. 'Anyway, Jolyon would fit in anywhere. He's much more confident than Edward.'

'That's not what you said when I suggested that he should go to prep school at eight. If he goes away to boarding school in September he'll be two years behind all the other boys and he'll find it very difficult to make friends–'

'I've thought about that,' she interrupted. 'I think he should go to Herongate. Jamie and Bess will look after him. I shall move to Salisbury and you can be at The Keep whenever you can't get home. Then we're all happy.'

'Are we?' Hal murmured. He looked at her thoughtfully, watching the colour rise in her cheeks. 'Are we indeed?'

'Why not?' she cried, embarrassed but still angry. 'It was you who said that Jolyon ought to go away to school. Well, you spend enough time going over there to see the twins so why shouldn't Jolyon go, too? The twins didn't start until they were ten. It's a different setup there from prep schools. And I can look after Edward properly and still get over to see Jolyon. It wouldn't be that much further away.'

'And how do you think Jolyon will feel when you tell him that you're going to pack him off to school now, after all the awful things you've said about boarding schools, when he's very happy where he is and looking forward to moving on eventually with all his friends? How do you think he will feel, Maria, when you tell him that?'

'I'm afraid it's just too bad,' she answered sulkily. 'I can't please everyone.'

'Have you asked Elaine whether Edward could live with her during the term?'

'No,' she said, frowning. 'I haven't. Mum's too old now to have that kind of responsibility. It wouldn't be fair to ask her. She'd feel obliged to say yes. I've thought it over very carefully and I still think that this is the best way for everybody. Of course, it's not perfect. What is, in this life?'

'I thought you really liked this house.'

'I do but there are other houses. Salisbury's lovely. We might get a town house. They're often much cheaper than country places. You can get really big houses very reasonably.'

'And I suppose you're not confusing Salisbury's attractions with those of Adam Wishart?'

She swallowed, the colour rushing back into her face, but when she looked at him her eyes were cold.

'I don't know what you're talking about.'

He raised his eyebrows in polite disbelief and she bit her lip. Turning away from him she began to put the china away, slamming drawers and banging the doors of the fitted pine furniture which had cost so much to instal.

'You said that when I was made Captain you would join me,' he reminded her. 'Remember?'

'Oh, don't be so bloody selfish,' she shouted. 'Edward isn't yet eight. Do you seriously expect me to put you before him? You'll be at sea for most of the time anyway, and you'll have your delightful family to wait on you when the ship's in. You don't need me the way Edward needs me. You never think about anyone but yourself, do you? God, you make me sick.'

Hal sat down again at the table. 'Well, that certainly makes things very clear,' he said. 'Are you so very certain that this is something that Edward wants and not simply something that you and Elaine want for him?'

She stared at him. 'What are you suggesting?'

He shrugged. 'It's very difficult for someone like Edward to refuse something which you and his grandmother have glamorised and made very desirable in his eyes – and yours. Edward likes to please you but he's only a small boy. Being a chorister is very gruelling, you know. It's like a vocation. It'll have to become his whole life until his voice breaks. And what then? He'll just be an ordinary little boy again, having to start somewhere new. Are you certain that it's right for him?'

'You're jealous,' she said contemptuously. 'That's what it is. You can't bear for him to have all this attention or to be better at something than Jolyon is. You can't bear him having everyone's attention, can you?'

He closed his eyes for a moment – and presently he laughed. 'Have it your way,' he said. 'But I shall have a talk with him just the same. I want to be absolutely certain he knows what's going on.'

'If you put doubts in his head and make him change his mind I shall never forgive you,' she hissed. 'And you can take that any way you choose.'

She went out of the kitchen and he heard her running up the stairs, her voice raised, calling to the boys. Hal sat quite still, staring at the cold remains in his coffee cup. When Jolyon appeared he glanced at him absently and then smiled quizzically. Jolyon was looking upset.

'Mum says she's phoned Grandma and we're going to Salisbury. Grandma's taking us out to lunch and then we're going to decide what we're going to do after that.'

'Well, that will be fun,' said Hal, only slightly surprised by this new turn of events. 'There's lots to do over there.'

'It's not that.' Jolyon lifted Hal's arm and put it around his shoulders as he'd always done ever since he was little. 'She says that you've remembered that you've got work to do and that you can't come. Oh, Dad . . .'

'Never mind,' said Hal after a very long moment. 'We'll do something tomorrow instead. I promise. Something special.'

'Will we?' He was looking happier. 'Certain sure?'

'Certain sure,' agreed Hal. 'I'm sorry, Jo. You know how it is.'

'Is it something to do with being Captain?' he asked eagerly.

Hal hugged him. 'Something like that. I'll make it up to you tomorrow, I promise. You and Edward think something out between you.'

'OK. See you, then. Mum says to say goodbye.'

'Take care,' said Hal. 'Look after Mummy and Edward for me.'

He heard the noises of departure, the front door closing, the car starting up, and after a while he stood up and switched on the kettle.

Chapter Forty

Hanging out the washing beyond the utility-room door, Susanna kept a cautious eye on the dark clouds massing yet again in the west. She was hoping to take advantage of a brief respite in the weather, knowing that if the rain would hold off even for an hour the strength of the late March wind would dry the clothes very quickly. She sang as she worked, blessed with the happy awareness of the person who is in the right place at the right time. Even in a few short years the barn had acquired a mellow appearance; the garden and trees growing up about it, hiding the rawly turned earth, covering any remaining evidence of the builder's traffic. A hedge of mixed shrubs and trees was tall and dense, already giving some protection from the road that ran at the end of the track, and the courtyard which Gus and Susanna had built within the L of the barn walls was a delightful place, an area of complete safety for the children.

As she pegged out the small garments, Fred's dungarees and Podger's pinafores, her mind was already planning her planting for the coming spring. This year they intended to start work on the plot at the west end of the barn that looked out across the fields to the moor. It could be a cold windy spot, exposed as it was, but Susanna refused to agree to anything which might obscure the glorious views. She liked to stand at the window of the sitting room, watching the sun, partially obscured by great ramparts of cloud, cream, amber, gold, rolling down behind the high bleak granite tors. Long after the sun had disappeared the sky remained stained with scarlet and crimson banners, fading at last to a golden luminosity which filled her with a kind of wordless poignant joy. Nothing, she told Gus, *nothing* must shut it out, no matter how much the wind might hurl itself against that end of the barn or the rain beat against the sitting-room windows. After all, she argued, they had the courtyard if they wished to be warm and out of the wind.

In the end they'd decided to start with a lawn, bordered by a beech hedge where the ground began to drop away a little to the west. The hedge would take a long time to grow but it would be worth it to see the tender green leaves unfurling in spring and to enjoy the splendour of the autumnal colours. She planned to plant daffodil and blue-bell bulbs beneath the turf of the new lawn and perhaps crocus and squills that would flower into a tender tide of colour, washing over the grass just as it did in the orchard at The Keep each spring.

Susanna dropped the peg-bag into the wicker basket and went back inside. Janie was coming for supper and she had yet to decide what they might eat. As she rooted amongst her cookery books, she felt a sense of pleasure that things had worked out reasonably well for her old friend. Janie loved the flat above the studio and she and Gus worked happily together, the business continuing to flourish. She'd slowly recovered from the break-up with her boyfriend and seemed quite content with occasional dates with one or two of the local males although she never allowed them to become too serious. When Mole was home on leave they tended to partner off together, although here Susanna suspected that Janie might have been quite ready to settle into a more intimate relationship had Mole ever given her the least encouragement. Mole, however, had shown no such inclination. For the last two years he'd been First Lieutenant of HMS *Osiris* based in *DOLPHIN* and his journeys home from Gosport had been few and far between, mainly because he'd been at sea for most of the time.

Susanna pushed the kettle on to the hot plate of the Esse and perched on a high stool at the quarry-tiled working surface, her cookery books spread out about her. How long ago it seemed since she had slipped out of school and gone to meet Mole after his AIB. Even now, fourteen years on, she could remember the expression on his face as they'd stared across the water at the long black boats rocking gently at their trots. 'That's the future of the modern Navy and that's where I'm going, Sooz,' he'd said and she'd felt a shiver of mingled pride and fear and absolute confidence in him. This confidence had not been misplaced. His captain on *Osiris* had recommended him for Perisher – the commanding officers' qualifying course for submariners – and having passed it he had been given his own command: HMS *Opportune*, a conventional submarine, running out of Devonport.

He'd hidden his pride – or tried to – when she and Fliss had gone down to the dockyard to see him, but his sisters had found it more difficult to dissemble. As they were shown over the submarine and were introduced to his First

Lieutenant Susanna couldn't decide which was the most impossible to believe: that Mole was thirty-one years old or that he was the Captain of this warship and its complement of men. She'd squeezed his arm privately as they'd left. 'Even further from the spinney,' she'd whispered and he'd remembered and smiled. With another shock, she'd seen that his smile reminded her of Uncle Theo's, crinkling his eyes but barely touching his mouth, and she'd thought for a dreadful moment that she might actually burst into tears. When she'd looked at Fliss, once they were back in the car, she'd known that Fliss was feeling exactly the same. She'd stared out across the driving wheel, lips pressed tightly together, and when Susanna had touched her arm she'd turned to look at her, her face clenched with pain. 'Grandmother would have been so proud of him,' she'd muttered . . .

Susanna slipped off the stool and began to make some coffee. At moments like these it was as if her body simply couldn't cope with inactivity but must hurry into action; anything to prevent her from giving way to the grief that welled up when she thought of her grandmother and how much she still missed her. As Fred and Podger grew she longed for her, to share her pride and her fears, to feel once more that steel at her back as she faced out into life. Swallowing fiercely Susanna made her coffee and went back resolutely to the cookery books. As she brooded over the evening's menu, however, her thoughts kept returning to Mole. *Opportune* was on a visit to Copenhagen and his postcard, pinned to her cork notice board – he'd chosen, with a certain unoriginality, a picture of the little mermaid – suggested that he was enjoying himself. She sighed, focusing her mind more firmly. If she didn't stop day-dreaming Janie and Gus would be having no supper at all.

A handful of rain pattered against the window as a swirl of wind raced round the barn. Groaning with frustration, Susanna set down her mug of coffee and hurried out to retrieve the washing.

The pinging could be clearly heard on the underwater telephone. In the silent control room Mole stood motion-less, head bent, mind busy. Somewhere close at hand, in the cold waters of the Baltic, the two Russian frigates were cruising, waiting and watching. HMS *Opportune* was in the area to carry out an exercise with a Danish submarine, and Mole had no intention of being tracked to the rendezvous. He could feel the sweat prickling on his forehead as he clamped down on the old terrors of ambush, of sudden death striking out of a bright sunny day – or a cold dark night. At moments like these he was still prey to his childhood fears. The First Lieutenant, standing beyond the periscope, shifted position, distracting him, and their eyes met. Mole's nod was almost imperceptible – an acknow-ledgement of solidarity, of accepted responsibility for the little team around him. He clasped his hands behind his back, imagining the Officer of the Watch up on the bridge, sweeping the swelling stretches of black icy water through his powerful binoculars.

Mole thought: He'll be bloody freezing up there tonight . . .

The visit to Copenhagen had been fun, especially the trip to the Tivoli Gardens. Mole liked the English-speaking Danes, who smoked like chimneys and drank quantities of

Gammel Dansk which, in his view, tasted exactly like cough medicine, but the arrival of the Petya and Krivak class frigates had been a bit of a shock. Their presence, nevertheless, generated an air of subdued excitement amongst the submarine's crew, and Mole, rising to the occasion, had even gone so far as to seat his First Lieutenant on a bollard on the edge of the harbour so as to take his photograph – as well as that of the Russian frigates moored behind him. It was an act of cheerful bravado which the First Lieutenant, a sound, reliable officer who was certainly going places, entered into with tremendous panache.

The frigates sailed during the afternoon but it was after midnight when *Opportune* slipped her mooring and crept out of harbour, turning east, keeping close to the coast. It was too shallow to submerge and she was travelling on the surface, going slowly, using the two diesel generators. Down below, the crew went to action stations, getting quiet, getting set, checking the trim; the control room lit by red lighting, the atmosphere electric with nervous tension.

The parallel ruler rolled across the chart table, toppling on to the deck. In the silence the sudden clang was thunderous. Everyone tensed, fingers crisping into palms, the embarrassed Navigation Officer gesturing apology as he bent to capture the offending item. Mole glanced at the intent, listening face of his First Lieutenant and experienced a sense of comradeship; he knew that he could trust him absolutely and he felt a sudden surge of confidence, of almost schoolboy daring. No British submarine had ever been tracked by a Russian frigate and he wasn't going to allow that record to be broken. Mole breathed deeply and unclenched his fists. His hands were sweaty and he dug them into his pockets as he wandered across to the Navigation Officer who now leaned over the chart table, the yeoman beside him.

'Are we in deep enough water to be able to dive yet?' he asked quietly, watching as they checked the echo sounder.

'We're heading into deeper water, sir,' the yeoman murmured. 'Give it five minutes and the depth'll be two hundred feet.'

He nodded, turning away with relief. They would all breathe more freely once they were dived, moving silently, secretly, beneath the surface of the waves. As he made the rounds the pinging faded and he moved across to the sound room to check with the sonar officer, who shook his head. 'Nothing, sir. The Russian sonar transmitter has just ceased.'

Mole experienced a private easing of tension. Odd that, although he'd been with these men for barely six months, there was the familiar small-ship sense of family, engendered by their dependence on each other, strengthened by the knowledge that their safety was grounded in a common bond of trust. Odd that, at this moment, he would not choose to be anywhere else in the world.

The radar team, at the aft end, looked up at him. 'No Soviet radar transmissions, sir.'

He crossed to the Outside Wrecker. 'Ready to dive?'

'I'm happy, sir.'

The engineer officer sitting behind the planesman prepared to check the trim and, heart beating hard, Mole picked up the handset.

'Officer of the Watch, this is the Captain. I have the ship. Clear the bridge. Come below. Shut the upper lid.'

They waited in silence until the officer climbed down the ladder inside the fin and appeared in the control room.

'Captain, sir. Officer of the Watch. Bridge cleared. Upper lid shut. Two clips, two pins. Two fishermen on the starboard bow, three miles away, sir. No sign of any other ships.'

The general feeling of relief was palpable and a surge of triumph washed through the control room.

'Open main vents,' said Mole. 'Six degrees bow down. Eighty feet back to periscope depth.'

The waves washed over the casing, lapping about the tall fin as it slowly submerged until the waters closed over it and the surface of the sea was smooth again, empty beneath the black starless sky.

As the diesel generators were switched off the only sound now was the low hum of the electric motor, propelling the submarine forward into deep waters. Mole's periscope revealed a comforting dark emptiness and he heaved a sigh of relief as he clipped up the handles and swung round on the seat. The crew were grinning at one another, relaxing, stretching. Mole made certain that they were safely at periscope depth and prepared to pass control to the Officer of the Watch.

'I can see the fishermen,' he told him, 'but there's nothing else. Keep an easterly course for a couple of hours. Let them get used to being dived. Are you happy?'

'I'm happy, sir.'

'You have the ship.'

'I have the ship, sir.'

With a few words of congratulation to the watch, Mole gestured his thanks and went out, along the passage to his cabin. He had yet to write his intentions for the next twelve hours in the night order book and make a report of proceedings. He drew the curtain behind him and sat down for a moment on the edge of his bunk. This small rectangle contained his desk, cupboard and wash basin and was the only place where he might snatch a few moments of privacy and peace. As he sat, letting the adrenalin slow, beginning to relax, his gaze fell on the framed photograph on his desk. Susanna beamed out at him, Fred in the circle of her arm, Podger balanced on her knee. It was impossible not to smile back at her, this companion of his childhood. The children watched him; Fred with a faintly censorious frown of concentration; Podger, thumb in mouth, with a friendly thoughtfulness.

Mole experienced the familiar sensation of anxiety for their vulnerable innocence. How terrifying it must be to bring children into the world, exposing them to its dangers and its pain. Yet Susanna and Gus were so confident, so *sure*. He knew how much they longed for him and Janie to get together, so as to be able to experience this happiness for themselves, but Mole resisted any efforts to propel him into matrimony. He had no such confidence in his ability to make a good husband – apart from which it was necessary to be in love for such an undertaking. He was very fond of Janie but nowhere near fond enough to make such a commitment . . .

The steward banged on the bulkhead beside the curtain and, responding to Mole's shout of 'Come', thrust the curtain aside and set a mug of coffee on his desk. With a murmured word of thanks Mole stood up, stretched mightily and sat down to make his report.

Chapter Forty-one

In the living room, waiting for Miles to return with the morning paper, Fliss folded her letter from Bess and put it back in its envelope, holding it on her lap as she looked about her. With their small portable belongings back in place the house had lost the impersonal quality of which she'd been aware during those quick visits between tenants. Even so she was glad that at last Miles had agreed that they should sell. It was too small a house to contain the growing twins; not suitable that at nearly twelve they should have to share a bedroom. Had they stayed this living room would have been made into a bedroom, the furniture going to The Keep or to be sold, but it was a relief not to have to contemplate such an upheaval. For the coming Easter holidays Miles had agreed that Jamie should use the dressing room as he had at Christmas but, even so, there simply wasn't space for their toys and books or their bicycles. A lot of the twinnies' belongings were at The Keep but this wasn't a very satisfactory arrangement once the holidays arrived.

Fortunately Miles was in very good spirits and was making light of being turned out of his dressing room, something which might easily have irritated him. Tempers had become somewhat strained during the Christmas holidays and it was a relief to take the twins over to The Keep for periods of time so that Miles could have some peace and quiet. Fliss stirred a little in her chair, anxiety tinging her happiness at the thought of having the twins home again; at the balancing act required to keep everybody happy. It was necessary to remember that Miles was fifty-three and the twins could be very boisterous and noisy. They came home for such short periods that she longed for it to be fun but Miles found it difficult to remain tolerant whilst they played pop music or clattered up and down the two flights of stairs between kitchen and bedroom. They were all too much under one another's feet . . .

She thought: The trouble is that this house has never really felt like home.

Even here, in her favourite room, she did not feel so much at ease as she had in some of the quarters and married hirings she'd lived in during the last fourteen years. She longed to settle down at last, for them to become a real family living in a comfortably careless way without the pressure of knowing that in two years' time they'd be moving on.

'At least constant moving saves you collecting rubbish,' Miles had said when an argument had arisen about whether the twinnies' baby toys and books should be kept. 'It's silly to hang on to a lot of useless stuff that no one will ever want again.'

'But they will want to look at it all from time to time,' she'd argued. 'And they'll like to keep these things for their own children. It's not rubbish, it's part of their history.'

'Honestly, darling.' He'd shaken his head, laughing at her, patting her shoulder. 'As if their children would want it. If they *have* children, that is. Just because *you* hang on to a rose-coloured vision of childhood doesn't mean that they will.'

'But they might,' she'd protested, refusing to be brow-beaten by this attempt to make her feel foolish, sentimental, childish. 'Look how all the children love the toys and books that are kept at The Keep. Those things aren't just mine or Mole's or Sooz's. Some of them were Daddy's and Uncle John's and some even belonged to Grandmother and Uncle Theo. It's a kind of continuity.'

'Have it your way,' he'd said tolerantly. 'But I'm not paying to cart it all with us from place to place and there's no space for it in Dartmouth.'

'It can all go to The Keep,' she'd said. 'There will be room for it there,' and she'd boxed up the Ladybird books and the Richard Scarry books and the Fisher Price toys and driven them down to Devon herself. However Pudgie and Binker, the teddy bears which Kit had given them, remained with them and had gone off to Herongate with a name tape sewed to each left-hand paw. She'd noticed, too, that on their visits to The Keep, sooner or later Jamie and Bess made the pilgrimage up to the nursery quarters where she'd find them kneeling beside open boxes, their books and toys about them on the floor.

As she reached to put Bess's letter on the table beside the other post, her glance fell on the ginger jar, back in its place on the small bookcase. She remembered how she'd found it damaged and the sadness she'd felt, sadness and shame that she'd been so careless as to risk it to strangers.

After that she'd taken it with her as a kind of talisman, a reminder of the value of loyalty and friendship and how easily these qualities can be neglected and damaged. Getting up she went to look at it more closely, studying the frieze of figures, absently tracing the crack with her fingers, thinking of Remy, the little Filipino amah . . .

Miles came into the hall, closing the front door behind him, and she turned, calling to him.

'*There* you are,' he said, as if she had been hiding from him, and threw the *Telegraph* on to the table. 'Any coffee left?'

'Of course there is.' She passed him in the doorway, indicating the letters on the table. 'One from Bess for us and a couple for you,' and she left him to open them whilst she went into the kitchen.

When she returned with the coffee he was standing by the window, reading a letter. His attitude, tense, alert, concentrated, drew her attention, and as she half frowned, half smiled at his intensity, he swung round to her, his face alight and eager. She smiled at him, eyebrows lifted enquiringly, and he gave a laugh that was partly a breath of relief.

'It's come at last,' he said. 'I've been waiting for this. It's the final confirmation.' He shook the sheets of paper at her, smiling broadly. 'I've got a job.'

'Oh . . .' The familiar sensation of hurt and irritation that she'd been excluded from the secret, combining with the instinctive desire to encourage and support him, made her response only slightly enthusiastic. 'I had no idea things had got this far.'

'I didn't want to say anything until it was a certainty.' He was ebullient, unable to contain his delight, and she was reminded of that former occasion when he had told her about his posting to Hong Kong. 'It's from Richard telling me that my formal application's gone through and a contract will be following shortly.'

'Richard?' she interrupted him, puzzled.

'Richard Maybrick, darling,' he answered in that faintly impatient tone which implied 'Don't be silly, darling.' 'You can't have forgotten Richard and Mary?'

'Of course not,' she replied. 'It's simply that I didn't associate him with getting you a job. Not with them out in Hong Kong. So what's it all about?'

'Well, that's the whole point.' Miles put the letter down and seized his coffee mug. He took an enormous swig of coffee and in that moment Fliss felt a trickle of fear, of premonition.

'What's the whole point?'

'Well, it was Richard who suggested it, you see. He knew how much we loved it out there and he's always talked of us moving out once I'd finished with the Navy. He's been making enquiries for me, dear old lad. D'you remember meeting James Perowne at a party when we were in London? Well, his brother Peter owns Preselli Enterprises out in Hong Kong. It's an import-export business, mainly exporting liquid propane gas and small diesel generators and so on into China. Old Richard's been pulling strings for me and I've been offered the job of acting manager, light engineering. Pretty good, eh? It's a very fair salary and I get commission. Shan't know the details until the contract comes with the letter from Peter but I'm sure there won't be any problems. God, it'll be good to be back out there again, won't it, darling? We had such fun, didn't we?'

Beyond him the ginger jar was lit by a sudden gleam of sunlight. Staring at it she remembered the noisy streets, the neon lights, the busy harbour, the hot fragrant smell of root ginger . . .

'You should have told me.' It was oddly difficult to move her lips and she clenched her hands behind her back. 'You had no right—'

He frowned. 'No right?'

'No right to plan all our lives as if I didn't exist.' She closed her eyes, shaking her head, suddenly angry. 'It's unbelievable.'

'But you loved Hong Kong.' He could barely understand her reaction. It had been his dream for so long that it had never occurred to him that she would not be as excited as he was. This was the start of their new life together, a picking up where they'd left off when Jamie and Bess had arrived: a new life, a new job, a new country. 'You loved it,' he repeated, as if the words would make it so, certain that this was a momentary qualm born out of surprise. 'We know quite a few people out there and we can buy a lovely flat and you can have help. The social life is terrific.' He laughed. 'You'll have to buy yourself some decent clothes and smarten up a bit. Seriously, it's a brilliant opportunity, Fliss.'

'Wait,' she said. 'Wait. Hong Kong was fine as a two-year posting and I *did* love it, some of it, although I missed everyone so terribly. But that doesn't mean I want to live there permanently. I take it that this is what's in your mind? This isn't just a two-year job or something?'

'Of course it isn't,' he said impatiently. 'Do you realise how lucky I am to be offered such a job at my age? For

God's sake! Most wives would leap at it.'

'But I don't want to live in Hong Kong, Miles. I can't believe that you thought that I would. I'm English. I want to be here in my own country. And to be so far from the twinnies and the family—'

'Oh, I wondered how long it would be before we came round to that,' he said irritably, turning away from her. 'I thought that just for once you might put me first.'

'That's unfair,' she said, stung by such injustice. 'I've moved about with you for fourteen years, I've been glad to, but I'm not prepared to contemplate spending the rest of my life in Hong Kong. And what happens when Great Britain's lease runs out in the nineties?'

He shrugged it off. 'Nothing will happen. Do you honestly see Margaret Thatcher handing it back to China? According to Richard there's massive building going on out there. High rises are going up on every available square inch of land. He says we'll hardly recognise it.'

Fliss shuddered slightly. 'I can well believe it,' she said.

He was cross with himself for letting this negative information slip. 'I'm sure it won't make any difference to us,' he said. 'Don't be foolish about this, Fliss, please. The twins can travel to and fro for holidays and they can go to The Keep or to Hal for exeats and half terms. We simply can't let them stand in the way of this fantastic opportunity. I know how you feel about your family but we must put us first. There will be plenty of opportunities to come over to see them and they can come to us if they want to but we have to think of ourselves here.'

Fliss tried to smile. 'The trouble is,' she said, 'that you're assuming that we want the same thing. I don't want to go to

Hong Kong, Miles. Even if the twinnies and my family were out of the equation I still shouldn't want to go. I've been to Hong Kong and to Brussels and we've moved round this country and it was fun. But I want to stop now and settle down. Here in England, preferably in Devon, but certainly not in Hong Kong.'

He stared at her disbelievingly. 'I don't understand you,' he said at last. 'I've plotted and planned for this. Richard and I have talked about it almost ever since we left Hong Kong. It's our new start. Our new life. Most people would be out of their minds with excitement.'

'Perhaps you should have discussed it with me as well as with Richard,' she said – and watched his lips tighten at this criticism. 'If you don't understand *me*, Miles, even less do I understand *you*. How is it possible that you know me so little as to think that I'd like the idea? Why did you never consider telling me about it?'

Miles tried to push down his instinctive anger at being questioned in such a way. Perhaps he had been a touch autocratic in arranging things without consulting her but this was the way he'd always behaved. She was so young and inexperienced, so foolish about the twins and her family. He still suspected that this lay at the root of the problem and he decided to try a different approach. She was watching him, chin high, eyes wary, and he was reminded of old Mrs Chadwick.

'Look,' he said, and his voice was conciliatory now, 'I admit I've probably been a bit high-handed but you know me, Fliss. I'm just one of those people who like to be in control. It was silly to want to get it all arranged before I told you but you have to believe that it never occurred to me for a single moment that you wouldn't love the idea. In fact I was afraid to tell you unless it fell through and you were disappointed. Clearly I misjudged the situation. I've allowed myself to get a bit carried away.' He sighed, part regret, part self-pity, expecting her ready sympathy to respond to this admission. 'But I can't tell you how terribly I've looked forward to this, Fliss.' His voice grew louder again now and his face was eager. 'I've thought about nothing else for months, ever since I knew there might be a job with Peter Perowne. Can't you see how I felt? It was for *us*, Fliss, not for me. It's the beginning of our new life together.'

'But I don't want a new life.' Her voice was cool. 'I like the old life, Miles. I know you've left the Navy and I know that it might be difficult to get a job but it's not that urgent. We can live on your pension and my allowance quite easily until something turns up. I can get a teaching post if it comes to that.'

He was frowning, cautious and alert. 'What d'you mean?'

She clenched her fists with frustration. 'You say that you planned it for us, Miles, but now that you can see that I don't want it, can't we think again? If this is really the beginning of our new life together shouldn't you have planned it with me rather than with Richard Maybrick?'

'Look,' he said grimly, 'I've apologised for not taking you into my confidence, no doubt it was wrong of me, but let's not bother with that now. Don't let hurt pride spoil this for us—'

'Hurt *pride*,' she burst out. 'Yes, fair enough, it does hurt that you never mentioned this to me at all but I'm not playing hard to get, Miles. This isn't some kind of act to punish you for treating me as if I'm a backward child instead of your wife. It's simple. I don't want to live in Hong Kong. That's all there is to it.'

She stared at him, willing him to understand. He shook his head, as if she were speaking some language that he couldn't understand.

'So what are you suggesting?'

She took a deep breath. 'I'm suggesting that this isn't going to work. I'm saying that I'm not going to Hong Kong. I'm suggesting that we think again. Make other plans.'

'You can't be serious?' He looked outraged. 'You don't think that I'm going to turn down this opportunity, do you?'

There was a silence. 'You told me,' she said carefully, 'that this wasn't for you but for us.'

'So I hoped,' he said with a short laugh. 'It seems that I was wrong.'

'Yes,' she said, after a moment. 'You were wrong. Are you saying that you will go to Hong Kong whether I go or not?'

'But why do we have to talk like this?' he shouted. 'I might never get another chance as good as this one. Why should I turn it down?'

She bit her lip, fighting an urge to give in, to agree that he must have his opportunity, that she should be ready to support him. 'You don't have to,' she said at last – and watched the tension go out of him as he gasped with relief that she had come to her senses. 'It would be wrong to ask you to sacrifice your career, just as it would be wrong to ask me to sacrifice my life. I can't go to Hong Kong, Miles. I'm sorry. If you want to go I shan't stop you and I can understand what it means to you but I can't face the thought of living there permanently. Don't misunderstand me. It's not because of the twinnies or the family, although they enter into it, it's because I don't belong there. It was one thing being a naval wife and going where the Navy sent you but now we have choices and Hong Kong isn't my choice.'

'Are you threatening me?' he asked quietly.

She laughed. 'Don't be silly. I'm simply telling you the truth. It's up to you—'

'Oh no,' he said quickly. 'Don't put it on me. It's up to you. I'm continuing to offer you a home and my support in Hong Kong. If you don't choose to take it then it's your decision, not mine.'

'Very well,' she said gently but quite firmly. 'I don't choose it.'

'I think you'd better think it over,' he said. 'You need to be on your own for a day or two to have time to consider. I have to go up to London to sort out a few things anyway so as to be ready to fly out at the end of the month.'

'The end of the *month* . . .?'

'Quite,' he said. 'Naturally I wasn't expecting you to come with me that soon – you'd have to follow later – but think about it, Fliss. It's our lives we're talking about here so don't be too hasty. I'm going to pack a bag and be off, give you some space, but don't be melodramatic about it, for God's sake. OK?'

He went out and up the stairs and she was left alone, staring at the ginger jar.

Chapter Forty-two

Yawning, Kit tied her dressing-gown belt tightly about her and stumbled out of her bedroom. Outside the bathroom door she paused. Strange sounds issued forth, as though someone might be cutting his – or her – throat in the bath and she stood, trying to concentrate beyond the dull aching of her own head, listening intently. After a moment or two she realised that it was merely Sin singing. Unmelodic strains of 'I Feel Pretty' rose above the plashing of water and the strangled gurgles of the antique cistern. Kit passed on, groaning aloud as she groped her way into the kitchen and stood looking about her. Indications of the previous night's revelry met her wincing gaze and she tried to fill the kettle with her eyes closed lest the sight of such carnage should depress her too utterly. She tried to remember the party but most of the details remained outside her present cerebral capabilities. Andrew and Clarrie had been there, of course, as well as other friends, celebrating Sin's birthday; her fortieth birthday.

Kit spooned instant coffee into a mug, opened a cupboard door and peered inside for some aspirin. To begin with, poor Sin had been rendered practically suicidal at the idea of forty. Depression had set in months before the dreaded day and it had taken everyone's co-operation to persuade her that this wasn't simply the end of everything.

'Forty,' she'd moan at regular – and often quite inappropriate – intervals. 'Oh God. Forty years old. I'm over the hill. Middle-aged. Might as well top myself and have done.'

Kit, whose own fortieth birthday had been last autumn, attempted to persuade Sin that forty was a mere nothing. 'Look at Clarrie,' she'd said. 'Look at Uncle Theo.'

'They're men,' Sin had replied morosely – and then almost overnight, her depression had changed to this cheerful jollity which resulted in throwing impromptu parties and singing in the bath.

'And we all know why,' muttered Kit bitterly, swallowing several tablets quickly with gulps of coffee and burning her tongue in the process. 'It's love. Dear God, it's pathetic. We just never learn, do we?'

The bathroom door slammed and Sin pattered into the kitchen wrapped in a huge towel, her hair in a turban, her face radiant.

'Coffee!' she cried. 'Great!'

'Hush,' whispered Kit furiously, closing her eyes in agony. 'Don't *shout*!'

'Sorry.' Sin modulated her voice to a more reasonable level but couldn't help grinning. 'I told you to go gently on the vodka.'

'Shut up,' muttered Kit grimly. 'I was commiserating with Hal . . .' She fell silent, eyes still closed, marshalling her thoughts. 'Hal,' she repeated carefully. 'Was Hal here last night?'

'He was indeed,' said Sin cheerfully, though still quietly.

'He dropped in quite by chance. He'd been seeing some bigwig at the Ministry of Defence and decided to visit us afterwards. When he knew that it was my birthday he went round to the off-licence and brought back lots of booze.'

'Aah.' Kit nodded – and stopped abruptly, frowning painfully. 'I remember now. He was telling me his problems and we were comforting each other.'

'You certainly were,' agreed Sin. 'He's still sleeping it off on the sofa. It was really good to see him.'

'Poor old Hal,' mourned Kit, sounding now if she might burst into tears at any moment. 'Isn't life hell? He's got all these problems with that cow Maria, and then there's Fliss phoning up to say that Miles wants her to go and live in Hong Kong. And now there's you and Andrew—'

'But that's good,' interrupted Sin. 'Me and Andrew, I mean. It's great. I've never been so happy.'

Making a supreme effort Kit raised her eyelids a little, gazing at Sin through the lower part of her eyes.

'How can it possibly be great?' she demanded scornfully. 'He's married. Terribly, terribly married. What sort of future does that leave you?'

Sin heaved a sigh of happiness and beamed upon her flatmate. 'But it doesn't matter,' she explained. 'He loves me. It's working. I'm not certain that I'd want to marry him anyway. This way I keep my independence. I like the idea of keeping my job and my friends separately. I like the way you and I go on together. It's what I'm used to. Then again, I love my evenings out with him and our walks on the heath and Sunday lunchtime down the pub. Just knowing that we love each other, being able to admit it and share it, is enough.'

'At the moment,' assisted Kit cynically as Sin paused, either for breath or for inspiration. 'And how will you feel every time he goes home to wifie?'

Sin shrugged. 'All I can say is that it doesn't bother me at the moment. We all know her, don't we? I believe Andrew when he says that he loves me but I quite understand that he doesn't want to hurt her. I'm not certain that I could cope with the whole marriage bit. It's too late. I'm too independent. This suits both of us.'

'If you say so,' said Kit morosely. 'I just don't want him using you, that's all.' She gave a faint scream as the door opened suddenly and Hal put his head round. 'Don't *do* that, little brother.'

He raised his eyebrows at Sin, who nodded significantly. 'Coffee?'

'Definitely,' he said, coming in and chuckling at Kit's pained expression. 'That was a really good thrash, girls. I should come to your parties more often. Pity I've got to go back down to Hampshire or we could all have gone along to the pub for some hair of the dog. That would have set you up in no time.'

Kit shuddered artistically. 'Please,' she begged. 'Be content with the knowledge that all night I've suffered what I believe you call the whirling pits. My bed has rocked and heaved relentlessly through the long watches of the night. Let that be enough for you. Just drink your coffee and go.'

'I was hoping to see Clarrie before I dash off,' said Hal, accepting his mug gratefully. 'Sound man, Clarrie. He's had the most amazing life.'

'Don't believe everything he tells you,' warned Kit darkly. 'He's a skilled liar, like most men, and he'll stop at nothing to cause a sensation or win sympathy. No lie is too outrageous, especially when he's had a bit to drink.'

'Quite right, too,' said Hal comfortably. 'Never let the truth get in the way of a good dit, as we say in the Navy. Hell, is that really the time?'

'I'm late.' Sin put down her mug and flitted away.

Kit sighed with mingled anguish and relief. 'Thank God I haven't got an office to go to,' she murmured. 'It's crazy to give a mid-week party but she would have it. Do you really have to dash off? Aren't you on leave?'

'I am,' he agreed, 'but I must get back.' He hesitated. 'Sorry to bend your ear last night. It was just such a relief to get it all off my chest.'

Kit looked at him properly. 'Don't give it a thought,' she said lightly. 'I'm sorry though . . .'

'If only I could be certain that it was right for Edward it wouldn't be so bad but it's gone too far now. Maria and her mother have completely brainwashed him so we must just pray that he'll cope.'

'And you'll move to Salisbury?'

He hesitated. 'I think we'll have to. Like I said last night, it's Jolyon that's really worrying me. Obviously nothing's going to happen just yet. We don't want to disrupt their schooling any more than we have to but we'll have to be in Salisbury ready for the new school year. I know it's five months away but we must start looking at houses soon. Jolyon's going to have to know what's in store for him.'

'Poor Jolyon.' Kit finished her coffee and switched the kettle on again. 'Ooh, my poor head. So who's going to tell him?'

Hal looked grim. 'Maria's shirking it. I told her that since it's her decision she should do the dirty work but actually part of me doesn't want her to do it. I'm afraid she'll just blurt it out. She loves Jolyon, don't get me wrong, but she doesn't have the same sensitivity towards him as she does towards Edward. To do him justice he could be making much more mileage out of it than he is, poor little chap, but even so, old Jolyon's taking a real back seat. It's going to be even worse when he hears that he's going to be packed off to boarding school. The trouble is that Maria has become totally tunnel-visioned over this choir school business. She can see and think of nothing else. It's so vital to her that other people's feelings have ceased to exist, even Edward's. She honestly thinks that it's important enough for everything else to go by the board.'

'Sounds like Miles over this Hong Kong business.' Kit made more coffee. 'Honestly! How can he possibly have imagined that Fliss of all people would want to upsticks and emigrate to Hong Kong? Like Maria he simply got totally carried away by the whole idea.' She glanced at her brother. 'Better not mention it to anyone, by the way. I don't know how much of a secret it is at present.'

'Sure.' Hal nodded reassuringly. 'I must say that I agree with you. It seems impossible but having seen Maria over this business I know how single-minded people can get. They want something so much that it becomes inconceivable that everyone else doesn't want it too. Poor Fliss.'

'And as for not even telling her about it.' Kit snorted. 'It's outrageous. But then he's always behaved as if he were her father. This time, however, he's overstepped the mark. She's absolutely determined not to go.'

'What will she do?'

Kit shrugged. 'She hasn't got that far. Poor old Flissy. Oh Hal . . .'

'Don't,' said Hal. 'We did that bit last night when we'd both drunk too much.'

'She's just trying to work through it at the moment,' said Kit gently. 'I'm sure she'll tell you about it.'

'Yes,' said Hal. 'Yes, I'm sure she will. Actually, I might be seeing her soon. I've got a vague plan about Jolyon. There's an open day at the school for Edward during the Easter holidays and I'm wondering whether I might leave it to Maria and take Jo down to see the ship in Devonport. Perhaps try to break the news to him during the course of the day and spend a couple of nights at The Keep? What d'you think? The twinnies will be home and I thought I might ask Fliss to tell them the situation and then drop in to see them while we're down there . . .' He gestured impotently. 'Oh hell, I just don't know how to deal with it.'

'That sounds a great idea,' said Kit. 'Honestly. The twinnies will boost Jolyon's confidence and make him feel that it will be fun. After all, he's often been down to Herongate with you to see them, hasn't he?'

Hal nodded. 'If Maria hadn't been so set against it I think he would have been quite happy to go a couple of years ago when Bess and Jamie started. Now, of course, she can see that it's an obvious way out but she's said such awful things about boarding school that it's rather embarrassing for her to eat her words.'

'He's only got to look at the twinnies to see that it isn't awful,' Kit pointed out comfortingly. 'It'll be OK. And he'll be thrilled to be taken down to see *Broadsword* all on his own. But, Hal, make sure he sees Fliss and the twinnies at

The Keep, not at that house in Dartmouth. And warn Ma and Caroline. It's a brilliant idea and I'm sure it'll work.'

'Bless you.' He smiled at her and glanced at his watch. 'I really must go but I'll be in touch. Thanks, Kit . . .'

'Think nothing of it, little brother,' she said casually. 'We also serve who only stand and wait but don't think I haven't noticed that everyone's dashing off and leaving me with the washing-up.'

He hugged her, laughing. 'Will Clarrie be up if I go to say goodbye?'

'Definitely,' said Kit. 'He has a head of iron and will have been out with his dog at dawn. Tell him I shall expect to see him shortly to help with the clearing-up but tell him that if he values his life it would be foolhardy to ring the bell.'

They parted amicably, Sin and Hal leaving together, and, feeling a little more human, Kit trailed away to her bedroom to get dressed. Her headache was subsiding but she felt depressed. On several occasions during their lives Hal had unburdened himself to her, seeking advice and sharing his fears, but never before had she seen him quite so angry as he'd been last night. It was clear that his anxiety was as much for Edward as for Jolyon, fearing that his younger son wouldn't be able to cope with the rigorous demands ahead, but his bitterness was very plain. As the evening had worn on he'd told her that he believed that Maria was having an affair with a man she'd known very well just before he himself had met her.

'I think her mother's encouraging it,' he'd said thoughtfully. 'The truth of it is they thought that I would inherit The Keep when Grandmother died and when I explained it all properly they became somewhat disenchanted. Maria likes the idea of being the lady of the manor but only once everyone else has been chucked out. Part of the attraction of moving back to Salisbury is that Adam Wishart is there. He's her father's partner now. I expect they feel it would have been better to have kept it in the family.'

Even now, Kit felt a sense of shock at the thought of it. When she attempted to analyse her feelings she realised that she felt annoyed with herself for underrating Maria. She and Sin had often joked at Maria's preciousness, at her adoration for Hal, her jealousy . . .

'I don't believe it,' she'd exclaimed.

But Hal had shaken his head sadly. 'Things are not good,' he'd said quietly

It was then that they'd begun to reminisce, to talk of the past, of their childhood, of Fliss.

'It's my fault,' he'd said. 'Fliss would have stood firm but I was undecided both for me and for her . . .'

Later, she'd told him about Miles's bombshell and Fliss's determination to stay in Devon.

'Perhaps,' she'd said, having drunk enough to speak her mind, 'perhaps you and Fliss will get together after all. What with Maria playing the field and Miles going to Hong Kong.'

She'd felt his reserve return, then, the barriers rising. 'It's not that easy,' he'd said shortly – and begun to talk about Mole.

By the time she was dressed and ready for action she found Clarrie in the kitchen already clearing up.

'Come live with me and be my love,' she said, kissing him fulsomely on the ear, 'and we will all the pleasures prove . . .'

'As long as I do all the work,' he finished for her, flapping her away with a soapy hand. 'Useless woman! Get hold of that tea cloth and never mind the cupboard love.'

'Love causes nothing but problems,' she said, picking up the tea towel. 'Oh, Clarrie, I don't think I know one happy person in the whole world.'

'You know me,' he answered indignantly. 'I'm happy, dammit.'

'True,' she said, brightening a little. 'I suppose it's a start . . . Clarrie?'

'Mmm?' he answered cautiously.

'I've had a good idea.'

'Mmm?'

'When we've finished let's go down to the pub.'

'Now you're talking,' he said. 'Get moving with that cloth then. This is only the tip of the iceberg. Have you seen the sitting room?'

'Shit,' said Kit. 'I'd forgotten the state of the sitting room. Never mind . . . Clarrie?'

'Mmm?'

'Thanks for being there.'

'Don't talk daft, woman. Take that tray and go and fetch the dirty glasses or we'll be here all day . . . and, Kit?'

She paused at the door, tray in hand. 'Mmm?'

He grinned at her. 'I love you, too, you know,' he said.

Chapter Forty-three

The room was quiet, full of April sunshine whose glancing brightness slid across the faded Chinese rugs and lit the titles of the books ranged on the shelves of the mahogany bookcase. A bee, enjoying the unexpected warmth, lumbered lazily in through the open, south-facing window and buzzed inquisitively beside the brocade curtains before landing heavily, clambering over their thick folds.

'But have I got the right?' asked Fliss into the silence. 'Have I got the right not to go, if you see what I mean?'

She continued to stand by the other window, which looked east over the hill. One knee was resting on the broad seat and her eyes were fixed on the spinney where new leaves were transforming the bare branches with a tender misting green. In the ivy below the window the sparrows were busy, chattering noisily together, whilst in her hidden, secret nest the blackbird guarded her eggs, waiting for the return of her mate.

Theo stirred. Sitting with his arms folded on the battered leather-topped desk he attempted to find words with which to help her. He'd listened carefully whilst she told him about Miles's plans for the future, trying to hear what she wasn't saying as well as what she was actually telling him, praying for guidance. As usual he felt all the weight of his own inadequacies and wondered why it was that she thought he might have the wisdom to help her. He realised that she was feeling her way through a kind of moral maze and he wondered whether she really expected him to explain that there was a clear-cut path; a definite choice of right and wrong. He gave a deep internal sigh. If only it were that easy and, even if it were, why did she assume that he would have the right to help her decide?

She'd gone to great lengths to put both sides of the argument, to explain Miles's character to him, to be as fair as possible. He could understand this. Ultimately, there was never any point in cheating, whether it was yourself or other people. He knew how frighteningly easy it was to distort truths to justify one's actions, often at the expense of someone else. How tempting it was to drug one's conscience until it dwelled contentedly in a shadowy land beyond the reach of the bright searching beam of self-knowledge.

'The trouble is,' Fliss was saying, still with her back to him, 'that's it's almost too late. If only he'd discussed it with me earlier it wouldn't have made it seem so desperate – but it's all fixed. There's no time for me to put my point of view calmly or sensibly, no time to consider other options. I had a letter from Mary Maybrick before I left home this morning, telling me how delighted she was that it was all arranged and that she's got somewhere lined up for us to live until we sort ourselves out. Part of me wants to think that he's bounced me into it because he suspected that I wouldn't want to go. I sometimes think that it's almost impossible not to, if you see what I mean. It's like a kind of awful nightmare where you find yourself being swept along and you can't shout or move. I feel that one day I'm going to wake up in Hong Kong and that will be that. But to be fair to Miles I honestly don't think it *was* that. It just took hold of him and obsessed him. He genuinely can't imagine that I'm not thrilled to bits. He thinks it's because of the twinnies and all of you here.'

'And is it?' asked Theo gently.

Fliss looked out at the sweep of the hill. In her mind's eye she saw Fox, with the dogs running ahead, climbing the sheep tracks with Susanna astride his shoulders and Mole coming along behind. Down by the river the blackthorn blossom was bridal white whilst marsh marigolds glowed, splashes of gold in the fast-running waters, and she heard voices from long-past summers, calling and laughing as dams were built and picnics unpacked on the bank. A yaffingale was laughing in the woods and, as she watched, Caroline appeared from behind the spinney with Rex, nose to ground, pursuing an elusive rabbit.

'Only in part,' she said at last, trying to be completely honest with herself. 'It's too closely bound up together to be absolutely clear about it but it's not just because I can't bear to leave you all, it's because of all that.' Her gesture embraced the scene beyond the window. 'I'm just too English, I suppose. I love the changing seasons and everything that goes to make the countryside what it is. I'm like a fish out of water in a place like Hong Kong. It was

OK for a year or two, knowing I was coming back, but I can't face it for the rest of my life.' She turned back into the room, the small frown fixed between her brows. 'But how do you work out something like this? Does Miles sacrifice his job or do I sacrifice my need to be where I belong?'

Theo emptied his mind and prayed for guidance. It came at once.

'There is a difference,' he said slowly, 'between this new situation and being a naval wife. When you marry a man, assuming that he is the provider, you go where his work takes him cheerfully and bravely. I can imagine that it might not be simple for Miles to find another job immediately but I'm sure that this is not the only opportunity open to him. He should have discussed the future with you. It belongs to both of you and to your children. Compromises might have to be made but to take a decision of this enormity knowing you as he does – or should – and without asking your opinion is overstepping the mark. Now that he knows how strongly you feel about it, I think he should be prepared to reconsider.'

'He doesn't want to stay in England,' said Fliss miserably. 'It's a kind of impasse and neither of us wants to back down.'

'If you had never been to Hong Kong,' Theo said carefully, 'I might have suggested that you tried it for a short time but since you spent two years there then I think we can take it that you know your own mind. If Miles has set *his* mind against this country that certainly presents problems. It comes down to this: do you love your country and family more than you love Miles? Or, to look at it the other way –

which is only proper – does Miles love the idea of this new job more than he loves you?'

Fliss did not hesitate. 'The answer to both questions must be yes,' she said, 'since we're each of us considering these options.'

Theo leaned his chin upon his folded hands. The bee had finished its inspection of the curtains and was droning gently as it buffeted itself against the window pane. Fliss went across to open the window wider, to allow the bee its freedom.

'The answer might only be "probably".' Theo's voice was thoughtful. 'It is probable that both of you are mistaken in your assumptions. Each of you might miss the other more than you suspect.'

Fliss shrugged. 'Obviously that could be true. I wouldn't want you to imagine that we are indifferent about this.'

'Clearly not or there wouldn't be all this soul-searching, but I think that perhaps a period of separation might give us the real answer. Why shouldn't Miles go to Hong Kong? Give it a trial for, say, two years, a time to be agreed between you both, anyway. Plenty of naval postings last that long and families are often separated for even longer. Give yourselves the space and time for your true feelings to emerge. What do you say?'

'It sounds terribly sensible,' said Fliss. 'Much better than acts of martyrdom or irreversible divorces.'

'I don't approve of the first,' said Theo. 'Such acts invariably lead to resentment and self-pity. As for the second, I believe that there are valid reasons for such action but only as a last resort. I'm not certain that you and Miles are far enough along that road just yet. Well?'

He pushed back his chair, smiling at her, and she smiled too, relief smoothing away the frown as she nodded.

'It's worth trying,' she said. 'Miles won't be very pleased but it's better than making a decision we might both regret. Bless you, Uncle Theo. I knew you'd help me see things straight.'

'I can't imagine why,' he murmured, 'but we won't go into that.'

They stood together at the window, his arm about her shoulder, looking out at the spring morning and listening to the cuckoo calling across the valley.

'I simply can't bear the thought of leaving it,' she said suddenly and with great vehemence. 'I just can't. Why does he treat me as if I'm a child who can't possibly know her own mind? For heaven's sake, I'm thirty-eight years old in September.'

Theo thought: I am nearly fifty years older than she is. She still seems like a child to me, too, but I can remember how offensive it was when old people refused to take me seriously when I was a young man.

He said, 'It's true that people think wisdom only arrives at the age they are at the moment and that anyone younger is, therefore, foolish. That age might be twelve or thirty or it might be eighty. We each like to imagine that we are superior to someone and age allows us this illusion more easily than almost anything else. Each generation thinks it is the last to possess real taste or genius or sound moral judgements.'

Fliss laughed. 'I'm afraid that's so,' she said ruefully. 'I'm guilty of that myself with the twinnies' pop music. Oh dear, now you've made me feel bad.'

His grip around her slim square shoulders tightened.

'Is there time for a moralising lecture on motes and beams?' he murmured provocatively.

'No there isn't,' she said tartly, 'but there's certainly time for a drink before lunch. I think I need one after all that.'

She looked and sounded so much like Freddy that he laughed delightedly and went away to find some glasses and to inspect the contents of his drinks cupboard.

Downstairs Prue was laying the kitchen table when Caroline came in with Rex at her heels.

'That was just heavenly,' she said. 'Sorry to leave you to it but I couldn't resist. Is Fliss still with Theo?'

Prue nodded. 'I can still hardly take it in,' she said. 'Poor Fliss. Just as she was getting so excited about buying a house and settling down at last. I can't believe that Miles can be serious. It makes him sound so insensitive and I've always thought that he was so nice.'

'I can believe it,' said Caroline grimly, shooing Rex into the dog basket and bringing a tray of warm rolls out of the oven.

Prue stared at her in some surprise and Caroline smiled back at her affectionately. Prue had put on weight in these last four years at The Keep and her fluffy short hair, a pretty silvery grey, gave her an oddly youthful appearance. She'd yielded gracefully to a plump middle age and, resisting Kit's spasmodic attempts to make her fashionable, had settled happily into kilts and guernseys which underlined the aura of classic timelessness which surrounded her. Looking at her, Caroline was aware of her own more angular shape. The necessity to help out in the grounds and to exercise Rex had made the wearing of trousers a habit and her mild disinterest in clothes had hardened now into complete indifference.

'You're lucky to be thin enough to wear trousers,' Prue had said recently with a certain amount of envy. 'I stopped when Hal said my behind looked like two poodles in a sack.'

They'd laughed together, Prue quite unresentful at such an unchivalrous remark.

'Whatever do you mean?' she was asking now, almost indignantly, and Caroline was surprised to find that she was ready to talk about something which had been a secret for nearly twenty years.

'I was in love with Miles once myself,' she said almost carelessly.

Prue sat down at the table, spoons and knives still clutched in her hand.

'*No!*' she breathed, sounding suitably shocked but quite ready to hear the details. 'When?'

'When I first met him.' Caroline gave the saucepan of soup a good stir. 'He was Hal's divisional officer, remember? He used to come here quite a bit and we used to make up parties for end-of-term balls and Ladies' Nights. Because he was so much older I used to be partnered off with him. He paid me a bit of attention and I fancied I was in love with him. After a while I thought that he felt the same way about me.' She laughed. 'It was a terrible shock when I realised that he'd never noticed me in that way at all. I still remember how I felt when he phoned to say that he was coming out here to talk to Mrs Chadwick. He said he knew I'd guess why and I was convinced that he was coming to ask if she had any objections to his proposing to me. I went off for a long walk to try to calm myself down and when I got back Mrs Chadwick told me that he was in love with Fliss.'

'How perfectly awful.' Prue was taking it very seriously, ignoring Caroline's lightness of tone. 'You poor darling.'

'It was a shock,' admitted Caroline. 'Only Mrs Chadwick knew. My pride couldn't take everyone feeling sorry for me. I came and stayed with you for a bit. During the Easter holidays, if you remember? Good grief, I can't imagine why you should remember.'

'I think I do, though,' said Prue, who could remember the whole thing perfectly well. She could also recall the shock she'd had on receiving Freddy's letter, taking her into Freddy's confidence, asking her for her assistance in this attempt to save Caroline's pride. It was about the same time that she'd discovered that Fliss was in love with Hal . . .

'I thought at the time that he must be pretty insensitive not to notice how I felt,' Caroline was saying, 'but it might be sour grapes, of course. After all, I never noticed that he was in love with Fliss but then she was always so devoted to Hal . . .'

Her voice died away and she sat frowning at nothing in particular.

'She was in love with him,' said Prue sadly. 'Poor little Fliss. And Hal loved her, too. Freddy and I came down very heavily on Hal, their fathers being twins and all that, but now I wonder if we were right. I was so afraid they might have funny children, oh, all sorts of things, but I sometimes

461

wish we'd never interfered.' She looked at Caroline, eye-brows raised. 'Did you never guess?'

Caroline shook her head slowly. 'No. Oh, I knew she had a sort of childish infatuation for him but I imagined that he was a kind of replacement for her brother Jamie. Well, that will teach me to talk about Miles being insensitive. All these years and I never knew.' She struggled not to feel hurt. 'And Flissy and I are so close.'

'We wanted to save her pride,' explained Prue gently. 'Only the four of us knew. Me and Freddy, Hal and Theo. Fliss still has no idea that anyone guessed. Hal told her that they were too young and that it was too much of a risk when it came to babies.' She sighed heavily. 'Poor children . . . And poor Caroline.'

'I feel such a fool now,' said Caroline gloomily. 'Sitting in judgement on Miles and then being caught out in the same fault myself. What does it say in the Bible? Some-thing about "judge not lest ye be likewise judged".' She began to laugh. 'I remember when Mrs Chadwick told me that Miles was in love with Fliss I was so shocked and humiliated that she actually gave me a glass of whisky in an attempt to cheer me up.'

'I think that's an excellent idea,' said Prue, rising with alacrity and leaving the knives and spoons in a heap. 'Just a small drop before lunch will do us both good. Why not?'

'Whisky before lunch,' murmured Caroline, with an apologetic grimace to Ellen's shade. 'Whatever next, I wonder.'

Theo and Fliss came in together and she smiled at them, relieved to see them looking so cheerful.

462

'Lunch is very nearly ready,' she told them. 'Prue and I are feeling rather guilty. We've been making moral judgements and then discovering that we're just as bad ourselves. We decided that we needed a drink to make ourselves feel better.' And wondered why they both began to laugh.

Chapter Forty-four

The train from Paddington was late. Glancing at her watch for the third time, Fliss tried to quell the churning in her stomach and, in an attempt to distract herself, began to rehearse all the things she wanted to say to Miles. It was vital that everything was decided and agreed upon before the twinnies came home for the holidays in three days' time. It would be terrible if they suspected that there was a serious falling out between their parents. The train slid slowly into the station and Fliss's heart jumped with fear as she scanned the alighting passengers, watching for Miles's familiar form. He was one of the first off, hefting his grip, stepping aside as a woman leaped into his path to embrace another passenger. He smiled briefly, acknowledging their apologies, and Fliss felt a painful tugging in her breast, a terrible tenderness. She hadn't noticed until now how grey his hair was, how much more vulnerable he looked out of uniform.

She thought: I can't do it. I can't let him go all that way on his own. Underneath his bravado he must be terribly nervous at such a huge change. And he was so excited about it. Oh *hell* . . .

She opened the door and slid out as he came towards her, knowing that he always preferred to drive himself, and he smiled and kissed her quickly before throwing his grip on to the back seat. Once they were together in the car she was seized with a paralysing shyness, only capable of uttering banalities whilst he negotiated the milling crowds and finally turned out of the station and headed up Kingsbridge Hill. Hands clenched between her knees, she waited for him to speak but even now he maintained an adult approach.

'No point in discussing anything important while I'm driving,' he said. 'We'll wait till we get home. Any other news?'

As the car fled through Harbertonford and turned left at Halwell on to the Dartmouth road they conversed as if they were strangers. Never had a journey seemed so long. Anxious though she'd been at the thought of his return, Fliss was almost relieved when they finally arrived home. She switched the kettle on ready to make some tea whilst he parked the car and presently she heard him close the front door. She made the tea with trembling hands and was suddenly aware that he had come in silently behind her. The thick strokes of her heart beat made speech almost impossible but she managed a smile as she turned to look at him.

'I thought you'd like some tea,' she said, and continued to look at him smilingly despite the lack of expression in his face.

'Why not?' He shrugged. 'Bring the tray through to the living room.'

She was glad that he had not chosen the drawing room for this confrontation. Somehow the drawing room had remained very much Miles's territory. At least here she took some measure of comfort from the things around her. As she set the tray down her glance alighted on the ginger jar and she felt another pang of uncertainty. The jar had become a symbol of love and friendship, its jagged crack reminding her how easily both these gifts could be damaged. The jar might be carefully repaired but it would never be as strong and this principle applied to relationships. Once trust was smashed could it ever be replaced? Feeling her resolutions wavering she poured the tea, handed him a mug – and waited. He took a sip and then raised his eyebrows.

'Well?'

Afterwards, Fliss believed that it was this 'Well?' uttered in a tone which blended impatience with a tinge of tolerance that swung her emotions back into focus and enabled her to retake possession of her own life. The vision of an uncertain Miles who might need her support faded and she squared her shoulders. For a brief moment she fought down the desire to meet him with matched weapons, no holds barred, but for some reason a vision of Uncle Theo slid into her mind and she found herself attempting to approach him calmly.

'I've thought it all over very carefully,' she told him nervously. 'Please don't think that I've taken this decision lightly . . .'

'But,' he prompted as she hesitated. 'That sort of statement most certainly has a "but" attached.'

'Yes,' she said. 'You're right, it does . . . *But* I'm still not coming to Hong Kong.'

She swallowed, turning to take a sip of tea, wishing that her hands would stop trembling, and he watched her consideringly, wondering how to deal with this reaction. As soon as he'd seen her he'd known that she hadn't changed her mind. His waiting tactic had been an attempt to unsettle her, to force the strength of his personality upon her in the hope that she might weaken. He'd imagined that once she was alone she might think carefully about what her future might be without him and be ready to admit that she couldn't cope. Yet suddenly, as though a veil had been gently removed, he saw the square set of her shoulders, the lift of the chin as she turned to look at him, the steady, level gaze, and his hold on the future suddenly felt infirm and his confidence was momentarily shaken.

'I love you,' he said, surprising them both, and saw the tiny frown appear between her brows. A stab of exultation pierced his heart.

He thought: I've got her. I'm playing this all wrong. I'm a damned fool . . .

'I do love you, Fliss,' he repeated rapidly. 'But surely you know that after all these years? I've only wanted to protect you, you know, to look after you. Is that so wrong? I only ever wanted you . . .'

She was looking quite desperate now and he knew quite surely that her defences were crumbling. It was important that he should breach them; important for both of them and for the children. This was his wife and he was determined that she should remain so.

'Oh, Miles,' she said sadly. 'I love you, too.'

'Well, then,' he said, his confidence returning. 'What's the problem? Surely that's all that matters? I love you more than anything.'

'Do you?' she asked with an odd intentness. 'Do you truly?'

He felt a rush of triumph. This had been the problem then. She simply needed to be reassured. Perhaps he had been too enthusiastic about the job, taken too much for granted. Well, he was quite prepared to make amends, to do what was necessary to soothe her hurt pride and put things right. Relief made him expansive.

'Of course I do,' he said tenderly, stretching out his hands to her. 'Silly girl. I love you more than anything in the world.'

'Do you?' She still held on to her mug, ignoring his hands. 'Are you sure, Miles? More than the job in Hong Kong, for instance?'

His expression changed so quickly that it was almost ludicrous but Fliss felt no desire to smile. She waited. His hands fell to his sides and he stared at her grimly.

'Are we really going to play stupid games?' he asked harshly.

'No,' she said. 'No, truly we aren't. I'm sorry, Miles, but you do see what I'm getting at. We love each other but not quite enough it seems. You don't love me quite enough to be prepared to stay here and I don't love you quite enough to leave England permanently.'

'Is this some kind of blackmail?'

'Of course not.' She tried to smile at him. 'I just want us to be able to be honest with each other. At this moment, that's where we both stand.'

'So what then? I have no intention of putting this job in jeopardy, you know.'

'You've made that very clear.' She put her mug back on the tray, folding her arms across her breast. 'I have a kind of compromise to suggest, if you're prepared to listen.'

There was a silence. Fliss watched him, praying that he would co-operate, willing him to be understanding. He set his mug beside hers on the tray and sat down in one of the cord hammock chairs, legs stretched out, ankles crossed, hands thrust down into his trouser pockets.

'Very well,' he said. 'Go ahead. Let's hear this compromise.'

She could feel that his mind was shut against her, that he required nothing less than an absolute agreement, but she was determined to try to break down his resistance to her.

'My idea,' she began carefully, 'is that we should each have a kind of trial period. A sort of sabbatical. We've been very lucky that you haven't spent long periods at sea, although we've moved about a great deal. I know that you did your sea time before we met but it means that we've been together for most of the time we've been married. What I'm suggesting now is a separation of, say, two years. Not *that* long in naval terms, really. It will give us both time to sort out our feelings. I might find that I don't want to be here without you or you might discover that the job doesn't suit you— Wait.' She held up her hand as he made a gesture which indicated disbelief at such a ridiculous idea. 'I know how excited you are about it, Miles, and I can see that it's a great opportunity but there's a faint possibility that it might not be as good as you hope. That might be a negative approach but at least it's a realistic one. I, on the other hand, might well find that living in Devon with the twinnies and my family close at hand is no substitute for being with you in Hong Kong. Neither of us can absolutely say that these scenarios are not possibilities. I think that we should approach it like that. It might not take as long as two years but I think that a limit should be set.'

She fell silent, thinking again of Uncle Theo and their talk in his study. After he'd poured them each a Scotch, he'd hesitated whilst she took a sip.

'I think that I should make one thing quite clear,' he'd said. 'What I have suggested is not to be misinterpreted as some kind of an easy option. It's not an opportunity to simply postpone the rupture to a point in time when it will probably be less painful for both of you. During those two years you should both behave as if you are absolutely committed to each other. You should still be working at it even at so great a distance. Forgive me for underlining this but I shouldn't want you to misunderstand me. If you decide to take my advice I should like to be sure that you are under no misapprehension as to exactly what I'm suggesting.'

Now, as Miles sat watching her, Fliss felt that it was important that he, too, should understand this.

'Look,' she said urgently. 'This isn't some kind of brush-off, Miles. I'm not going to send you a Dear John letter once you're safely in Hong Kong. This is a genuine attempt to make our marriage go on working despite the fact that we both feel unable to give in to each other at present. I promise you that there are no traps or deceptions.'

'No, I see that.' His tone was mild but cool. 'I shall need time to think about it, of course.' He laughed abruptly at her puzzled look. 'Did you imagine that I would agree at once? Why should I? I might not care to start a new life with such conditions attached.' He shrugged. 'It has its merits, I suppose, given that your whole attitude is so absurd, but I shall want to think it over. So . . .' He hesitated for a moment. 'It's only fair to tell you that whether you come or not I intend to sell this house. Naturally there will be a home for you and the twins wherever I am but I can't afford to run two establishments, I'm afraid. This *isn't* the Navy, you see. I shan't be living on a ship or in a base, subsidised by a grateful government. Just a tiny point but I have to make it.'

He saw that she was not going to rise to this proffered bait. He'd wondered whether the thought of not having her own place might panic her but he knew it was a vain hope. The wretched Chadwicks at The Keep would welcome her back with open arms . . .

'I accept that,' she was saying quietly. 'My proposal was, I admit, made on the supposition that you would continue to support us.'

'I'm sure it was,' he burst out angrily. 'But can you give me a good reason as to why I should? You're my wife. Your place is with me wherever that might be. I've found a good job which offers us a very satisfactory level of living and you have no right to offer me terms and conditions when you decide to refuse to accompany me.'

'Very well.' She turned to look at him and, once again, he was struck by her likeness to her grandmother. 'That's quite fair. I have my allowance from the family and if I can find a teaching post I should be able to support myself and the twinnies but I'm not sure that I could manage their school fees, too. Would you be prepared to finance that?'

'Oh, for God's sake,' he said, his anger evaporating. 'Of course I'll continue to pay the bloody school fees. I'd have done that if you'd come with me so what difference does it make? It's just all so disappointing, Fliss. It's been my dream for so long and now it's just turned to ashes.'

He dropped his head forward, chin to chest, but this time his expression had no power to move her.

'Of course you must think it over,' she said gently. 'I quite see that. But try not to reject it out of hand,' and picking up the tray she went out to the kitchen.

Chapter Forty-five

The Little Chef on the Honiton road was almost empty. Having taken some time in choosing his breakfast from the menu Jolyon sat back, swinging his legs, looking about him. His cheeks, although cold when he actually touched them, seemed to be burning after the journey all the way from Hampshire with the car's hood down. It had been really great, sitting beside Daddy in the front, with the wind rushing over his head. Mummy hadn't been all that keen when he'd pleaded to have the hood down very early that morning as they were getting ready to leave.

'It could pour at any moment,' she'd said. 'Oh, really, Hal, you're just encouraging him . . .' but Daddy had given him a private little wink and gone on putting it down. Ed had jumped about saying things like, 'You *are* lucky,' and, 'I wish I could come,' but they both knew that he was looking forward to his Open Day. They'd talked about it already, he and Ed, because he'd wanted to be certain that Ed didn't really mind about them not being there or whether he was upset about missing the visit to the ship. Mummy had sounded almost cross when Daddy said he was taking him when he went down to the ship. He, Jolyon, had heard them talking in the kitchen when they thought he and Ed had gone off on their bikes to a friend just down the lane.

'It's bad enough,' she'd said, 'not coming to the Open Day but to take Jolyon as well.'

'I don't suppose that Jo will mind missing the Open Day,' Daddy had answered, 'and anyway, I thought we agreed that it was I who had to do the dirty work.'

He'd wondered what the dirty work was. After all, with Daddy being the Captain there couldn't be anything for him to do on the boat that would be dirty.

'It doesn't have to be then,' she'd said in her cross voice. 'There will be plenty of other opportunities.'

'Possibly, but I've taken the decision now.' Daddy had what he and Ed called his 'don't care' voice. Mummy often got cross these days and at some time or other they'd all pretended that they didn't really care even if, inside, they felt knotted up and a bit anxious really. It was nice to think that Daddy felt just like they did but somehow a bit scary, too, because it meant that though he was grown up he could be just as frightened as they could. It made him, Jolyon, feel rather grown up himself because sometimes it was as if he and Daddy were the same age, like when Daddy winked and went on putting down the hood and Mummy stood there looking angry but not being able to stop him.

'He must have his hat on *all the time*,' she'd said and he'd hastily dragged it out of his little overnight bag and put it on so that Daddy didn't get into any more trouble. Ed had taken hold of her hand then, as if to calm her down a bit, and she'd smiled down at him but anyone could see that she wasn't absolutely thinking about Ed, not properly.

'Give my love to your family,' she'd said with the same

rather hateful sarky note in her voice which the Geography master used at school when the boys got quite easy things wrong, and Daddy's face had gone all still and empty. Ed had come running round to the side of the car then, hanging over the door and saying, 'Give my love to Jamie and Bess,' while Mummy and Daddy kissed goodbye. They didn't kiss like they used to, once, with Daddy kind of wrapping her up and them both going into one person, but just giving each other a quick sort of dab on the lips while Ed had gone running back to Daddy's side of the car and he'd swung him in the air and wished him good luck . . .

Now Daddy was watching him across the table and he grinned at him quickly and said the first thing that came into his head.

'I'm glad that Jamie and Bess will be there. They've spent all the Easter holiday at The Keep.'

'Yes, I know.' Daddy was pouring his coffee as if he were thinking about something else. 'I think they might be living there permanently for a while. Miles is going to Hong Kong for a couple of years, did Jamie tell you when he phoned?'

Jolyon nodded, feeling important. Daddy never bothered to call people Uncle and Aunt like Mummy did and it made him feel very grown up when his father talked about people as if he and they were all the same age.

'They've got to sell the Dartmouth house because Miles needs the money to buy a flat in Hong Kong and anyway it was too small for them all.' This is what Jamie had told him when he'd phoned to say that he was looking forward to seeing him and did he mind sharing the bunk bed. Jamie said he could choose whether he went on the top bunk and that they'd told Rex he was coming to see him. 'They're lucky to live at The Keep, aren't they? I wish we could, then we'd be near you when the ship comes in.'

'Well, you could be there for some of the holidays, I suppose.' He sounded as if he were thinking it through. 'If you didn't mind being there with the twinnies.'

Jolyon tucked his right foot under his left thigh, remembered that he wasn't allowed to do it because of spoiling the chairs and let it swing free, looking round quickly in case anyone had noticed. The waitress smiled at him and he grinned back at her with relief.

'I like the twinnies,' he said, leaning back in his chair. 'They make me laugh and they play really good games.'

'I think they do quite a lot of acting and things at school.' Daddy smiled, as if he were remembering something. 'Mole and Susanna were at school at Herongate, you know, and they used to love the Pioneer camp best. They had tents and camped out in the grounds and cooked stews over the campfire and Matron had to judge which group had made the tastiest stew.' He laughed out loud. 'How they loved it. They used to pretend they were the Famous Five. Well, two of them.'

'Jamie and Bess do things like that.' His breakfast was arriving and he looked at it with pleasure. 'I'm starving,' he said, surprised at how hungry he was, and Daddy and the waitress laughed.

'Of course, you can't do things like that at a day school.' His father picked up his knife and fork. 'In some ways it's not so much fun as boarding school.'

'But they can't go home each night.' He put some sausage in his mouth and had to jiggle it about because it was so hot and was burning his tongue. 'I wouldn't like that much.'

'It makes the holidays a lot more special, though.' Daddy didn't seem to be very hungry after all, fiddling about with his food and not eating it properly. 'Every situation has its pluses and its minuses, I suppose.'

'I don't blame Ed for not wanting to be a boarder.' Jolyon guessed that his father was worrying about the school thing again and he wanted to make him feel happy. 'I don't mind that we've got to move to Salisbury, really. It's only that I shall miss my friends at weekends but I shall see them at school and they can come and stay in the holidays.'

The fried bread was delicious. He pierced a piece with his fork and dug it into the soft yellow yolk of the egg. It was a pity that Daddy didn't seem to be enjoying his breakfast at all.

'Arc you feeling all right?' he asked anxiously.

His father sighed. 'Look, Jo. I've got a problem.'

Jolyon's stomach churned a bit, like it did when he had tests at school. He swallowed the last of his bacon and tried to look grown up.

'Is it about the ship?' He tried to make his voice casual. When *he* had a problem he liked the grown-ups to sound like that when he told them about it, then he imagined that it couldn't be too bad after all, but it wasn't like Daddy to be anxious. He began to think that perhaps he wasn't too hungry either but he finished up the sausage and the baked beans anyway.

'No, it's not about the ship.' His father was smiling a little. 'It's about you, old chap.'

'Me?' He drank some of his Coca-Cola, wondering if he'd had a bad report from school. 'Why? What's wrong?'

'Well, it's difficult to explain but sometimes, in families,

479

things happen and one person has to be looked after a bit more than the others.' Daddy was fiddling about with his coffee cup. 'It's not that the others are less important or not loved as much but it's just the way things work out. I'm not absolutely certain that it's right for Ed to be going to his new school but he's been offered the chance and so we think that he should take it.'

'But I don't mind. Honestly . . .'

'I know you don't. It's not that. The real problem comes when we move to Salisbury. Mummy— *We* think that Edward's a bit too young to board. You have to be very grown up and able to take care of yourself and he's simply not that sort of boy, not yet. The trouble is that with me away at sea and based down in Devon, Mummy's going to find it difficult getting you both to different schools.'

'But we shall be living quite close to Ed's school.' Jolyon felt frightened without quite knowing why. 'That's why we're moving. It'll only be me . . .' Quite suddenly he knew what his father was trying to say and he had the feeling that the world had been moved round a bit and all the things he knew and felt safe with had disappeared. 'Can't I go to the school in Winchester? But why can't I?'

He could tell from his face that Daddy was just as upset as he was. It was as if he wanted to say something really, really badly but something else was stopping him. He put his hand across the table and Jolyon took it. It was warm and strong and he stared down at it, playing with the long fingers.

'I feel we're all letting you down very badly, Jo,' Daddy said. 'You see, I shall be too far away to help and Mummy will be going in two directions at once.'

'But what will I do?' He tried to stop the wobble in his voice and swallowed hard.

'There are two things you can do.' Daddy was holding his hand tightly. 'You can go to a day school in Salisbury—'

'But I shan't know anyone.' Jolyon could feel his lips trembling a little bit, as if he might cry. He pressed them together hard, still staring at his father's hand.

'I know. So the other thing would be to go to Herongate with Jamie and Bess. They'd look out for you and make sure you were OK and they'd also make certain you make lots of good friends.'

'Board?' He could hardly believe it. 'Go away from home?'

'Well, yes. For the term times. It could be lots of fun and I have a feeling you'd love it once you settled in but you don't have to go. You can stay at home and go to school in Salisbury. You'd soon make new friends. I'm truly sorry, old chap. It seems terribly unfair on you.'

Even through his own misery he could feel that Daddy was angry. Not at him but at someone else. At Ed, perhaps? But it wasn't really Ed's fault, it was Mummy and Grandma who were the keen ones. Poor old Ed was scared stiff about it . . . Something was edging about in his brain like when he was at school doing problems. He could almost see the answer but not quite, although there were all sorts of clues. The clues here were a bit different though; Mummy's cross voice, Daddy's silences, not kissing properly . . . He didn't want to think about it but something made him know that he could make it better or worse. One of his friends had told him that his father had left them, gone off, and now he had another wife and he hardly saw them any more. David cried

481

when he was telling him, and he, Jolyon, had felt terribly helpless and upset and had given him his new set of crayons. Mummy had been furious with him . . . Jolyon's heart gave a terrific jump. Suppose Daddy went off or supposing Mummy did? She might go off with that horrible Adam Wishart who always seemed to be dropping in when Daddy wasn't around . . .

'I don't really mind.' His voice seemed to come from nowhere, all of its own accord. 'Whatever makes things easiest. I don't want you and Mummy getting . . . upset . . . or . . . or going off with other people or anything.'

'Oh, Jo.' Daddy's face looked odd, as if he might cry, which was terrible. 'I love you very much and I want you to be happy. You don't have to decide now. Just think about it all, will you?'

Still clutching his father's hand, he slipped off his seat and went round to sit beside Daddy, who put his arm about him, holding him tightly.

'But you and Mummy are all right, aren't you?'

'We're perfectly all right. We love each other. I promise. It's only because everyone's worked up with getting Edward sorted out and me going to this new ship down in Devon. Poor old you is the one who's dipping out.'

'But you and Mummy are OK? Certain sure?'

'Certain sure. It's you I'm worried about.'

'I'm OK.' He was feeling better already. 'But I don't know what I'll do.' He hesitated, fiddling with Daddy's plate. 'What do *you* think's best?'

Daddy gave a really big sigh and settled him more comfortably.

'It's all a question of whether you think you could cope

away at school. If you could it might be nicer for you. Otherwise you might get swallowed up a bit in Ed's routine. Because of being at the cathedral so much, weekends and Christmas and Easter, it might be a tad busy until he's settled down and gets a bit older, if you see what I mean. Now, if you were away, you'd have your own life, your own plans. Matches and school plays and things like that. You might decide you wanted to go down to The Keep with the twinnies for the odd weekend or half term if the ship's in, and then you and I could do things together. And Granny's there, too, of course and she always loves to see you, doesn't she? And dear old Rex. But if you can't face being away from home we'd all quite understand that. It would be perfectly normal and natural.'

Jolyon leaned against him. Deep inside he felt a tiny flicker of excitement. He could quite see that being in Salisbury, trailing in Ed's wake might be a bit boring.

'Have a think.' Daddy was signalling to the waitress. 'Talk to Bess and Jamie when we get to The Keep later on. But remember that we want you to be as happy as you can be with this new situation changing things. Now, let's get this show on the road, shall we? Do you need the heads? So do I. I'll go and settle this first. Don't forget your hat.'

He grabbed his hat, still feeling alarmed and unsettled but the excitement was there, deep down. After all, going away to boarding school was just as important as going to the choir school. There would be lots of plans to make and new uniform and things to buy – and Daddy and Mummy would be happy again . . . Jolyon took a deep breath, grinned at the waitress and followed his father across to the cash desk.

Chapter Forty-six

Hal stirred restlessly, rolled over and peered at the luminous face of his watch: twenty past four. He groaned softly, covering his face with his forearm as he listened to the stirrings of the birds in the caves. His dreams had been a confused muddle: scenes with Maria, travelling with Jo, the tour of the boat, their arrival at The Keep. All these happenings had become a ludicrous kaleidoscope with no relevance to the actual events and he'd managed to rouse himself out of one nightmare only to fall headlong into another. Yet, given the circumstances, everything had gone very well. He felt a confusion of emotions when he thought of Jo, sitting across the table, listening whilst he told him how he was to be sacrificed to Edward's musical abilities.

He thought: Mole's right. Having children is a terrifying responsibility. I don't blame him for opting out. By the time parents know whether they've got it right or wrong it's too bloody late. Poor old Jo . . .

He'd loved the tour of the ship, though, and the wardroom had treated him as if he were an honoured guest instead of a small boy of nine. Well, rank hath its privileges and all that, and if his being Captain made Jo feel special, all well and good. Of course, once they'd arrived at The Keep everything had fallen into a calmer perspective and the tension evaporated.

Hal turned on to his side, smiling at the remembrance of his mother greeting Jo as if he were some warrior returning from battle whilst the twinnies, clearly forewarned, had hustled him off immediately after tea to their own amusements. As for Fliss . . . He closed his eyes, wondering why it should have felt so right that she'd been there, waiting for them; smiling at Jo but not fussing him, enabling him to realise that he was one of the family rather than a guest, helping him to find a book to read before he went to sleep, laughing with him at young Fred's latest attempt with the Lego.

That's where he'd found them, together in the playroom.

'It's supposed to be a lorry,' she was saying, 'just in case he turns up tomorrow and shows it to you himself. I wouldn't like his feelings to be hurt,' and she'd smiled at Hal over Jo's head. 'Fred hasn't developed a great sense of perspective yet.'

'He's only three.' Jo had defended his small cousin, turning the odd Lego shape in his hands, and then he'd set it down and gone running out to find the others. She'd raised her eyebrows questioningly and Hal had nodded.

'I think it's going to be OK,' he'd said, moved as always by the sight of her. How familiar she was, how very dear. 'Bless you for warning Bess and Jamie. They're doing splendidly.'

'They're very fond of Jo.' She put some books back on the shelves and he knew that she was feeling just as he did.

'Thank you for letting us use The Keep as our home while Miles is . . . away.'

'It's just as much your home as mine, you know that,' he'd answered, 'but I'm very glad that you'll be around whilst I'm driving *Broadsword*. Oh, Fliss, I'm so sorry about Miles and Hong Kong and . . . well, everything.'

'It's not as if it's the end,' she'd said rapidly. 'We're giving it two years to see how things work out. I've got to keep trying. I've promised Uncle Theo . . .'

He laughed, stretching out a hand. 'And I've promised Jo. So where does that leave us?'

'Friends?' She put her hand in his and he held it tightly, aware of her fears, acknowledging their shared weaknesses, their shared love.

'Friends,' he said gently, and raised her hand briefly to his lips before going back to the others in the hall . . .

Now, listening to the noisy sparrows, he groaned again, knowing how difficult it would be.

He thought: Uncle Theo and Jo will keep us up to the mark if we start to waver.

He settled himself more comfortably and, as the early morning light filtered between the curtains, he fell at last into a deep and dreamless sleep.

Bess woke suddenly. She lay quite still, with her eyes shut, until she remembered where she was. It always took her a little while at the beginning and end of the holidays, or at exeats and half term, to get used to the change, and she liked to do this little test; feeling the shape of the mattress beneath her, aware of the direction of the light, listening to the different sounds. She wriggled about, pulling her quilt right up over her head, making a kind of tent. Keeping her eyes closed she imagined this room which was to be her bedroom while they lived at The Keep. It had been her mother's room when she'd been a child and Bess liked it much more than the bedroom at the house in Dartmouth. She and Jamie had slept in lots of different beds considering that they were only eleven and a quarter. They were always moving about – well, every two years, anyway – and it could get a bit muddly after a bit. It would be awful if they had to change schools as often as they changed houses. That's why she and Jamie felt sorry for poor old Jo. It was horrid for him to have to suddenly leave all his friends and go to a school where he didn't know anybody. She'd been glad that she'd had Jamie with her when they went off to Herongate and they'd promised that if Jo decided to board that they'd look out for him.

'Poor old Jolyon's had his nose put out of joint with Edward getting this scholarship,' Mummy had said to them and she'd felt quite envious of Ed getting a scholarship to a choir school. Not for the singing but for all the other music. There was a lot of interest in music at Herongate but it wasn't as good as a choir school. 'He's coming down with Hal to see *Broadsword*, and then they're coming here for a day or two so please be specially nice to him. Tell him about Herongate if he asks. And try not to frighten him to death, please, he won't be in the mood for jokes.'

James had asked, 'Why "nose out of joint"?' and she'd just known that he was imagining Jo with his nose pushed sideways. Mummy had laughed. 'It does sound silly, doesn't it?' she'd agreed. 'It means that Edward's getting all the attention at the moment and Jolyon's being rather left out of things.'

There had been that usual awkward bit when he and Hal had first arrived. The 'not quite knowing what to say' bit while the grown-ups told you that you'd grown and asked how school was and all those things but almost at once Hal had asked to see Rex and they'd all gone into the kitchen and everything was suddenly easy. Aunt Prue and Caroline had made loads of really nice things to eat and they'd had a huge noisy tea round the kitchen table. She was glad that they all knew that she hated playing the piano in front of them. It was difficult to describe how she felt inside but it was as if her music was very private and that if she talked about it too much it would disappear. Sometimes she had tunes in her head, little bits and pieces which she could imagine quite clearly written down on manuscript paper, but she'd learned that it was best to keep it inside, private even from Mummy or Miss Pearson who taught her at school. She'd play a few party pieces if pressed but she liked best to be alone, shut in with the piano and no one else about. If people went on about it she could hear herself getting all gruff and rude. She simply couldn't help it. She guessed that it was because it was so important, more important than anything – so precious that it might disappear at any moment unless she guarded it carefully.

'So what about a recital?' Daddy had said when he came over to The Keep to see them settled in. 'Let's hear what all the fuss has been about,' and when she'd refused he'd laughed – well, it wasn't really a laugh because there had been no fun in it but it was a *kind* of laugh – and said, 'Thank goodness I didn't waste my money on a piano if you won't play for me.'

Bess pushed herself up in bed, still clutching her quilt, feeling uncomfortable inside. She knew that she should have played for him. He'd gone away for two whole years to Hong Kong and they weren't going out to be with him. Mummy had explained that this was sensible, just in case he didn't like the job or he wasn't happy out there and decided to come back before the two years were up. Moving the whole family would be much more difficult and so she would stay here with them until they knew whether it was going to work out.

She and Jamie were privately glad that Mummy wasn't going. It was such a long way off and although it might have been fun flying to and fro for holidays it was much nicer to think that she would be here at The Keep and that they would all be together, not just for the long holidays but half terms and exeats as well. It would be much more fun than being stuck in a flat in Hong Kong. Daddy's flat was on the third floor so he didn't have a garden or anywhere to play and he certainly wouldn't have a piano . . .

She wished she'd played for him. He'd been rather quiet during the last week before he went and she'd had the feeling that he was cross in some way with her and Jamie. A few days after the holidays started it was decided that she and Jamie should stay at The Keep while Mummy and Daddy packed up the Dartmouth house. They'd been so pleased to go although they tried not to show it. The trouble was that Daddy seemed so . . . well, as though he wasn't really quite with them. He'd never really joined in anything or taken much interest in them . . . She clutched her quilt miserably because then, when he *had* shown an interest and asked her to play, she'd refused in her gruff voice, frightened that she might be made to perform. Mummy had driven him to Heathrow to catch the plane and when she came back the next day she looked awful and she and Jamie knew that she'd been crying . . .

Bess scrambled out of bed, knowing she might cry too if she didn't think about something else. Outside the birds were singing. One bird in particular sang a whole range of notes, far more than the other birds, and she kneeled up on the window seat, trying to follow them until it blended with another tune in her head . . .

She was still sitting there, wrapped in her quilt, when the boys came in to see if she were ready for breakfast.

'Did you hear the stormcock earlier?' asked Caroline, slicing cooking apples. 'He was singing in the orchard when I woke up. Hope it's not going to rain.'

'Stormcock?' Prue was mashing potatoes for the shepherd's pie, Rex sitting beside her, watching hopefully. 'What on earth is a stormcock?'

'Ellen used to call the thrush the stormcock,' said Caroline, smiling at private memories. 'Country people called it that because it continues to sing even when it rains. You know, I was wondering whether we ought to rethink where we should eat if Fliss and the twinnies are going to be here for a while. It's going to be a real squash round the kitchen table with all of us here. Do you think we should start using the breakfast room again when everyone's together?' She sighed happily. 'It's lovely to think that the twinnies are up with me in the nursery quarters. Just like old times.'

'I thought that we'd never persuade Fliss into Freddy's rooms.' Prue chuckled a little. 'Mind you, I know just how she felt. I couldn't have used them myself but I think it's right for Fliss to take over her grandmother's rooms, don't you?'

'Quite right.' Caroline was very definite about it. 'My only fear is that she'll be afraid to change anything. Mrs Chadwick would have been delighted to know that Fliss was in those rooms but she'd have wanted to think that she could put her own stamp on them.'

'I wonder.' Prue reached for the dish of minced beef, fried with carrots and onion and a hint of tomato purée, and deftly covered it with the creamy potato. 'Oh, not that she'd have minded Fliss using the rooms but whether she would have approved of Fliss not going with Miles. She was rather strict about things like that, wasn't she? Your place is with your husband and all that.'

'I think she'd have been more disappointed that Hal and Maria aren't moving down now that he's been posted to Devonport. It was always her dearest wish that he should make The Keep his home.'

Prue sighed. She felt as if it were all her fault that Maria and Hal were not fulfilling Freddy's hopes.

'I can see that Maria is unhappy about Edward boarding,' she began excusingly. 'He's a very shy little boy, isn't he? A tiny bit of a Mummy's boy if we're honest, and not really ready to board. But it's such a splendid opportunity . . .'

'Of course I realise that.' Caroline didn't want Prue to feel guilty. After all, no one could plan other people's lives for them with any real hope of success. 'It's just a pity, that's all. Never mind. We'll have Fliss instead and we're bound to see a lot of Hal with him being based down here.'

'It'll be such fun,' agreed Prue, brightening up at the

prospect. 'And if Jolyon decides to go to Herongate he might come home sometimes with Bess and Jamie. Oh, it would be such a treat. I see so little of my grandsons.'

'It's just what we need.' Caroline began to line a pie-dish with pastry. 'It'll stop us getting old and fuddy-duddy. Thank goodness you have a light hand with pastry, Prue. Mole could use mine as ballast. Do you remember Ellen's pastry? Light as a feather and quite delicious. Which reminds me. Susanna phoned earlier. She's bringing Podger and Fred to tea. Thank goodness there's some cake left over from yesterday. It's like the feeding of the five thousand . . .'

'I just have this feeling,' Prue said to Theo when she took up his morning coffee, 'that Miles will never come back. It's odd. Like a premonition.'

She pottered about, picking up a book and putting it down again, screwing up the top of his fountain pen, straightening his blotter. He watched her compassionately, guessing what might be at the back of her mind. In this new situation, with the inevitable future proximity, might not the love between Hal and Fliss flare up again? He knew Prue, like Freddy, had questioned their earlier joint determined belief that the two young people should be separated, had even regretted their interference, but now there were the children to consider, as well as Maria and Miles.

'I'm quite certain that Fliss doesn't feel the same way,' he said gently. 'She is looking upon this exactly as she might any naval posting except that there isn't the naval safety net if anything goes wrong. If the job works out she might well decide to join him much sooner than planned but I think it's sensible to give themselves a moratorium rather than disrupting the whole family for what might be a false step. It's a big change for Miles, after all.'

'I'm sure you're right.' Prue smiled at him, reassured. 'These children. Such a worry. Miles going off to Hong Kong and poor Jolyon trying to decide whether he can cope with boarding school. By the way, Susanna's bringing the children over for tea so we shall be a houseful . . .'

When she'd gone Theo sat down at his desk and emptied his mind of the worries of his family. Closing his eyes he opened his heart to his own source of strength and courage: the quiet, secret inflowing of God.

Chapter Forty-seven

In the small sitting room overlooking the courtyard Fliss sat on the window seat and communed silently with her grandmother. Here, in this room which had been her private sanctuary, Fliss was aware of her personality and presence all about her and was comforted. A cool, quiet hand was laid upon the confusion and anxiety which seethed in her mind; her thoughts flowed more peacefully. During the last two weeks she'd clung to Uncle Theo's advice; her determination to abide by it surrounded her and held her from tumbling into the abyss which yawned continually before her feet. Although Miles had accepted her compromise, this acceptance had not prevented him from attempting to break down her resolve. It had been hard – oh! how hard – to resist him.

Fliss drew her feet up on to the edge of the window seat, wrapping her arms about her knees and resting her chin upon them. Would Grandmother have approved of her resistance? Would she not have persuaded her that her place was with her husband? Yet the room held no such reproach. The bow-fronted bureau was empty now of her papers, and Fliss's own writing pad with other odds and ends lay on the blotter, but the tall glass-fronted bookcase still held Freddy's favourite books just as the corner cupboard contained her precious pieces of glass and china.

Slipping from the window seat, Fliss went to look at these treasures. Some of the pieces had come to The Keep with her grandmother so many years ago but she recognised the pretty candlesticks in Bristol blue glass, remembering that they had been a birthday present from Uncle Theo. It was the year that the twins had been eighteen and she'd worn her first real grown-up dress to dinner that same evening. Even now she could remember the apprehension she'd felt as she'd hesitated outside the drawing-room door. Plucking up her courage she'd pushed the door open and stepped inside – and seen Hal's expression: surprise, puzzlement and a dawning awareness. That had been a wonderful moment and she remembered, too, her own reaction: joy, the sense of power, overwhelming love.

Fliss turned away, staring up at the two great Widgerys, one each side of the fireplace. Seeing Hal here with Jolyon, talking to him in the playroom last night, aware – how terribly aware – of the love flowing silently between them, had jolted her confidence. She could cope as long as she was not faced with temptation. At this thought she laughed aloud, imagining her grandmother's impatience at such feebleness of character. Miles had tried to 'persuade' her – at the time it had seemed more like blackmail – by evoking her grandmother's memory. One night in bed he'd held her tightly after an emotionally disastrous lovemaking, his face pressed against hers, and she'd been quite unable to think of any suitable words, except for those which now seemed to swim permanently in the uppermost layers of her thoughts.

'*I'm so sorry. I'm so sorry.*' However she was not sorry enough, not enough to back down, to give in ... She'd hugged him closely, tears threatening, hanging on desperately to her resolve, and he'd turned his head a little, freeing his mouth from the long strands of her hair.

'I wonder what your grandmother would have thought about all this?' he'd murmured. 'She always rather approved of me, didn't she? Dear old Freddy. She told me to take care of you and I've tried to do my best. I wonder what she's thinking now?'

Just as earlier his 'Well?' had released her from her guilt, so had this assault on her love for her grandmother renewed her strength. She'd felt herself grow heavy in his embrace until she'd been unable to bear his proximity for another moment. She'd slid out of his clinging arms, saying that she was going down to make coffee and to her enormous relief he had not followed her with more recriminations. Instead, to her surprise – and relief – on her return she'd seen that he'd fallen asleep. Clearly his distress had not been enough to keep him awake. Yet it was a pattern that had been repeated at intervals during those last few days. He'd been quite happy for the twinnies to be sent on to The Keep whilst the house was cleared. Not only would they be out of the way but it would give him time to be alone with her. It was no longer hurtful that he had no desire to be with his children during this short time left to them and, anyway, she'd found it easier herself not to be obliged to keep up certain pretences for their benefit. With them gone she and Miles had been able to be perfectly natural together, hiding nothing, and she'd been able to concentrate utterly upon him.

Dealing with the house had given him other opportunities to lay siege to both her guilt and her love for him. She'd continued to remain firm in her belief that after the two years – or even before – there was a real possibility that they would be together again, although she would not be drawn on *where* this reunion might take place. Nevertheless, he'd decided to sell the furniture. This brought the chance to reminisce, to invoke the past, but here he'd had no power to move her. They had chosen nothing together; no reminders of cheerful shopping trips or hopeful plans could be brought forward here to touch her heart. The house and its contents had been Miles's own and she had been nothing more than a very welcome guest. She'd collected together the few possessions she'd brought with her and they'd agreed to keep the portable belongings which had made their naval quarters homely. These she would take with her to The Keep.

The drive to Heathrow had been agonising. At the end they'd both been equally upset, pride and anger dissolving finally into other gentler emotions, and he'd held her tightly just before he'd boarded the plane.

'I do love you, Fliss,' he'd said, his voice muffled against her hair. 'You must believe it.'

She'd reassured him as best she could and, when the plane could no longer be seen, she'd stopped waving and returning to the car had sat for some time, crying bitterly. She'd managed the drive back to Dartmouth and had written to him that same evening in another attempt to comfort him, to underline her continuing support and love, but, once she'd achieved this, grief overtook her again and the night was a long and miserable one.

The next morning the last of the furniture had been collected and she'd been free at last to drive to The Keep. As she'd walked about the empty house she'd been oddly glad that their last day together had culminated in her night alone here. It was fitting that it should finish in the little house in Above Town but she'd been filled with an overwhelming relief at the knowledge that now, with Miles gone, she need not return. If they were to go forward at some distant time then it would need to be a completely new start, conceived and planned together.

Thinking of Miles, that next, final, morning, she'd stripped the bed, packed up the few remaining odds and ends and then gone from room to room making her own private farewells. Several days before he flew out they'd gone together to The Keep so that he could say his good-byes and had taken with them most of the small items, but there'd still been a few things which had been required up until the last moment. In the kitchen, beside the boxes to be put into the car, had stood the ginger jar. She'd stood, holding it between her hands, remembering, and she'd wept again, for the small losses, for the tiny bitter failures and for the inadequacies of love. At last she'd put the boxes in the car, taking the ginger jar last of all, wrapping it about with a rug and placing it carefully on the floor in front of the passenger seat.

By the time she'd arrived at The Keep she was exhausted. As she'd driven in beneath the arch of the gatehouse she'd seen that Uncle Theo was sitting on a bench in the courtyard and she'd known that he was waiting for her. Swallowing, lips pressed together, she'd climbed stiffly, wearily, out of the driving seat and stood looking at him. He'd risen to his feet

and, leaning on his stick, had come towards her, hand outstretched, smiling his own particular smile. As her hand
found his, clinging on tightly, he'd drawn her close and
kissed her.

'Welcome home, Fliss,' he'd said.

Now, remembering, her courage returned. 'I've promised
Uncle Theo,' she'd said to Hal last night in the playroom,
when their love had threatened to engulf them.

'And I've promised Jo,' he'd answered.

Well, there was no doubt that these two would prove
powerful consciences should they be needed: Theo with his
direct, clear-seeking look: Jolyon with his innocent, childish gaze. Between the man and the boy they should be able
to run straight.

Fliss turned away from the Widgerys and glanced at
her watch. She and Hal had promised the children that
they'd all go for a walk before tea and, with one last
grateful glance about her, she picked up her jacket and
went out.

Out on the hill the late April sunshine was hot. Across the
valley on the round green hills, sheep grazed, lambs at foot,
straying over the new growth of sun-warmed grass. Beyond
the hedge, where the pink and white hawthorn blossom hid
the chaffinch's nest, the rooks wheeled in a ragged flock
behind the tractor. The newly ploughed earth was a dark
pinky red, almost maroon in its damp richness, contrasting
sharply with the bright emerald of the turf. From the shelter
of the woods the cuckoo called, clear and evocative in the
quiet of the afternoon.

The children were already far ahead, racing after Rex

who had put up a rabbit and was in hot pursuit. Strolling more slowly, Hal and Fliss watched them reach the banks of the river and pause to paddle in the shallows where the rippling water was clear and the sunlight shimmered in the green depths.

'Remember all those dams we built?'

His voice broke the companionable silence between them and she took a deep breath, straightening her shoulders and frowning slightly as though she were returning from some distance.

'Of course I do. And Susanna tumbling over and getting soaked to the skin.'

'We stripped her off and dried her with my shirt . . .' he said cheerfully.

'. . . and dressed her in Mole's jersey to bring her home,' she finished.

'Ellen wasn't all that pleased,' he remembered.

' "Going swimming and not even May yet",' quoted Fliss. ' "Whatever next, I wonder." Susanna was a terror. I fear that Podger is destined to be just such another.'

'What a wretched girl Kit is,' said Hal, chuckling. 'Poor Podger. No one will ever recall that she was named Alison for your mother.'

'I'm afraid you're quite right . . . So you went to Sin's fortieth birthday party. And how was it?'

He shook his head, wincing. 'Don't ask. What a crazy pair they are. I like old Clarrie, though. He's really good news.'

'Too old for Kit?'

'Oh!' He frowned as if surprised by the suggestion. 'I should have said so. He's like a mother hen looking after them both. They're clearly very fond of one another but no more than that I should have thought. Not that I'm a very good judge of other people's feelings.'

'Well,' she said lightly. 'It was just a thought. She still misses Jake, even after all these years.'

'If you really love someone,' he said, after a minute or two, 'I don't think that time has anything to do with it.'

The silence held a different atmosphere now. Fliss dug her hands into the pockets of her jacket, forcing herself to think about Miles, knowing how important it was that he should remain vividly in her mind.

The children were running along the river bank, disappearing into the spinney and, as they approached, Hal and Fliss could see the bluebells' luminous glow within that dim interior, the rippling, spreading azure lake which carpeted the earthy floor, lapping the tall smooth boles of the beech trees.

'Remember Mole running round the spinney?' murmured Hal. 'Who would have believed then that one day he'd be a Commander of one of Her Majesty's submarines.'

'Superstition is a very powerful thing,' she answered. 'I remember that just before I went out to Hong Kong I came down here by myself. I was so frightened about going, hating the thought of leaving everyone behind. I decided that if I ran round the spinney everything would be OK.' She shook her head and fell silent.

'And was it?' he asked at last.

She shrugged. 'Well, except for Ellen dying while I was away. But then it might have been so much worse, mightn't it? If I hadn't, I mean.' She began to laugh. 'What a twit I am. What difference can it possibly make, after all?'

HOLDING ON

'You never know,' he said, slipping an arm lightly about her shoulder. 'Let's not take the chance, shall we?'

The children and Rex came running out into the sunshine and overtook them, climbing the hill towards home and tea, whilst somewhere high above them a lark began to sing.